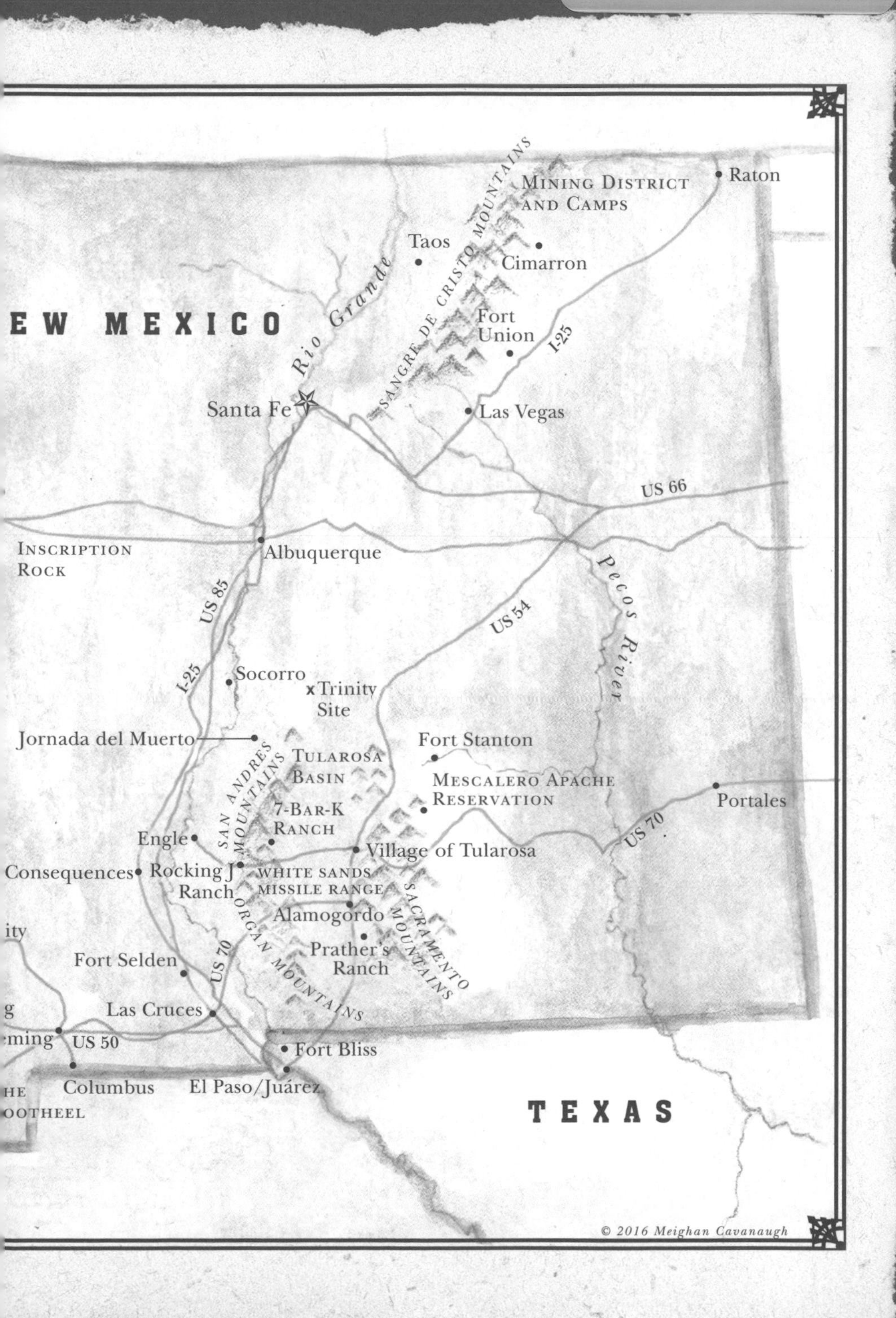

Raton
Mining District and Camps
Sangre de Cristo Mountains
Taos
Cimarron
Rio Grande
Fort Union
I-25
Santa Fe
Las Vegas
US 66
Inscription Rock
Albuquerque
Pecos River
US 85
US 54
I-25
Socorro
Trinity Site
Jornada del Muerto
Fort Stanton
San Andres Mountains
Tularosa Basin
Mescalero Apache Reservation
Portales
7-Bar-K Ranch
US 70
Engle
Village of Tularosa
Consequences
Rocking J Ranch
White Sands Missile Range
Alamogordo
Sacramento Mountains
Organ Mountains
Prather's Ranch
Fort Selden
US 70
Las Cruces
US 50
Fort Bliss
Columbus
El Paso/Juárez
TEXAS
© 2016 Meighan Cavanaugh

THE LAST RANCH

ALSO BY MICHAEL McGARRITY

Tularosa

Mexican Hat

Serpent Gate

Hermit's Peak

The Judas Judge

Under the Color of Law

The Big Gamble

Everyone Dies

Slow Kill

Nothing but Trouble

Death Song

Dead or Alive

Hard Country

Backlands

THE LAST RANCH

A Novel of the New American West

MICHAEL MCGARRITY

DUTTON
— est. 1852 —
An imprint of Penguin Random House LLC
375 Hudson Street
New York, New York 10014

LIBRARY OF CONGRESS CATALOGING-IN-PUBLICATION DATA
Names: McGarrity, Michael, author.
Title: The last ranch : a novel of the new American West / Michael McGarrity.
Description: New York : Dutton, [2016] | Series: American West trilogy ; 3
Identifiers: LCCN 2015047686 (print) | LCCN 2016000366 (ebook) | ISBN 9780525953258 (hardcover) | ISBN 9780698409736 (ebook)
Subjects: LCSH: Ranch life—New Mexico—Fiction. | Family life—New Mexico—Fiction. | New Mexico—History—20th century—Fiction. | BISAC: FICTION / Westerns. | FICTION / Sagas. | FICTION / Action & Adventure. | GSAFD: Western stories. | Historical fiction.
Classification: LCC PS3563.C36359 L37 2016 (print) | LCC PS3563.C36359 (ebook) | DDC 813/.54—dc23
LC record available at http://lccn.loc.gov/2015047686

Printed in the United States of America
3 5 7 9 10 8 6 4 2

BOOK DESIGN BY ALISSA ROSE THEODOR

The place of infinite possibility is where the storyteller belongs.

—N. Scott Momaday

ACKNOWLEDGMENTS

A tip of the hat and *muchas gracias* to Stephanie Kelly at Dutton, who resolutely and enthusiastically helped me get to the finish line. And much thanks to Brian Tart. Without him the American West trilogy would have been nothing but a haunting, chimerical dream.

THE LAST RANCH

ONE

Matt Kerney

1

In the pale moonlight that floated through her bedroom window, Anna Lynn Crawford studied Matthew Kerney's face. Fortunately for both of them, tonight he slept quietly. Whenever he stayed the night at her house, he often woke with a start from bad dreams that left him shaking, and she would find him sitting silently alone on the front porch at first light. When he was restless, Anna Lynn took to curling up on the floor with a pillow and comforter in the hope her absence would have a calming effect on him. Sometimes his breathing eased and the night passed peacefully. But most mornings, she found him on the porch in her rocking chair, unmoving, his hands clutching the armrests, his face moist with sweat.

Six months earlier, Matt had returned home from the war with a patch covering his left eye, which had been destroyed in a landmine explosion during the Allied invasion of Sicily. He only removed it at night. As he lay quietly sleeping, Anna Lynn snuggled close to examine the wound Matt insisted made him ugly.

His upper-left eyelid was missing completely, shredded during the explosion, and there were tiny, jagged shrapnel scars around the socket of the eye, which was covered in a murky film. There was a slight puffiness under the eye she hadn't seen before. She wondered if it was causing him pain.

You're still a handsome man, you fool, she thought to herself. *You still look like you.*

She'd told him that if he stopped wearing the patch, folks would soon pay the injury no mind. But Matt immediately dismissed the suggestion the two times she'd made it, the second time so vehemently that she hadn't mentioned it since. She had to try again to persuade him to listen to reason, but dreaded his reaction. He was, and he wasn't, the man she knew before he went into the army.

What she knew about Matt's war experience came mostly from an army press release printed in every New Mexico newspaper the week after his discharge from Fort Bliss, the army post outside of El Paso. He'd been decorated for bravery under fire for clearing a fortified enemy position above a beachhead, where troops had been pinned down and taking heavy casualties. His actions had allowed a battalion of men to move inland without suffering further serious losses. He'd been promoted to platoon sergeant on the spot and was later awarded another medal for using captured enemy horses to carry equipment through rugged, mountainous terrain, which aided the Allied advance against a large, retreating enemy force. He'd lost his eye in the final push to liberate the island and had been evacuated to a hospital ship, where he'd received the Purple Heart from a general after his surgery.

She snuggled closer and gazed at Matt's face, remembering the only time he'd talked about those experiences. After making love early one morning, they'd sat quietly together on the veranda of his ranch house overlooking the wide expanse of the Tularosa Basin, her daughter Ginny sound asleep in bed and Matt's father, Patrick, away in town. She'd broken the silence by asking Matthew to finally tell her what had happened to him in Sicily. It earned her a sad-faced grin and a loud chuckle.

"What's so funny?"

"It was all a big frigging joke," he answered without rancor.

"How so?" Anna Lynn asked.

Still smiling, Matt rose from his chair. "Wait here and I'll show you."

He returned and gave her two cartoons from the pages of an army newspaper. One showed a sergeant with a shiny medal pinned to his uniform explaining to a ragtag private that he'd been decorated for scaring the enemy away by speaking "Eye-talian" at them. The second cartoon displayed a grizzled sergeant pointing a finger at a sorrowful-looking horse, demanding to know if, as a POW, the animal would abide by the Geneva conventions.

Anna Lynn looked up from the cartoons. "I don't see what's so funny."

Matt smiled at the only two memories of Sicily that brought him any pleasure to recall. "What makes them funny is they show exactly what happened to get me decorated like some kind of hero. On the beachhead, all I did was talk some Italian soldiers into not shooting at us anymore. They withdrew from their position and we were able to move inland. There was nothing heroic about it. Later on, when we were in the mountains, my platoon stumbled on a herd of abandoned enemy ponies that we commandeered for the regiment to use as pack animals in the high country. Because it helped force the Germans into a hurried retreat, I got another medal, and it wasn't even my idea in the first place. That's the sum total of my so-called bravery."

Anna Lynn gazed at his face and his eye patch. "That may well be, but it doesn't make you less of a hero. You were smart and saved lives, and besides you were gravely wounded."

Matt's mood shifted as he thought about the men in his platoon he'd lost. His expression turned somber. "I didn't save enough lives. And I lost an eye for being stupid and not paying attention to what I was doing."

The image of Pvt. Joey Cohen taking a bullet in his head, twirling around, and dropping dead at Matt's feet replayed through his mind as it did at least once a day. He shook it off and pointed at the signature on the bottom-left corner of each cartoon. "I thought you would have noticed by now who drew these," Matt said, trying to sound lighthearted. "They're both signed, 'Bill Mauldin—Sicily.'"

"Bill Mauldin!" Anna Lynn squealed in surprise. "Our very own little Billy Mauldin?"

Matt smiled and nodded. "Yep, the one and same scrawny kid who peddled his drawings and cartoons to folks up and down the west slope of the Sacramento Mountains. I still have a stack of them put away somewhere. He sends you his regards."

"Oh, that sweet, lovely boy," Anna Lynn said, blinking away a tear. "Is he a war correspondent?"

"Nope, he's a soldier in the 45th Infantry Division, if he isn't already among the dead from all the casualties we took in Italy."

Anna Lynn's face clouded at the mere thought of it. "Oh, please don't let that be true."

"I sure hope he survived," Matt agreed. "I figure he's gonna become rich and famous if he comes through the war alive and intact. The troops already love him."

Matt took the cartoons from Anna Lynn's hands. "That's all the talking I want to do about my time in the army. I'm home now and that's the end of it. Understand?"

Anna Lynn nodded. "If that's what you want."

"It is."

Matt had countenanced no more talk about the war after that morning, although he diligently followed the battlefront newspaper and radio reports, especially the ones from Europe, which often threw him into a funk. As time passed, his interest waned in anything or anybody other than the war, Anna Lynn's five-and-a-half-year-old daughter, Ginny, and the ponies on his ranch. He withdrew, turned inward and silent. His visits to her farm became less frequent, their conversations, once so engaging, became awkward, their lovemaking, always passionate, turned perfunctory at best.

The changes between them chilled Anna Lynn. Here, close to him in her bed, his warm breath against her cheek, she wondered if she'd lost Matt completely because of the terrible war. If so, it would have been far less of a heartbreak to have lost him to another woman.

The next day he was to travel to William Beaumont Army Hospital at Fort Bliss for a follow-up physical disability examination. If he failed to keep the appointment, his monthly pension benefits might be suspended, and Anna Lynn knew he could little afford the loss of that income. She wanted to go with him, but he wouldn't hear of it. She fell asleep hoping the army doctor might have a miracle in his pocket to restore Matt's eyesight. If he were made whole again, at least in some psychological way, perhaps her constant fear of trying to endure an unhappy future with a man who'd once filled her heart with so much happiness and joy would vanish.

* * *

In the morning, Anna Lynn fixed steak and eggs for Matt and pancakes for Ginny, who sat next to Matt with syrup dripping down her chin as she chewed a bite and stared at Matt's eye patch. She reached up with sticky fingers to touch it and he yanked her hand away.

"Don't touch," he snapped.

"Why not?" Ginny demanded, shocked at Matt's scolding.

Matt took a deep breath to calm his annoyance and forced a smile. "Because I look like the bogeyman without it and that would scare the dickens out of you."

"It would not," Ginny replied bravely, not completely sure of herself or of Matt's warning.

"Well, it sure would scare the hell out of me," Matt said, tousling Ginny's hair. "Now, eat, and don't be such a pest."

Reassured, Ginny put another big bite of pancakes into her mouth, closed her left eye, put her hand over it, and looked around the room. She saw her mother's jars of honey she got from the bees lined up neatly on the shelves above the kitchen cabinet and sink, her mom's reading chair next to the table with the lamp and radio, the box under the window with her toys and books that had to be put away neatly every night before bed, and the open front door with the screen gently flapping in the cooling morning breeze.

"I can see okeydokey with one eye," she announced matter-of-factly.

"But it's better with two eyes," Matt countered, forking the last of his steak. "Don't you think?" he asked after his last bite.

"Yeah," Ginny agreed with a grin.

"We'd like to keep you company today," Anna Lynn said casually as she cleared Matt's plate.

"Can we?" Ginny pleaded, clapping her hands. She loved trips to town.

Matt shook his head and wiped his mouth with a napkin. "There's no need," he replied, ignoring Ginny's pout. "I'll stop by on my way home to the ranch tonight and tell you what the army doc had to say."

Anna Lynn dipped Matt's plate into the soapy dishpan at the sink. "You'd better," she cautioned.

She turned her head from the sink to look at him, and he grinned at her in agreement. A forced grin, she thought, trying her best to smile in return. The left side of his face twitched involuntarily. She was sure he was in some pain. She was also sure he knew that he couldn't hide it completely from her.

"Stop worrying about me," Matt ordered gruffly.

"I just want you to be okay."

"I am okay." Matt pushed back from the plank-board kitchen table. "And I'm trying my damnedest to stay that way."

He exchanged hugs with Ginny that left her sticky syrup fingerprints on his shirt-sleeve, kissed Anna Lynn quickly goodbye, and headed out the door. Below the small village of Mountain Park, the Tularosa Basin sat under a cloudless, brilliant blue sky with blinding sunlight that swept clean all color except for the gypsum dunes at White Sands National Monument and the foreboding dark uplift of the San Andres Mountains forty miles westward.

War had brought serious gasoline rationing to civilians, and most country folks had parked their cars and gone back to traveling by horse. In his pickup during the short drive to Alamogordo, Matt passed a dozen or so people in buggies or ahorseback clip-clopping along the highway heading to town. Only two passenger cars, an army truck, and a delivery van breezed by him, traveling northbound on the two-lane concrete road that gave way to gravel shy of Three Rivers. It was as though time had reversed to the early 1920s, when horses and wagons had still dominated the mostly rutted, hard-packed dirt roads of rural New Mexico that became mud pits after a heavy rain.

At the Alamogordo train station he bought a ticket to El Paso and waited on a bench in the shade of the covered platform watching warplanes rise up from the army airfield outside of town, grouping into formations high above to practice bombing runs at the north end of the basin.

Just about every rancher on the Tularosa had filed claims with the government to get reimbursed for livestock that had been killed by trigger-happy turret gunners eager to shoot anything on the ground that moved. Matt was still waiting on payment for two old ponies he'd found riddled with bullets and half-eaten by coyotes in a high country pasture on his San Andres ranch.

After boarding the train for the ninety-mile trip to El Paso, he fished a lapel button out of a pocket. Given to him as an afterthought by a personnel clerk at Fort Bliss the day he'd mustered out of the army, it was a small button made of brass depicting an American eagle with wings spread beyond the confines of an encircling wreath. It identified the wearer as having been honorably discharged from the armed services, and was jokingly known as the ruptured duck.

Matt attached it to the top buttonhole of his long-sleeved work shirt. Soon after the train left the station, two MPs on the train looking for AWOL soldiers entered his coach compartment. They scrutinized his eye patch and the ruptured duck, and gave him a nod and a smile of acknowledgment as they passed by.

In downtown El Paso, the ruptured duck and his medical appointment letter to see Dr. S. Beckmann at William Beaumont

Army Hospital got him a free ride on an army bus to the fort. Matt rubbernecked on the ride up the hill with the Franklin Mountains towering close by. Not long ago El Paso had nestled quietly along the Rio Grande across from the Mexican town of Juárez. Now the city was spreading north along newly paved streets lined with bars, diners, pawnshops, and motels that catered to the soldier boys stationed at Fort Bliss. The war economy had brought new life to the once dusty, somewhat dismal town. Matt guessed that the bars, nightclubs, and whorehouses in Juárez were also thriving during the boom times.

The bus driver dropped him off outside the old Spanish colonial brick-and-stucco hospital building now used for offices, where a clerk directed him back outside to one of the army-style barracks buildings that served as hospital wards, rehabilitation clinics, surgical theaters, and medical specialty centers. Considered temporary construction, each building was a long rectangle, two stories high, with a gable roof, horizontal wood siding, double-hung windows, and an external staircase to the second floor. Dozens of the buildings, marked with numbers and signs, stretched out in long, neat rows with the brown, barren Franklin Mountains as a backdrop. After presenting his appointment letter to a receptionist in the Ophthalmology Clinic, Matt was led to an examination room, where he was greeted by an attractive older woman with eyeglasses perched on her nose and captain's bars on her uniform shirt. She had blond curly hair cut short; warm, brown eyes; and a small raspberry-red birthmark above her right cheek.

"Take a seat, Sergeant Kerney," she said, smiling and motioning to a stool as she looked up from a medical chart. The nameplate on her desk read Capt. Susan Beckmann, MD.

"I'm Dr. Beckmann, and I'm new to this man's army," she said with a hint of humor in her voice. "I've been told by my commanding officer, who is still instructing me in matters of military etiquette, that you must call me ma'am, Doctor, or Captain."

Matt nodded as he sat on a gray metal stool. "I didn't expect to be seeing a lady doctor for my exam, Captain."

Beckmann's smile froze as she paused to study her patient. He was tall, in his early thirties with square shoulders, a darkly tanned face, and intelligent features. "We're a rare commodity, I'll grant you. Do you have a problem with that, Sergeant?"

Matt touched the ruptured duck lapel button on his shirt and shook his head. "No, ma'am, and since I'm a bona fide, one-hundred-percent honorably discharged civilian, you can drop the 'sergeant' moniker. Call me Matt, Dr. Beckmann."

Beckmann's smile warmed. "Fair enough, Matt." She left her desk, sat on a stool, scooted it close to him, and said, "Now, let's take a look at that eye."

As she lifted his eye patch her smile faded. There was no doubt the loss of sight in the eye was permanent, but the surgery to remove the shrapnel had been neatly done. The worrisome thing now was redness and swelling around the orbital cavity that suggested the possibility of infection.

"See, Doc, it just doesn't work right," Matt joked lamely.

"Does it cause you any discomfort?" Beckmann asked as she slipped her hand into a sterile glove and probed gently with a finger above and below the eye.

Matt shrugged. "Not much."

Dr. Beckmann paused and gave him a quizzical gaze. "Really?"

Matt's jaw tightened. "I do okay."

"You aren't a very good straight-face liar," Beckmann scolded with a sigh. "I've never understood why some men have a hard time being honest with doctors. You didn't strike me as that type."

"What type is that?"

"The stupid type," Beckmann explained, softening her criticism with a smile. "Let's start over. Do you experience any pain?"

Chagrined, Matt nodded.

"Describe it to me."

"Sometimes when I move my eye, it feels like I've been stabbed in the eyeball and it hurts like hell."

Susan Beckmann nodded and continued her questioning. Matt reluctantly admitted he sometimes had severe headaches that laid him low for an hour or more. Occasionally his head tingled as if insects were crawling on his scalp, or he sensed a slight trembling of his head, almost like a palsy that was hard to control. The bad eye just ached dully much of the time, but the pain often intensified and spread to the entire left side of his face. It got worse if he had a beer or some whiskey. Taking aspirin frequently helped but it usually took a long time for the pain to lessen.

"How much do you drink?" Beckmann asked.

"Not much," Matt allowed. "Maybe twice a week I'll have a beer or a whiskey before supper."

"How's your memory?"

"I don't have trouble remembering things."

"Not even little things?"

Matt shook his head. "Nope. What are you getting at here, Doc?"

"The orbital cavity around your eye is inflamed and possibly infected. And I'm thinking the optic nerve behind the eye may be involved, which is partially causing your pain."

"Partially?"

"Yes. You received excellent surgical care for the eye injury, but you also suffered trauma to your brain when the shrapnel penetrated your eyeball. That could be causing some of your symptoms as well."

"Can you fix it?"

Susan Beckmann paused before responding. "Yes, by removing the eyeball and fitting you with a prosthetic eye." She didn't mention that some patients who'd suffered the traumatic loss of sight in one eye eventually lost vision in their sighted eye. It could happen within months or it could take years and there was no way of predicting who went totally blind or when. For the time being, she wanted Matt focused solely on the immediate need for surgery and not the unknown future.

"A glass eye?" he asked.

"Yes, but you could always continue to wear the patch if you like. At this point, doing nothing is not an option. If there is an infection, I don't want it to spread to your brain. It could kill you. If I find only inflammation, surgery is still our best option and I can treat it immediately. It should significantly reduce your episodes of pain and discomfort."

Tired of the pain and the headaches, Matt didn't hesitate. "When can you do it?"

Susan Beckmann returned to her desk and consulted her calendar. "Early tomorrow morning; you'll be first up in the operating room," she said. "I'll arrange for you to be admitted to our pre-surgical ward this afternoon. Be back here at four o'clock. Eat a good lunch, because it will be the last food you'll have before I operate." She waved a finger at him. "And absolutely no alcohol."

Matt nodded and stood. "How long will I be stuck here after you saw my bones, Doc?"

Beckmann smiled. "Two to three days, depending on what I find."

"See you at four, Captain."

Matt shook her hand and headed out the door for the NCO club, stopping first at the Post Exchange, where he bought postcards and stamps, and scrawled notes to his pa at the ranch and Anna Lynn in Mountain Park, writing that his doctor had ordered some tests that would hold him over for a few more days but it was just routine and there was no need to worry.

He doubted the postcards would be delivered much before he returned home, but since neither his pa nor Anna Lynn had telephones, it was the best he could do.

At the NCO club he ordered a hot turkey sandwich, mashed potatoes, green beans, and apple pie. As he sipped coffee and waited for his meal to arrive, Matt wondered why Dr. Beckmann had hesitated when he'd asked her if she could fix him. Had she given him the whole scoop or was she holding something back? He had reason to be a little wary about medicos. He'd seen too many army doctors and medics tell dying men they were going to be all right.

* * *

Groggy from the general anesthetic, Matt Kerney woke up to find a young, cute brunette in a crisp white nurse's uniform with gold second-lieutenant bars on her collar taking his pulse. Her name tag read LT. R. HARTMAN.

"Hi, Matt," Nurse Hartman said brightly. "You'll be just fine. Your surgery went perfectly. The doctor will be here in a jiffy to give you the once-over. And your wife and daughter are waiting to see you."

"My wife and daughter?" Matt asked, still scatterbrained from the heavy dose of painkillers used to knock him out.

Hartman looked up from her wristwatch. "Yep, Anna Lynn and Ginny. What a cutie that little girl is. I want one just like her someday."

"You shouldn't have any trouble finding willing suitors ready to volunteer," Matt predicted.

Lt. Hartman almost giggled. "I sure hope not." She patted Matt on the shoulder. "You just rest and stay put now. We'll get you moved to the post-op ward in a little while, as soon as the doctor gives the okay."

The nurse's perky, friendly manner made Matt smile. "What's your first name?"

"Raine," she answered. "Bet you didn't expect a handle like that."

"Nope, I didn't," Matt allowed, as he watched Raine Hartman swish out of the room. He wondered how in the blazes the postcard he'd sent yesterday could have arrived in Anna Lynn's mailbox the same day. That was impossible. He was still only half-awake when Captain Beckmann breezed into the room, smiling broadly.

She took a quick look at his chart before speaking. "Good news, no infection. You'll be out of here in no time. How are you feeling?"

"Dopey," Matt replied.

Beckmann nodded. "I'll check on you again later in the day." She told him how long the bandages needed to stay on, how he was to care for his face until his next outpatient appointment in a week, and when he would be scheduled to return to be fitted with his new eye. "I'll go over all of this with you again," she added.

"Is all this what you weren't telling me yesterday?"

Beckmann looked surprised. "Why, yes," she lied. "I didn't want to overwhelm you with too much information."

Matt laughed. Beckmann might be new to the army, but she already had the right stuff when it came to keeping the troops in the dark.

"Why is that funny?" Beckmann asked.

"No reason, Doc," Matt replied, figuring only another dogface would see the humor. He wondered what kind of cartoon Bill Mauldin might have dreamt up about it. Matt couldn't come up with anything, but with his mile-wide funny streak Mauldin would have thought of something hilarious.

Beckmann shook her head in puzzlement and left.

As the fog from the anesthetic lifted, Matt's mood continued to improve, and when the orderlies wheeled him to the post-op ward he got to thinking that maybe Doc Beckmann had not only fixed the problem of his awful pain and headaches, but had also rid him of his sulky temperament. More likely he was just giddy from the heavy dose of drugs.

No other patients had come out of surgery so far that morning, and all the other beds were empty. One of the orderlies, an older private with a pronounced limp, gave Matt a sharp look as he helped move him off the gurney onto the hospital bed. Before he left, he took another close look at Matt, paused momentarily to glance at the chart, and seemed about to say something. Instead he retreated silently down the corridor as Anna Lynn and Ginny came hurrying to his bedside.

Matt didn't recognize the man at all, but he looked vaguely familiar. He gave up trying to put a name to his face and turned his attention to his visitors, smiling broadly. Tongue-in-cheek, he said, "Well, if it isn't my own little loving family come to visit."

Anna Lynn wrinkled her nose at his wisecrack and kissed him on the lips. "Your doctor wouldn't have let us near you if I hadn't lied and said we were married. So I'm your wife, but only until we can take you home."

"I've got no complaints with that," Matt replied, grinning. He asked her how she'd found out about his surgery.

Anna Lynn smiled. "You're the most reliable man I've ever

known, and when you didn't return as you promised I knew there had to be a reason. So we drove to Alamogordo and I called the hospital from the train station and learned you were scheduled for surgery this morning. We drove right down."

"We slept in the truck, and we're going to stay over in the city until we take you home," Ginny said excitedly, as if it were a grand adventure, looking up at Matt from his bedside. "But you still have only one eye," she announced with great disappointment.

"My doc says I'm gonna get a new one soon," Matt said.

Ginny smiled at the prospect. "Then will you stop wearing that patch? Mamma hates it."

"Maybe," Matt replied.

Footsteps down the corridor announced the impending arrival of Lt. Raine Hartman.

"I think we're about to be shooed away." Anna Lynn gave Matt another smooch. "We'll leave you in the hands of your pretty, young nurse. Don't flirt with her too much."

"Why not?" he asked, feigning confusion.

The lighthearted tone in Matthew's voice, missing for so many months, brought a warm smile to Anna Lynn's face. She kissed him again. "On second thought, go ahead. A little flirtation might be good for you."

* * *

With the realization that Doc Beckmann's first surgery patient of the day was quite possibly none other than Matthew Kerney, *his* Matthew Kerney, Pvt. Fredrick Robertson Tyler forgot about keeping his nose clean and getting out of the army with an honorable discharge. Known as Fred to his buddies on the base, Tyler stood outside the ophthalmology ward, lit a cigarette, and mulled over his discovery. First off, he needed to make damn sure that he wasn't mistaken about the man he'd helped wheel from surgery to post-op. If it was Kerney, it would be stupid to reveal himself to the woman and little girl who were visiting him at his bedside. A closer look at Kerney's medical chart should do the trick, and if Tyler needed more proof about the patient's identity, a pal in personnel could let him have a look-see at his service jacket.

Tyler took a long drag on his smoke, hoping the woman and little girl would come out of the building before his cigarette break was up. He wanted a closer look at Kerney's happy little family for future reference.

When the war started, Fred figured he was too old, too lame, and too undesirable to be drafted into the army. But at age forty-four, with an armed robbery conviction on his sheet and a smashed foot courtesy of a fellow inmate at the New Mexico State Penitentiary in Santa Fe, his local draft board classified him as acceptable for limited military service. A month later he was inducted into the army, put through an abbreviated Basic Training course for men unfit for combat assignments, and sent to Fort Bliss along with a few other semi-cripples, misfits, and miscreants to serve as medical orderlies.

Years of living in prison surrounded by dangerous men made the army a cakewalk for Fred Tyler. He figured he'd remain safe and sound stateside at Fort Bliss, frequent the Juárez whorehouses when he had money and some leave, maybe earn a stripe or two, and get out with everyone else who'd been drafted for the duration plus six months. Then he'd return to the business of robbery.

But if he was correct about the man in post-op, he had to change that plan some. Years earlier, he'd been expecting to rob a kid named Matthew Kerney living alone in a house his mother had left him, only to have the kid scald him with boiling hot coffee, stab him in the arm, knock him unconscious with a frying pan, and get him arrested by the cops. Later in open court, Kerney had accused Tyler of killing his friend Boone Mitchell, which Tyler had done, though it couldn't be proved at the time because no dead body had been found.

Kerney's accusation caused the presiding judge to hang two consecutive sentences on Tyler, doubling his prison time. For that alone he needed to settle accounts. Moreover, it gnawed at him that a punk kid barely out of high school had gotten the best of him. Now, miraculously, here was an opportunity for a reckoning. Tyler figured something much more painful than a bone-breaking beating or a slow, agonizing death for Matt Kerney was in order.

The price Kerney paid needed to be steep. As Kerney's wife and daughter stepped out into the hot early-morning sun, he got the idea that maybe Kerney losing his family might just be the ticket. As they approached him, that notion became even more appealing.

He field-stripped the cigarette butt, smiled, touched a finger to his fatigue cap, and said as the woman and child drew near, "Don't you worry none about your man, ma'am. We'll take good care of him and get him back home to you in a jiffy."

The woman took a half step back, gave him a studied look, smiled through thin lips, and thanked him rather stiffly, as if he were some lowlife crud looking for a handout.

The tight-assed bitch's reaction pleased Tyler. He watched her hurry to the visitor parking lot clutching the little girl tightly by the hand. *This just might be a lot of fun,* he thought.

* * *

Anna Lynn drove through downtown El Paso past the ritzy, ten-story Hotel Paso Del Norte that soared over the nearby plaza. Several years earlier, she'd stayed there with Matt on an unforgettable romantic weekend that still brought a smile to her lips every time she thought about it. But with money tight, she couldn't afford such luxury. Instead, she stopped at a motor-coach inn on the street to the Rio Grande, where the international border separated El Paso from the Mexican city of Juárez. She rented one of the brick bungalows with attached garages shaded by a grove of trees and sheltered behind an adobe wall. Each bungalow came with a double bed, radio, telephone, hotplate, and coffeepot.

At a nearby market run by a Mexican couple, Anna Lynn stocked up on some groceries. Back in the bungalow, she gave Ginny a bottle of cold soda pop, along with several children's picture books she was using to teach her to read that she'd hurriedly packed in her suitcase before leaving Mountain Park. Then she brewed a pot of coffee.

Ginny sat at a small table under the window that looked out at the walled courtyard, happy with her soda and books, reading aloud the words she'd already learned as she turned the pages. Recently, she'd started reading some of the Sunday funny papers all by herself. When the pot finished perking, Anna Lynn sipped her coffee and thought about the soldier who had greeted her outside the hospital ward. The man's leer masquerading as a smile, the belligerent look in his eye, and his aggressive tone disturbed her. Had he been deliberately waiting for them? For what reason? To stop them solely to reassure them about Matt's care made no sense.

He'd given her the willies. Her instincts warned her that he was dangerous. Did it have something to do with Matt, or was he one of those monsters who raped and murdered women, or kidnapped and molested young girls like Ginny? She could think of no other reasons why a complete stranger would behave in such a threatening way.

Anna Lynn decided not to bother Matt about it, but she'd keep a watchful eye out for the soldier with the angular, mean-looking face and long scar below his cheekbone. She turned on the radio just in time for the hourly news broadcast and joined Ginny at the table. After lunch and a nap they'd go to see Matt again and visit with his doctor. She wanted to know exactly how to care for Matt after his return home.

2

Two days after his surgery, Dr. Beckmann discharged Matt from the hospital with strict orders that he was to be under Anna Lynn's constant care throughout his recuperation, up to and including the fitting of his new eye. She wrote out instructions for Anna Lynn to follow, warned Matt against strenuous physical activity, and gave him appointments for follow-up visits at the hospital.

Eager to go home, Matt's only demand was that he be allowed to recuperate at the ranch. Anna Lynn readily agreed. Aside from her own Mountain Park farmhouse, she loved no place better than the 7-Bar-K headquarters perched on the remote eastern slope of the San Andres Mountains overlooking the Tularosa.

At the ranch, Matt's spirits continued to improve so much so that Patrick, who filled his free hours doting on Ginny, thought Matt was finally pulling out of the dark funk that had settled over him since his army discharge. Patrick even went so far as to suggest to Anna Lynn that it would do Matt a world of good if she gave up or rented out her Mountain Park farm and moved permanently to the ranch with Ginny. When she asked if this brilliant idea was his or Matt's, he stammered something about it being a darn good notion nonetheless and huffed off to care for two of his old ponies, who lulled, fully retired, in the near pasture next to the corral.

Over the years Anna Lynn had warned Matt that she neither wished to marry nor live full-time with any man. Having learned that arguing about it made no difference to her firmly held point of view, Matt hadn't said a word about making their relationship permanent. Nonetheless, he seemed to be enjoying Anna Lynn's constant attention, companionship, and care, and she'd noticed the lovely little spark of sexual tension that had been missing between them for so long had returned.

For Anna Lynn, the week had been so pleasant she'd come to realize that *almost* being a wife was actually quite enjoyable. It also struck her that she'd spent more time sharing a bed with Matt, and more time in his company, than with any other man ever. He'd truly become the love of her life. The ironclad truth of it warmed her heart. And to cement matters, Ginny, who loved Matt almost as much as she adored Patrick, had been acting as though she'd stepped into the midst of her natural family. Anna Lynn had never seen her happier.

She made no mention of her private thoughts to Matthew or Patrick. But the idea had begun to rattle around in her head that perhaps she should reexamine her need to preserve her fiercely held notion of independence at all costs. She'd lived by that one rule for so long the idea of possibly changing it was simultaneously appealing and disquieting.

By the end of his first week home and their return from his initial follow-up appointment with Dr. Beckmann, Matt's restlessness caught up with him. In a voice that brooked no argument, he announced to Anna Lynn that it had been too long since the small herd of mares and foals pastured in a mountain meadow had been looked after. He suggested an outing by wagon to the high country cabin in the San Andres, and proposed that they ask Patrick to come along to keep an eye on Ginny and her pony.

The idea thrilled Anna Lynn. She asked him to put off the journey for a day so she could prepare a picnic basket for the trip up to the cabin, assemble groceries she needed for meals while they were there, get clothes and bedding packed, and put together a kit of bandages and ointments for the treatment of Matt's eye. He agreed without complaint, but said he'd wait only one day.

When she told Ginny they were going on an adventure to the cabin and she'd be allowed to ride her pony there, she whirled and skipped around the kitchen table like a pint-size tornado and wanted to leave immediately. Patrick curbed her exuberance with chores in the barn that included brushing and currying Ginny's pony, Peaches, in preparation for the trip.

That night on the veranda, Anna Lynn complimented Matt for his wonderful idea. "Everybody's so happy you suggested it," she added.

"I reckon it is a good one," he allowed with a slight smile. "And those mares and foals do need looking after."

"You seem to be more your old self," she ventured, reaching for his hand.

Matt nodded. "I didn't realize how deep a hole of self-pity I'd dug for myself. It took a while to climb out of it." He suddenly laughed. "But I still have a hole to deal with, except now it's the one in my head. I tell you, it's a strange feeling to have an eyeball gone missing."

"It must be, but you're handling it wonderfully," Anna Lynn replied. Every day she applied ointment and put a fresh bandage over Matt's eye socket as Dr. Beckmann had ordered, and it *was* strange and somewhat unsettling to see the empty space where his left eye had been. She wanted to tell him how brave he was but instead added, "You'll have a new eye soon, and then you'll look just fine."

"Not soon enough," Matt groused.

Originally his new eye was to have been ready in three weeks, but swelling from the surgery had made Dr. Beckmann extend her estimate of how long it would take. Now it would be four weeks until Dr. Beckmann made the cast for the eye, and another three weeks to get the finished eye back from the lab.

"She did apologize for the delay," Anna Lynn reminded him.

"She'll learn fast in the army it's all about hurry up and wait." He leaned against the veranda railing and watched the first hint of moonlight crest the Sacramento Mountains. "Let's change the subject."

"Okay," she said as she pressed against him and whispered conspiratorially in his ear. "I have an idea. What would you say to a little hanky-panky, if I did all the work so that your head wasn't jarred by any sudden, strenuous physical activity?"

Matt slid his hand around her waist. "Well, it would be ungentlemanly of me to refuse such a polite request," he whispered in return. "But you'll have to be very gentle with me."

Anna Lynn nibbled his ear. "I think I can manage that."

Through the open living-room window they could hear Patrick reading Ginny the magazine story Gene Rhodes had written about Matt's mom, Emma Kerney, making a hand on a cattle drive back in the old days. "Do you have a place in mind?" he added.

Anna Lynn smiled seductively, grabbed his hand, turned on her heel, and led him toward the veranda steps. "A horse blanket spread on some hay in the barn will do nicely, Sergeant Kerney."

* * *

By the dint of hard experience, Pvt. Fred Tyler thought himself to be cautious and cunning. In the old days, before prison, he'd always looked at all the angles before pulling a heist, doing a burglary, or strong-arming some drunken idiot stumbling out of a saloon. Until the day he encountered Matthew Kerney, Tyler had never been arrested or charged for a crime. So for starters, he wanted to make absolutely sure that the Matthew Kerney he'd wheeled out of post-op was the right guy before he embarked upon taking his revenge.

One look at Kerney's discharge papers slipped to him by a buddy in personnel proved he hadn't been mistaken. Kerney had been born in the same house in Las Cruces where Tyler had waited on a cold, cheerless morning to rob him, only to wind up with the stuffing knocked out of him, arrested, sent to prison, and deprived of over ten years of freedom.

But Kerney's army records raised some questions Tyler needed answered before he hatched a plan. Enlistment paperwork showed him entering the service as a single man, and there was nothing in his file showing he'd gotten married while on active duty. Also, the only life-insurance beneficiaries on Kerney's GI policy were his father, Patrick, who lived at the 7-Bar-K Ranch along a state road east of the village of Engle, New Mexico, and a minor child, Virginia Louise Hurley, living with Anna Lynn Crawford at a PO box address in Mountain Park, New Mexico. Although Captain Beckmann's medical-chart entry showed Kerney's authorized visitors were his wife, Anna Lynn, and his daughter, Ginny, Tyler now had doubts about who they really were.

He wondered if Kerney was simply shacking up with the woman

and her kid. If so, did Kerney truly give a damn about the skirt and her brat? Did he care enough about them that seriously punishing the woman and little girl would cause the suffering Kerney deserved? And what was making the kid a beneficiary on his life insurance policy all about? Was little Ginny blood kin? Was the woman an in-law or something? Was she like some war widow related to Kerney by marriage? Tyler needed to know more.

Kerney's service jacket had contained the citations for the medals he'd won in Sicily. Included was a copy of an army press release about his exploits overseas, which made him out to be a hero. All that hero stuff about Kerney annoyed Tyler. Maybe he'd been lucky in battle, but there was no way he could've stood up to ten years living with cold-blooded cons at the state prison. On the inside, he would have either been shanked or made somebody's bitch within a month. The thought of Kerney being violated by some hairy goon soothed Tyler's irritation about his war record. The one-eyed hero wasn't a hard case like the badasses Tyler had gone up against in the pen. He'd still be locked up serving a life sentence if the screws had been able to prove he'd killed the con who had mangled his foot with a claw hammer during a brawl in the prison wood shop.

Because of weekly medical appointment postings, Tyler had no problem keeping track of Kerney's follow-up visits with Captain Beckmann. He always came accompanied by the woman, which made Tyler wonder who looked after sweet little Ginny. And aside from Kerney's old man, were there other people in the picture at the ranch he needed to know about?

Although he was sure Kerney hadn't recognized him, Tyler made it a point to steer clear of him and the woman on his appointment days so as not to jar any recollection from the past. Once, as he hurried by pushing a wheelchair-bound patient, he saw them from a distance outside the Ophthalmology Building. The woman turned and looked back in his direction, but Tyler had been too far away to be recognized. Besides, he figured they'd only met briefly one time and she probably didn't remember him at all.

Nurse Raine Hartman, who'd become friendly with Kerney and the woman during his time in post-op, told Tyler that they always came to town a day before his scheduled appointments and stayed at a motor inn downtown. She didn't know which one. Tyler almost asked if she knew who cared for their little girl while they were gone from home, but decided against it. Too many questions might raise suspicions as to why he was so interested in Kerney, and he'd be hard-pressed to give a plausible reason other than he wanted to permanently ruin the SOB's life.

Determined to learn what he could from a distance about Kerney's home ground, Tyler visited the post library to consult an atlas and study road maps. From what he estimated, Kerney's ranch was about a hundred miles north of El Paso and forty miles west of the village of Tularosa, off a state highway that ran through the San Andres Mountains to Engle—another small settlement in the desert along the Santa Fe Railroad tracks. Good news in terms of not having to travel very far.

In the library stacks he also located an official US Government Land Office book from the 1930s that contained a foldout map showing all of the state of New Mexico's federal, state, tribal, homestead, and private landholdings. The 7-Bar-K Ranch was clearly marked on a big swath of land along the east slope of the San Andres Mountains. He could see by the contour lines on a Geologic Survey topo map that the ranch ran from the Alkali Flats on the Tularosa Basin into deep, tangled canyons and up rugged mountain peaks.

Tyler knew absolutely nothing about ranching, but he could tell from the maps that Kerney owned a whole lot of land, and people with that much property usually had things worth stealing. The possibility of coming away with some good loot made it all the more appealing to take a close look-see at Kerney's ranch, as well as find out more about Anna Lynn Crawford's digs in Mountain Park. Once he knew all the players and saw where and how they lived, then he'd decide what move to make. What he needed now was time to reconnoiter and the money to pay for it.

Tyler thought about going AWOL, but ditched the idea as plain stupid. That would only serve to put the MPs on his tail. Instead, he'd do it legit and take some accumulated leave. As a buck private, he earned fifty dollars a month and was down to a ten-spot in his wallet with three weeks to go before pay call. He'd borrowed from a sergeant in the motor pool once before who lent money at 20 percent interest per week compounded. How much more moolah he needed depended on when Kerney was scheduled for his next visit.

After hours, when the offices in the Ophthalmology Unit were empty, he slipped into Beckmann's office and flipped through her appointment book. A note in her neat script showed Kerney was scheduled to be fitted for his glass eye in two weeks. That was perfect. It was SOP for patients getting glass eyes to be held over an extra day to make sure everything fit. That would give Tyler even more time to poke around the 7-Bar-K Ranch.

He found Maurice Michelet, the motor-pool sergeant, in his barracks room hosting a poker game, and arranged to borrow thirty bucks in two weeks, which would cost him over forty when the loan came due on payday. He'd worry about being almost tapped out then. If he had to, he'd do some stealing on base and fence the merchandise in Juárez.

In the morning after breakfast, before reporting to his duty station, Tyler stopped by the company HQ, filled out a leave request, and turned it in to First Sgt. Leland Childs.

"You just want five days, Tyler?" Childs asked, flicking his cigarette in the direction of the ashtray on his desk. He was tall, skinny, and had an acne-scarred face along with a sour disposition. "What for?"

Tyler shrugged and smiled slyly. "I got a skirt coming to see me. That's all the time she can spare from her factory job in California."

Childs grunted and signed the request. "Don't get so nookie-whipped you forget to come back. You're due for a stripe next month."

Tyler laughed. "I sure wouldn't want to mess that up, Sarge."

Childs grunted and handed Tyler the form. "What are ya standing there for? Your leave doesn't start for two weeks. Go to work."

Tyler grinned and turned on his heel. Two weeks couldn't pass fast enough.

* * *

The day before Matt and Anna Lynn were to leave for Fort Bliss, a corporal in an army jeep from the Alamogordo Army Air Field ground to a stop at the ranch house, knocked on the open door, asked to speak to Matthew Kerney, and handed him a sealed envelope.

"Is this the check I'm owed for the two dead ponies the flyboys killed?" Matt asked, waving the envelope at the young soldier standing on the veranda, looking miserable, uncomfortable, in perfect health, and no more than nineteen. Matt had no sympathy for any able-bodied GI sitting out the war stateside.

"I don't know, sir," Cpl. James Barko replied with a nod to a woman who had joined Mr. Kerney on the veranda. He'd driven from the airfield to the ranch in a hot car with the windows down, and his face was crusted with dust and his uniform shirt damp with sweat. "I was just told by my lieutenant to bring this to you right away."

The enclosed telex message from Dr. Beckmann read:

> *Due to an unexpected problem, your appointment tomorrow is rescheduled for 8 AM, June 6. The laboratory shipped a green eye instead of blue. My apologies for the mix-up.*
>
> *Capt. S. Beckmann, MD, USA Medical Corps*
> *William Beaumont Hospital*
> *Fort Bliss, TX*

Matt laughed and handed the message to Anna Lynn. "Seems our trip to Fort Bliss is delayed until June sixth."

Anna Lynn scanned the telex and said, "You're taking it lightly."

Matt shrugged. "There's nothing I can do about it."

"One green and one blue would be an interesting combination," she suggested.

"Certainly eye-catching, wouldn't you say?" Matt said.

Anna Lynn suppressed a giggle and smiled at the young soldier, wondering why Matt hadn't shown the boy, who looked decidedly nonplussed by the exchange, any hospitality. "Can I get you a cool drink?" she asked him.

"No thank you, ma'am," Corporal Barko replied, desperate to depart. Born and raised along the Delaware Bay, he hated the desert, the heat, the dryness, the absence of water, and the boredom of New Mexico. He also hated the army that sent him to such an awful place. "Do you want to reply to the message, sir?" he asked Matt.

"Nope, just tell your general or whoever is in charge of the flyboys to pay me for my two dead ponies."

"I'll pass that along, sir." Barko nodded again to the woman, retreated to the vehicle, and quickly drove away. In the pasture, the tires of his car threw a billowing cloud of dust that veiled a horseback rider approaching at a fast trot.

"Now what?" Kerney asked, trying to identify the rider.

Anna Lynn searched Matt's face. "Why were you rude to that boy?"

"I wasn't rude, just unsympathetic." Through the diminishing dust cloud, Matt made out Al Jennings Jr. approaching on his gelding. "Al Jr. has come calling and I don't think he's got good news."

* * *

Al's news wasn't good. Someone in a vehicle had busted through the gate to the 7-Bar-K high pasture where Matt was grazing his mares and foals and scattered them onto the desert scrub of the Jornada west of the San Andres. Al rounded up two that had strayed onto his land, but the rest were nowhere to be seen. From the tracks he'd found, it had probably happened about a week earlier.

"I figure it was some army boys from the airfield, out joyriding in jeeps," Al added. "The sheriff says he's had half a dozen reports from ranchers that have spotted them trespassing and spooking their livestock."

"Well, I'd better go fetch them critters back," Patrick said from the living-room couch.

"I'll lend a hand," Al offered, which was about all he had, having lost a thumb and forefinger in a roping accident. It hadn't slowed him one mite.

"That's mighty neighborly," Matt said, perched on the edge of the desk. "But you two aren't going anywhere without me."

"You shouldn't," Anna Lynn cautioned. "Besides, it could be dangerous."

Matt fell silent for a moment and then burst out laughing.

"What's funny?" Patrick asked.

"Think about it," Matt said. "You with a stove-up leg from when you crashed the truck, Al missing some fingers, and me with one good eye. Now who, pray tell, would be foolish enough to rile us?"

"I didn't crash the truck," Patrick grumbled. "A buck deer ran into it."

"I like our odds," Al said, grinning.

"So do I." Matt rose to his feet. "Let's get packing."

Ginny, who'd been quiet during the grown-up conversation, tugged Matt's sleeve. "I can go too," she announced, smiling hopefully.

"Not this time," Anna Lynn replied. "Us girls get to stay behind. And don't you dare pout."

Ginny pouted anyway and stomped out of the room.

Within an hour the three men were on their way, Patrick and Matt trailing pack animals. With Ginny at her side still pouting,

Anna Lynn stood wet-eyed on the veranda and waved goodbye as the riders moved up the ranch road that led to the high country cabin. She'd wanted to argue strenuously with Matt not to go, but outmatched by three true-blue cowboys who weren't about to be dissuaded from doing what was best, she held her tongue. And besides, all the lust for life that the war had drained out of Matt was back in full force, and was such a tearful joy to see.

3

The day before Matt Kerney's scheduled appointment with Dr. Susan Beckmann at William Beaumont Hospital, Pvt. Fred Tyler started a five-day leave from Fort Bliss. Dressed in civvies and carrying a small satchel containing a change of clothes and an army-issued model M1911 .45-caliber semiautomatic he'd stolen from an MP soldier's footlocker, he caught a midmorning bus to Alamogordo.

Once there, he had a sandwich, apple pie, and coffee at a luncheonette before hitchhiking his way to Mountain Park through the Mexican village of La Luz along a winding gravel state road that hugged canyon walls. At the village post office, he told the portly postmaster he was Anna Lynn Crawford's cousin just back from the war on convalescent leave and looking to find her. The story and his limp from his badly damaged foot got Tyler sympathy and directions to Crawford's farmhouse, although the postmaster added he didn't think she was home, as she hadn't picked up her mail for some time.

Tyler thanked the man with a wave and a smile, stepped outside, and started down the steep road that cut through the village. He could see for miles across the empty desert to a hazy mountain range, and wondered exactly where Kerney had his ranch. The distance across the valley looked daunting but the thin ribbon of the state highway reassured him. He was sure to catch a ride.

There wasn't much to Mountain Park. It was just a sleepy spot on the map, with a general store, a church, a small schoolhouse, and some homes scattered on a hillside and in a narrow valley sprinkled with apple orchards. There were shuttered roadside fruit and vegetable stands along the way, stands of tall evergreens in the high, forested country above the settlement, and a long wooden railroad trestle that loomed over the far side of the pinched valley. Tyler reckoned the citizens were mostly poor and struggling. Other than knocking over the general store or the post office, he figured doing robbery in Mountain Park wouldn't be worth the effort.

Anna Lynn Crawford's tidy farmhouse sat in the mouth of a shallow side canyon on a nice piece of grassy land. An empty corral sat fifty yards or so from the front porch and there was a row of handmade wooden white-painted beehives out back. Tyler called out from the front porch to make sure no one was home before trying the door, which was, as he had hoped, unlocked. He slipped inside and took a quick look around the orderly front room, the kitchen, and two adjacent bedrooms—one for a child, the other containing a large, comfortable bed with fluffy pillows. A framed pencil drawing under glass of a younger-looking Matthew Kerney hung on the wall above the headboard. In a tall, ornate wardrobe he found a couple of pairs of pressed men's jeans and long-sleeved work shirts on hangers. Inside the drawer of a bedside table was a stack of letters tied with a ribbon that Kerney had written to Anna Lynn while in the army. He paged through them. Some were downright lovey-dovey.

Tyler smiled. The question of whether Anna Lynn Crawford was more than just a skirt to Kerney had definitely been answered. He considered busting the pencil drawing and scattering the glass on the bed but thought better of it. Best to leave things as they were. He started an exhaustive search looking for valuables, carefully putting everything back in its place.

The house was filled with homey things women accumulate: kitchen pots and pans, enough dinnerware and utensils for a squad of soldiers, letters from relatives, family photographs—some showing Kerney with little Ginny as a toddler or with an old man who looked like his father—and an amazing number of books. There were also sewing baskets, a hamper filled with unfinished needlework, several kitchen shelves of home-canned fruits and jars of raw honey, shoeboxes crammed with old receipts and sales slips, a small wooden box filled with inexpensive jewelry, and a nice sterling-silver tea service, each piece wrapped in protective cloth, tucked away at the back of the top pantry shelf.

It took the better part of an hour to finish his search. He came away with thirty dollars in greenbacks from the pocket of a ladies' winter coat in the bedroom wardrobe and two dollars and seventeen cents in a piggybank in the kid's room. He pocketed the money, pleased that he now had enough cash to cover the entire loan minus the interest he owed Master Sergeant Michelet. He made a mental note to return for the tea service after he'd disposed of the bitch and her brat.

With the day fading and the sun hanging low in the western sky, Tyler hitchhiked down the road, getting a ride within ten minutes from a grizzled Forest Service worker on his way home to Alamogordo. The man had once been a supervisor at a CCC camp in the nearby national forest, and on the trip down the mountain he jawboned about the hardships of the Great Depression before the war. Tyler let him ramble on without interruption. He got dropped off at the junction to the US highway and was told Tularosa was seven miles north, where a rundown village hotel rented cheap but clean rooms.

In the cool of the evening, he hoofed it for a mile before a Mexican farmer named Miguel Chávez, who spoke good English, gave him a ride in his wagon the rest of the way. As Chávez slowed in front of a dilapidated hotel, he told Tyler it had once been owned by an Irishman named Coghlan, who'd been known throughout the basin as the king of Tularosa—a man now long dead and almost forgotten.

"My father told me that in its day the hotel had the best saloon, the best restaurant, and the best whores on the whole Tularosa," Chávez added, gazing at the listing veranda that fronted the hotel. "He said it was the most elegant place in town. Soon they will tear it down, I think."

Tyler, who was not well disposed toward Mexicans, Negroes, foreigners of any stripe, or snobs who thought themselves his betters, grunted his thanks as he climbed off the wagon seat. He was tired, wanted a drink, food, and a bed, and didn't give a hoot about some long-dead Irishman and his once-ritzy hotel.

"Know a good place to eat?" he asked Chávez.

Chávez pointed down the quiet street to a blinking electric sign a quarter mile away. "Where the road forks there is a bar and diner. The food is okay and they stay open late."

Inside the hotel, the threadbare carpet in front of the reception desk, several burned out electric lightbulbs in the table lamps, and the scruffy lobby furniture didn't faze Tyler at all. From his time in the prison woodshop, he could tell the dingy wainscoting on the walls was first-class carpentry and the dinged-up furniture had been handmade. The Mexican had been right about the hotel once being grand.

Tyler paid for one night, climbed the squeaky stairs to his room, dumped his satchel on the bed, and hoofed it up the street to the bar and diner. Over a whiskey and a hot meal, he'd study the New Mexico road map he'd picked up at an Alamogordo service station, estimate the miles he had to travel to reach Kerney's ranch, and decide if he should keep hitchhiking in the morning or steal a car.

* * *

At sundown, Matt, Patrick, and Al Jennings made camp at an old Bar Cross horse camp on the Jornada not far from the Camino Real that once stretched from Mexico City to Santa Fe. They'd cut trail on the mares and foals twice, only to lose it on a volcanic rock field and again at a perilous lava break that flowed around a stand of petrified tree stumps. To the west, the Fra Cristobal Mountains rose up, masking the Rio Grande. To the east, basalt-capped black mesas hovered in the foreground with the Oscura Mountains beyond.

Earlier in the day at the high pasture, Al's conclusion that joyriding army boys in jeeps had busted the gate and spooked and scattered the herd proved true. They followed the trail to a yucca grove on the edge of the Jornada where the jeeps had turned back, and tracked fresh hoofprints north over some faint tire tracks that ran through desert scrub and stopped in the middle of nowhere at the base of a low mesa. There the footprints of four men led from two parked vehicles to the top of the mesa. The party had tromped around for a time, pausing to look in all directions before descending to their vehicles, where they turned around and went back the way they came.

The pony tracks veered east toward the bald face of the Oscuras, but low hummocks hid from view the sight of any animals that might be loitering, and there was no telltale dust floating skyward to signal movement of the herd. The riders pushed on, hoping to find the ponies at the abandoned Bar Cross horse camp where a steady trickle of water from a creaky old windmill filled a rusty tank, but all they found were signs the herd had recently moved eastward.

Patrick speculated the ponies were looking for browse, drifting toward the old McDonald Ranch that ran hard up against the Oscuras. "We'll catch up to them in the morning," he predicted as he put the coffeepot on the campfire to boil. "But answer me this: Why were four men driving around in the middle of this forlorn country for no good reason? It makes no sense."

"The tire tracks came from army jeeps," Al said as he joined Matt and Patrick at the campfire. "Maybe some soldier boys were treasure hunting or sightseeing."

"Except for the old, played-out Spanish mine in the Fra Cristobals there's no treasure here to be found," Patrick remarked as he gingerly sat on the chair he'd rescued from the dilapidated, varmint-infested cabin. At sixty-nine, his gimpy leg and the long day in the saddle had left his body sore and aching. "And while it can be a pretty slice of country at times, there ain't that much to see."

"They were looking at something," Matt said.

"Like what?" Al asked.

Matt shrugged. "I don't know, but they drove straight to that mesa, took a long gander, and went back the same way they came."

Patrick filled his cup with boiling coffee and passed the pot around. "If they weren't treasure hunting, rubbernecking, or joyriding, then why bother? It's plumb mystifying."

"Stupid or smart, the army always has its reasons," Matt said.

Having served as a Rough Rider under Teddy Roosevelt in the Spanish-American War, Patrick nodded in agreement. "I wonder what dumb thing it could be," he added.

"It's too far from anywhere civilized to make any sense," Al noted.

"But if you want to do something on the sly, this big empty is just about the perfect place for it," Matt conjectured.

"That's savvy thinking." Patrick opened the hamper of food Anna Lynn had packed and pawed through the contents. "There's a canned ham in here and some of Anna Lynn's homemade muffins that look inviting, and I'm a mite hungry. Let's chew on it over supper."

During supper, and to no one's satisfaction, the men tossed around notions of what the army was doing on the Jornada. Then they turned in under the blanket of a million stars in a clear night sky with the first hint of a full moon touching the tips of the Oscuras. Before sunup they struck camp and were trailing the ponies at a good clip when they came upon Billy McDonald, who was driving Matt's mares and foals toward the Bar Cross horse camp they'd just vacated.

"Howdy and I'm glad to see y'all," Billy called out with a pleased smile. No more than sixteen, young McDonald had left school after the fifth grade to help on the family ranch. "It saves me the trouble of herding these renegade mares and their babies back home to you."

"*Buenos dias,*" Matt replied as he drew rein and gave his ponies a quick once-over. They all looked healthy, including the little ones. "We're glad to see you as well. Where did you find them?"

"In the pasture near my grandpa's old place, none the worse for wear," Billy answered as he drew alongside the three riders. His cowboy hat hid his red hair but not the freckles on his face. "I watered them good and let them graze overnight. I'll ride with you a spell to the horse camp."

"I'm in your debt, and your company is most welcome," Matt said.

Patrick tipped his hat. "You done good and we're obliged."

"That's the truth of it, Billy," Al echoed with a grin.

"No need for all of that," Billy said, unable to hide his pleasure at the compliments.

The riders fell into place side by side and as they pushed the little herd along, Matt asked Billy if he'd seen anything unusual lately on the Jornada.

Billy nodded and explained that for several months soldiers had been driving a bunch of civilians around in jeeps taking pictures with big cameras, floating large balloons in the sky, and doing all kinds of strange stuff with instruments the likes of which he'd never seen before. Once, when he tried to approach them neighborly, MPs had shooed him away with stern looks.

"Has anybody talked to them?" Al asked.

Billy shook his head. "Appears not. My pa says the Socorro County sheriff was told the government is looking for a safe place to store a lot of military ammunition."

"Now, that makes good horse sense," Patrick said. "Put it out here where no one gets hurt if it blows up."

"Mystery solved," Al said as he guided a skittish foal back to its mama.

At the horse camp, the riders watered the ponies, parted company with Billy McDonald, and started the trek back to the 7-Bar-K. Matt figured they could get home before the next sunup if they made an early stop for a cold supper and kept the ponies moving once the full moon broke over the mountains.

Al allowed that even though the ponies had been found safe and sound, he'd ride along for a spell before heading home. Matt thanked him again for his neighborly help. Patrick winced at the thought of his aching bones come the end of another day and a full night in the saddle and glanced west. Thick clouds had gathered above the Black Range, swirling into towering columns that pierced the turquoise sky.

"Best we get moving," he said, stifling a groan. "Storm's a-coming."

* * *

After an early breakfast in Tularosa, Fred Tyler decided it would only draw unneeded and unwelcome attention if he stole a car in the village. He slung the strap of the satchel over his shoulder and started out under the cool shade of big cottonwoods that bordered large adobe haciendas and adjacent irrigated farmland fed by dirt ditches that drew water from a slow-running stream. Outside the confines of the village, both the stream and the shade disappeared and the morning sun burned the back of his neck. He walked along the graveled state road, switching his gaze from the distant mountains to the broken, green-gray valley floor of greasewood, mesquite, prickly pear cactus, and occasional yucca groves with stalks ten feet high topped by dry, dead blossoms.

For a good hour he kept expecting to hear vehicles approaching from the village, but the only sound was the crunching of his shoes on the gravel underfoot. Ahead, the mountains seemed no closer. A huge, puffy white cloud hung over the highest peaks, crowned by a fanlike cloud that spread across the entire range. From the underbelly of the cloud an angry sheet of rain closed like a gray curtain over the mountains.

The storm, so far away, taunted Tyler with the luxury of unavailable shade and coolness. He trudged on. Starting out, he'd figured to catch a quick ride along the state road, which he'd assumed would be well traveled. So far, not one vehicle had passed in either direction.

He hadn't thought to bring water. His mouth was dry and the sun scorched his face. A harsh, gusty wind from the storm stung him with sand. He used his satchel to shield his face and had to turn around to protect himself when a dust devil came down the road and pelted him with gravel.

In all directions the land offered no escape or protection from the elements. Crouched at the side of the road, Tyler stopped walking until the winds abated and the storm drifted north, gradually returning the mountains to view. He knew from the maps he'd studied at the post library that Kerney's ranch was off the state road somewhere in foothill and mountainous terrain, but he could only guess how far he'd come and how many more miles he'd yet to travel.

Behind him, the village of Tularosa had long disappeared from view. Already running out of steam, Tyler decided to turn back if a vehicle didn't come his way in the next ten minutes. If he did manage to thumb a ride west, he might just take it straight on to Engle, get a room, and strike out again in the morning to Kerney's ranch.

He started his retreat to Tularosa just as a black Buick coupe came into view. Tyler stuck out a thumb, faked a gimpy limp with his bad foot, and gratefully watched the Buick coast to a stop beside him. He looked inside the open window and a man with a sweaty, red face leaned across the car seat and opened the passenger door. "Climb aboard," he said.

Tyler cracked a smile. "Thanks. I was starting to think nobody used this highway."

"It's desolate, that's for sure. Where are you heading?"

"To a ranch my buddy owns." Tyler got in, closed the door, and laid his satchel on his lap. The backseat of the coupe was filled with boxes. "It's off the highway up in the foothills. You moving?" he asked.

The man chuckled and nodded. "California bound. Got a new job as a procurement agent for a company in San Diego that does business with the navy. I decided to take the scenic route. Name's Mark Behr."

Behr extended his hand and Tyler shook it. "I'm Fred."

"Saw you limping a bit, Fred."

Tyler nodded. "Wounded in Italy," he lied.

Behr gave him a quick once-over. "Sorry to hear it. You look a little old to have served."

Tyler shrugged nonchalantly and kept lying. "I signed up right after Pearl Harbor. It was the right thing to do—fight for your country and all. I figured since I have no kin, my age didn't matter."

Behr nodded his approval and gingerly touched his chest. "I would've done the same myself except for a bad ticker. I'm sorry I've missed out."

"Be glad you didn't have to go," Tyler replied, trying to sound as world-weary as possible, remembering his years in the shit-heap state prison in Santa Fe. "There's nothing good about war."

"Yeah, I suppose you're right." Behr peered through the windshield at a bank of dark clouds that had descended over the mountains, moving in his direction. "Looks like more bad weather is coming. Do you know what the road is like up ahead? I sure wouldn't want to get stuck out here."

"Can't say that I do."

Behr gave him a thin, worried smile, tightened his grip on the steering wheel, and slowed the Buick in the face of the oncoming storm. "If the road turns real nasty, do you think your buddy would let me lay over at his ranch until it clears up?"

Tyler smiled broadly and nodded enthusiastically. Behr's request had just made his fishing expedition a whole lot simpler. "Sure he will. He's a good guy. Why, he'll put you up overnight if need be."

Behr's expression lightened. He was a beefy guy, maybe forty, with a soft gut and small hands that didn't match the rest of his body. "That's a relief. I'm glad I stopped to pick you up."

"Me too," Tyler replied with genuine appreciation.

Behr offered Tyler water from a jug on the front seat. He took several big swigs before returning it to the seat cushion just as thick raindrops splashed against the windshield. The rain turned to hail, pounding the roof of the Buick with the relentless *rat-tat-tat* sound of a machine gun.

"Jesus," Behr said, between clenched teeth.

Tyler's thoughts raced ahead. Maybe he should make this trip more than a simple fishing expedition. Kerney and his lady friend were in El Paso at Fort Bliss, which probably meant his old man was looking after the little girl at the ranch. Why not kill the old man and snatch the girl? That would surely cause Kerney enough harm and anguish.

He glanced at Behr. If he eliminated him as well, he'd have a getaway car plus the bonus of whatever money the man was carrying. Tyler grunted with satisfaction. He'd kill both Behr and Kerney's pa, and when he was finished with the girl, he'd dump her body in the desert. He'd abandon the car in Las Cruces and return to Fort Bliss as though nothing had happened. It was a perfect plan. He grinned at his sound thinking.

Behr had tensed up, his knuckles white on the steering wheel as the torrent came down in sheets. He cast a nervous glance at Tyler. "What ya grinning about?"

"I'm looking forward to seeing my old pal and his family, that's all," Tyler answered gleefully.

* * *

Matt, Patrick, and Al kept the small herd of ponies moving through the first pulse of the storm, but the second one stopped them in their tracks with a driving rain and lightning that lit up the ominous charcoal dark clouds. They threw up a rope corral to pen the agitated animals and hunkered down in their rain slickers under the bellies of their mounts to wait it out. In between the thunderclaps, wind, and pummeling rain, they could hear the throaty roar of water rushing in a nearby arroyo.

Although they were cold and wet, not a word of complaint passed among them. Monsoon season was still more than a month away and this unexpected, welcome, early storm was filling dry dirt tanks with water, soaking pastures of still-dormant native grasses, making sluggish mountain streams run fast, and replenishing the dry, cracked earth baked by the sun. There would be mud-soaked flatlands, washed-out trails, eroded ranch roads, leaky roofs, some flooding, and critters scattered everywhere, but for every rancher on the basin the storm was a boon rather than a burden.

When the rain slackened and the western sky cleared, Patrick rose slowly, clutching his stomach, a sour look plastered on his face.

"What's wrong?" Matt asked.

"Nothing." Patrick grimaced and turned away to re-cinch his saddle.

Matt stepped over to Patrick and looked him in the eye. "Don't lie to me."

"Gut ache, that's all," Patrick snapped. "Let's get these mares and their babies home." He started to mount, grabbed his stomach, and sank to his knees in pain. "Dammit," he moaned.

"I'm taking you to town to see the doctor," Matt said.

Patrick rose slowly and climbed on his pony. "No, you ain't. It's a gut ache, is all. I'll be fine. Just give me a minute. If I start feeling worse, I'll ride home on my own. You two can handle these mares and their babies."

"We can throw these ponies over into my pasture and you can ride on home with him," Al proposed to Matt.

Patrick shot Al a dirty look.

Al flashed him a smile. He'd lived on and managed the 7-Bar-K while Matt was in the army. Patrick's sourpuss didn't faze him a bit. Besides, the old-timer looked downright ill. "It will save a bunch of time."

Matt gave Patrick another worried glance. At a steady pace, in two hours they'd have the ponies settled safely on the Rocking J pasture. From there, they could go straight home over the mountain. He nodded at Al. "Okay, and once again I'm obliged."

"No need for the thanks," Al replied.

Patrick undid one end of the rope corral and shooed the mares out, the foals following alongside their mamas. "Well, stop jawboning and let's get going," he snapped, fighting to control his expression. The pain in his gut felt like a hot poker.

Matt had never seen his pa look so poorly. He wondered if Patrick was in a hurry to get home and die in his bed. He eased his pony behind the last mare and hurried her and her chestnut foal along. "You ride alongside, where I can see you," he ordered Patrick, who did as he was told.

* * *

In the storm, Tyler would have missed pointing out the ranch turnoff if it hadn't been for the 7-Bar-K wrought-iron sign at the side of the road. Several miles in, Behr got the right front wheel of his Buick stuck in a deep muddy rut on the ranch road. Flustered and red in the face, he gunned the engine, spun the wheels, and sank the tire deeper. He gladly turned the driving over to Tyler, who freed the Buick by slowly backing it up in reverse.

After ten more miles bouncing along the muddy, rutted road cut by fast-running rivulets, Tyler began to wonder exactly how far in the ranch house was from the state highway. The storm had cleared the basin and he could see nothing up ahead but uninhabited land with mountains to the west and desert to the east. He topped a small rise and the Buick nose-dived into a steep washout that had sliced across the road. Thrown forward, Behr cracked his head on the dashboard. Tyler left him whimpering in the car, holding a handkerchief to his forehead to stem the bleeding, and inspected the damage. Ankle-deep in muddy water, he bent down and checked the undercarriage. The Buick was high-centered on an exposed boulder half the size of the car. At the rear bumper he pushed the Buick to see if it would move. It didn't budge. Several more tries convinced him it would take a tow truck to dislodge it.

He reached through the open driver's door, killed the engine, and grabbed his satchel from the floorboard. He glanced at Behr, who looked miserable as he held the blood-soaked handkerchief against his face. Plans change. The man and his car had suddenly become useless.

"What do we do now?" Behr whined.

"I'll walk on ahead to the ranch house and get help."

Behr took the handkerchief away and shook his head. It was a nasty-looking gash. "I need medical attention. I'm not staying here to die by myself."

Tyler reached inside the satchel for the .45 semiautomatic. "You ain't dead yet," he said. He shot Behr twice in the chest, puncturing an artery that splattered blood across the dashboard. "Now you are," he added with a smile.

Tyler searched him, found a wallet containing a windfall hundred and eighty-four dollars, put it in his satchel, grabbed the half-full water jug from the car, and considered his next move. Being so far from anywhere, he figured Kerney had to have some sort of farm vehicle at his ranch. That would have to do for his getaway. He regretted that he wouldn't have much special time to spend with the little girl.

He glanced at the car. Nothing connected him to Behr or the Buick. Still, why take any chances the cops might find something? From the backseat of the coupe, he took one of Behr's shirts from a suitcase, tore it into strips, tied the strips together, and snaked them into the gas tank. He lit the end of the jerry-rigged fuse, made sure it kept burning, and hurried away from the car, the inside of his muddy shoes sloshing wet.

When he stopped and turned fifty yards from the Buick, wondering if the fuse had gone out, it exploded into a ball of fire.

* * *

The distant sound of two gunshots brought Anna Lynn to the veranda with Matt's binoculars. She'd been at the kitchen table schooling Ginny in her numbers, a subject she did not easily take to, when the shots rang out. With Ginny at her side, she scanned south, east, north, and west, wondering if joyriding soldiers in jeeps were once again shooting up the countryside, although she doubted anyone, no matter how idiotic, would have been outside by choice in the violent storm that had passed over the basin. She hoped Matt, Patrick, and Al had found shelter during the worst of it.

It wasn't hunting season and the ranch was posted, so gunfire made no sense unless someone was in trouble or up to mischief. She considered getting in her truck to see what had happened, but decided it best to stay put and remain alert.

"What do you see, Mama?" Ginny asked, tugging at Anna Lynn's jeans.

"Just a lot of beautiful country, sweetie," she answered. The ranch road was dotted with pools of muddy water and closer in she could see where the downpour had washed it out in places. The stream through the near pasture ran full, spilling its banks and fanning out across the coarse ground of the Alkali Flats. In the sunlight the basin sparkled with glistening wet mesquite, yucca, greasewood, and cactus, and the air felt moist and sweet, no longer dusty and dry. Off the veranda, the branches of the old cottonwood trees, soaked by the storm, bent lower to the ground.

"I'm gonna go see Peaches," Ginny said.

"Peaches is fine," Anna Lynn said. "We put her in her stall before the storm broke, remember?" They'd moved Peaches and Patrick's two old ponies into the barn from the near pasture minutes before the first downpour.

"She may be scared," Ginny argued.

"The ponies are fine. You stay right here with me. We'll check on them later. Okay?"

Ginny nodded. "Let me see," she said, reaching for the binoculars.

An explosion rang out before Anna Lynn could give Ginny the binoculars. It was followed by a cloud of smoke and flames that curled into the air. She focused on the smoke plume and guessed it to be three or four miles distant, out of sight behind a rise but somewhere near the ranch road. She swept the area looking for any movement. Other than grass waving in a gentle breeze, all was still. She couldn't imagine what had caused the blast, but combined with the gunshots it made her apprehensive and a little worried. A sudden misgiving that something bad was coming washed over her.

"What was that?" Ginny asked.

"Just a really big bang, honey. Maybe the army planes from the airfield mistakenly dropped a bomb or something. Let's go inside."

"A bomb?" Ginny said excitedly. "Let's go see."

Anna Lynn took Ginny's hand. "Not now. The ranch road is too muddy and we'd get stuck."

Ginny tried to tug free. "It scared Peaches, I just know it did."

"Peaches is just fine." She guided Ginny into the kitchen. "When Matt and Patrick get home, they'll be hungry. We should bake something special for them. What will it be? You decide."

Ginny's eyes lit up. "Sugar cookies!"

Her distraction worked. Sugar cookies were Ginny's favorite. She loved to use the star-shaped cookie cutter on the rolled-out dough. "Perfect. Get the flour tin from the pantry and we'll get started."

While Ginny got the flour, Anna Lynn put on her apron, went to the living room, and from the gun case got the horse pistol Patrick's father had brought to New Mexico after the Civil War. She checked to make sure it was loaded before slipping it into her apron pocket. If trouble showed up, she'd scare it away.

In the kitchen, she lit the firebox in the cookstove, sprinkled some flour on the table, and with Ginny's help began to make the dough. Occasionally she glanced out the open door, still half-convinced trouble was coming. But by the time the dough was ready for Ginny to cut into star-shaped cookies, there had been no sign of any unexpected or unwanted visitors approaching on the ranch road. She felt silly for putting the old pistol in her apron pocket. She could always bean an intruder with a frying pan if need be.

She usually did not cook in the kitchen during the heat of the day, but the passing storm had cooled the morning and a pleasant breeze wafted through the open doors and windows of the house. She checked the stove firebox and decided more wood was needed to keep the oven at the right temperature while they baked six batches of cookies.

She left Ginny at the table busy with the cookie cutter, went to the walled courtyard, and startled a blue jay that was parading on top of the woodpile. It squawked in displeasure and flew away as she gathered an armful of logs. Back in the kitchen she found the room empty and Ginny gone from her chair.

"Ginny!" Anna Lynn called loudly, letting the firewood tumble from her arms to the floor near the stove. She rushed onto the veranda. Ginny was nowhere in sight.

"Young lady!" Anna Lynn shouted as she hurried down the veranda steps. Ginny's small footprints in the wet ground led directly to the barn. Relieved, she slowed her pace. Although she admired her daughter's concern for Peaches, she'd still earned a scolding for disobeying. "You come out here right this minute," she ordered.

A man stepped out of the shadows of the barn, holding Ginny in one arm, a gun in his free hand. His clothes were wet, his shoes were caked with mud, and his hair was plastered against his forehead.

"Let me down," Ginny wailed, struggling in his arms.

Tyler squeezed her tight against his chest and leered at Anna Lynn. "Well, well, this is better than I expected."

"I know you," Anna Lynn said hotly. "You're the orderly from the Fort Bliss hospital."

"That's right. Name's Fred Tyler. I want you to remember that."

"Put my daughter down," she demanded.

Tyler pointed the semiautomatic at Anna Lynn. "Or what?" he snarled. "Don't give me orders."

"You've got no cause to hurt her."

Tyler laughed. "You don't know the half of it. Where's your lover boy and his pa?"

"They'll be here any minute."

"I don't think so."

"Did you shoot somebody and blow something up?"

Tyler bared his teeth in a smile. "Aren't you a nosy bitch? Just maybe I did have to kill me someone. Maybe you're next. Or your little girl."

"You don't have to do that." Anna Lynn dropped her shaking hands in front of the apron pocket. Unless Tyler put Ginny down, the horse pistol was useless. "I'll do anything you want if you promise not to hurt my daughter."

"Is that so?"

"Yes." Anna Lynn switched her gaze to Ginny. She was crying, her face contorted with fear. "It's okay, sweetie," she said, forcing a smile.

"Look at me, not her!" Tyler thundered. "And do exactly what I say."

Anna Lynn stiffened. "Tell me what you want me to do."

"First, food," Tyler replied, as his leer reappeared. "Then you and me are gonna have a little party."

"I'll do whatever you want," Anna Lynn said. "Anything. But please, please, let Ginny come to me. You're scaring her."

The bitch was his now, he could sense it. He couldn't remember when he'd had so much fun. He put the kid down. "Since you asked so nice."

Sobbing, Ginny ran straight to Anna Lynn, who scooped her up. "Thank you."

Tyler smirked, looked her up and down hungrily, and waved his gun at her. "Now, turn around and go to the house. I'm right behind you."

Anna Lynn nodded, turned, and carried her terrified daughter, who clung fiercely to her, into the kitchen. She heard Tyler's footsteps at her back, the scraping of a chair as he pulled it away from the table, and creaking sound of him sitting down.

"Get me something to eat and drink," he demanded.

Anna Lynn lowered Ginny, and holding her tightly by the hand, turned. Tyler's gun was resting on the table.

"Send that little girl over here to me," Tyler said huskily, wetting his lips. "I want her to sit on my lap."

Smiling to hide her disgust, Anna Lynn nodded, figuring she had just one chance. She squeezed Ginny's hand even tighter to keep her from moving. "You heard the nice man," she said.

Fixed only on Ginny, Tyler's eyes lit up.

Anna Lynn shot him dead between the eyes from four feet away with Patrick's horse pistol.

4

The last ten miles home, Patrick rode with his gut ache worsening by the minute. The shooting pain in his bloated stomach nagged him relentlessly and he felt god-awful sour in both mind and body. He let his pony, Ribbon, do most of the work and rested in the saddle as best he could.

After midnight, clouds masked the full moon and slowed their pace in the canyons where flooding from the storm had tumbled rocks and boulders across the trails. Darkness allowed him to hide his discomfort from Matt, who eyed him worriedly as they entered the last canyon to the 7-Bar-K headquarters. When the ranch house came into view, every room was lit up, lamplight winking through the windows and open doors.

"Something's wrong," Matt said, spurring his pony into a fast trot, maneuvering around a soggy pool of mud at the lip of the stream that flowed into the near pasture close to the barn. He splashed across the rushing water and broke into a fast lope with Patrick following apace, grimacing in pain.

In front of the veranda on the muddy ground near the hitching post, a body lay covered with a blanket. Matt took one astonished look at the dead man's face, realized who he was, and climbed the stairs two at a time, anxiously calling out for Anna Lynn and Ginny. He found them on the living-room couch, Ginny fast asleep, her head on her mother's lap, Anna Lynn awake and wide-eyed, Patrick's old horse pistol close at hand on the lamp table.

"Are you all right?" he asked, searching her face.

"I couldn't get all the blood up," Anna Lynn replied dully, gently stroking Ginny's hair. "I scrubbed and scrubbed, but there's still a big brown spot on the kitchen floor."

Matt knelt at Anna Lynn's feet. "What happened?"

"I shot him, but I couldn't stand to see him dead inside the house. I dragged his body to the yard and covered it. He was going to kill us both." She searched Matt's face. "Why did he come here?"

Matt took her hand in his. "Revenge, most likely. Fred Tyler tried to rob me years ago in Las Cruces. After I testified against him in court, he threatened me. At the time, I figured he was shooting off his mouth. How did he even know where to find me?"

"From your medical records, probably," Anna Lynn replied. "He was one of the army orderlies at Fort Bliss. After your surgery, he waited outside to speak to me. At the time I thought it was creepy, but I never saw him again and forgot all about it."

"Don't dig a hole and bury him," Patrick advised from the open living-room door, remembering with great clarity his failed attempt to hide Vernon Clagett's body from the law after justifiably killing him. "Get the sheriff out here, pronto."

"Yes, we must," Anna Lynn replied. "I think he may have killed somebody before he got here. I heard two gunshots and an explosion on the ranch road about an hour or so before he arrived.

That's why I got the pistol. When Ginny went to check on Peaches, he was hiding in the barn. He came out carrying Ginny in his arms with a gun in his hand."

"Where's his gun?" Matt asked.

"On the kitchen table," Anna Lynn answered. "I didn't give him a chance to use it."

Patrick considered his pappy's old horse pistol on the side table. "Well, from the bullet hole in his head, you surely corrected his misdeeds."

Anna Lynn winced at the reminder, and Patrick, embarrassed by his words, turned his attention to Matt. "Best you wrap the body in an old horse blanket and weigh it down with rocks so some hungry critters don't come and make a meal of him before we can get the law out here."

Matt rose to his feet. "I'll take care of all that, and fetch a doctor to take a look at you." The ranch, so remote and isolated, was still without electricity or telephone service.

"No need," Patrick said as he made his way to his bedroom door. "This gut ache will pass and I'll be fine come morning."

Matt looked out the window at first light touching the Sacramentos. "Morning is upon us, and I'll be the judge of what's needed."

Carefully, Anna Lynn shifted the still-sleeping Ginny from her lap to a couch cushion and gently picked her up. She didn't stir. "After I put her in bed, I'll fix you a hot water bottle and some warm lemon tea to settle your stomach."

"Don't put yourself out on my account."

Anna Lynn brushed a stray strand of hair away from Ginny's cheek, smiled weakly, and whispered, "I need to do something, otherwise I may just fall apart."

Patrick smiled in return. "Much obliged." He waited until

Anna Lynn left the room carrying Ginny, shook his head in admiration, and said to Matt, "That gal of yours is some pistol."

"Don't I know it," Matt agreed with a worried sigh. Anna Lynn looked as if she could fall apart at any moment, and he'd never seen her like that before.

* * *

Matt wrapped Fred Tyler's body in a horse blanket, piled rocks on top of it, and left to fetch a doctor and the law. On the ranch road, he stopped for a look-see at the burned-out Buick with the charred body inside before continuing cautiously to town on the state highway that had been badly damaged in the storm. Six hours later, he returned leading a small caravan of vehicles containing Sheriff Riley Dodson in his patrol car and Dr. Edwin Slattery in his Chevy. At the twisted metal wreckage of the Buick, Dodson stopped to investigate while Matt and Doc Slattery drove on to the ranch. There, Slattery did a thorough examination of Patrick, pronounced him to be suffering from a severe case of appendicitis, and ordered him to the hospital immediately. He drove off with Patrick in the passenger seat of the Chevy protesting mightily just as Sheriff Dodson arrived to inspect his second dead body of the day. A tall, thin man with a square face and thick lips, Dodson had come up through the ranks, serving as undersheriff before winning the election after his predecessor retired.

Matt helped him expose Tyler's remains and in the harsh light of day he looked at the face of the man who'd wanted to kill Anna Lynn and Ginny out of pure meanness and revenge. In town, he'd told Dodson about his history with Tyler and what had happened at Fort Bliss and the ranch, and he repeated it briefly once again as the sheriff looked through Tyler's wallet.

"He's an army private all right," Dodson remarked, holding up a military ID card. He stuck the wallet and card in his shirt pocket, flipped the horse blanket back over Tyler's body, and allowed that the bullet hole in the victim's forehead was some damn fine shooting for a woman. He asked to speak with Anna Lynn.

"She's inside," Matt said, bringing Dodson into the kitchen, where he pointed out Tyler's semiautomatic pistol lying untouched on the table. He gave the sheriff a cup of coffee and went to fetch Anna Lynn. He found her sequestered in the casita with Ginny, both of them lying on the bed with the curtains closed.

"We're going home, if the sheriff will let us," she said before he got a word out. "I can't stay here."

Matt sat on the end of the bed and nodded agreeably. "We'll all go to your place. I need to check on Patrick at the hospital anyway."

Anna Lynn smiled. "Good."

"First, Sheriff Dodson wants to talk to you."

Anna Lynn swung her legs off the bed. "Stay here with Ginny."

"Are you sure you don't want my company?" He held out his arms and Ginny eagerly scooted over to him.

"No, I'll be fine."

Anna Lynn left and Matt snuggled with Ginny, unsure of what to say, wondering if the horror of what had happened was too fresh in her mind to risk discussion. He decided to forgo words and hold her quietly in his arms. For a long time, they stayed silent, Ginny's head against his chest.

Finally, she looked at Matt and asked, "Is Patrick gonna die?"

Matt didn't have an answer. "Doc Slattery will take good care of him."

Ginny's eyes filled with tears. "He's gonna die, I just know it." She started sobbing.

All Matt could do was gather her closer and hold her tight. "Hush now," he said.

* * *

Before leaving his office for the murder scenes at the 7-Bar-K ranch, Sheriff Riley Dodson made several important telephone calls. He called Fort Bliss to advise the army that one of their soldiers had been killed, told the county coroner to meet him at the 7-Bar-K, where there were two alleged murder victims, let the district attorney know about the crimes, and lastly spoke to the editor of the local newspaper, who readily agreed to send his best reporter out to cover the story.

Killings, once somewhat common in the early frontier days, had become rare events for sheriffs in the rural southern counties of the state, and Dodson, who was up for reelection in November, wasn't about to let any free publicity slip away. He took Anna Lynn's statement knowing full well that the coroner, the district attorney—who was also up for reelection—an army officer, and a newspaper reporter would soon be arriving at the ranch. And although he was inclined to believe her story, he wasn't about to let her leave for her home until everyone, including the reporter, had a crack at her—although he'd didn't put it to her quite that way.

Dodson's decision to have Anna Lynn and Matt remain until he released them raised Matt's ire. "That's unnecessary," he snapped, staring at Dodson, who had called them out to the veranda. "This was self-defense, plain and simple. For chrissake, there's no good reason to keep us here. Can't you see that?"

"I understand how you feel," Dodson said calmly. He had no desire to rile a homegrown war-hero veteran or his lady friend, saw no benefit to it, but wasn't about to get hornswoggled, although he appreciated Matt Kerney's concern for the woman. He eyed Anna Lynn, who appeared shocked, numb, and deflated; almost like a department-store mannequin, which was understandable given the fact she'd killed the man lying outside the house mere hours ago. "Ma'am?" he asked, offering her the chance to make her case.

"If we try to leave, will you arrest us?" she asked unemotionally, her face blank.

Dodson toyed with the notion of arresting her if she tried to leave and decided not to risk it. Instead he tried persuasion. "I've got to get this job done right, ma'am, and as material witnesses, I need your and Matt's help. So, I'm detaining you both. It's a lot more polite than an arrest."

"How long do you plan to keep us here?" Matt inquired.

On the ranch road a line of vehicles appeared that included the coroner's car, an ambulance to carry off the remains of the victims, the DA's automobile, an army jeep, and reporter Ed Julian's old Studebaker. "It may take a while, I reckon," Dodson replied. "I'll push it along as fast as I can."

"We'll wait inside," Anna Lynn said. For a long moment, she stared at Fred Tyler's covered body before retreating to the casita, where Ginny, forbidden to venture outside until Tyler's body had been removed, impatiently waited.

* * *

Anna Lynn's ordeal didn't end until darkness, when the last of the men who'd descended on the ranch left, taking with them Fred Tyler's body, the blackened remains of the unknown person in the burned-out car, and all the evidence, photographs, and sworn statements Anna Lynn and Matt had been required to make.

In full moonlight casting long, silver shadows across the basin, the twisted wreckage of the car, high-ended on the crest of a precipitous washout that cut across the road, had an eerie look about it that chilled Anna Lynn to the bone. On the passenger side of the bench seat to the truck, with Ginny nestled at her side, she closed her eyes against the sight of it as Matt slowed to take a look when they passed by. She had no desire to see anything more that spoke of violent death. The stain on the kitchen floor was reminder enough.

The ranch, once so dear to her as a delightful hideaway, now felt ominous. She wondered if that mood would last. Just then it felt indelible. Since the moment Fred Tyler fell dead on the kitchen floor, an obsessive desire to flee the 7-Bar-K dominated her thoughts. She desperately wanted to be alone with Ginny in her own home. Even the prospect of Matt's company in her bed, recently so welcome and agreeable following the long absence of intimacy after his return from the war, felt bothersome.

"Sheriff said he'd have that wreck towed away in a day or two," Matt noted.

Anna Lynn didn't respond. She turned her face to the passenger window and said not a word on the drive to Mountain Park.

* * *

After five days in the hospital and minus a ruptured appendix, Patrick was discharged, lucky to be alive, and told to recuperate in bed for a week and avoid any physical activity that would put the slightest strain on his abdomen. He was even to avoid laughing or coughing if at all possible. Because of his age and slow recovery from surgery, Doc Slattery specifically forbade him from doing any ranch work for three weeks and told him to gradually increase his physical activities by an hour a day after that.

Although in pain and crabby, Patrick was having none of it, determined to get back to his normal routine as soon as he could put his boots on and go about his business. In order to enforce Doc Slattery's regimen and keep Patrick from literally working himself to death, Matt and Anna Lynn decided he would convalesce at her home, under her watchful eye and care.

As Anna Lynn helped him dress to leave, Patrick groused about it, but not convincingly, as he was secretly delighted by the prospect of being cared for by a woman he truly liked and in the company of a child he adored. He'd lost a few pounds on hospital food, and with a fresh haircut, a shave, and some color in his cheeks, he actually looked good for his years.

Outside, several newspaper reporters waited, including Ed Julian, who'd interviewed Anna Lynn at the ranch, hoping to get additional comments about the killings on the 7-Bar-K. Not once had Anna Lynn, Matt, or Patrick spoken to the press since the day of the shootings and with the dead man in the car now positively identified and the DA yet to decide whether to press charges against Anna Lynn, the story was front-page news again. The reporters took pictures and called out questions as Matt hurried Patrick in a wheelchair to the truck with Anna Lynn and Ginny close behind.

At the farm, Patrick, under protest, was put up in Anna Lynn's bedroom, which had been prepared for him in advance with a wooden step Matt had built for him to use to get in and out of bed and a chamber pot nearby for nighttime emergencies.

"This is putting you out and I just won't have it," he grumbled as he stretched out on the soft bed.

Anna Lynn adjusted his pillow and kissed him on the cheek. "We'll all be fine. I'll sleep with Ginny, and Matt can use the couch when he's here."

"Which won't be that often for a spell," Matt added, opening the bedroom wardrobe. "You've got fresh duds in here, and your shaving gear is on the top shelf. Try to keep yourself presentable for the womenfolk."

"I ain't no imbecile," Patrick retorted. "They took my appendix, not my thinking cap or manners."

From the foot of the bed Matt nodded in agreement. "I'm glad to see they also left your tetchy nature alone." He patted Patrick's leg. "You heal up good, old man. I still need you at the ranch."

"I'm in good hands with these two," Patrick replied, cracking a smile as Ginny climbed up on the bed to be with him. He took her outstretched little hand in his calloused mitt.

"Rest," Anna Lynn ordered. "I'm fixing you a nice supper."

In the living room, Matt kissed her goodbye and left hurriedly for the ranch, where his ponies had been unattended since the night he'd driven Anna Lynn and Ginny home. From the front door, Anna Lynn watched him go, knowing that his animals needed care but wondering how he could seem so nonchalant about returning to a place where there had been so much recent violent death. She returned to her chores as the image of Fred Tyler falling dead on the kitchen floor floated through her mind.

* * *

Matt stopped in Tularosa to speak with Miguel Chávez and over coffee at his house asked if he might be willing to hire on at the 7-Bar-K for a month at top-hand wages. His offer made Miguel's wife, Bernadette, beam with delight as she refilled his cup. Farm families always welcomed the opportunity to earn cash money, especially when harvest time was several months away.

"*Si*," Miguel replied, suppressing a smile. "In my absence, I can have my brothers tend to my crops and my animals."

"I mostly need help with the ponies," Matt explained. "And caretaking the ranch while I'm in town on business and such."

"I'll come out tomorrow." Miguel paused. "We were sorry to hear of the killings."

Matt shook his head. "It was bad business."

Miguel's expression turned somber. "I'm reluctant to ask about your *padre.* Is he not well?"

Matt laughed. "That tough old hombre is just fine. He had his appendix out and is mending nicely at my lady friend's home in Mountain Park. He can't do a lick of work for at least another month."

"I am happy to hear he will recover."

"Me too." Matt finished his coffee and pushed back his chair. "I'll see you tomorrow. Be careful on the ranch road—it's rough in spots."

Miguel offered his hand. "*Mañana, mi amigo.* Adios."

"Adios." Matt thanked Bernadette for her hospitality and left the casa. Across the pasture, under a thick canopy of old cottonwood trees stood the sprawling Chávez hacienda. The sight of it brought pleasant memories of Teresa Magdalena Armijo-Chávez, Miguel's mother and Matt's surrogate aunt, and of the fiesta they threw at the ranch for his mother, Emma, days before she died.

It brought a smile to his lips. He desperately needed pleasant times to remember. The killing of Fred Tyler had opened up a slew of unhappy reminiscences about his younger years, most painfully the death of Beth Merton, a girl he'd truly loved. It still hurt when he thought of the loss of her.

On the state road, he left the shade of the village and drove into the glaring hot desert scrublands, now awash from the recent storm with blooming cactus flowers and occasional patches of silky green native grasses. No matter how many times he drove across the Tularosa, it was always different and new.

He turned his thoughts to work. The ranch road needed grading, leaks in the stock tank needed patching, a windmill needed fixing, and of course there were the ponies. It was time to get cracking. He had a week to get all the maintenance work done before he went to see Dr. Beckmann to get his new eye.

* * *

The week passed quickly for Matt, and he left the 7-Bar-K feeling good about the work he'd accomplished with Miguel's assistance. Miguel's easygoing nature, his willingness to work hard, and his pleasant companionship had helped Matt get his thinking about past heartaches and recent calamities squared away. He drove straight to Mountain Park to check on Patrick, Anna Lynn, and Ginny, and found the threesome in high spirits, about to sit down to a noon meal. Over homemade soup and fresh corn bread, they caught up and made small talk. Patrick complained a mite about his slow recovery, Anna Lynn reported he was mostly being a good patient with only an occasional lapse, and Ginny proudly displayed new reading skills honed by many hours of schooling by Patrick, who obviously enjoyed all the attention he got from Anna Lynn and Ginny. The gruff, mean-spirited man Matt had loathed for so many years seemed to have completely vanished.

Matt described the work at the ranch he'd done with Miguel's help, which included sanding away the bloodstain and refinishing the entire kitchen floor. He'd thought Anna Lynn would be pleased by the effort, but she seemed barely appreciative and not at all interested in doings at the ranch.

With a promise to return promptly from Fort Bliss to show off his new eye, Matt continued on to Alamogordo, where he stood on the train station platform surrounded by a contingent of high-spirited flyboys from the airfield on seventy-two-hour passes who were impatiently awaiting the southbound train that would carry them to El Paso. When they arrived in the border city, the boisterous GIs, most of them kids not old enough to vote, piled into taxis for the short drive to Juárez, where sins and pleasures of the flesh abounded. He marveled at their innocence and exuberance, knowing for those who survived, combat would quickly wash it all away.

At Fort Bliss, as an authorized civilian on post, he secured a billet at the BOQ, which came with a pass to the Officer's Club. Never having been allowed in officer country before, he couldn't resist the temptation to take a look. He showed up with happy hour in full swing, found an empty stool at the far end of the bar, and with a cold beer in hand watched a swarm of junior officers barraging a trio of pretty army nurses, one of whom was Lt. Raine Hartman.

She turned in Matt's direction, smiled in recognition, and approached, followed by a slightly drunk, persistent captain, who wasn't about to cut off his pursuit.

Matt raised his glass in greeting.

Raine settled on an empty stool. "What a nice surprise. I didn't expect to see you until your appointment tomorrow morning."

"I'm here on my own this time, Lieutenant," Matt replied. "I see you haven't lost your allure."

Raine shrugged a shoulder. "They're just a bunch of eager Boy Scouts with dishonorable intentions. I'm holding out for a true gentleman."

"Good for you," Matt said.

The relentless young captain, who had carrot-red hair and a freckled nose, butted in between them and eyed Matt suspiciously. "What have we here?" he rudely demanded.

"This is Lt. Colonel Matthew Kerney," Raine lied, straight-faced.

Color drained from the young captain's face as he erased his insolent sneer and straightened up. "Colonel, sir."

"At ease, Captain," Matt said, enjoying the moment and his sudden unexpected promotion. "If you'll allow me to have a private conversation with Lieutenant Hartman, I'll return her to your custody shortly."

"As you wish, sir," the captain replied, discreetly retreating.

"You're a bold gal," Matt said with a grin when the young man had departed.

"So my father says." Raine giggled. "Are you really married?"

"Why do you ask?"

"Neither you or your wife wear wedding rings."

"That's very observant."

"Well?"

From Raine's tone and expression Matt gathered it was a serious question deserving a truthful answer. "In spite of my best attempts to change her mind, Anna Lynn doesn't believe in the institution of marriage."

Raine grinned and clapped her hands. "Goody. I knew it."

"You approve?"

"Completely. If I have to marry, I plan to do it five times."

"Five times?"

Raine nodded in strenuous agreement. "I get bored easily."

Matt laughed, drained his beer, and stood. "In that case, I want an invitation to each of your weddings."

"I promise," Raine said, reaching for Matt's hand. "You don't have to release me from your custody tonight."

Her tempting suggestion made Matt hesitate. "I think I'd better," he finally said.

Raine leaned close and kissed him. "I'll see you tomorrow. But if I forget, tell Anna Lynn that she might want to reel you in permanently, otherwise I could decide to give her some serious competition."

"Knowing her, I can guarantee she'd applaud your best efforts."

* * *

In the morning, Raine Hartman assisted Dr. Beckmann, and when the glass eye was installed, the three of them took a good look at it.

"The lab did a nice job," Susan Beckmann said approvingly. "It's a perfect fit."

"You're now more handsome than ever," Raine added, flashing him a brilliant smile.

"I just might get used to it," Matt allowed, looking in the mirror. The skin around his left eye, so long hidden by the patch, was pale white in contrast to his suntanned face. "Once I stop looking like a circus clown," he added.

"I'll loan you some of my makeup," Raine offered.

"No thanks."

Dr. Beckmann smiled and glanced at her watch. "Raine, please check to make sure my next patient has been prepped for surgery. I don't want to keep him waiting."

As Beckmann turned back to Matt, Raine gave him a big wink on her way out the door.

"Now I'm going to teach you how to remove and insert your eye," she said, scooting her stool closer. "We'll practice together until you're comfortable."

After ten minutes, Matt had it down. "Do you really need to

keep me over another day?" he asked. The enticing and dangerous prospect of once again encountering Raine at the Officer's Club during happy hour made him determined to go home.

"I should, but I think you're going to adjust nicely." From her desktop, she handed him a typewritten paper. "Care instructions for you and the eye. Follow them and you'll do just fine. Goodbye, Matt. Have a good life."

"Thanks, Captain Beckmann. I appreciate all that you've done."

In the reception area, nurses and orderlies clustered around a radio. The allies had invaded Europe and troops were on the beaches of Normandy. It was June 6, 1944.

5

Anna Lynn Crawford's uneasiness about returning to the 7-Bar-K proved impossible to overcome. Her best efforts to conquer it met with no success, nor did the passage of time. Knowing she'd done the right thing to protect Ginny and herself made little difference. Eventually, she stopped making excuses about her continued absence from the ranch, and simply ignored the subject when it was broached by Matt. He, in turn, soon gave up trying to change her mind, rarely visited, and no longer stayed overnight. She knew full well she was the architect of the growing breach, but did nothing to repair it.

Since killing Fred Tyler, she'd retreated from the notion of establishing a more permanent relationship with Matt. She'd always believed no man was completely trustworthy. It had been one of the linchpins in her desire to remain independent and free. Although it took a month for her to realize it, that one irreversible moment of putting a bullet in Tyler's head had wiped away all ideas of having an enduring connection with any man, Matt included. She'd killed another person because of him, and that would always cloud their relationship. She doubted that she would ever be able to be completely comfortable with him again.

Unwilling to hurt him, she'd begun to think how much better it would be if he found someone else. And due to his almost complete disappearing act, Anna Lynn thought it quite possible another woman had already turned his head. She'd considered flat-out asking him about it, but had put it off. Given enough time, she would know.

Patrick, on the other hand, visited often, frequently staying overnight, bunking on the couch. The grandfatherly pull of his relationship with Ginny was irresistible and he was perfectly comfortable with Anna Lynn's strong reluctance to revisit the "scene of the crime" at the ranch as he crudely but jokingly called it. In an attempt to make her feel better, he told her the story of getting attacked in the barn by a hired hand named Vernon Clagett and busting his head open with a hammer. Intended as an object lesson to help her overcome any lingering doubts about killing Fred Tyler, it only stiffened her resolve to completely shun the ranch.

After the astonishment of what happened had worn off, Patrick's cavalier outlook and Matt's equally blasé mind-set about the killing bewildered her. It didn't make any sense until she realized that war had made both men either immune or tone deaf to human violence and brutality. She wondered if they were even aware of how combat had affected them. If so, they certainly never talked about it.

To entertain Ginny, Patrick had trucked her pony, Peaches, to the farm, along with his gelding, Ribbon, to ride. They went out often, much to Ginny's delight. When Patrick wasn't at the farm, Ginny stayed happily occupied after her homeschooling, caring for Peaches and Ribbon. Occasionally, in the cool of the evening, Anna Lynn and Ginny would ride down the narrow canyon after supper. It was just about the most perfect time imaginable for the two of them.

For the time being, having Patrick in Ginny's life and Matt absent from her own served Anna Lynn well. Aside from the anguish, bad dreams, and the constant recurring memory of what she'd done, killing Fred Tyler had taken an unexpected physical toll on her. She'd lost her appetite, suffered from persistent bloating and cramps, had become disinterested in sex, and for the first time ever her menstrual cycle had gone completely off kilter. She considered it nothing more than a temporary aftershock. Time might never completely erase the mental distress of killing another human being, no matter how justified, but she was certain her body would rebound. It always had in the past.

* * *

The 7-Bar-K stayed afloat because of wartime government beef purchases, Matt's military disability pension, and Patrick's pension from the Spanish-American War. The loss of any one source of income would put Matt in the hole if he continued to keep breeding and training cow ponies and cutting horses, which was the part of ranching he loved best.

For the moment, cattle were the moneymakers, and the ponies were eating into the profits. Ranch ponies had mostly been replaced by trucks, the war had forced the rodeo operators to either fold up shop or scale way back, and the small outfits that still relied on horseflesh weren't interested in high-priced ponies. Maybe after the war the demand for cow ponies and cutting horses would improve, but for now it was time to reduce the herd and concentrate on beef production.

In the silence of the living room at dusk, Matt sat at his desk by lamplight, made a note to hire a trucker to take most of his ponies to market in Fort Worth, and wrote a letter to a livestock broker there authorizing him to handle the sale and setting a fair minimum price for each animal. He put it on a small pile of letters to be mailed in the morning, leaned back in his chair, and listened to the breeze whispering through the cottonwoods off the veranda.

Six weeks had passed since Miguel Chávez drew his pay and returned to his family in Tularosa, and the day before Patrick had left on one of his frequent visits to Mountain Park. Matt usually enjoyed his solitude but in the growing darkness he felt lonely and restless. The ranch had been a happy place before Fred Tyler arrived to get himself killed. These days, not so much.

He shrugged off a wistful thought floating through his mind about Anna Lynn. Maddeningly, she'd turned stone-silent on him, and he wasn't about to try to cajole her out of it. To clear his thoughts of her, he paged through the plans for the ranch he'd prepared before he'd enlisted in the army. In retrospect, the list was laughable, a testimonial to unbridled optimism and wishful thinking. He'd hoped electricity would come to the ranch, maybe even telephone service, but as far as he could tell both were still years away. He'd wanted to build some new ranch roads to get around the spread more easily, but it hadn't gotten done. A garage, automotive tools, and a gasoline storage tank were also on the list, as was a new hay barn. Again, *nada.* Even more outrageous had been his wild-hair notion to get indoor plumbing and an honest-to-God bathroom installed in the house.

Matt pushed the list aside. In the middle of a modern world he was still living in the nineteenth century. It felt ass backward and ridiculous. He decided the hell with it; he'd spend the money on plumbing and a bathroom when the ponies sold. Patrick might pooh-pooh such an extravagance, but to Matt it would be worth it.

Patrick had slowed down some since surviving his ruptured appendix. Matt figured he'd probably never pull his full weight again. But that was okay; nearing seventy, the man had given a lifetime of bone-crunching, backbreaking work to the ranch and had earned the right to ease off if he so desired. If it played out that way, as Matt expected it would, best to let it be an unspoken arrangement. Patrick's pride would never allow him to admit to giving less than a hundred percent to the homestead.

In a desk drawer where Matt kept the ranch ledger was a pile of unopened mail Patrick had fetched and failed to mention. In among the bills, stud bull auction notices, and correspondence from the Stockman's Association was a letter addressed to Matt in flowery penmanship postmarked from El Paso, Texas. It read:

Dear Matt,

Remember me? I was your nurse at William Beaumont. I'll be starting leave soon with another nurse (we're both from San Diego) and we've decided to visit nearby places like the White Sands National Monument, Inscription Rock, and some of the mountain villages. We'd love to get some ideas from you of the best places to explore. We'll be starting our adventure at the Park Hotel in Las Cruces next Saturday. If you're in town, we'll buy you a drink and dinner for your trouble. I hope to see you again soon!

Yours Truly,
Raine Hartman

Matt crumpled the letter and discarded it in the wastebasket. The next day was Saturday and he had no business leaving the ranch and his livestock unattended to drive to Las Cruces to play tour guide for two army nurses on leave. It would be plain foolishness. Still, the invitation intrigued him and Nurse Hartman was a looker.

He retrieved Raine's letter, smoothed it out, and read it again. On the other hand, why not go? In spite of his best efforts to become one, he wasn't a married man, and Anna Lynn seemed even more disinterested in the subject of matrimony than ever before. She'd never once pledged faithfulness to him, so the only thing holding him in check was his own notion of loyalty to her.

What could be more fun than squiring two pretty nurses to a nice dinner in town while they picked up the tab? Hell yes, he'd do it. He just might act like a true gentleman and for the pleasure of their company pay for dinner himself. If he got off his duff and did the next day's chores that night, he could leave in the morning with the livestock in good shape, the barn and corral mucked clean, and new salt licks put out. He'd have a night on the town with the gals and be back home by Sunday afternoon.

Matt pushed back from the desk and headed for the barn with a smile on his face, all listlessness and loneliness washed away.

* * *

Las Cruces was no longer the sleepy town of Matt's childhood. An agricultural boom fostered by the war economy had turned the town into a center for crop storage and distribution. There were factories to grade and sort onions, compress and bale cotton, tag and bag seed stock, sort and bag pecans, and package chili. Along the railroad tracks, new warehouses stored commodities awaiting shipment, and a big livestock shipping pen had recently been thrown up.

Spreading out east and west, downtown Main Street bustled with commerce. Outside the J.C. Penney store, a war-bond booth festooned with stars and bracketed by American flags was staffed by ladies handing out flyers to passing pedestrians. With no new cars being built, used car lots had proliferated on street corners at the edges of town near mom-and-pop motels, garages, and gas stations. Most citizens were either on foot or in vehicles, but an occasional horse-drawn wagon clip-clopped down paved Main Street while two saddle horses languidly waited, hitched to a light pole outside a popular dry-goods store.

Matt had half a mind to drive by his old home on Griggs Avenue, but decided to save it for later, perhaps on Sunday morning before heading back to the ranch. He parked on Court Street and walked past the city park, green and lush compared to the natural desert landscape, with a large gazebo in the center surrounded by a canopy of mature, pleasantly cooling shade trees. Nearby, the Park Hotel, a two-story brick affair with tall arched windows, a parapet concealing a flat roof, and an entry porch with a latticework enclosed balcony above, looked out over beautifully tended grounds.

At the front desk, he asked for Raine Hartman and learned she'd checked in but had gone out a short while ago. Thinking it might be a good place to dine, he asked the clerk if the Castle nightspot was still in business.

The man, fortyish, overweight, and with a wheezy voice, winked conspiratorially and said, "It's real popular again since our new sheriff has turned a blind eye to gambling, so I'd make reservations if I were you. And the food is still good."

Matt registered for a room, slipped the clerk a buck to make dinner reservations for three at the Castle, and asked him to call his room when Raine Hartman returned. The upstairs room had a view of the park, a full-size bed, and a bathroom with hot and cold running water. Matt didn't care that it was ninety degrees inside the room; he ran the tub full and sank into the hot water, letting the warmth seep into his bones. He'd just finished shaving when the phone rang. He picked up and was greeted by Raine's voice asking to speak to Colonel Kerney.

Matt laughed. The sound of her voice was a tonic. "I'm afraid I've been cashiered."

"All the better," Raine replied. "I don't like being ordered around. Give me ten minutes to freshen up and I'll meet you in the lobby."

"Yes, ma'am," Matt said in a snap-to-attention tone of voice.

Raine giggled and hung up.

Dressed in fresh duds, Matt made it down to the lobby with five minutes to spare. Raine kept him waiting for ten minutes more. She arrived dressed in gray, pleated, beltless slacks, and a white short-sleeved cotton blouse that accented her slender figure. She kissed him lightly on the cheek and gave him a top-to-bottom once-over.

"You clean up nicely," she said teasingly. "I half expected you to still being wearing the eye patch."

"I don't think to wear it much anymore," Matt replied. "Where's your traveling companion?"

Raine hooked her arm in his. "She's here, but otherwise engaged. It's a long story. Buy me a drink and I'll explain everything."

They stepped into the hotel bar, quiet and cool with ceiling fans pushing a steady breeze through the long room. At a corner table Matt ordered drinks from a waitress who looked glad to have two more customers in the almost-empty establishment. While they waited, Raine explained that she was accompanying her friend, Sue Van Amberg, to provide cover for her affair with a married army major.

"She's in love, or at least she says she is." Raine paused to stir her drink when it arrived. "But she's done this before. I think she just likes the sneaking around and having illicit sex. He's a rogue and a ladies' man who will never leave his wife."

"Why is that?"

"Because he's career army and his wife is a general's daughter." Raine shrugged. "It doesn't matter; it will soon be over. He's shipping out to the European theater in two weeks. His wife thinks he's at the Alamogordo Air Field on a training mission for the weekend. This is their goodbye tryst; Susie will soon move on to a new lover." She paused and sighed. "Sometimes I wish I could be that carefree."

"I'd like to meet her," Matt joked.

Raine punched him lightly on the arm. "No, you're with me."

"So your letter was a ruse. Why?"

Raine smiled apologetically. "I'm sorry for tricking you, but I didn't think you'd find it very ladylike if I wrote and asked you for a date. I didn't want to stay in my room alone while Susie and the major played house down the hall from me."

"Is that what this is, a date?" Matt asked.

Raine leaned provocatively close. "Yes, please."

She smelled slightly of jasmine and lavender. "I'd better change our dinner reservations for two."

Raine flashed a brilliant smile. "Where are we going?"

"It's a nightspot with a good restaurant, bar, and an illegal gambling casino."

Raine clapped her hands. "Oh, goody, I'll dress up. Until then, will you take me on a drive? I'm falling in love with the desert, and those mountains nearby with the spires are awe-inspiring."

Matt put money on the table and stood. "They're called the Organ Mountains. Let's take a look."

Raine remained seated. "One more thing; you're still not married, right?"

"Right," Matt replied.

"Perfect." She stood and took his arm again. "I'm glad you showed up."

"So am I."

As they walked out the door, Matt felt the pressure of Raine's arm against his side, saw the sparkle in her eyes, caught the subtle scent of her, and knew his day was going to be just as she said: perfect.

* * *

Their day together passed quickly. After admiring the Organ Mountains from the foothills above the town, Matthew drove the rutted dirt road to Dripping Springs, deep in the mountains, where they explored the ruins of an old resort hotel and sat in the cool shade near a waterfall that ran down a polished, sheer rock face. Back in town, they had burgers, Cokes, and fries at the lunch counter of the Las Cruces Drug Store and wandered in and out of several curio shops before returning to the hotel, where they parted company.

In his room, Matt examined the clothes he'd packed and found them sorely wanting for a classy night on the town with a pretty woman. And a careful look in the mirror made him realize that more than his wardrobe was lacking. He left the hotel on foot and returned an hour later sporting a fresh haircut, wearing polished boots, and carrying a package containing a new white cowboy shirt and Levi's dress jeans. He laid everything out on the bed and gave his cowboy hat a brushing. Fortunately, he'd worn his good, go-to-town hat.

On his way back, to make sure he had enough money to pay for a night on the town, Matt had cashed a check at Sam Miller's Grocery Store, now owned by Sam's son, Steve. The store hadn't changed all that much over the years and it brought back memories of shopping for his ma, when she was sick in bed, and hurrying home with the provisions to their little adobe casa nestled in an old Mexican neighborhood a few blocks behind Main Street.

He counted out his money and tried not to gulp at how much he would spend if he emptied his wallet at the Castle Restaurant. Although Raine had proposed in her letter to pay for his dinner, as a gentleman he couldn't let her do that. He hoped she didn't turn out to be a heavy bettor in the backroom gambling parlor.

From a housekeeper, he borrowed a broom and a rag and cleaned out the inside of his truck. The outside was dust-coated and had a dented fender, but it would have to do. Instead of returning to his room, he had a drink in the hotel bar, eyeing a snuggling couple in a back booth who had to be Raine's friend Susie and her married lover. The realization hit him that he was acting like a smitten teenager. What made him think Lieutenant Hartman had any interest in a one-eyed ex-sergeant other than using him as an alternative to an otherwise boring Saturday night alone in a hotel room? He should have stayed home at the ranch where he belonged.

As the sun lingered on the horizon, he spruced up in his new duds, checked his appearance in the bathroom mirror, and parked himself in a lobby easy chair with a clear view of the staircase. Raine appeared at the head of the stairs right on time, dressed in a simple, sleeveless cotton dress gathered at the waist by a thick black rope belt tied at the hip. All thoughts of foolishness about coming to Las Cruces flew out of Matt's head. There was absolutely nothing wrong with a night out on the town with a stunningly good-looking young woman, no matter her reasons.

* * *

The Castle was named for the owner and had no resemblance to a royal palace or an ancient fortified stronghold. Housed in a rambling old adobe a few blocks from the Loretto Academy, a Catholic girls' school, the restaurant and gambling parlor had a décor reminiscent of the Casa Blanca, the best, most expensive whorehouse and nightclub in Juárez. A front gate in the street-side adobe wall opened onto a lovely flagstone courtyard filled with tables and chairs for dining under the heavy branches of old trees. Open doors and windows spilled light from chandeliers onto the patio. From the saloon that boasted a long walnut bar, laughter and conversation mixed together with the music of a jazz trio playing softly on a small bandstand.

At a small table within earshot of the musicians, Matt bought Raine a drink, his thoughts wandering to the night he'd taken Beth Merton to the Casa Blanca.

"You seem far away," Raine said.

"Just listening to the music," Matt replied. "Are you hungry?"

"Are you eager to be done with me and deposit me safely back at the hotel?" Raine teased.

Matt looked into her light-green eyes and saw a fleeting hint of uncertainty. "Not at all; let's have another."

"Goody."

They talked for half an hour, mostly about Raine growing up

in San Diego, raised by a grandfather whom she adored, and how she loved being an army nurse. They moved to a candlelit patio table, where Raine ordered the roast pork loin and Matt chose the breaded veal cutlet. For dessert, they shared a slice of cheesecake and dawdled over coffee. When the waiter brought the check, Raine reached for her clutch purse.

Matt plucked the check from the waiter's hand. "This is my treat."

"But I promised."

"Please, allow me." He counted out the money, added a nice tip, and placed the bills on the table. It had cost less than he'd anticipated. "Save your money for the gambling tables."

Raine reached out and touched his hand. "Thank you. This is lovely."

"It's my pleasure."

"I've never gambled before."

"The first rule is to decide how much you're willing to lose."

Raine gave it some thought. "Ten dollars."

"Okay, we'll both wager ten dollars. If we lose, we leave. If we win, we split the take. Agreed?"

"Wager on what?"

"I think roulette would be best. I'll bet on black, you bet on red. We'll watch a few games so you can get the hang of it. Take ten dollars to buy chips and tuck the rest of your money away. I'll do the same."

Raine feigned a sharp look. "Do you think I lack willpower, sir?"

Matt shrugged innocently. "I don't know. Gambling can become addictive real easily."

Raine lifted an eyebrow. "Like sex?"

"Now, that's an interesting question. What would your friend Susie say?"

Raine smiled seductively. "I thought you'd ask what I would say." She quickly brushed off his attempt to respond. "Don't ask now—I want to gamble first."

She took a ten-dollar bill from her purse, tucked the rest of her cash in her bra, and took Matt's hand. "Let's go win some money."

"I'd like that," Matt said.

An hour at the roulette table had Raine up sixty bucks and Matt down to his original ten-dollar betting money. They took a break for a drink at the bar and Matt handed her five two-dollar chips. "You're on a hot streak, bet this for me."

Raine jiggled the chips in her hand. "Fifty-fifty split?"

Matt nodded. "On anything above what you've already won."

"It's a deal." She slipped the chips into her clutch, shook Matt's hand, downed the rest of her drink, and stood. "Let's get back to the table," she ordered, her face flushed with the excitement of winning.

Two hours later, Raine stopped gambling and watched the cashier count out her winnings. Cash in hand, she peeled ten dollars off the stack, divided the rest equally, and gave half to Matt. He tried to give her fifty back, but she refused it.

"Nope, fair is fair," she said as she slipped her share of the winnings into her clutch. "I'm flush with more money than I make in a month as a second lieutenant. But if it will make you feel better, you can buy me a nightcap at the hotel bar."

"I'd like that." Feeling flush as well, Matt put the money in a shirt pocket and guided Raine out of the noisy, smoky gambling parlor into the late-night coolness.

In the truck, he detoured to show her his old neighborhood, and parked across the street from the house where he'd been born. Behind the picket fence, the cottonwood now loomed over the front of the small adobe casita. Matt had forgotten how small the place was. In the quiet of the night, he told her about Emma and all she'd done on her own to raise him before her untimely death.

Over cordials at the hotel bar, Matt took his time sipping his drink, not wanting to say good night. He talked about Raine's exciting run of luck at roulette. He mentioned how pleased he was she'd written to him and what a fine time their evening had turned out to be. He told her that if he hadn't found the stack of unopened mail in his desk, he would have not known to show up until it was too late.

Through all his small talk, Raine smiled pleasantly until she suddenly put down her half-empty glass, looked him straight in the eye, interrupted, and asked, "Are you ever going to get around to inviting me to your room?"

Caught off guard, Matt smiled sheepishly. "I've been working up to it."

She stood and pulled him out of his chair. "Not quickly enough."

In his room, they eagerly undressed each other, impatient to touch, taste, see, breathe each other in, and explore the hidden places. They made love explosively and did it again almost immediately, only more slowly, deliciously. Snuggled in his arms, Raine asked when he planned to return to his ranch.

"I was thinking to leave in the morning."

She wiggled a hand free and found him erect and ready. She straddled him, let him slip inside her, and began to move. "Can I convince you to stay until noon?"

"I'll consider it."

She bent down and kissed him, her nipples touching his chest as he began to thrust deep inside her. "I'd be most grateful," Raine gasped.

* * *

After a late Sunday breakfast in the hotel restaurant, they went to Raine's room and made love again until it was almost checkout time. Susie called while they were dressing, and urged Raine to hurry up, as the major was anxious to return to El Paso. They kissed one last time outside Matt's door.

"Let's do this again, real soon," Matt suggested lightheartedly, happier than he'd been in months.

Raine smiled, tight-lipped, her eyes suddenly sad. "Maybe we can after the war is won. I ship out for England in a week. I was going to tell you, but . . ." Her voice trailed off. She touched his cheek. "I'll write."

The news stunned him. Somehow he found the willpower to force a smile. "I'd like that. Stay safe, Raine."

"I will, promise." She picked up her suitcase and walked down the hallway. Turning once to look back at him, she waved and smiled before disappearing down the stairs to the lobby.

From his room, Matt watched the married major load Raine's luggage into the trunk of his car. Raine got in the backseat, with her girlfriend Susie up front next to her lover. As the trio drove away, Raine never looked up.

Matt drove home in a stew, trying to figure out why he felt so let down. It had been, after all, nothing more than a weekend fling. No promises or pledges had been made, no words of love exchanged. That he was a hundred and fifty dollars richer didn't console him. Such a weekend might not come his way again for a long, long time. Maybe he was grateful, maybe he was sad. Maybe he was both.

With the sun dipping to the west, he approached the ranch house surprised to see Ribbon and Peaches lolling in the pasture near the water tank. If Patrick had brought Anna Lynn and Ginny to the ranch along with the ponies, the timing couldn't be worse. He found him alone on the veranda, feet up on the railing, smoking a cigar.

"Are they here?" Matt asked.

"Where have you been?" Patrick countered.

"In town. Are they?"

Patrick shook his head and handed Matt an envelope. "She sent this."

Matt tore it open and read:

Dear Matthew,

I've been asked by my sister Danette to come to Idaho and help her move to California. You may remember I wrote you when you were overseas that she'd lost her husband in an Air Corps training accident and was about to have a baby. She stayed with us for a while and had a lovely baby boy named Joshua, before she returned home.

I'm not sure how long we'll be gone, but I think it's good for us to get away, especially with all that has happened. The timing is perfect now that the district attorney has finally decided that he has no reason to charge me with a crime.

Hopefully, I'll come back more like my old self and we can sit together and have a long talk.

Ginny sends you a hug that's as "big as the whole world."

Love,
Anna Lynn

Matt looked at Patrick. "She's going to Idaho to help her sister move. Did she say anything more to you than that?"

"Nope, except I figure she ain't planning to make it a quick trip. She sold all her hives to a beekeeper, parked her truck behind the house, and locked the place up tight before they left. I gave them a ride to the train station and promised to look after Peaches while they're gone."

"Did she leave you an address where I can write to her?"

Patrick shook his head and dropped his feet to the floor. "I didn't think to ask. You hungry?"

Matt shook his head.

"I'm gonna fix me some grub," Patrick said. He plodded off to the kitchen.

Matt stayed alone on the veranda until he finally figured it out. One way or the other, starting with the death of his mother, all the women in his life who cared about him eventually vanished. He decided it had to be a curse.

6

Several weeks passed before Matt received another letter from Anna Lynn: a chatty note about all the headaches she'd faced helping Danette—who wasn't a very well-organized person—prepare for the move to California, how excited they all were to see the Pacific Ocean, and how Ginny had eagerly taken on the role of big sister to her little cousin Joshua, reading him stories and entertaining him while Anna Lynn and Danette packed, sorted, and cleaned in anticipation of the move. She made no mention of when she planned to come home.

Matt expected to hear from her again upon their arrival in California, but when a month passed with no further word, he drove to Mountain Park hoping she might have been in recent touch with some of her neighbors. Nobody had heard from her, and her mail at the post office had piled up. At the farmhouse, Matt got the spare key from under the porch step and took a look inside. Everything was neat and tidy as she'd left it, just dusty from the wind that found its way through cracks in the walls and window frames. Her truck, parked behind the house, was undisturbed as well. He left feeling both a little worried and a little put out by her careless disregard of their friendship, which remained at least that, if nothing more.

He'd also hoped for a letter from Raine Hartman and was disappointed by her silence. Maybe their overnight fling didn't warrant any acknowledgment other than a goodbye hug and a peck on the cheek in a hotel hallway, but Matt wouldn't have minded more. At the ranch he shared his frustration about women with Patrick.

He snorted and said, "Hell, boy, you're better with the ladies than I ever was."

"True, but that doesn't mean I understand them at all."

Patrick grimaced slightly at Matt's cut. "Give it time before you start fretting. Truth be told, I surely miss Anna Lynn and that little dickens of hers. They sure beat your company by a mile."

"And yours as well," Matt retorted as he put on his spurs. The truck hired to take the ponies to auction in Fort Worth was due in the morning. He wanted to move the stock he'd cut out for shipment from the pasture to the corral, where he'd feed and water them overnight.

Patrick rose from his chair. "I'll get Ribbon saddled and go with you."

"No need."

"I'll come along anyway," Patrick announced, unwilling to miss out on a last goodbye to the ponies.

The two men rode out and silently brought the herd into the corral, chasing down a few frisky colts that needed to be coaxed along. The following day, the 7-Bar-K would be out of the horse business, maybe forever, and it was a sad prospect to consider. Neither man wanted to talk about it, but the pastures were so poor that in spite of a normal monsoon season the land couldn't carry both cattle and horses.

They watered and fed the ponies, staying at the corral until the animals quieted down for the night. In the barn, they unsaddled their horses and gave them a good wipe-down and bag of oats before jingling their spurs into the house, where a cold meal of bacon, biscuits, and soggy gravy left over from breakfast awaited them.

Feeling as stale as the slice of bacon he munched, Matt remembered the time not so long ago when he saw himself running the best cutting horse outfit in the West, supplying rodeo cowboys and ranchers with top ponies with proven bloodlines. It would have given him a life larger than the 7-Bar-K. He'd be traveling to auctions to buy breeding stock, making the rounds to visit ranch managers and owners at larger spreads throughout the west, attending regional and national rodeos to sell to the promoters and stockmen who produced the events. He'd once thought it possible, but not anymore, leastways not until peace, prosperity, and wet weather returned in significant amounts.

If he could only figure out a way to go back to college, maybe get a degree in animal husbandry or range management. If he expected to keep the 7-Bar-K, he needed something that could earn him a dependable living besides ranching. He couldn't see parting with the ranch, so something had to change.

Matt eyed Patrick. The years were telling on him more and more. As long as the old man drew a breath and kept his senses, he'd never want to live anywhere else. Keeping Patrick happy on the land he loved, taking care of the ranch and livestock, and at the same time going back to school seemed almost like an impossibility. Maybe he was stuck on the basin for the duration.

He shook off doldrums that were sneaking up on him. There were a lot worse places—Sicily, for one—and not as many beautiful and soul-filling spots on the good Earth as the Tularosa.

* * *

Fall works kept Matt occupied. When he'd finished gathering his cattle and culling the herd, he jumped right in and helped Al Jennings do the same. He left Al in good shape, gave a hand to Earl Hightower, and then worked with Preston McDonald, Billy's father, to gather some of his strays scattered across the Jornada, west of the Oscura Mountains. The long grueling days and hard work kept Matt fully occupied. He especially enjoyed having his mind clear of anything other than the tasks at hand. It didn't matter that September had turned blistering hot; getting cows to market trumped having the juices sucked out of you every day, sunup to sundown.

Patrick had lent a hand at the 7-Bar-K works and was about to do the same at Al's Rocking J Ranch when the check from the sale of the ponies arrived in the mail. Instead, Matt put him in charge of overseeing the construction of a new well, installing a holding tank for gravity-fed water to the house, and building an indoor bathroom, complete with tub and toilet.

Patrick had groused about being left out of all the fun during fall works, but gratefully took on the new assignment. He simply didn't have the staying power to spend sixteen hours in the saddle or behind the wheel of a truck chasing cows. Although he didn't do a spit of work for his neighbors, he was invited to all the feeds they put on to thank the hands and celebrate the end of the selling season, where he was feted for being one of few surviving old-time Tularosa pioneers. Growing old was no damn fun, but getting a few minutes of royal treatment from friends and neighbors pleased and tickled him.

On his trips to buy materials and supplies and hire all the men needed for the work on the ranch house, he always made a swing by Anna Lynn's locked and shuttered place hoping to find her home. He was starting to think she wasn't ever coming back. He'd stopped talking about her prolonged absence to Matt, who had taken to turning away at the mere mention of her name.

In October the heat wave broke and the nights got cold. One afternoon, Matt was in the barn, looking after Stony, an old packhorse who had thrown a shoe and come up lame. In the kitchen, Patrick poked embers in the cookstove to get a fire going to fix some grub for dinner. The sound of a vehicle brought him to the veranda. He whooped with pleasure at the unexpected sight of Anna Lynn and Ginny climbing out of her truck. A tall, middle-aged Mexican fella was with them. Ginny screamed his name and flew up the stairs into his outstretched arms.

"By God, you're almost all grown up," he said, twirling Ginny around in his arms.

"I know," Ginny giggled. "We're gonna live in California."

Patrick planted Ginny on the floor. "Is that a fact?"

Ginny nodded. "Forever."

"I'll be," Patrick said, amazed and disheartened.

"Hello, Patrick," Anna Lynn said as she approached. The Mexican didn't follow.

Patrick smiled to hide the shock of what he'd just heard. "Here I've been missing the sight of you two, and from what Ginny just told me, I'm gonna have to get used to it permanently."

Anna Lynn smiled with regret. "I'm afraid that's true. I came to tell you and Matt in person. Is he here?"

To Patrick's eye, she looked a little worn down. He nodded at

Matt, who'd stepped out of the barn. "He's coming. Who's the Mexican with you?"

Without answering, Anna Lynn turned to face Matt, her expression empty of pleasure. She remained silent as Ginny dashed down the veranda steps and gave him a big hug.

Tugged along by Ginny, Matt approached. He stopped in front of Anna Lynn, pointedly looked back at the man standing next to her truck, and said flatly, "What a surprise."

"They're moving away for good," Patrick said before Anna Lynn could react. It earned him a stern look.

"That's true," she said, searching Matt's face for a reaction.

"Who's the guy?" Matt asked.

"Alejandro."

"Just Alejandro?"

Anna Lynn's back stiffened. "What else do you need to know about him?"

Matt shrugged. "Whatever you want to tell me."

"He's here for Peaches. He'll take her to California for us. That's if she's still Ginny's pony."

Patrick's jaw clamped shut before he answered. "That wasn't called for. I gave Peaches to Ginny free and clear and you know it."

Her words came in a rush. "I'm sorry, you're right. It was a stupid thing to say." She glanced remorsefully from Patrick to Matt.

"No harm done," Patrick replied, warming a mite. "Come in and sit a spell."

"Stay for supper," Matt added, with a nod toward Alejandro.

Anna Lynn hesitated. "No, no thanks. We need to get going. Alejandro will help you load Peaches."

"You folks will have to wait a while," Matt said. "I have to bring her in from the pasture."

"Can I come?" Ginny asked.

Matt nodded and took Ginny's hand. "Sure you can. Help me saddle up and we'll go fetch her. You can ride her home bareback."

Ginny stomped her feet in delight. "Let's go, let's go."

"I'll put a fresh pot on while we're waiting." Patrick gestured at Alejandro and invited him in Spanish to come inside and have some coffee. He didn't move until Anna Lynn nodded her approval.

* * *

Matt hoisted Ginny up, put her in front of him on the saddle, and trotted his pony out to the pasture. He knew exactly where Peaches liked to laze about in the evening and took a roundabout way to her location in order to give Ginny a chance to talk. Because Ginny was so excited about reuniting with Peaches, he didn't get a lot of specifics about why Anna Lynn was leaving Mountain Park, other than some elderly relative had died and left his California farm to Anna Lynn and her sisters. From what Matt knew about the family, he figured it had to have been the bachelor uncle who'd lived on a farm outside Modesto in the San Joaquin Valley.

When he asked Ginny if she liked Alejandro, she simply shrugged, said he was nice, and that he sometimes stayed with them in California. Matt didn't need to hear more.

He found Peaches, put a bridle on her, gave Ginny a leg up, and watched her break into a big, beautiful smile as she loped away on her pony. After Ginny had a good twenty-minute ride, he cajoled her into returning to the ranch house, where he learned that Anna Lynn and her sisters had indeed inherited their uncle's farm.

At the kitchen table over coffee, he sat with Patrick, Alejandro, and Anna Lynn as she explained that she and Danette were buying out their other sisters' inheritance in the farm. She would pay her share of what was owed with proceeds from the sale of the Mountain Park property. Danette would use the army life-insurance payments she received from her husband's death in a military training accident to do the same.

Pending the settlement of the estate, Anna Lynn, Danette, and the two children were living on the farm, which consisted of half a section of prime agricultural land with good water rights, and they were busy fixing up the house, repairing fences, shoring up the hay barn, and building beehives for Anna Lynn's planned raw-honey enterprise.

Matt kept his questions to himself, especially ones about Alejandro. He also held back on asking Anna Lynn if she'd been planning her move before she left to visit Danette. He thought it likely; she had always been good at keeping secrets.

She seemed uneasy with him, keeping her attention focused mostly on Patrick, who was trying his best to be positive. Her face was drawn, her eyes were tired, and she was thinner.

Across from Matt, Alejandro remained mute, quietly drinking his coffee. Matt studied him surreptitiously with several quick glances and decided he wasn't subservient, just diffident in an uncomfortable situation. All in all, he wasn't bad-looking either, with strong features and a long Spanish nose. He could see the appeal he held for Anna Lynn.

Silently, Matt wished Alejandro well, surprised at how comfortable it felt to be letting go of Anna Lynn to another man. He felt no remorse, no anger, just a subdued gratefulness for all that she'd meant to him over the years. She'd brought a lot of love into his life at a time when he'd badly needed it. He would have married her if she had allowed it.

Anna Lynn used Ginny's eagerness to depart as a pretext to cut short the socializing. After saying thank you and goodbye, she stood with Matt on the veranda while Alejandro and Ginny installed the side boards on the truck, walked Peaches up the ramp, secured her in the bed by way of a guide rope, and latched the tailgate. Patrick had stayed in the kitchen, where he was irritably rattling coffee cups in the new sink.

She waited to speak until Alejandro and Ginny got in the cab, Alejandro settling behind the steering wheel. "You're not angry?"

Matt shook his head. "I don't think so. He's a good hand with ponies."

"Yes, just like you." Anna Lynn looked in Matt's eyes. "I never promised . . ."

Matt cut her off. "I know. How sick are you?"

Anna Lynn stiffened. "What do you mean?"

"I mean you're not well, I can see it."

"It's just a female problem. Change of life, the doctor says."

"That's all?"

Anna Lynn nodded.

"You're sure?"

Anna Lynn pursed her lips, signaling the subject was closed. "Yes."

She didn't look like she wanted to be kissed, but Matt did it anyway, right on her lips. She yielded and caressed his face with her hand before breaking away.

"Goodbye, Matthew."

"Adios."

She walked carefully around the spot where Fred Tyler had lain dead and got in the truck. Until that moment he'd wanted to know why she'd soured on him. Now he knew. If Tyler hadn't come looking for him, they might still be together. No one ever forgets the people they've killed, nameless or otherwise, or the places where it happened, and for Anna Lynn, if she'd stayed, the constant reminder of what she'd done at the ranch would have haunted her forever.

They drove away with Peaches prancing in the bed of the truck, Ginny's face pressed against the back window watching her pony.

Patrick eased to his side. "It's a damn shame."

"Yep."

"I want you to hire me a housekeeper."

"Nope, you'd just want to marry her and screw it all up."

Patrick snorted. "Then find a way to get us some female companionship out here once in a while. Or maybe we could adopt a kid."

Matt laughed. "There's a fat chance of that happening."

The truck disappeared in the gathering darkness.

"It's a damn shame," Patrick repeated remorsefully.

Matt sucked in a deep breath. "Yep."

7

December brought rainsqualls to the Tularosa, not enough to give Matt an optimistic outlook for a wet winter, but enough to slightly raise his hopes. It also brought an unexpected letter from Raine Hartman, who was stationed at a field hospital somewhere on the Continent. She couldn't tell him where because the censors wouldn't allow it, but she assured him that she was absolutely safe.

She apologized for not writing sooner, but hadn't had a moment of free time since arriving at her duty station. Except for one three-day weekend pass to London, she'd been working long hours every day, eating her meals half-asleep, and collapsing into bed exhausted. She'd taken up smoking.

She spent her waking hours nursing gravely wounded soldiers who were more courageous than any men she'd ever met. It made her realize how brave Matt had been and how little she had known back in the States about how awful war really was. The movie newsreels or the army propaganda films didn't come close to the truth. She'd begun to understand why the combat veterans she'd met at Fort Bliss rarely talked about their experiences.

She told him that Susie, her nurse pal, who was still stationed stateside, had gotten a "Dear Jane" letter from her married officer lover, who'd dumped her as soon as his promotion to lieutenant colonel came through along with command of a battalion. Supposedly he was fighting somewhere in France and probably bedding Parisian hussies in between battles. She pitied his poor wife, the general's daughter.

She also mentioned she was now a first lieutenant and that through the grapevine she'd learned Dr. Beckmann had been promoted to major and reassigned to Walter Reed Hospital in Washington. She asked him to write and closed with the hope she would see him again when the war was over, but didn't know where or when.

Raine's letter made Matt smile, and knowing how much mail had meant to him in Sicily, he immediately wrote her back, keeping it light and chatty, offering her another night out on the town if she so desired.

In the middle of December, Matt's already-diminished holiday spirits were battered by word of a German counterattack in Europe. Headlines in the newspapers called it the "Battle of the Bulge." He wondered if his old outfit was in the thick of the fighting, but had no way of knowing. Reports mentioned the Allied and German army corps engaged in the battle and identified several besieged army regiments fighting for survival in blizzard conditions with dwindling supplies and no air support. Stories of Germans capturing and executing hundreds of American soldiers made Matt boil with anger. He felt miserable about not being with his unit, no matter where they were.

January 1945 brought better news. The Allies stopped the

counterattack in the Ardennes and routed the German forces; the Russians continued to advance eastward, rolling up Nazi divisions, and in the Pacific the US Army had returned to the Philippines and was pushing back the Japanese in fierce fighting.

On the Tularosa, due to paltry winter rains, spring works started early. Much of the land from the Rio Grande to the east side of the basin remained open range and cattle roamed freely in search of browse and water. In March, when ranchers began gathering, reports soon started circulating of run-ins with military police patrols denying them access to several hundred square miles of land west of the Oscuras. A group of stockmen made a request to the Alamogordo Air Field commander for permission to round up their stray cows. It was quickly rejected, in spite of the fact that cattle had been spotted in the restricted area.

New roads on the government-seized land were being built by construction crews from sunup to sundown, and miles of electrical wire had been strung on low poles from power lines adjacent to the Rio Grande. Jeep and truck tire tracks crisscrossed the scrubland, and dust thrown up by the dozens of trucks coming and going daily filled the sky, along with two tall steel towers poking up like beacons into the big empty near the old McDonald Ranch.

In the middle of the restricted land a small compound had been built to quarter twelve MPs, who patrolled the perimeter of the newly established federal reservation in jeeps. Because there were no fences, signs on posts placed every hundred yards or so warned that there was no trespassing on government property.

The lack of twenty-four-hour MP patrols and the absence of fencing was sufficient incentive for Matt, Patrick, and Al Jennings to mount an early March predawn raid to gather a sizable bunch of cattle that had congregated for water at the abandoned, now-officially-off-limits Bar Cross horse camp. After camping overnight outside the perimeter, they gathered the critters without a hitch under the cover of darkness and were two miles from the boundary with the sun blazing down on them in a cloudless sky when four MPs in two jeeps converged on them. The soldiers ground their vehicles to a stop and two rifle-toting privates in combat fatigues jumped out, weapons at the ready. Startled by the commotion, the cattle began to break away and scatter. Paying no attention to the GIs, Matt and Al went after them at a gallop, Matt veering left, Al to the right, hoping to turn the lead steers back and get the bunch milling before the scattering became a stampede.

Astride Ribbon, Patrick watched while the two nervous army boys—kids, really—held him at bay with their M-1 rifles.

"Make those men stop," the MP sergeant ordered him, waving his .45. A stubby little fella, no more than five-foot-five, the sergeant had a beak for a nose and almost no eyebrows.

Patrick slowly unholstered his horse pistol and placed it on his leg. "They can't do that until the cows decide to quit," he answered peaceably.

The sergeant held out his hand. "Give me that pistol."

"Nope. You give me yours."

The sergeant pointed his .45 at Patrick's chest. "Don't be stupid, old man."

"You gonna shoot me?" Patrick demanded. Matt and Al had turned the lead steers. In a dense dust cloud that hid the two riders from view, the cows began to wheel back toward Patrick, a good sign the scattering had been halted.

"I just might have to," the sergeant growled.

"I'd wait, if I were you," Patrick replied calmly. The cows slowed to a walk and the dust lifted, revealing Matt and Al flanking the sergeant, their Winchesters pointed directly at him. "That is, unless you're hankering to be shot dead where you stand."

The sergeant glanced left to right at the two riders and slowly holstered his sidearm. "Lower your weapons," he ordered his troops. They did so in great relief.

Patrick eased the horse pistol into the holster. "Let us pass and we'll trouble you no more today." Matt and Al took his cue and returned their rifles to their scabbards.

The sergeant shook his head and got a clipboard from his jeep. "First, I've got to make a report about this."

Patrick looked down kindly at the sergeant and smiled. "I reckon you do. Tell your commanding officer or whoever is in charge that Patrick and Matthew Kerney from the 7-Bar-K and Al Jennings from the Rocking J came and rescued their privately owned property that was illegally impounded by the government. If he needs to know more, he's invited to come and visit. He can look up how to find us on a map. You got that?"

The sergeant hesitated then nodded.

"Good." Patrick started to urge Ribbon forward and paused. "What are you people building out here?"

"I don't know," the sergeant replied sincerely.

"An ammo dump?" Patrick proposed.

"I can't say," the sergeant answered.

"Is it a big secret?" Patrick prodded in a mock whisper.

"I can't say because we don't know." The sergeant punctuated his ignorance with a shrug. "None of us do. Technically, we're not even out here on this godforsaken desert. But if I were you, I wouldn't come back. There are gonna be a whole lot more of us real soon."

Patrick nudged Ribbon forward. "I'll keep that in mind. Adios, Sergeant."

* * *

Seven of the rescued cows belonged to the McDonald family. They threw them over onto a home pasture on their way to the Sweetwater Canyon Pass, where they parted company with Al Jennings, who continued with his bunch southwestward to the Rocking J.

With Salinas Peak towering to the north, they came out of the rock-strewn pass on to the Tularosa flats with the Malpais in full view, bedded the critters down for the night at an occasional spring that still ran clear at the foot of a rock outcropping, and made camp an easy ten miles from home.

"Those army boys ain't building an ammunition dump," Patrick announced as he eased onto his bedroll and stared up at the black, star-filled sky. "If that was all they were up to, that MP sergeant would've told us. An ammo dump is no big secret."

Matt opened a can of peaches, drank the juice, and forked the halves into his mouth. "Got any ideas what it is?"

"Nope, but it bodes no good for the likes of us," Patrick ruminated. "Once the government gets its talons into something, chances are they won't let go."

"Most of our land we own free and clear, unlike other folks who proved up a section for a homestead and were leasing the rest of their land from the government," Matt countered. "Besides, our landholdings aren't part of the bombing range or this new hush-hush whatever-the-hell-it-is. Way I see it, we're okay."

Patrick gave Matt's comments some thought before responding. "Let's hope it stays as simple as that. But the Tularosa has a way of serving up a passel of perilous surprises, and on this slice of country I count mankind as the most dangerous critter of them all."

A squadron of B-17s on a night bombing-raid exercise roared overhead in formation, lights blinking fore and aft, punctuating Patrick's point. His aching bones kept him awake long after the last faint whisper of the aircraft engines had faded away.

* * *

In the morning they arrived home, settled the cattle in the fenced pasture, and were greeted by two men waiting next to an army jeep parked in front of the ranch house. The man in an army uniform, a stern-jawed fella, wore first lieutenant's bars and crossed-pistol insignias on his jacket, signifying military police. His companion, a tall man in a suit and tie with a sunburned face, had a deputy US Marshal badge pinned to the handkerchief pocket of his suit jacket. Neither man offered a handshake or attempted an introduction. Hoping Patrick had the good sense to sit on his pony and stay quiet, Matt dismounted and asked the men to state their business.

"You're one of the Kerneys?" the officer demanded.

"Yep." Matt nodded in Patrick's direction. "And that old boy is the other one."

The lieutenant glanced quickly at Patrick and returned his attention to Matt. "I'm here to give you both a warning: stay off government land. The next time you trespass, you'll be taken into custody, arrested, and jailed without bail until a hearing can be scheduled before a federal judge."

Patrick snickered at the thought of it. "Trespassing is a petty misdemeanor. You get a fine, not jail time."

"It isn't as simple as that," the deputy marshal retorted briskly. "This is serious government business. You'd better heed the lieutenant."

"Is that so?" Patrick moved Ribbon closer to the lieutenant, who stepped back. "What are you boys cooking up out there?" he asked.

The officer gave Patrick's pony a wary look, climbed behind the wheel of the jeep, and cranked the engine. "Take this warning seriously, gentlemen, or be prepared to suffer the consequences."

Patrick dismounted as the men drove away. "They weren't very neighborly. Think they'll send a bomber to blow us to kingdom come if we don't do as we're told?"

"More likely it will be a platoon of heavily armed soldiers in half-tracks."

Patrick uncinched his saddle. Ribbon snorted with pleasure. "Best we stock up on ammo next trip to town."

Matt rolled his eyes and unsaddled his pony.

* * *

That afternoon, a trip to the mailbox brought a typewritten letter from Matt's former first sergeant, now captain, Roscoe Beal, sent from a military hospital in England. It read:

> *Matt:*
>
> *I'm sitting on a thick rubber cushion in the hospital day room at this typewriter writing to you this way because a German 88 shell blew a hole the size of a half dollar in my ass and took a chunk out of the upper arm of my writing hand, so it's hunt and peck one letter at a time. As you can tell by the envelope, I'm not a first sergeant anymore due to getting a battlefield commission in Italy. Be glad you weren't there with us. Only eleven of us who shipped out with the company survived Italy intact. Our regiment really got chewed up.*

You're getting this letter because this morning I was reading the Stars and Stripes *and saw the newest Bill Mauldin cartoon in the paper. When I told my pretty army nurse, Raine Hartman, about the hilarious cartoons Mauldin did about you in Sicily and mentioned your name she was flabbergasted. Apparently, she was your nurse at Ft. Bliss before she shipped out. Small world, isn't it? She transferred to England from a field hospital just a week before I got blown up by that Kraut 88. I got your address from her. She sends her best and promises to write.*

I'm hoping to get fixed up enough to rejoin the regiment although rumor has it now that fighting in this theater is winding down, those fit enough to return to combat may be held in reserve to fight Tojo. Maybe we'll all get some leave at home before then. Sure would be nice.

There's already talk going around in the division about holding a reunion in Oklahoma once the war is over. Maybe we can get together then and lift a glass. I'd like that.

Sincerely,
Roscoe

To give Roscoe news of a normal life at home, which he knew would be a welcome distraction, Matt wrote back about cattle prices, making improvement to the ranch, and putting up with his often testy old man. He didn't mention the army, rationing, national politics, the war, or the hush-hush military doings on the Jornada.

Over the next several weeks he expected to hear from Raine, but a letter never came. He soon put it out of his mind, figuring a good-looking woman in London wouldn't be missing a one-eyed veteran on a dusty New Mexico ranch when there were legions of horny soldiers to occupy her attention. In April his reckoning proved right when a brief, formal note arrived announcing her marriage to Maj. Harry Stanford Barrett IV, MD, known to all as Bill. After the war, Dr. and Mrs. Barrett would live in New York City, where the good doctor would resume his private psychiatric practice.

Disappointed that another weekend rendezvous with Raine wasn't going to happen in either the near or distant future, Matt wrote a congratulatory note to the happy couple, wondering if he'd ever attract a woman who wanted to stick around. The day he mailed it, Adolf Hitler and Eva Braun committed suicide in Hitler's Berlin bunker. A few days later, on May 6, 1945, the war in Europe ended.

Although it was only half a victory, with the war in the Pacific still to be won, Matt broke out a bottle of Kentucky sipping whiskey to celebrate, and for the first and, he expected, the only time in his life, he got stinking drunk with his father.

8

Just as the MP sergeant predicted, after their raid to liberate the cattle stranded on the land seized by the army, activity there soon increased. Dozens of watchtowers were built along the perimeter and quickly staffed by armed GIs. Along certain sections of the boundary where errant cattle had been known to illegally wander, fencing had been thrown up with No Trespassing signs nailed to posts every several hundred feet. On the new roads that cut straight across the raw, sun-blasted land, truck convoys brought troops, supplies, equipment, civilian workers, and tons of construction materials. Within weeks, swarms of workers reassembled Civilian Conservation Corps barracks that had stood vacant in the old forest camps and created a post laid out in a typical military configuration. Gasoline engines powered huge floodlights so work could proceed at night. Water wells were dug, latrines built, and electric generators installed. At night from mountaintop vantage points, it seemed that a new town had miraculously dropped down from the sky onto the desert floor, along with a host of colonists embarked upon mysterious undertakings.

Matt saw it all as he rode the Oscura Mountains high country in search of 7-Bar-K strays. Before the army kicked McDonald off his ranch early in the war to use it as a bombing range for the Alamogordo Airfield, there had been no need to ride so far north. But with no one left to gather the wandering critters, he periodically rode an upcountry circuit looking for livestock that had gone missing, invariably chasing home a few half-wild steers and an elderly dry cow or two—mostly 7-Bar-K cattle, but occasionally a critter carrying a neighboring brand.

Matt enjoyed the outings not only for the solitude it provided in a pretty slice of mountain country, but also for relief from Patrick's company, who'd become reasonably easy to tolerate but still prone to crankiness.

From horseback, he always paused on a protected shelf to scan the encampment below him in the distance. Even with binoculars it was hard to see the goings-on in detail, but he could clearly make out huge concrete bunkers under construction and two tall towers, one of steel and one of heavy timbers, being thrown up. It was all a puzzle.

One Sunday morning he watched in astonishment as soldiers on horseback played polo on a dusty field near the base camp. On another occasion, as he was chasing a belligerent steer out of a slot canyon, a huge explosion, louder than anything he'd ever heard before, brought him at a gallop to a western crest to find a thick plume of dense, black smoke swirling skyward and a large, smoldering crater in the desert floor where the wooden tower had once stood. At home, he told Patrick the army had blown up a wooden tower with enough high explosives to wipe out most of Alamogordo for no apparent reason.

"What was the tower for?" Patrick asked.

"As far as I could tell, it was just a tower," Matt replied.

"Was it an accident?" Patrick asked, turning down the volume on the portable radio Matt had bought from a bomber pilot who had deployed with his outfit to somewhere in the South Pacific.

"I don't think so," Matt replied.

"Maybe it was just a quick way to make a big hole in the ground," Patrick ventured.

"But what for?" Matt asked.

Patrick shrugged indifferently. "Your guess is as good as mine, but since the army did it, I figure it has to do with finding new ways to kill the enemy. After all, that's what they do." He turned up the volume on the radio and promptly lost interest in the conversation.

With the war in Europe won, rumors at the airfield whispered of massive preparations for the invasion of Japan. Earlier in the year, Tokyo had been firebombed, killing tens of thousands. The Philippines had been reclaimed, Okinawa captured with staggering losses on both sides, and in China, Burma, and Borneo the Japanese forces were in retreat. Folks were getting optimistic that maybe the war in the Pacific would be over in a year, and the gung-ho flyboys who'd yet to see combat were eager to kill their share of Japs before it ended.

Matt didn't doubt that soon a lot more Nips would be dead, and after hearing the reports of Japanese atrocities committed against Allied POWs, especially the New Mexico boys who had been captured on Corregidor, the notion didn't trouble him one bit.

The portable radio Matt had purchased, a Zenith Trans-Oceanic that received five shortwave bands as well as AM broadcasts, was a honey of a radio that quickly became Patrick's prime source of entertainment. After supper, he settled into his easy chair in the living room and listened to the news and his favorite comedy and variety shows, including Abbott and Costello, Fred Allen, and Bing Crosby. Occasionally, he'd scan the shortwave bands, fiddling with the antenna until he got an overseas station, sometimes from Australia, sometimes an English-language broadcast from as far away as India. The mountains frequently blocked reception, which left only a Juárez music station to listen to after the college station in Las Cruces went off the air. By then, Patrick was usually asleep in his chair.

Matt frequently joined Patrick in the evening, sitting at his desk while going over the ranch books, lazing on the couch as he mended a piece of tack, or reading the latest bulletins from the National Livestock Producers Association. He always paused and paid particular attention when the war news came on. Roscoe Beal had written him while stateside on medical leave, saying scuttlebutt had the division rotating to the Pacific theater before the end of the year. He worried about his old army buddy. How much war could any one man hope to survive?

One evening the college station aired an interview with New Mexico US Senator Dennis Chávez, who discussed the GI Bill of 1944 that he'd helped get passed in Congress. Matt's interest peaked when the senator explained the educational benefits available to eligible veterans. Not only was tuition fully covered, but every veteran enrolled as a full-time student received a fifty-dollar-a-month subsistence allowance during the school year. Matt wrote the information down and told Patrick he was going to look into it next time he had business in Las Cruces.

Patrick guffawed and said anything other than land that the government gave away for free probably wasn't worth the bother. And even then, they could come and take it back like they did to McDonald. It made Matt wonder if the entire Tularosa would get permanently swallowed up by the army.

* * *

On the first Monday in July, Matt drove to the campus of the New Mexico College of Agricultural and Mechanical Arts in Las Cruces. He hadn't been there in years and the changes were dramatic. During the Great Depression, the campus had been used by the Civilian Conservation Corps, and later on, in the early years of the war, it had served as an Army Special Training Center. The main core of the campus, with its array of stately classroom buildings, large gymnasium, dorms, and the grand administration building, remained the same. But the surrounding grounds were dominated by temporary military-style barracks and Quonset huts spread out over once-empty fields and pastures.

In an old single-story CCC administration building propped up on concrete pillars and converted into a veteran's service center, Matt met with James Kendell, a one-armed navy veteran with a ruptured duck button pin on the lapel of his suit jacket. After introductions, he sat at a small desk in a tiny office and quickly reviewed Matt's paperwork. When he finished, Kendell took out a lined tablet and started writing, pausing to look up information from a thick binder embossed with a Veterans Administration logo. Matt silently waited.

After a few minutes, Kendell put down his pencil and smiled. "You're gonna be in good shape. In addition to your service-connected disability pension you'll get a monthly fifty-dollar subsistence allowance during the school year. That goes up to sixty-five dollars next year."

"Great," Matt said, figuring he'd be able to hire a ranch hand who could also keep an eye on Patrick and have enough left over to cover his room and board expenses in town.

Kendell reached for a pack of cigarettes, lit up with a Zippo lighter bearing the navy emblem, and blew a smoke ring. "You're going to have to provide a copy of your advanced army language training record to the provost's office so they can determine how much college credit to allow you. But from what I've seen so far, guys with foreign-language proficiency rack up the credits. With a year of college already under your belt before your enlistment, you just might be enrolled as an upperclassman. Are you planning to start back in the fall semester?"

"I have some things to work out first," Matt said.

Kendell pushed blank forms across the desk. "Fill everything out and return it to me so I can get the process started." He turned to a small file cabinet, pulled out some mimeographed sheets of paper, and handed them to Matt. "Here's some general information about the college. Who's who, where to go, and all that important stuff."

"Thanks." Matt barely glanced at the material before stuffing it in a back pocket. "Where did you lose the arm?"

"Leyte Gulf," Kendell answered. "I got shot down."

"Tough," Matt said sympathetically.

Kendell chuckled and stood. "From what I understand, Sicily was no picnic. It could have been worse for both of us."

"Roger that," Matt said as he shook Kendell's hand.

"Sooner you get the provost's office started evaluating your service jacket, the better," Kendell advised as he handed Matt his file.

"Aye-aye, swabbie," Matt replied, breaking into a grin.

Kendell grinned in return. "Get lost, dogface."

* * *

Matt made his way to the provost's office on the first floor of the administration building, where an older woman was sitting at a desk in front of an inner door talking to a man wearing a suit and tie. Three students, one boy with thick glasses, another scrawny kid who might have been sixteen, and a rather homey, serious-looking girl in a cotton dress, waited patiently on chairs along one long wall. Matt joined them, feeling very much like an old man. His glass eye earned quick stares. He returned their interest with a friendly smile as each kid looked away. When the man in the suit knocked on the inner door and stepped inside, the woman called the next student to her desk. The boy with the thick glasses hurried over, clutching a notebook in his hand.

Figuring he had a long wait before his turn, Matt got out the mimeographed information about the college that James Kendell had given him. Most of it was stuff he already knew, such as the history of the institution, the various degree-granting departments, the location of faculty offices, and the social clubs on campus. Included was a faculty directory. His old professor and friend Augustus Merton was listed as the college provost.

Augustus Merton had been Matt's favorite professor during his freshman year and, just as important, the uncle of Matt's first love, Beth. Augustus and his wife, Consuelo, had welcomed Matt into the family much like a son. During the Great Depression, when Patrick was laid up with a broken leg and Matt was desperate to find work, Gus had hired him to help the Forest Service scout locations for CCC camps in New Mexico and Arizona. Soon after, Gus accepted a temporary appointment with the WPA in Washington and left the college on loan to the government. Matt hadn't seen him since.

As more students came into the office and filled up the chairs, Matt waited patiently as the woman spoke to each of the kids ahead of him. When his turn came, he asked her if he could first speak with Professor Merton.

The woman shook her head. "He's very busy. You'll have to make an appointment."

"If he knew I was here, I think he might like to see me," Matt said pleasantly as he handed her the telephone. "Just ask, please. Tell him Matt Kerney would like a minute of his time."

For a very long minute, the woman glanced at his service records, his old college transcript, and his glass eye before replying. "Very well."

The telephone was barely back in its cradle when Gus Merton flung open the inner door and grabbed Matt in a bear hug. "My boy," he boomed, "come in, come in."

In the office, the man in the suit was bent over a large desk poring over stacks of architectural drawings. He nodded a vague hello as Gus made the introductions.

"When the war is over, there will be much to do," Gus said by way of explanation for his office clutter. He'd shrunk an inch from his five-foot-eight frame, his mop of curly brown hair had turned gray, and his round face was thicker in the jowls, but liveliness and curiosity still gleamed in his eyes.

"Come to dinner tonight at the hacienda," he ordered. "Six sharp for drinks."

"I don't want to impose."

"Nonsense, Consuelo would horsewhip me if I failed to demand your company tonight. We have much to talk about." Gus studied Matt's face. "And stories to tell, I would imagine."

Matt nodded agreeably. "Six o'clock."

Gus smiled happily and reached for the telephone on the credenza behind his desk. "I'll call her right now." He was gleefully informing Consuelo of their unexpected dinner guest as Matt closed the office door.

* * *

For Matt, there had been no more enjoyable home to visit than the Merton hacienda in the village of Mesilla. At the same time, memories of the thick adobe walls; the serene, lovely courtyard; the colorful tiled walls of the inviting kitchen; Gus's comfortable library so perfect for conversation; and the rambling rooms with low-beamed passages, weighed heavily on his heart. For a moment he hesitated at the hand-carved hacienda door before tapping the forged iron door knocker. Here, at Consuelo's ancestral home a few steps off the lovely plaza, he'd fallen in love with Beth, won her heart in return, and made plans for a life together, only to have it vanish with her death.

He took a deep breath and knocked. Almost immediately the door opened to reveal Consuelo, her dark hair now lightly streaked with gray, her face still as lovely as ever, her figure still girlishly slender. She greeted him in Spanish with a hug and a kiss, ushered him by the hand into the kitchen, where Gus waited smiling, pouring wine into glasses. Together in silence they raised a toast of reunion before adjourning to the library for conversation that veered away from Matt's war experiences—he suspected Gus had read his service jacket at his office and shared its contents with Consuelo—or any mention of Beth. Instead, Gus—first and foremost a teacher at heart—asked Matt about his plans to return to college. Matt explained that he definitely wanted to finish his degree, but first needed to get everything in order at the ranch.

Gus raised an eyebrow at the mention of the ranch. "The army didn't force you off the land for the air corps bombing range?"

"No, except for a small slice on the Alkali Flats, most of the 7-Bar-K is in the high country on the fringe of the bombing range.

Besides, thanks to my savvy grandfather and his partner, I own title to most of the land, unlike the other ranchers, who only held title to a section and leased the rest for grazing. The army would have a hard time forcing me out or offering only to pay a paltry amount."

Gus nodded in approval. "That's a definite advantage, although there is always the threat of eminent domain proceedings, which I'm sure won't happen. I've heard a number of the displaced ranchers are planning to return after the war ends."

Matt leaned forward in his chair. "I hope they can, but let me tell you it's not just a bombing range out there anymore."

He launched into the strange army doings he'd witnessed at the McDonald ranch, and the topic was carried into the dining room, where, over an excellent meal of tacos, salad, and melon, they speculated about the hush-hush military enterprise on the Jornada. The only conclusion they reached echoed Patrick's observation that armies, by their nature, specialized in blowing people up.

It was only then that Consuelo asked about Matt's war wound. He kept his reply brief, but it still brought tears to her eyes.

In the cool of the high-walled courtyard at twilight, Matt asked Gus and Consuelo about their son, Lorenzo, a West Point graduate who'd been a serving officer at the onset of the war. He learned Lorenzo was now a highly decorated brigadier general at the Pentagon after serving in North Africa, Italy, and France. He'd married before the war. Gus fetched snapshots of Lorenzo, his wife, and their three children. In the lamplight of the patio table, Matt declared them to be a handsome bunch.

As the evening wore down, Consuelo advanced the notion that Matt could live at the hacienda as their guest when he returned to school.

"Even when Lorenzo and his family visit, there will be empty bedrooms gathering dust," she added. "Although I will never give it up, this place is much too big for the two of us and we'd love your company."

Gus heartily endorsed her offer.

Matt thanked them and said he would give it some thought. Only then did Beth's presence briefly hover over them.

He left soon after, filled with renewed affection for Gus and Consuelo. Their good company and lively conversation made him realize all that had been missing in his life since the day Anna Lynn left for California. He'd been semi-comatose and hadn't even noticed it.

Just as Consuelo would never give up her hacienda, Matt could never let go of the 7-Bar-K. He'd worked too hard for too long to save it. Yet he needed more than ranching in his life. Without any clear idea of what to study other than range management or animal husbandry, he resolved to go back to school as soon as possible.

9

Matt returned home to find a package on his desk sent from an army post office in Europe. Inside was an inscribed copy of Bill Mauldin's book *Up Front,* along with the two original cartoons Bill had done about Matt's exploits in Sicily. A typewritten letter read:

> *Matt:*
>
> *Just about the time the Nazis threw in the towel I got the Pulitzer Prize for my first book of cartoons. Hell, I didn't even know what a Pulitzer Prize was until my publisher explained it all to me earlier in the year. I sure didn't expect to get it but I'm glad I did. My book is selling like hotcakes and my publisher says that I'm gonna be rich and famous, so you'd better hold on to all those drawings I peddled to you when I was a kid in Mountain Park. They're gonna be worth a lot of money someday.*
>
> *I thought you'd like to have the original cartoons I did about you in Sicily, so I've signed them and sent them along in this package as well.*

Anyway, I've got to run now because some journalist from the States wants to interview me for his Chicago newspaper. (There's a bird colonel assigned full-time to handle all my publicity and such. How's them apples for a lowly buck sergeant from New Mexico?)

Your pal,
Bill

Matt showed the letter to Patrick, and thinking it might be wise to find a better place to keep Bill's drawings—a bank safe-deposit box, perhaps—he went to the small blanket chest in the casita where he'd tucked them away before leaving for the army. They were all gone—two dozen drawings—along with Anna Lynn's letters he'd added after returning home.

Steamed, he stomped around the house calling for Patrick and found him in the corral with a pained expression on his face, shoveling horse apples into a wheelbarrow. It was not a chore he took to willingly—further evidence of his guilt.

"What did you do with them, old man?" Matt demanded.

"I don't know what you're talking about," Patrick mumbled, his face averted, hidden by the brim of his cowboy hat.

"Yes, you do: Bill Mauldin's drawings, Anna Lynn's letters."

Patrick dropped his shovel into the wheelbarrow. "When Anna Lynn and Ginny quit us, I burned all of it. Jesus, they were just some kid's drawings. How was I to know?"

"They weren't yours to burn, dammit," Matt snapped.

"I was mad at what she'd done to you."

"What she did to *me*?" Matt queried sarcastically.

A sad look flickered across his face. "To both of us, I reckon."

Matt almost felt sympathy for the old man. He'd watched Anna

Lynn win him over by the strength of her personality, and lovable little Ginny burrow her way into his heart. But he did not have the goodwill to grant him forgiveness, at least not yet. "You are the most inconsiderate person I know."

Patrick bit his lip before forcing out the words. "If I've done wrong to you I'm sorry."

Matt stared at his father trying to remember if he'd ever heard such an admission before. As far as he could recall, it was a first. He could either accept the apology or simply acknowledge it. "Let's leave it at that," he said sharply, walking away.

At his desk, he put Bill Mauldin's book, the cartoons, and his letter in a locked drawer along with the framed drawing of Patches, Matt's pony. It was the first sketch he'd ever bought from young Billy and he'd paid a whole dollar for it. The next time he went to town, he'd rent a safe-deposit box.

* * *

Breakfast the next morning was a silent affair, with Patrick dour-looking and Matt not quite ready to let him off the hook for his misdeed. After finishing his bowl of hot oatmeal, he left Patrick with the dirty dishes, loaded a salt lick in the pickup, and drove up the canyon where he'd hazed his cattle that were scheduled for market into a pasture near a clear water stream. They'd laze and fatten there for a week before he moved them up higher to the north pasture.

The monsoons were past due and there wasn't a cloud in the sky. Every day, he ranched hoping for moisture while keeping a watchful eye on the parched land. To avoid overgrazing, he routinely threw the cattle from pasture to pasture to let the grasses recover. Most times, he did it on his own and it was downright exhausting work.

He put out the salt lick and rattled back down the poor excuse of a ranch road in time to see two riders approaching the corral leading a packhorse. He sounded the truck horn to announce his pending arrival and the riders drew rein and waited.

Wondering who his unexpected visitors were, Matt punched the accelerator.

* * *

James Kaytennae sat on his pony, watched the truck slow to a stop, and studied the man who approached on foot. He was tall, broad-shouldered, blue-eyed, with the same features he remembered. But he was much too young to be Patrick Kerney. Perhaps he was a son. He scanned the ranch house, saw no movement, and softly in Apache told his young nephew, Jasper Daklugie, that their journey may have been in vain.

From the shoulder of Kaytennae's pony, the man looked up at him. Expecting a cool reception from the White Eyes, Kaytennae inwardly tensed.

Instead the man nodded a pleasant greeting, smiled, and said, "You gents are a far piece off the highway. Light and come in for some coffee."

Relieved by the neighborly reception, James swung off his pony. "Thank you. But first, I must ask, has Walks Alone gone to the Happy Place?"

"Who?"

James gazed up at the ranch house, which he remembered clearly. "Patrick Kerney—is he dead?"

Matt laughed and extended his hand. "No, he's too contrary to die. I'm his son, Matt."

James shook hands and said, "I am James Kaytennae. My young nephew is Jasper Daklugie. I have brought him here at his grandmother's request so he can work for you. You do not need to pay him. He has almost sixteen summers and is strong for his age. He wishes to fight in the war but is too young. I have told him he must wait for the next war, which will come when he has twenty summers."

Jasper Daklugie smiled at the prospect of becoming a warrior as he slid out of his saddle and stood by his pony.

Rendered speechless, Matt nodded a greeting in the boy's direction and returned his attention to James Kaytennae. He was Patrick's age, maybe a few years older. He wore his long hair in braids under his hat and was thick through the chest with a narrow waist cinched by a belt with a turquoise-and-silver buckle. Kaytennae had called Patrick by an Apache name Matt had never heard before, and had announced he'd brought his young nephew to the ranch to work for free, while offhandedly predicting with great certainty that another war would start in about five years. It was a hell of a lot of information to take in all at once.

After chewing on his choices for a moment, Matt picked the easiest topic to question. "You want Jasper to work here for free?"

James nodded. "Yes, for room and board."

Matt looked over his shoulder for Patrick. *Where was he? Probably in the outhouse, where he seems to be spending more and more time the older he gets.* He returned his attention to James Kaytennae. "What kind of trouble is the boy in?"

"No trouble," James replied calmly. "He has been chosen by tribal leaders to study cattle ranching. We need our young men to gain experience from ranchers like you and your father to help improve our herd."

"How do you know my father?" Matt asked.

Patrick's voice boomed from the veranda. "Don't answer that!"

Matt turned in time to see him adjusting his suspenders.

James Kaytennae smiled. "Ah, Walks Alone."

"Don't call me that," Patrick thundered.

"It is a good name," James countered. "You should be honored to have it."

Patrick thudded down the veranda steps on his bad leg. "I don't see why."

"Because not many White Eyes are given an Apache name," James answered.

Patrick stopped a nose short of Kaytennae's face. "It was you that gave me that damn handle."

James didn't budge. "That's even more of a reason for you to be happy with it."

"You're still uppity," Patrick said, breaking into a smile. "How long has it been?"

"Too long, Walks Alone," Kaytennae replied.

Still flummoxed, Matt turned to Jasper Daklugie. "Do you know what this is all about?"

Jasper nodded. "Yes, Uncle has often told me the story."

"Well, then I guess it's my turn to hear it," Matt said.

"He will do so if you ask," Jasper replied.

* * *

Over coffee in the kitchen, James recounted the story he'd obviously enjoyed telling many times. As a boy during the wars with the White Eyes, he'd hidden on the ranch with his sister, who was about to have a baby and had suffered a badly broken leg. Unable to continue their travels and without any food, James stole a chicken from the ranch house, only to be tracked down and captured by Matt's grandfather, John Kerney, and his partner, Cal Doran.

His sister went into labor before they could be taken to the ranch headquarters, and in spite of John Kerney's attempt during a raging thunderstorm to save the infant, it died in childbirth. Under watchful eyes, they were made prisoners at the ranch, although well treated and cared for, until his sister had recovered enough to travel home. While at the ranch, James, who knew no English, gave Patrick the name Walks Alone—although he kept it to himself during his captivity.

Accompanied by Patrick, John Kerney drove James and his sister in a wagon across the Tularosa and high into the forest to the reservation near the sacred mountain. As they approached the fort they were met by more than thirty Apache warriors who showed their silent gratitude for sparing James and his sister by accompanying the wagon to the post headquarters. It had been an honor conferred upon few White Eyes.

Years later, after John Kerney's death, James became a tribal police officer. Ordered to guide Patrick and Cal Doran to Pine Tree Canyon, where they were to deliver a hundred and fifty head of cattle purchased for the tribe, James had kept silent about his identity until the journey was almost over. Only then did he reveal himself and tell Patrick how he'd come to give him an Apache name so many years ago. Insulted to be called Walks Alone, Patrick had ridden off in a huff.

James paused to smile at the memory of Patrick's bluster. He had no humor then and probably very little now.

"While we were at Pine Tree Canyon, Patrick met the girl who was to become his wife and your mother," he continued, looking directly at Matt. "She was living there with her sister and brother-in-law, but not happy. When we left, she came with us."

James avoided mentioning the names of the woman and brother-in-law, long dead, to keep their spirits from becoming ghosts and spreading sickness.

Taken aback by information he'd never heard before, Matt held up his hand to stop James and quickly turned to Patrick. "I never knew how or where you met Ma, or about her living with a sister on the reservation and leaving with you and Cal."

Patrick shrugged as he glanced pointedly at James. It would not do to tell Matt the whole truth. "It never crossed my mind to tell you. I guess your ma felt it wasn't important either."

James nodded to signal his understanding, but his enjoyment in telling the story had vanished. It was rude to interrupt a speaker, even more so a storyteller in the middle of his tale. Perhaps Matt and Patrick knew no better. He fell silent.

"Please tell me more," Matt prodded.

To convey his displeasure James remained mute. He considered recounting how, some moons after helping Walks Alone rescue his future bride, he'd returned and killed the brother-in-law for stealing from his people and badly mistreating the young woman. It was a well-deserved killing that he'd relished then and still relished now. He'd never admitted the killing to anyone before and decided to say nothing of it, although he knew Walks Alone would be happy to know the truth.

He waited until Matt lowered his gaze before continuing. But since it no longer pleased him to continue the story in his usual great detail, he drastically shortened it. "Some time passed before I saw Cal Doran again, when he was the law hunting for the killers of Judge Fountain and his son," he said. "More summers later, He Who Steals Horses told me of his dream that Cal Doran and Patrick needed me, so I came and worked here until I had money to buy enough ponies to get married."

He pushed his empty coffee cup aside. "And that is the story of how we came to know each other over these many years."

Jasper raised an eyebrow, as his uncle had left much unsaid, especially the part he liked best of how he had tracked two horse thieves who'd stolen ponies from the ranch and shot them out of their saddles dead.

The steely look in James's eyes kept him silent.

Matt quietly mulled over what he'd heard. Though a firm believer in reality, he had a hard time shaking off the feeling that his grandfather's long-ago act of human decency had created some sort of magic for his family. He sensed it more than knew it, but the Apache people—who continued to maintain a singular disdain for the white man—simply didn't mysteriously show up twice at the ranch over a span of many decades offering their help when none had been asked for. Yet here sat James Kaytennae and Jasper Daklugie at his kitchen table at a time when Matt wanted nothing more than to find a way to go back to college. It was all very perplexing to his logical mind.

He waited, hoping for more from James, but the look on his face made it clear he had finished. "Why do you call Patrick 'Walks Alone'?" Matt asked. "You never explained."

"Because it is who he is," James replied, feeling no further need to elaborate.

This time, Patrick didn't grouse about the moniker. He glanced at Jasper and without consulting Matt said, "The boy will get wages just like any other hand." He figured to pay it out of his veteran's pension if need be.

James nodded his approval.

The deal had been struck. Jasper beamed with pleasure.

As it was exactly what he'd intended to propose, Matt didn't say a word. Instead, he thought it wise to shut up and pour James and Jasper another cup of coffee.

* * *

By the end of the week it was clear to Matt that Patrick and Jasper had hit it off. Jasper's deference to elders was part of it, but mostly it was his easygoing nature and sly sense of humor that won Patrick over. As for Jasper, it was apparent that he held Patrick in the highest regard for his role in the legendary rescue of James Kaytennae and his sister during the wars with the White Eyes.

Patrick basked in the boy's respect and seemed rejuvenated by it. Matt noticed a lot more energy in the old boy when it came to doing his share of the chores. Additionally, he'd taken on the role of schooling Jasper in the finer points of ranching, and when it was his turn to cook, suppertime meals improved vastly.

Matt got to thinking that Patrick seemed to get along better with folks who weren't his blood kin. That sure had been true with little Ginny, Anna Lynn, and now with Jasper. He made that observation to Patrick one night after Jasper turned in.

From his seat on the living room couch, Patrick frowned and turned off the radio. "Why are you licking at old wounds?"

"That's not what I'm doing," Matt replied as he scanned the bank statement that had come in the mail. "I'm glad to see you taking an interest in Jasper, that's all."

"I know I weren't much of a pa to you, but I thought we had a truce about that."

"We do," Matt slipped the current bank statement into the top desk drawer and leaned back in his chair.

"Then what in the blazes are you saying?"

"Haul in your horns; I'm not looking to argue with you. Maybe it's just that you're less ornery in your dotage." Matt smiled to signal he meant no offense.

"That's a hell of a thing to say to me," Patrick replied in an injured voice. He'd turned seventy earlier in the year and with his bum leg, his old war wound, and his worn-down body, he wasn't enjoying getting older one damn bit.

Matt laughed. "I take it back. Are you game for riding along when I take Jasper on a tour of the ranch? There's a lot of backcountry for him to get familiar with. I figure we'll be three days in the saddle camping out."

"Hell yes, I'm game," Patrick said with gusto. "Just try to leave me behind and see what happens."

Matt rose from his desk chair and stretched. "I wouldn't dare want to rile you. Get a good night's sleep. We leave after breakfast."

* * *

They left in the morning on horseback, heading south with Patrick in the lead and a pack animal carrying victuals and supplies trotting alongside Jasper.

Matt hung back with Jasper to point out some of the prominent ranch landmarks, the hidden canyons where live streams ran year-round, the pastures where the grass was scant and short in the spring, where deeded land gave way to leased land owned by the state, and the western boundary to the southern section of the Army Air Corps bombing range.

They skirted the desolate Alkali Flats and paralleled the state road westward toward Rhodes Canyon before veering north into higher country in the direction of the 7-Bar-K line cabin, where they would spend the night.

Jasper asked a lot of good questions about the land, and Matt liked that. Tall, lanky, and smart, he had high cheekbones and a narrow nose reminiscent of his uncle's, and thick, almost perfectly straight eyelashes above dark, oval eyes that gave his face a serious cast and made him look older than his years. It was easy to forget he was only approaching sixteen.

They ate their noon meal of hardtack and beef jerky in their saddles, stopping only to give their ponies a good blow after hard climbs up rocky trails. At sunset, they arrived at the cabin pleasantly cloistered in an oval clearing. Built by Cal Doran while Patrick was fighting with the Rough Riders in Cuba, it had a stove; two cots; a small table with two chairs; a pantry stocked with emergency provisions; and a cord of split, seasoned, and stacked firewood convenient to the front door. A sturdy corral a few steps away enclosed a small hay shed with a barrel of oats. Fresh water flowed to a galvanized metal trough, gravity-fed by a pipe from a nearby stream. It was always agreeable in late spring and summer to leave the searing heat of the basin for the relative coolness of the cabin.

Matt set about fixing supper while Jasper and Patrick tended to the ponies. He cut up and sautéed potatoes, onions, and a small can of green chilies in bacon drippings; mixed in a large tin of corned-beef hash; added salt, pepper, and garlic salt; let it simmer for a time; and served it up. After supper, while Jasper did KP, Matt and Patrick wandered over to the corral and checked the ponies for any sores or bruises. To the west, through a gap in the mountains, clouds hovered above the distant Blank Range, burning bright orange in the sunset.

"From what I see, he makes a hand," Patrick ventured. "At least he knows his way around the ponies."

"I agree," Matt allowed. "He'll do to help you run the spread."

"You're fixing to go back to college, aren't you?"

Matt nodded. "As soon as I can."

"You're the boss of this outfit, so do what you want."

Matt ignored the dig and kept silent.

Patrick scanned the sky. "Storm coming our way late tomorrow," he predicted.

"Best we get an early start so we can hunker down when it hits," Matt suggested.

They turned back to the cabin in time to see Jasper spreading his bedroll under the low branches of a nearby juniper tree.

"We wore the boy out some, I reckon," Matt said.

"He's no more worn-out than me," Patrick said, yawning.

* * *

Throughout the following day, Patrick's prediction of a storm appeared sadly farfetched. The three riders traveled the vast high desert tableland of the Jornada under a starkly blue cloudless sky in sweltering heat. By the time they'd turned east to enter the soft foothill trail through Mockingbird Gap, Matt had completely given up on any chance of rain.

They plodded along, men and ponies alike weary and thirsty. To the south, Salinas Peak signaled the northerly thrust of the San Andres Mountains, home to the 7-Bar-K Ranch. North lay the Oscura Mountains overlooking the bombing range, where the military had thrown up the mysterious army post in the middle of nowhere.

Matt had planned to take Patrick and Jasper into the Oscuras for a look-see at the military goings-on, but instead he veered toward a little-known spring in a half-forgotten slot canyon that cut into the westerly backside of the Little Burro Mountains.

Luckily, a trickle of live water from the springs filled a shallow pool in a polished stone crevice hidden by a leafy old desert willow. The narrow valley chute between the Little Burro and Mockingbird Mountains provided a clear nighttime view of the distant lights from the army encampment. Matt decided to make camp there so that Patrick and Jasper might have a glimpse, however remote, of what he'd seen.

After supper, clouds rolled in and hurried nighttime. Jasper made a small fire, more for enjoyment than for warmth. As the night deepened and the fire became a bed of glowing embers, the three men watched dozens of lights flickering and twinkling miles away at the old McDonald spread. Behind them deep, rolling thunder sounded the promise of rain but brought only a slight drizzle to the camp, barely enough to dampen their hats.

Matt recounted to Jasper how he and Patrick had been chased away by soldiers when they'd gone looking for stray cattle, and about the big explosion that had brought him willy-nilly out of a canyon in the Oscuras in time to see a huge crater where once a wooden tower had stood.

The drizzle continued. They turned in on bedrolls covered with their rain slicks, serenaded by distant thunder and an occasional bolt of lightning that danced across the sky. Long before morning the uneasiness of the ponies brought Matt out of a restless sleep. Low clouds hid the stars, but the promise of dawn eased the darkness.

Thinking Patrick and Jasper were still asleep, he sat up and quietly pulled on his boots, only to hear them moving about and shucking off their rain slicks. He was ten feet away from the ponies when the earth trembled, the wind roared, and the sun seemed to fall from the dark sky, exploding into a brilliant whiteness that rose up to become a massive, roiling, ravenous cloud.

He stood blinded, convinced he was consigned to permanent darkness, never to see again. He didn't begin to breathe until his good eye—his only eye—began to register the image of an enormous mushroom-shaped cloud in the distance rising to the heavens.

Momentarily mesmerized by the spectacle, the three men quickly struck camp and silently rode away from the horrifying sight.

* * *

Back home, the event was reported on the radio as the explosion of a large munitions dump in a remote southern New Mexico desert that had caused no injuries and only negligible damage. That preposterous lie was laid bare mere days later when atomic bombs dropped by army flyboys destroyed the Japanese cities of Hiroshima and Nagasaki, ending the war.

TWO

Mary Ralston

10

Chief Petty Officer Mary Ralston, age twenty-four, the only daughter and youngest child of Clyde and Shirley Ralston of Santa Fe County, New Mexico, approached the Quonset hut Personnel Office at the Treasure Island US Naval Station carrying her duffel bag and small suitcase. With mixed emotions she was about to leave the navy after four years on active duty.

In the summer of 1943, she'd arrived at the base in the San Francisco Bay as an apprentice seaman clerk-typist. She worked hard, used her brains, was tactful and diplomatic with her superior officers, and quickly mastered whatever tasks were assigned to her. As a result she rose steadily in rank and when the war ended she was a petty officer first class and secretary to Capt. Alexander Gilmore, the newly appointed base commander. She assumed that she'd be discharged when the navy ordered the immediate separation of all eligible enlisted personnel including most WAVES, but instead Captain Gilmore asked her to extend her tour of duty and promoted her to chief. With the promotion,

Mary Ralston became one of the youngest women in the navy to attain that rank.

She never regretted her decision to stay on. Her job helping run the naval station for her boss held much more appeal than the notion of returning to college. She'd enlisted after completing her sophomore year at the University of New Mexico, not knowing what to expect. It became an amazingly liberating adventure that did far more to help her outgrow her family and her past than college ever had.

Leaving home for college had put some distance between her and her parents—who ranched on the fringe of the Galisteo Basin outside Santa Fe—but not nearly enough to suit her. Clyde and Shirley were pious, pompous, and old-before-their-time churchgoing Baptists who'd been painfully unhappy with each other ever since Mary could remember. Whatever affection they possessed for their two children was reserved for Mary's older brother, Tom, a bully who could do no wrong. It didn't take her long to figure out that she was a mistake, not a blessing.

Her greatest measure of happiness came from the freedom the ranch provided. Twenty-four thousand acres gave her plenty of opportunities to escape her parents' constant dissatisfaction and her brother's relentless taunts and pestering. Until her teenage years, as long as she obeyed, did her chores, went to church every Sunday, and got good grades in school, Clyde and Shirley let her roam on her pony as much as she liked. She'd pack a lunch and leave her cares behind, loping her pony across rocky pasturelands, up low-lying mesas, and down wide, shallow arroyos until she knew every nook and cranny of the ranch. She'd be gone for hours and it didn't matter. Or she'd call from her best friend Patty's house, who lived on a neighboring ranch, to say she was staying overnight. Most of the time, her parents didn't care if she was home or not.

That all changed when she started high school, stopped acting like a tomboy, and got interested in boys. Her parents reined her in hard, worried and suspicious that she might be hanging out with the wrong crowd and, as they put it, letting boys take advantage of her. They were so vexed by all the sinful trouble she could get into that she was obliged to participate in a special family Bible study hour after every Sunday dinner that made her want to scream. It didn't matter that she was an honor student, president of the Spanish Club, was liked and respected by teachers and friends, and had won an academic scholarship to the University of New Mexico. The fear that she might become pregnant and disgrace the family name dominated their minds.

One Saturday night near the end of her senior year, she stayed out way past her weekend curfew at a pre-graduation party thrown by Patty's parents. She made it back to the ranch road at two in the morning in a pickup truck driven by the Elkins brothers, walked four miles home, and crawled into bed thinking she hadn't been caught, only to be dragged almost naked into the kitchen by her father, who accused her of being nothing but a whore. She sat frozen in a kitchen chair, arms crossed to cover herself, shivering while he ranted, threatened to send her to their minister for counseling, and demanded to know who she was sleeping with, while her mother glared at her in unforgiving disgust for a sin she'd yet to commit. It was the worst day of her life.

Sent to bed, locked in her room, and ordered not to come out until called, Mary dressed quietly, snuck out through the window, and in the predawn light rode her pony to Patty's, thinking she'd run away forever, never to be found. She was huddled with Patty in her bedroom when Clyde showed up red-faced and riled, yelling and yanking her into his truck. He drove her away, with Patty and her parents standing dumbstruck in the dust thrown up by the tires. Grounded, virtually imprisoned except for school and church, terrorized by a regime of silence, her worst day turned into her worst month.

One Monday afternoon at school, the last week before graduation, she fell apart and ran sobbing out of her Spanish class to the guidance counselor's office, where she babbled to Miss Scoville about her miserable family and her unhappy life. She was a good person, had done nothing wrong, had never gone all the way with a boy, but now she would, she would, she would, yes, she would.

Miss Scoville, who knew Mary to be a smart and well-mannered girl, said nothing for the longest time. When she finally spoke, her advice was direct and simple: trust who you are, get out and on your own as soon as you can, and don't look back. It was advice Mary never forgot. Only the prospect of college made that summer at home bearable.

At the university she used her part-time job at the college bookstore as an excuse to shorten her visits home. At the end of her freshman year, she took classes in the summer session that also cut into her time at the ranch, which made being with her parents slightly more endurable. Her relationship with Clyde and Shirley became an armed truce verging on open rebellion. She survived flare-ups by avoiding doing anything to rile them.

As the end of her sophomore year approached, she was told by her parents she couldn't take summer classes because of the cost. The idea of being under her parents' thumb at the ranch for three months distressed her so much she lost weight and couldn't sleep. And with her brother Tom now back home from his defense job in California with a deferment to help run the family ranch, it would only be worse. Patty, who was also at the university, suggested she stay with her for the summer, but Mary knew her parents would never allow it. The time had come to take Miss Scoville's advice and move on. Two weeks before the semester ended she enlisted in the navy. Ordered to report for induction the day after final exams, she had Patty drive her to the ranch for a quick goodbye. Her mother feigned tears, her father sank into one of his famous pouting silences, and Tom flashed a frosty smile in her direction as she eagerly climbed into Patty's car for the getaway. She left knowing that she wanted very little to do with any of them ever again, suspecting they felt exactly the same way about her.

She turned to look back as they drove away and saw them frozen like wooden statues on the front porch, not waving, just watching. The thought struck her that they were strangers. Characters in some melodrama totally unrelated to her.

Over the next four years, she wrote home only once, after finishing basic training. A letter soon came from her father wishing her good luck in the navy and letting her know everyone at home was praying for her. A week later a copy of the King James version of the Bible arrived with a note from her mother encouraging her to study the Scriptures daily and attend church regularly. She gave the Bible to the base library. As she expected, her brother never wrote, but a year later she received a wedding invitation from his bride-to-be. She replied with a card of congratulations and never heard back.

As her time on active duty grew short, Mary gave serious thought to the navy as a career, but reached the conclusion that she wouldn't be happy remaining in the enlisted ranks. Only as an officer could she advance, but that required either a college degree or a nursing certificate. She wasn't keen about becoming a nurse, so finishing her degree seemed the best thing to do. After that, if the navy still held her interest, she'd put in for a direct commission or consider reenlisting for Officer Candidate School.

Minutes away from becoming a civilian and eight weeks away from starting her junior year of college under the GI Bill in Las Cruces at the New Mexico College of Agriculture and Mechanical Arts, Mary felt eagerly adrift. She didn't know if she'd like Las Cruces, had no idea where she would live when she got there, had yet to think seriously about selecting a major, and was unsure if she'd enjoy being a lowly college student again without any rank or prestige. All she knew for sure was that it was the start of another new adventure in her life. Once again it was time to never look back.

She finished signing the final paperwork and received her honorable discharge papers that included the citation for the Navy Commendation Ribbon, the Good Conduct Medal, two World War II service medals, and her Pistol Marksmanship Ribbon.

Lt. Mabel Salisbury, the personnel officer and Mary's good friend, attached a ruptured duck to her uniform lapel, gave her a warm hug, and walked her to the base commander's car, where the driver waited to take her to the city.

Mary kept smiling and held back tears as she gave Mabel one last hug and a kiss on the cheek. She slipped into the backseat suddenly feeling sad. Leaving the navy was much harder than she imagined it would be. As a teenager, she'd been overjoyed to leave home for college and later wildly excited to drop out of college for the navy. Why was this departure so wrenching?

Maybe it was because of the friends and colleagues she was leaving behind. Or the sad memory of those she'd lost in the war, especially one handsome sailor she'd fallen in love with. Or maybe it was all the fun she'd had exploring San Francisco and California with her navy girlfriends, most of them since leaving the service married and starting families. Or those glorious good times with the soldiers and sailors she'd dated, drinking and dancing late into the night at the city hot spots. And surely some of it came from the satisfaction of doing an important job well enough to gain the recognition and appreciation of her superior officers. The Navy Commendation Ribbon for meritorious service was not an award given lightly, and she was proud to wear it.

She shook off the glum feeling and smiled as the driver entered the ramp to the Bay Bridge, headed for San Francisco. She needed to stop reliving the past and look to a bright future, even if she had no idea what it would bring.

At the Mark Hopkins Hotel on Nob Hill, she checked into her room, tipped the bellhop, and left her canvas duffel bag and small suitcase untouched on the bed. After a quick look out the window at the Coit Tower on Telegraph Hill and Alcatraz Island in the bay, she freshened up in the lovely bathroom she had all to herself with its inviting claw-foot tub. She promised herself a long soak later.

In the lobby she debated taking a taxi to shop for clothes at the Emporium Department Store on Market Street, but instead decided a walk down Powell Street to enjoy the lively city atmosphere would do her good. The mild, sunny afternoon raised her spirits. She enjoyed the glances her uniform attracted from an occasional passerby. With the war over these last two years, women in uniform were once again a rarity.

The noise and bustle of the city felt liberating and she quickened her pace to keep up with the people flowing around her. The squeaking brakes and the clanging bells of passing cable cars added a festive rhythm to the day. Right at that moment she had half a mind to forget New Mexico and stay in San Francisco instead. It was an expensive city, but it had breathtaking views, lovely old neighborhoods, a good university, a great nightlife, and it was teeming with young people—many of them veterans like her. With her secretarial skills, she could surely find part-time work to supplement her GI Bill while she continued her studies.

She crossed busy Market Street to the Emporium. She'd discovered the vast department store on her first weekend liberty from Treasure Island and always poked her nose inside whenever she was in the city, sometimes just to have lunch at the mezzanine café with her girlfriends. With its arched two-story Greek revival entrance bordered by tall pilasters, the soaring, welcoming rotunda, the grand staircase, and the acres of merchandise, it was far beyond anything that existed in Santa Fe or Albuquerque. Sometimes she'd wander the aisles of clothing racks for hours and leave empty-handed. More often she'd come away with an appealing blouse or a stylish dress to wear on dates.

Frugal with money, with each promotion Mary had saved most of her pay increases, and now she intended to spend some of it. She started in ladies' fashions, trying on and buying an assortment of skirts, dresses, tops, and slacks before moving on to the shoe department, where she picked out several pairs that went nicely with her new wardrobe. In the lingerie department she bought three new pairs of nylons, and mostly practical underpants and bras but couldn't resist purchasing several lacy sets to wear when she got dressed up to go out. She finished in the leather-goods section, impulsively adding a shoulder purse that went perfectly with her luggage.

A taxi took her and her pile of bags and boxes back to the Mark Hopkins, where she generously tipped the smiling cabdriver who unloaded everything, as well as the eager bellhop who carted it all to her room. She hurried out of her uniform, tossed it over the bed railing, and spent the next hour in front of the mirror trying on her new outfits. It was cocktail hour when she finished. She paused in front of the mirror before leaving for the hotel's famous Top of the Mark bar and lounge that provided a panoramic view of the city.

She was pleased with her new look. The pleated, tan skirt cinched at the waist by a wide brown belt went nicely with the white, high-collar blouse and the dressy brown pumps. The skirt ended just below her knees, showing just the right amount of leg, and the belt gave an appealing accent to her hips and tiny waist. At the door, she smiled at the huge pile of clothing, boxes, and shopping bags that littered the bed. It certainly didn't look like former chief petty officer Mary Ralston's spit-and-polish billet on Treasure Island.

At the Top of the Mark she sat in a comfortable upholstered club chair close to the bar with a view of the Golden Gate Bridge and the Pacific Ocean beyond and ordered a martini. She didn't want to think about the night in 1944 when she'd sat at the bar with Petty Officer Second Class Brian Sullivan and helped him celebrate his impending departure to Pearl Harbor, where he'd join the fleet. For a year—almost the entire time they'd been lovers—Brian, a six-foot, brown-eyed rancher's son from Montana, had been trying to get into combat. That night, they drank to his safekeeping, made plans to get married when the war was over, and decided to blow their savings and spend their honeymoon in a suite at the hotel. After dinner they returned to their room, and with the curtains open to a view of the Golden Gate lit by a full moon, they made love and fell asleep, spent and exhausted.

A hospital corpsman, Brian died in combat on Iwo Jima in March 1945. If he'd survived the war, they'd be married, probably with a baby, and either living on his family's Montana sheep ranch or in student housing in Bozeman while she worked and he finished his degree in animal science at Montana State University.

She still had all his letters and snapshots of their weekends together touring up and down the California coast. It especially broke her heart to look at the photos from the short trip they took to Seattle for his sister's wedding to a marine pilot. Brian's whole family had assembled for the nuptials, and Mary had instantaneously fallen in love with all of them. His parents, sister, and kid brother were warmhearted, happy, outgoing, and affectionate. It was as if she'd met the man and family of her dreams all in one.

When the waiter asked if she'd like another drink, she shook her head, paid the bill, and returned to her room. Fighting off sadness, she filled the tub, wiggled out of her clothes as the bathroom filled with steam, and sank into the deliciously hot water. In the morning she would be on a train to Los Angeles, where she'd stay with her best pal from the navy, Erma Fergurson, who was married and living in Hollywood with an ex-soldier named Hank Evans, who was trying to break into show business and using his GI Bill to take acting classes and voice lessons. Although Erma had hoped to study art after leaving the navy, she was supporting Hank by working as a waitress at an expensive steak house. Mary couldn't wait to see her.

She soaked until the water in the tub turned chilly and spent the next hour packing for her departure and setting out her clothes for the morning. Suddenly she was exhausted. She arranged her cosmetics on the small shelf below the bathroom mirror, brushed her teeth, snuggled into the luxuriously big bed, and fell into a dreamless sleep.

11

After a scenic train journey down the California coast, Mary arrived at Union Station in the growing dusk of a warm Los Angeles summer evening. Erma had agreed to meet her at the station, and she was surprised to not find her waiting. It wasn't like Erma to be forgetful or late. Mary called, got no answer at her home, and, concerned something bad might have happened to her friend, made arrangements to have most of her luggage shipped ahead to Las Cruces and hailed a cab to take her to Erma's as quickly as possible.

The cabbie got her there in a hurry and pulled to the curb in front of an old two-story Queen Anne house on a hill tucked behind Hollywood Boulevard. It had a full gable roof with delicate spindle work, and had been divided into apartments—two upstairs and two down. Only one light was visible from a front upstairs window.

Mary paid the cabbie, grabbed her small suitcase containing essentials and an overnight change of clothes, rushed up the walkway, and rang the bell in the foyer to Erma's first-floor apartment. There was no answer. She rang repeatedly before trying the apartment across the hall, again with no success. Upstairs, only one resident was home, an elderly man who smelled of cigars and whiskey. He gruffly said he didn't know his neighbors and didn't care to before closing the door in Mary's face.

She sat on the front porch step in the deepening darkness, the sounds of traffic on Hollywood Boulevard wafting up the hill, and considered what to do. Since she had no other way to contact Erma or her husband, she decided to stay put for a while in the hope one or the other would appear. Soon she heard footsteps approaching on the sidewalk and, thinking it might be Erma, she got to her feet only to be disappointed when an older woman, stocky and winded, walked by.

The chilly night had Mary about ready to leave for the warmth of a hotel room when a car stopped in front of the house. A woman slammed the door on the driver's side and came around the front of the vehicle, her heels clacking on the pavement. In the pale light of a rising half-moon Mary recognized Erma and called out to her.

"Thank God you're here," Erma replied, relief flooding her voice as she rushed up the walkway. "I'm so sorry I wasn't there to get you."

"Not to worry," Mary said as she hugged Erma. "What happened?"

"It's just a big mess," Erma said, the words spilling out of her as she broke away. "Come inside."

A half a dozen boxes were on the floor in the front room, some packed, some empty, and the walls were bare. Erma threw her purse and keys on a lamp table next to a saggy upholstered armchair and stepped toward a galley kitchen that contained a small table and two folding chairs jammed in a nook under a window. "I'll make some coffee and we'll talk."

Mary followed her and stood in the kitchen archway. Erma, who was always a bundle of energy but calm by nature, seemed uncharacteristically agitated. Slender and five-foot-two, her long brown hair was pinned up carelessly, strands cascading haphazardly down her neck, and her pretty face with her wide-set eyes, arched eyebrows, and thin lips looked haggard and pained.

"What's wrong?" Mary asked.

At the sink, Erma filled the coffeepot with water. She turned, pot in hand, eyes hard and angry, and bit her lip. "That son of a bitch husband of mine has been screwing some girl in his acting class for the last three months. I only found out about it last week."

"The coffee can wait." Mary took the pot from Erma's hand and put it on the countertop. "Let's talk." She marched her friend into the front room, and sat with her on the sofa. "Tell me everything."

"I should have known something was up," she replied, shaking her head at her own stupidity.

She had trusted Hank completely, believing when he came home late he it was because he was rehearsing scenes with members of his acting classes, or at an open audition at one of the semiprofessional theater companies, or he was working as a studio extra to earn money for his private voice lessons. On certain nights, when he needed the car to go to his twice-weekly improvisation class, he'd pick her up after work. But recently he'd kept her waiting for almost an hour, claiming he'd been cajoled to stay late to help a fellow student with an audition scene she was preparing for a screen test at a major studio's new talent department. A week earlier, when he failed to come for her, she took a cab home and found all his clothes gone and a note on the kitchen counter saying he'd moved out, wanted a divorce, and was keeping the car because he needed it more than she did.

Erma stopped to catch her breath. Mary gave her a moment before prodding her for more information.

"I darn sure wasn't going to let him take my car just like that." Erma snapped her fingers for emphasis. "I bought and paid for it with my own money. I didn't think he'd be hard to find, but he'd dropped out of all his acting classes, stopped going for his voice lessons, and wasn't hanging out with any of his usual drinking buddies. Everybody I talked to knew I was looking for him and why, but it was only this afternoon that I learned where he was shacked up with the bimbo from his acting class. I went there, but nobody was home and the car was gone. So I waited, hoping they'd be back in time for me to get to Union Station before you arrived, but they didn't turn up until an hour ago. After they went inside, I jumped in the car and drove straight home hoping to find you here."

Erma paused, took a deep breath, squeezed Mary's hand, smiled and said, "And I'm so glad you are."

"Me too," Mary replied. "But why are you packing to move?"

Erma pushed hair away from her forehead and laughed harshly. "It's just been one thing after another this week. My boss decided since my husband had left me I was fair game, so when he put his hands on me I quit. With next month's rent due at the end of the week, I can't afford to stay here. Besides, I hate this dump and don't ever want to see that SOB again. The place stinks of him."

Mary nodded sympathetically. The heavy odor of cigarettes hung in the air and Erma didn't smoke. "Where will you go?"

Erma shrugged. "I don't care. Anywhere away from L.A. will do for a start, and I really need to get going. Knowing Hank, he'll be here soon demanding the car back."

"Has he hurt you?"

"It hasn't gotten that far yet."

Mary looked at the boxes and furniture in the front room. There was probably a lot more in the bedroom. "Are you planning to take everything?"

"I was, but now it doesn't matter. Every stick of furniture we own I bought secondhand to save money. The dishes, pots, and pans too—even the cheap movie posters I hung on the walls. It can all stay behind."

"Then let's finish getting you packed, and go," Mary said.

"Go where?"

"Can your car make it to San Diego?"

Erma laughed. "Are you kidding me? My Olds is such a honey of a car even my mechanic offered to buy it. It will take us cross-country if we want. What are we going to do in San Diego?"

"We'll sit on a beach for a couple of days, eat, drink margaritas, and hatch a plan."

Erma grinned, reached over, gave Mary a quick hug, and stood. "I'm game until my money runs out. Let's get out of here before that jerk shows up."

In less than an hour, they had the trunk and backseat of the coupe filled with everything Erma wanted to take with her, mostly shoes, clothes, jewelry, cosmetics, personal mementos, and important documents. They quickly tidied up the apartment and put the trash in the garbage cans behind the house. Erma dropped the door key on the kitchen counter and scribbled a note to Hank. It read:

Hey, Jerk,
Help yourself to anything you want, just don't try to find me.

At the front door, Erma took one last look around, sighed, shook her head, and laughed. "What a dump. I think that two-timing bastard has done me a big favor. He has sure cured me of the marriage bug. I'm taking my maiden name back. Do you think you'll ever get married?"

Brian's face drifted through Mary's mind. A recipient of the Navy Cross for bravery on Iwo Jima, he was buried at Arlington National Cemetery. There would never be another like him. "It's starting to feel iffy," she replied as they walked to the car. "Have you got a bathing suit?"

"I need a new one," Erma slipped behind the wheel of the Olds and cranked the engine.

"Me too," Mary said.

Erma made a U-turn and headed for Hollywood Boulevard. "Maybe we should go shopping tomorrow. That will make me feel better."

Mary laughed over the throaty sound of the engine. "That's the spirit."

* * *

After midnight they arrived in the San Diego neighborhood of Pacific Beach and found a decent motel a short walk from the ocean. It was a single-story, Spanish Mission–style building with exterior brick walls painted white and a sloped red-tile roof topped by a fake bell tower above an arched portico. A Vacancy sign flashed in the window of the motel office. The room was clean, the linens fresh, and the twin beds were comfortable.

In the morning, after breakfast at a nearby diner, they drove downtown and roamed the streets window-shopping until the stores opened. It took diligent searching through the swimwear selections at four stores to find just the right suits. Erma picked a red maillot with a wraparound skirt, and Mary bought a strapless one-piece in black. After lunch at a Pacific Beach restaurant that served up a decent chef's salad, they hit the beach under a warm sun, where the whisper of a pleasant breeze and the sound of the ocean lapping peacefully at the shore lulled them into a languid daze. Occasionally, a group of noisy kids walked by, but mostly it was just the two of them on an empty stretch of sand.

Neither did much talking. Mary could tell Erma was smarting about being treated so shabbily by Hank, although she put up a tough front to hide it. She held back questioning Erma and let the quiet reign. Two pleasant hours passed, and when the clouds rolled in and cooled the day, they took a walk down the beach looking for seashells, went back to the motel, showered, changed, and found a friendly neighborhood drinking establishment several blocks from the motel populated by a few old men at the bar who were inclined to leave them alone. They settled into a back booth, ordered scotch straight with water chasers, and clinked glasses when the drinks came.

"Here's to new beginnings," Mary said.

Erma raised her glass high. "Amen to that, sister." She took a sip. "One of these is all I can manage." She glanced around the dimly lit, smoky, run-down bar. "Maybe I could get a job here waiting tables and mixing drinks. Think it's far enough away from L.A. and the jerk?"

"Is that what you want to do? Work in a place like this?"

"Heavens no, but San Diego seems like an okay town." Erma paused. "But maybe not. Being around a lot of sailors and marines might not be a smart thing for me to do. I was a sucker for a guy in uniform once. I don't need to make that mistake again."

"Where will you go?"

Erma sipped her scotch and sighed. "I know where I'm not going: back to Nebraska, where everything on the farm smelled like pigs, fertilizer, and manure; or to Des Moines, where I had a crummy job slinging hash until I enlisted."

"How about driving me to New Mexico?" Mary suggested.

Erma leaned back, considered the idea, and slowly grinned. "Why the hell not? You were always talking about how wonderful and beautiful it is, and boy do I deserve a vacation."

"Great!" Mary lifted her empty glass. "Shall we seal it with another?"

"Only if you agree to drive us to dinner, if I get too drunk."

They ordered another drink and made plans. Mary would cash in the unused portion of her train ticket to cover their gas and expenses. Erma insisted that they share all the costs fifty-fifty. They'd get a service-station road map on their way to dinner and look for interesting places to stop along the way. Both agreed that a side trip to the Grand Canyon would be a necessity, since neither had seen it.

At a busy, loud Italian restaurant inside a converted beachside cottage, Erma ordered veal scaloppini, Mary chose the spaghetti, and they shared a bottle of red wine with their meal. Over coffee, they studied the road map and discussed places to see. Erma wanted to visit the Painted Desert and the Petrified Forest. Mary thought Tucson, with a detour to the border town of Nogales, might be fun.

An impatient, hovering waiter with the bill interrupted their road-trip scheming. They continued their planning in the motel room until, sleepy from the booze and wine, they decided to chuck the whole notion of an itinerary and just roam wherever the spirit took them before heading to Las Cruces.

With the window open and the smell of the ocean gently coursing through the room, Mary snuggled into bed. Although completely sympathetic about the end of Erma's disastrous marriage to her despicable husband, she was truly delighted to have gained her company.

* * *

Over the next ten days, Mary and Erma crisscrossed the desert southwest. In Arizona they peered into the immense beauty and astonishing vistas of the Grand Canyon. They wandered along dirt roads in the Painted Desert and Petrified Forest before traveling south to the pretty town of Prescott, tucked into a mountain range, where Erma admired the cowboys and allowed that she might be tempted someday to wrangle one for herself.

After an overnight stay at a historic downtown hotel, they dipped south to Tucson for a few days and visited a nearby Indian reservation to tour an old adobe church before taking a day trip to Nogales, where they crossed into Mexico and meandered in and out of shops along the colorful main street. Mary haggled in Spanish with a merchant in a dry-goods store and came away with a lovely hand-tooled leather wallet, and then bargained on Erma's behalf for a coin purse she'd spotted that was etched with delicate dragonflies.

They drove on a dusty state road through rolling, grassy hills to the dilapidated village of Tombstone and on to Bisbee, a mining town filled with historic old buildings and charming Victorian houses. They spent the night in Douglas at an inexpensive motor inn and walked the streets of the Mexican border town of

Agua Prieta the next morning before crossing through thickly forested mountains into the New Mexico Bootheel, a vast expanse of grassland valleys with distant, shimmering mountains caressing the sky.

The landscape fired Erma's imagination and for the first time in years she began thinking about the personal dreams she'd put on hold for the sake of Hank's career. She wondered aloud if the college in Las Cruces had an art department. Mary didn't know. Erma figured it didn't matter; she'd been drawing and sketching since childhood and could learn on her own if need be. Suddenly, the unhappiness that had tied her stomach in knots over the past few weeks loosened and she felt a giddy rush of optimism.

They veered north on a gravel road past sprawling ranches and through tiny settlements until they reached the railroad town of Lordsburg. From there it would be a straight shot on a paved, two-lane highway to their destination.

The long drive through the heat of the day had left them thirsty, dusty, and weary. They got a room with a double bed at a small motel that fronted the main street and the train tracks, showered, went to a diner that served up a decent chicken-fried-steak dinner, and fell asleep early, serenaded by the sound of the passing freight trains.

Morning found them driving into a rising sun at dawn, the desert golden in the early light of day, the air swirling through the open windows, tasting dry and gritty. They had their first flat tire outside Deming, and after emptying all of the boxes Erma had crammed into the trunk, they were jacking up the car when two young cowboys in a pickup truck stopped and offered to lend a hand. Once the tire was changed they stuffed everything back into the trunk, smiled, doffed their cowboy hats, and drove off with Erma throwing them kisses.

Back on the highway, she glanced at Mary, grinned, and said, "I'm thinking cowboys are much more interesting than the Nebraska farm boys of my youth. We should have asked those two if they had eligible, handsome older brothers."

Mary shook her head in amusement. "You sound like you're well on the road to recovery."

"Is that where we're going?" Erma asked, feigning ignorance. "I thought it was Las Cruces. Although Recovery, New Mexico, does have a nice ring to it."

Mary's giggle soon had them both laughing and the joke kept their spirits high all the way to Las Cruces, where the spires of the Organ Mountains, the green ribbon of the Rio Grande bosque against the brown desert valley floor, and the towering white clouds in the turquoise sky took Erma's breath away. She started visualizing a palette of colors to capture the landscape; a vivid blue-green for the river, a bright-pink underbelly in the clouds, and deep charcoal for the cascading shadows across the nearby mountains that hugged the Rio Grande. The notion that she could paint the world in front of her eyes grabbed her like a vise.

"We're home," Mary said as the highway turned into Main Street.

"Yes, I think so," Erma replied softly.

They rented a room in the Park Hotel just off Main Street, which overlooked the cool oasis of a lush city park shaded by mature, stately trees. They freshened up, had a quick lunch at a Mexican café, drove to the college on the outskirts of town, and walked around the campus. The view was spectacular, with the Organ Mountains dominating the horizon to the east and the desert valley beyond the Rio Grande stretching as far as the eye could see to the west, promising mysterious peaks and promontories. A hodgepodge of old and new buildings dominated a horseshoe-shaped drive inside the main entrance, and within a short walking distance down a gentle incline stood neat rows of surplus military buildings that served as married-student housing.

In the administration building they collected information about degree programs and learned to Erma's dismay that there was no organized fine-arts program as yet, just a smattering of classes such as mechanical drawing and art appreciation that might fit her needs. Mary had already decided to explore degree programs in animal science and teacher education, and picked up a copy of the fall-semester class schedules to study. Enrollment started in six weeks.

At the student housing office they learned that the crush of adult students made off-campus housing almost impossible to find, to the point that older students were getting on waiting lists for dormitory rooms.

Outside, Mary turned to Erma. "I am not living in a college dormitory."

"Me neither."

"You're staying?"

Erma nodded. "I like it here."

Mary gave her an excited squeeze. "Oh, good. Let's start looking."

* * *

For two days they searched, driving by dilapidated farmhouses on the bosque, peering in the windows of tiny apartments converted from woodsheds and stables by homeowners eager for rental income. Several nice, large houses were available near the country club on the east side of town, but college students weren't welcome and the rents were excessive. Ten miles farther east in the tiny village of Organ, they toured a cabin several blocks in from the highway that came complete with a stinky outhouse and a kitchen with no running water.

On the third day at breakfast they looked through the daily edition of the local newspaper hoping for new listings in the classifieds. They found an advertisement for a new apartment building near the campus but when they got there all the units had been rented. Back at the hotel, they sat on the front steps debating whether to keep looking or simply give up and move on to another city, preferably one with a college or university.

A mailman on his rounds approached the hotel entrance, and Mary got the sudden idea that he was just the person who would know of any vacancies in the neighborhood. When he reached the porch steps, she stood and asked if he knew if there was anything for rent.

A pleasant-looking older man with curly gray sideburns showing under his regulation cap, he smiled and nodded. "Mrs. Lorenz's tenant is moving out. She rents a nice apartment that used to be her husband's medical offices. It's on the side of the house with a separate entrance and a nice covered porch. She's an elderly lady who won't put up with any college-student pranks, but you gals look like the responsible type. She lives two blocks on the other side of the park."

He rattled off the address. "Let her know that Teddy the mailman sent you."

Erma jumped up beaming. "Thanks, you're a real peach."

"And a lifesaver too," Mary added.

Teddy blushed. "No need for that. Good luck. If she takes a liking to you two, I'll see you around." He watched them hurry across the park, thinking any man who had a choice would be hard put to pick one over the other.

* * *

The house was a two-story Tudor with a steep roof, brick cladding, and a side gable above the entrance to the attached apartment. Vera Lorenz, tall, thin, and in her eighties, had a soft voice, lively eyes, and a warm smile. They inquired about the apartment and mentioned Teddy's name, which resulted in an invitation to sit in the parlor, where Vera politely interrogated them about their bona fides. They won Vera over with the mention of their naval service—the departed Dr. Lorenz had served as a navy physician during the Great War—and their ladylike deportment.

The apartment was charming, with two stories, a large front room, a good-size kitchen with all the necessary appliances, and two bedrooms and a full bath upstairs.

The current tenant was almost completely moved out, and the place would be available on Saturday. After Mary paid the deposit and a month's rent on the spot, they went furniture shopping the rest of the day.

It took a busy week to get settled in with enough furnishings, linens, kitchenware, and bedding to get by. Mary rescued her luggage from the nearby train depot freight office, and both of them opened accounts at a local bank on Main Street, a few blocks away from the apartment. For frugality's sake, they decided they needed only one car and that Erma's Olds would do nicely for their transportation. She had it serviced at a nearby garage by a mechanic who pointedly admired both her and her automobile. Because of the dry, dusty climate, he recommended frequent oil changes.

On the one-week anniversary of their occupancy, Mrs. Lorenz appeared at their door with a housewarming gift of homemade apple pie. They invited her in, made tea, had a celebration, and visited with her for an hour, after which they decided she would forever be their honorary great aunt.

On the following Monday, with the fall semester fast approaching, they hightailed it to the college and signed up for their GI Bill benefits, which they happily discovered when combined would be enough to easily cover their monthly expenses.

Erma went off on her own to explore the campus while Mary waited at the admissions office to have her college transcript evaluated for transfer credits. She came away with the good news that she'd enter as a second-semester junior, but she would probably need a full two years to finish a degree program. Still undecided, she tentatively selected elementary education as her major, although her heart knew that something to do with ranching would suit her better.

In front of the door to the provost's office, a good-looking cowboy, tall with square shoulders and a glass eye, stepped quickly into the hallway, bumped into her, apologized, smiled, and doffed his hat. Mary smiled back, thinking maybe she should wrangle herself a cowboy.

She laughed off the silly notion and went to find Erma.

12

Lt. Colonel Samuel R. Allen, commanding officer, White Sands Proving Ground, liked to tell the story of how two days after his arrival in Las Cruces with orders to establish a post on the Tularosa Basin for the purpose of testing captured German V-2 rockets, he was asleep in the Amador Hotel when the atom bomb went off at Trinity site.

"I slept through it like a baby," he noted to US Fish and Wildlife Service supervisor Rockwell Stanley, ignoring the bored politeness of Capt. Earl Potter, his XO, who'd heard the tale at least a hundred times.

"I had to read about it in the morning paper," Allen chuckled. "It was reported as a munitions explosion at the time, which of course none of the locals believed."

Rockwell Stanley had shown up to protest Allen's decision that Fish and Wildlife Service employees would henceforth be escorted by military police to and from the 57,000-acre San Andres National Wildlife Refuge, which was now completely surrounded by the proving ground.

What the military was doing besides testing V-2 rockets at the high-security, off-limits army base was anybody's guess. But with the local economy booming because of the new installation, only the out-of-luck, dispossessed ranchers who'd been promised their land back at the end of the war and Rockwell Stanley were complaining.

"That's a humdinger of a story to tell your grandchildren," Rockwell said, feigning geniality as he shifted his weight in his chair. A noisy, rotating fan on top of a file cabinet behind Allen's desk blew dusty hot air around the room. Midmorning, it had to be almost ninety degrees inside the post headquarters building, and Stanley's throat felt raw and dry.

Allen smiled, touched his neatly trimmed mustache, and looked down his long nose at Stanley. "Yes, I suppose it will be." He turned his attention to Earl Potter. "Is it possible we could have our range riders simply check in with the Fish and Wildlife personnel at the refuge from time to time?" he asked. "Find out if the War Department would approve."

Rockwell Stanley's smile of appreciation was thin-lipped. "How long would that take?" he asked Potter.

An accomplice in Colonel Allen's ruse to placate Rockwell, Potter smiled pleasantly at the bureaucrat. "No more than a week or two at the most, I'd guess."

Stanley stood. "Good. I'll expect to hear from you by then, otherwise I'm afraid the Secretary of the Interior will be asked to intervene."

Samuel Allen came around his desk and shook Stanley's hand. "No need to trouble the secretary. We'll try our best to work this out to everyone's satisfaction."

A somewhat mollified Rockwell Stanley nodded curtly at Potter on his way out the door. As Allen returned to his desk, Potter shifted his gaze out the window at the largest structure on the base, where German scientists and technicians—many of them former card-carrying Nazis who'd been secretly smuggled across the Mexican border by a covert intelligence operation—were busily preparing for the next launch.

Sadly, the colonel won't get to see it, Potter thought sarcastically, stifling a chuckle. In a week, Allen would turn command over to his successor, a brigadier general no less, who would have the enviable task of leading the army's missile program into the future. It was the summer of 1947 and already V-2 rockets had been successfully fired. Now the challenging process of designing, building, launching, and controlling large guided missiles had begun. A new era of weaponry was under way and the prospects looked extremely promising.

Earl Potter knew there was no chance Rockwell Stanley's civil servants working at the wildlife refuge in the San Andres Mountains would be allowed to enter the proving ground unaccompanied. Either they'd accept military police escorts or be denied admittance. The development of new and more powerful weaponry made security of paramount importance, and if the wildlife refuge had to get along without the tender loving care of naturalists and biologists, so be it.

Potter switched his attention back to Allen, who was still smarting from the news that a brigadier general would replace him as post commander, and he'd be leaving with the same rank he held when he arrived. Privately, Earl Potter rejoiced at the news. As the executive officer, he was filling a position authorized for someone with the rank of major, and Allen had yet to recommend his promotion.

He waited patiently for Allen to question him about the 7-Bar-K

Ranch situation, wondering if his response would cost him both the promotion and his career.

In his thirties and older than most company-grade officers, Potter had earned a battlefield commission to second lieutenant early in the war and by the summer of 1944 had been promoted twice to his current rank of captain. He hoped to stay in the army as an officer, which meant he needed to be wearing the gold oak leaves of a major on his collar shortly or face returning to his enlisted rank of staff sergeant.

The mere idea of it depressed Potter. Doing his job proficiently had meant nothing to Allen, who had consistently threatened him with ruination whenever he failed to meet any of Allen's harebrained ultimatums. And the 7-Bar-K Ranch boondoggle was most certainly among one of Allen's most pigheaded demands.

The privately owned ranch on the edge of the proving ground had been a thorn in Allen's side since the day he assumed command and raised the American flag on an uninhabited, empty cow pasture at the eastern foot of the Organ Mountains in June of 1945.

That thorn in turn became a cattle prod Allen had used on Potter to goad him into finding a way to get the rancher in question, Matthew Kerney, off his land. To date, Potter's efforts had been woefully unsuccessful. Kerney had rejected all offers to either lease or sell his ranch to the army, going so far as to recently turn back his grazing rights to three thousand acres of public land near the Alkali Flats to forestall any government action against him. Last week, Allen had given Potter the insanely impossible task of resolving the problem before his departure.

Allen tapped his pen on the desktop. "What about the 7-Bar-K?"

"The judge advocate has tied my hands," Potter replied, eyeing Allen carefully for a reaction. "As you know, all of the ranch is in mountainous terrain outside our boundaries and owned outright by Matthew Kerney. Presently, there is no legal way to move against him."

"Yes, yes," Allen said impatiently.

Deliberately, to irritate the old man who would soon no longer be his boss, Potter stretched out a recitation covering old ground: "Because of its location, the ranch was not included for lease or purchase consideration when the air corps established the Tularosa Basin Bombing Range during the war. Lacking a prior agreement, we must either negotiate with the owner, Matthew Kerney, to purchase or lease the ranch—which he refuses to consider—or take action to seize the land under eminent domain proceedings, which of course he can fight in the courts."

Allen glared at Potter. "Get on with it, dammit."

"He's a disabled war veteran with the Purple Heart, Bronze Star, Commendation Medal, and Combat Infantry Badge earned during the Sicily campaign," he reminded Allen pointedly. Potter proudly wore the same decorations on his uniform. Conversely, in Allen's thirty-some years of service, he'd never spent a day in a war zone.

"The publicity from any legal action against him on the part of the government would most likely be adverse," Potter concluded, waiting patiently for Allen to hurl another threat in his direction.

Allen huffed, twirled his pencil with his fingers, and glared at Potter through narrowed eyes. "If you don't want an efficiency report that kills any chance you'll ever have for a promotion, find a way to get that ranch under our control."

"There's possibly a way to overcome the problem without a drawn-out legal battle," Potter replied calmly, consulting his notes. "Originally in 1941, exactly 1,249,904.36 acres of land were either withdrawn from public use or appropriated by lease or purchase agreements to establish the Alamogordo Bombing Range. With the establishment of White Sands Proving Ground, those boundaries were expanded in 1946 using aerial photography. What if a mistake was made in regards to the 7-Bar-K Ranch boundary line?"

Allen raised an eyebrow in interest.

Potter continued: "What if all or part of the ranch already falls under our jurisdiction and we just don't know it? With that in mind, I've asked for a new aerial survey as well as a ground survey of the 7-Bar-K Ranch property lines to establish the actual boundaries. Unfortunately, the situation can't possibly be fully resolved by the day of your departure, but a final resolution to the problem will be well under way, and I predict it will most likely result in government seizure of land for the proving ground."

Potter fell silent and waited for Allen's reaction.

"How long would it take to get the results of the new survey?" Allen demanded.

"A month or two," Potter lied, having already learned from the Corps of Engineers that an accurate mapping would take almost a full year.

"Do it," Allen snapped.

"The Corps of Engineers will need a request in writing," Potter advised.

"Draft the letter and I'll sign it."

"Yes, sir," Earl Potter replied, delighted Allen had so willingly agreed to the letter. If Matthew Kerney decided to raise a stink about the land survey, he would have a copy of Allen's signed request to cover his ass.

"Good work, Potter," Allen said, breaking into a reluctant smile. "See me in the morning for your efficiency report. It just might get you those oak leaves you're yearning for."

Potter came to attention and snapped off a salute. "Thank you, sir." He executed a perfect about-face and left feeling damn good about one-upping Allen. It made his day; hell, it made his week.

* * *

Living in town and attending classes at the college limited the time Matt Kerney had to spend at the ranch, although he tried to get out most every weekend during the school year. Having Jasper Daklugie there had been a godsend. He'd quickly matured into a top hand and had all the makings of a fine ranch manager, so of course after two years the Mescalero tribal elders decided to bring him home to help run their cattle operation on the reservation. No one was more dismayed about Jasper's pending departure than Patrick, who'd come to prize the young man's company and appreciate his hard work.

Matt feared Jasper would be irreplaceable. He possessed a unique talent of keeping the 7-Bar-K running smoothly and making sure Patrick was looked after in a way that didn't bruise his pride. The old boy had turned seventy-three earlier in the year and while he still managed to lend a hand, his age and bad leg had slowed him down considerably, and that worried Matt.

Jasper stayed through fall works. After the cattle had shipped, he left for Mescalero with his last month's wages in his pocket, trailing a choice pony that Matt gave him as a bonus. From the veranda, Matt and Patrick watched him ride across Alkali Flats until he disappeared in the distance. With his foot planted on the railing, Patrick wistfully wondered aloud if he'd ever again chance to see a man on horseback crossing the Tularosa. With all the trucks and automobiles now clogging streets and highways, Matt doubted it.

After supper Matt looked through the mail he'd fetched earlier in the day to find a letter from White Sands Proving Ground advising him the army would be surveying for a high-voltage power line that would cross the basin near the 7-Bar-K boundary. Once the line was completed, under provisions of the Rural Electrification Act the government would provide electrical hookup service at no cost to all owners of private property adjacent to the transmission lines. Included was a form to be signed and returned granting permission for a land survey crew hired by the army to enter the ranch as needed to map the route.

"Don't trust them," Patrick warned, after Matt read him the contents of the letter.

Matt laughed as he signed the form and put it in the return envelope. For years he'd dreamt about having electricity at the ranch. "I'm not gonna pass up a chance like this. I don't see anything suspicious about the army stringing power lines."

"I thought you had more sense than that," Patrick chided. "Every time the army puts up a new building, or fires one of those Nazi rockets, or closes the highways while they blow something up, it means they ain't ever gonna leave. And running electric wires here and there on the Tularosa is no different. Don't let them on our land. It's a mistake. They'll come after us again someday, wait and see."

Matt put the letter away. "Maybe so, but they haven't been able to budge us so far, and I'll fight them again if need be."

* * *

A month into Brig. Gen. Lloyd N. Hulley's assumption of command at White Sands Proving Ground, Maj. John "Jack" Reynolds arrived at the post to serve as the general's XO. Expecting to be bumped from his job, Potter was reassigned as commanding officer of the Headquarters Detachment. Notified that he was on the promotion list for major and bearing the new XO no ill will, Earl assembled a comprehensive briefing document for Reynolds that included all the relevant information about the 7-Bar-K Ranch project he'd been ordered to initiate by Colonel Allen. Far too busy with a whirlwind visit from a four-star admiral and a British field marshal, Reynolds put the briefing document aside with a smile and a promise to revisit it with him soon. That was Potter's first and only private meeting with the man.

Two months later, Potter received a misdirected letter in his mailbox from the Corps of Engineers saying the aerial survey of the 7-Bar-K Ranch had been completed, the land survey was well under way, and there was preliminary evidence showing that part of the ranch was indeed within the boundary of the installation and therefore available for forced acquisition. The final mapping report would be completed by the summer of 1948. He had the detachment clerk forward it to Reynolds but heard nothing back in return.

In early December, Potter's promotion to major came through with orders sending him happily to Europe and gratefully back to an infantry outfit where he truly belonged. It was the best Christmas present he'd ever received. He considered reminding Jack Reynolds about the 7-Bar-K project but decided against it. Maybe like the perennial spring winds that scoured the Tularosa Basin, it would simply get blown away by more pressing command matters. Potter thought no more about it.

13

Before returning to his classes in Las Cruces, Matt hired Jim and Millie Sawyer as ranch caretakers and arranged to have Al Jennings manage the livestock operations for the ranch. Al would mingle the 7-Bar-K cattle in with his herd and use both ranches to pasture the stock, which would help reduce overgrazing. After expenses, Al would take a cut of the 7-Bar-K annual beef sale profits.

Jim and Millie Sawyer, an older, childless couple who'd lost their small sheep ranch to White Sands Proving Ground, would get room, board, and a salary to run the household, help look after the few remaining ponies, and do general maintenance and daily chores. They were happy to have the work and delighted to return to the Tularosa from town, where they'd languished and scratched out a living as a domestic and a handyman.

Because he knew and liked Jim and Millie and would be their boss in Matt's absence, Patrick didn't grumble about the arrangement. In fact, he seemed relieved to have their company and help, although he'd never admit to it.

For Matt, it was a financial strain, even with the fifteen-dollar-a-month increase in his GI Bill allowance and Patrick putting up part of his Spanish-American War pension to help pay Jim and Millie's salary. Without the GI Bill and his 50 percent veteran's disability check—he'd rather have his eye back than the money—the ranch would be a losing proposition once again.

Over the next two years, things ran smoothly with very few bumps in the road. Patrick and the Sawyers became fast friends and together kept the ranch headquarters and the six ponies on the spread in tip-top shape. Al managed the livestock and ramrodded the spring and fall gatherings. Decent moisture and rising beef profits brought the prospect of more of the same ahead.

Relieved of unnecessary worry about the ranch, Matt hunkered down and concentrated on his studies. He had turned down Gus and Consuelo's kindhearted offer to live with them at the hacienda, mostly because the memory of Beth would have haunted him there. But he continued to be a frequent dinner guest and always looked forward to attending their lively social gatherings and parties when he could. Instead, he'd rented a room from Rosella Gomez in his old neighborhood, which reminded him daily of his remarkable mother and his early childhood years living in the barrio.

A widow, Mrs. Gomez had a half dozen grandchildren between the ages of three and sixteen who were constantly in and out of her house, frequently accompanied by their parents, much to Matt's enjoyment, entertainment, and erudition. Since only Spanish was spoken in Rosella's household, Matt's command of the language improved considerably, to the approval of the entire clan. When the ruckus at the house got too loud and he needed to study for tests or finals, he decamped to the public library on nearby North Main Street and cracked the books there.

He'd turned thirty-seven earlier in the year and had started to think that boarding with Mrs. Gomez was as close as he'd ever get to a family of his own. He wasn't completely opposed to remaining a bachelor, but the prospect wasn't a satisfying one either. He'd dated a few town gals, several coeds, and more recently a neighborhood señorita introduced to him by one of Rosella's adult children, who was sweet, angling for marriage, wanted lots of babies, and wasn't interested in much of anything else. When Matt quickly proved indifferent to her well-laid plans, she moved on to a likelier candidate, a salesman at a downtown shoe store, and was planning her trip to the altar within the month.

After Thanksgiving of 1949, Gus and Consuelo Merton threw a holiday party that Matt decided was worth staying in town for over the weekend rather than returning to the ranch. He'd only been there ten minutes when Jimmy Kendell, the one-armed navy vet who'd signed Matt up for his GI benefits, arrived with Mary Ralston and Erma Ferguson in tow.

Over the last few years, he'd had a passing acquaintance with both women; mostly he saw them on campus, occasionally downtown at one of the Main Street stores, and sometimes at the social gatherings and parties thrown by the older crowd or by the couples living in married student housing. Because he was in classes during the week and at the ranch most weekends, he didn't know them well. All he knew was that they were best friends and roommates who had served together in the navy during the war. He would have liked to know more, particularly about Mary Ralston.

Her roommate, Erma, was petite, slender, and pretty, with long brown hair and wide, innocent-looking eyes that got her a lot of attention. But it was Mary who attracted Matt's interest. She was blond, blue-eyed, and leggy in spite of not being much taller than Erma, had an assured way of walking, a cheerful smile, intelligent eyes, and the seemingly natural ability to give everyone her full attention. All those qualities, plus a quiet reserve about her, captured Matt's curiosity.

He'd shared more than one beer with Jimmy Kendell, who aside from being a doctoral candidate in electrical engineering was a ladies' man in his spare time, so he kept his distance, trying to figure out which gal Kendell was wooing, hoping it wasn't Mary. He was about to reconnoiter directly when Consuelo Merton approached Mary, took her by the hand, and led her through the crowded room directly to him, beaming mischievously.

"I'd like to you meet Señorita Mary Ralston," Consuelo said in Spanish, her eyes twinkling with amusement at her own formality.

"I've had the pleasure," Matt replied, smiling brightly as he shook Mary's hand. "We've met on several occasions."

"But not often enough, I think." Consuelo's sweeping glance embraced them both. "Did you know that you both graduate at the end of this semester?"

"No, I did not," Mary replied.

Consuelo touched Mary's arm. "I didn't think so. Before you vanish into a classroom here in town and Matthew goes back to his ranch and disappears forever, I thought you two should get to know each other."

Matt started to agree, but Consuelo put her finger to his lips and silenced him. "No secrets have been shared." She turned and smiled at Mary. "If you'll excuse me, I've other guests to attend to."

Matt grinned at Consuelo's expertly played maneuver. "She's an amazing woman."

"I want to be just like her when I grow up," Mary said softly as Consuelo slipped away.

"If that's true, I'll follow you anywhere."

"You have secrets?" Mary asked, deftly deflecting the compliment.

"Not really, just some ancient history. Gus and Consuelo have been old friends for many years. What about you?"

Mary laughed. "No secrets, but there are some things I'd rather forget. How did you come to know the Mertons?"

"Therein lies the tale," Matt replied. "Can I get you a drink?"

"Yes, please, but only if you tell me the tale."

"Will part of it do?"

"For now," Mary replied.

"How about we adjourn to the library? I know where Gus keeps his private sipping whiskey."

"Do you propose to raid his liquor cabinet?"

Matt nodded. "That is my intention."

Mary cocked her head. "Are you inclined to be a law breaker?"

"Only on those very special occasions when I have the right accomplice."

Mary smiled winningly and linked her arm in his. "Lead on."

* * *

The prospect of a purloined drink from Gus's liquor cabinet quickly forgotten, they spent the next two hours closeted in the library sitting in comfortable easy chairs surrounded by walls of books, talking as though they were old friends reunited after a long time apart. Matt told her that Gus had been his professor before the war and had helped him find work with the Civilian Conservation Corps during the Great Depression. He left out the part of his brief fistfight with his father on campus that led to his first dinner invitation to the hacienda and made no mention of Beth. Both subjects were too personal for him to broach so quickly to anyone.

He briefly described the ranch, the Tularosa Basin, and the trials of keeping the 7-Bar-K afloat and operating while he was in school finishing his degree in animal science, but mostly he talked about his mother, Emma, and what a strong, capable woman she'd been. His obvious love for her charmed Mary.

Matt made no mention of his war service or his glass eye, and Mary didn't press it. She was surprised to learn he was thirty-seven, having figured him a good three or four years younger. Without dwelling on her family, she talked about growing up on the ranch outside Santa Fe, and how she'd loved it. Matt didn't even try to suppress a smile when she said that although she looked forward to teaching at the local elementary school after the Christmas break, she couldn't think of any better life than ranching.

To keep the 7-Bar-K solvent, Matt was hoping for an appointment as a New Mexico livestock inspector in the New Year, but he was up against some stiff competition. If that fell through, he was thinking of getting out of the cattle business for good and returning to what he liked best: training cutting horses and cow ponies for rodeo-circuit riders.

Mary's eyes lit up at the idea; she'd been a barrel racer at the county fairs while in high school and loved the sport. They talked ponies until Erma appeared in the library doorway with coat in hand, and said Jimmy Kendell was waiting for them in his car. When Matt offered to see Mary safely home, she readily agreed, and with a wink and a wave, Erma departed.

"What was that about?" he asked.

"Just Erma acting silly," Mary coolly replied. "Tell me more about the 7-Bar-K."

"It's on a pretty slice of country in the San Andres Mountains, east of the Jornada. Army land on the Tularosa sits at its feet.

There are mountains eastward, badlands to the north, and the White Sands National Monument to the south. The Rocking J and the 7-Bar-K are the last big spreads left in those mountains since the military forced the other ranchers out during the war. I'd be glad to show it to you, if you wish."

"I would like that very much."

"It's more than a day trip, so you should come for the weekend. I'll carry you out there if you like, and you can bring Erma along so she can ride shotgun."

Mary raised an eyebrow. "Do I need her protection?"

"Maybe so," Matt answered with a smile. "The Tularosa can be a dangerous place for man or beast. A lot of history has happened there."

"I should visit before I start my new teaching career," Mary suggested. "And I'm sure Erma will want to tag along."

"That's okay by me," Matt said.

Before he could say more, Augustus Merton opened the library door, smiled pleasantly, and said, "The party has ended, but I can offer separate sleeping accommodations for you two if you wish. I promise a delicious three-cheese omelet for breakfast if you stay."

Embarrassed, Matt scrambled to his feet. "Sorry, Gus, we got carried away talking. We'll get a move on."

Consuelo joined Gus at the open door. "We'd love to have you stay."

"I'll get my coat," Mary said as she stood and smoothed her skirt. "You're very kind to offer your hospitality, but I really must get home. Matt has offered to drive me."

With a twinkle in his eye, Gus stood aside to let them pass. "Another time perhaps."

"Yes, indeed," Consuelo echoed, her eyes dancing.

After the goodbyes at the front door, Matt and Mary walked to his truck parked on the Mesilla village plaza, the moon casting shadows from the church spires across the empty square.

In the middle of the plaza, Mary stopped, turned, and looked Matt squarely in the eye. "The Mertons are lovely people and your dear friends, so I'd appreciate it if you would tell me what exactly is going on."

"You didn't put them up to some matchmaking?" Matt countered, caught off guard by her accusation.

"Heavens no."

"Neither did I."

"Then what is this about?"

Matt took a deep breath before replying. "It's about a boy, a girl, her aunt and uncle, my two dear friends as you put it, and a terrible tragedy. Simply put, it's a love story."

In the pale moonlight Mary saw the pain in Matt's eyes. "Will you tell me?"

Matt paused. There was something about Mary he trusted. "Why not?"

He ushered her to his truck, silently considering how to start. As they left the village he told her about this young man he knew, still a boy really, who had been invited to dinner by his professor and upon his arrival greeted at the hacienda front door by a blue-eyed, redheaded girl, with creamy skin and a ridge of freckles across her nose, whose brilliant smile stunned him into silence.

"It was love at first sight," Matt added.

By the time he'd parked in front of Mary's apartment, she'd heard the story. Not all really, but the highlights, at least right up to the tragedy of Beth Merton's death that would never fully fade from his mind, no matter how many years might pass. Quietly he sat behind the wheel waiting for what seemed like an eternity for her reaction. Finally convinced that he'd made a big mistake, he turned to look at her just as she leaned over and kissed him on the cheek.

He almost flinched in surprise.

"Thank you," she said softly, her eyes moist with tears.

"What for?"

"Telling me who you are." She opened the passenger door and stepped out of the truck. "Can I visit your ranch next weekend?"

Matt nodded. "I'd like that."

"Me too. Good night, Matthew Kerney." She watched him drive away thinking that no man since Brian Sullivan had touched her emotions so quickly, so easily, and aroused her interest so thoroughly.

The light was on in Erma's upstairs bedroom. She hurried to the porch, eager to fill her in on the surprising events of the evening. As she put her key in the front door lock, it came to her that someday soon Matt would need to hear her story.

14

That weekend, Mary went with Matt to the ranch while Erma stayed at home feigning the onset of chills and a fever. It was a sweet ruse on her part to make sure Mary had Matt's undivided attention. The ploy was so blatant that Mary teased her about it on her way out the door. Erma stuck her tongue out in reply.

The long drive to the ranch started out uneasily, with Matt making nervous small talk and Mary chattering too much about nothing at all. By the time they were on the outskirts of town, they'd relaxed enough to enjoy each other's company. Matt mentioned tidbits of information about the landmarks and historical sites they passed along the way, which delighted Mary. On an unmarked farm road that paralleled the Rio Grande, he told her the true story of Consuelo Merton's ancestor, who moved his family to the west side of the river after the Mexican War so he could retain his Mexican citizenship only to lose it in 1854 when the United States bought millions of acres from the government of Mexico and promptly gave most of the land away to robber barons to build a railroad to Southern California.

They drove by the melting adobe ruins of old Fort Selden, where Matt's grandfather, John Kerney, finally found his lost son, Patrick, after many years of searching. At Rincon, a small village once a haven for outlaws and cattle rustlers during the territorial years, they turned east on a dirt road not shown on any map to the Point of Rocks, where early Spanish explorers camped before beginning the arduous journey across a hundred-mile stretch of desert, and where raiding Apaches waited in ambush for unwary settlers traveling north.

Along the remnants of the wagon road known as the Jornada del Muerto, Matt talked about the historic old ranches that had once thrown tens of thousands of cattle onto the range back in the day of the huge spreads; the Bar Cross, the 7-T-X, the Diamond A, the John Cross, and the Double K—now the 7-Bar-K.

Mary wondered about the brand change for the ranch, and Matt explained he'd been forced to sell the original brand during the Great Depression to keep from going under. It still rankled him to think about it.

He described Moongate Pass, a gaping, semicircular cut in the San Andres Mountains that on certain nights the rising moon filled perfectly. Back when Engle was more than a dilapidated semi–ghost town on the Jornada, folks would gather outside on a clear night to watch the full moon settle for a moment in the cradle of the cut. It was a breathtaking natural wonder to behold.

Without thinking, she almost asked him to bring her to see it some evening, but her good sense intervened. Until she knew if there was to be more to their relationship than a hastily agreed upon visit to his ranch, she didn't want to show too much eagerness to be with him, which might be off-putting. She quickly torpedoed any further speculation about the subject and returned her attention to the landscape.

To Mary's eye, it was a harsh and a beautiful land. Dry and dusty, worn thin by overuse, peppered by cactus and mesquite, it captured her imagination. She wanted to jump out and explore every mountain range, every thin ribbon of dirt track that disappeared into the vast tableland, every distant mesa. The sheer overwhelming power of the land deserved a major expedition, and since coming to Las Cruces she'd seen too little of it.

Matt had more stories as they entered the San Andres Mountains. The one about Eugene Manlove Rhodes publishing a short story about Matt's mother on a cattle roundup particularly intrigued her, and his surprising announcement that he personally knew Bill Mauldin as a young boy in New Mexico and as a soldier in Sicily made her impatient to see the cartoons he'd drawn about Matt's "war escapades," as he put it, and learn more about them.

Her first view of the astonishing Tularosa Basin from the heights of the San Andres took her breath away, and it was equally spectacular from the 7-Bar-K Ranch headquarters. As they drove past a line of power poles that marched down the mountainside to the ranch house, Matt happily noted that with some help from the army, which now controlled more than a million acres in the basin, they'd finally gotten electricity at the ranch last year.

The ranch headquarters sat in a horseshoe-shaped valley that dipped to low rolling foothills. A cottonwood-shaded stream wandered through a grassy pasture and disappeared into a wide, sandy arroyo that snaked down to barren Alkali Flats pressed against the base of the foothills. On a wide, level shelf nestled against the valley's north slope stood a house made of thick adobe walls with a pitched roof, a deep veranda, and a commanding view of the basin. It was protected by a lovely windbreak of old cottonwood trees, bare of leaves but still majestic with heavy, thick boughs bent low to the ground.

A mud-plastered, flat-roofed adobe casita was linked to the house by a courtyard wall. Above the enclave, a small family cemetery enclosed by a fence dominated a knoll with a clear view of distant mountains. A dozen or so steps below the house, a barn, two corrals, a chicken coop, a windmill, a water tank, and a water trough sat at the edge of the fenced pasture, where six fine-looking ponies lazily slapped their tails and grazed on winter hay spread along the ground.

Matt slowed to a stop next to an old 1920s Chevy truck and a newer prewar Ford pickup. He'd written ahead to say he was coming to the ranch with Mary as his guest, and waiting for them on the veranda were the Sawyers and Patrick Kerney, who was easy to pick out as Matt's father by his features, height, broad shoulders, and blue eyes, clearly discernable under the brim of his cowboy hat.

Matt put his hand lightly on Mary's shoulder and smiled. "Remember, you asked for this."

"No, you invited me," Mary corrected. "But I'm already enchanted. Can we go riding this evening after supper?"

"Yes, ma'am, the ranch is yours to do as you wish for the weekend."

On the veranda, hat in hand, Patrick greeted Mary with a smile and introduced her to Jim and Millie Sawyer. Jim wore thick glasses perched on a wide nose that had a downward slant, giving him an inquisitive look. Millie, in a checkered print dress and starched apron dappled with spots of flour where she'd wiped her hands, had a square face with a thick chin, giving her a truculent look that quickly evaporated in her warm smile.

Because Jim and Millie lived in the casita, Mary was to occupy Matt's bedroom, which had been cleaned and prepared for her with fresh bed linens, several soft pillows, and a set of neatly folded bath towels. He plopped her suitcase on the bed and told her the bathroom at the rear of the kitchen had indoor plumbing, a tub and a toilet, but cold water only, so if she wanted a warm bath, the kettle first needed to be heated on the cookstove.

"Where will you be sleeping?" she asked, looking around the room. On the dresser were the two framed, autographed Bill Mauldin cartoons he'd mentioned, and on the wall above the bed was a lovely pencil drawing of a saddled pony. A series of wall pegs held chaps, a battered cowboy hat, a pair of spurs, and an old, handmade hackamore. The room window looked out on the veranda and the basin beyond, the mountains lit up in delicate detail by the low afternoon light of coming winter.

"On my bedroll in the barn tack room. It's quite comfortable."

"I didn't mean to put you out."

Matt laughed. "You aren't. It's a sight better than bunking with my pa. I'm guessing Millie has something special cooked up for dinner. We'll have time before we sit down to eat to take a nickel tour of the old homestead."

"Just give me a minute," Mary said.

"Take your time," Matt said backing out of the open doorway. "I'll wait for you on the veranda."

After he closed the door, Mary took a close look at the Bill Mauldin cartoons that conveyed his classic tongue-in-cheek humor. It made her eager to know more about Matt's war service.

Humming to herself, she quickly unpacked, brushed her hair in the mirror above the dresser, freshened up in the bathroom, and went looking for Matt.

* * *

The tour was marvelous. Of all that she saw, she enjoyed the family cemetery best because of the stories Matt told of the kith and kin buried there, especially his older brother, CJ, killed in the Great War and buried in France. The pride he had about his family and the ranch, and his struggles to save it during drought and the hard times of the Great Depression, served to heighten her growing feeling of respect for him.

At mealtime, Millie served up a scrumptious dinner of corn bread, chicken-fried steak, baked potatoes, and canned string beans warmed in butter, which Mary, to her amazement, devoured. It was as if for years without knowing it, she'd hungered to break bread in the company of such people in a place exactly like the 7-Bar-K. It felt like home in the best sense of the word; a feeling she'd never truly had before.

Over dinner Patrick enthralled her with stories of being a young boy living through the Indian Wars, and his later experiences in Cuba with Teddy Roosevelt and the Rough Riders. He seemed friendly enough, but every time she looked directly at him, he dropped his gaze and paused before resuming his tale. It made Mary unsure whether he liked her or not.

After dinner she helped Millie with the dishes at the kitchen sink. When the menfolk adjourned to the living room, she learned that Matt had sent a letter to the ranch with clear instructions for Millie to make sure the house was spic and span with everything squared away before their arrival.

"I can't remember a time before when he was ever the least bit bossy with me about my housekeeping," Millie whispered conspiratorially. "Not once, mind you, so you must be pretty special. But don't you dare say a word that I told you."

Flattered to learn of her importance to Matthew Kerney, Mary crossed her heart. "I promise. You like him a lot, don't you?"

Millie nodded. "I'd claim him as my own kin if I could."

The squeaking kitchen door stopped their conversation. "The moon is up," Matt said as he stepped inside. Instead of his glass eye he wore an eye patch. "Are you ready to go riding?"

With a smile Millie relieved Mary of the dish towel. "You go on. I'll finish up here."

She thanked Millie, grabbed her jacket, and followed Matt outside, where he introduced her to his pony Maverick, a sorrel gelding with powerful legs suitable for scrambling up and down mountainsides, and Peanut, a pretty blue roan mare. Both were saddled and snorting impatiently to get going.

For a time they leisurely trotted up a well-traveled ranch road to the lip of the valley, where the mountain pressed against a narrowing passage. There they stopped to view the ranch bathed in moonlight below.

"It couldn't be more beautiful," Mary said.

"My grandfather had a good eye for the land."

"He did indeed," Mary replied. "Speaking of your kinfolk, I can't tell if your father likes me or not."

"He can be hard to read, but he does. He's cautious with his feelings. He got heartbroken by the little daughter of a woman I once cared about. He's never been the fatherly type, but that little girl sure got to him. I don't think he ever really forgave her mother for taking her away."

Mary waited for more, but Matt's silence signaled he wasn't ready to elaborate. She took a different tack. "Those cartoons Bill Mauldin gave you are a treasure. Every veteran I know would brag constantly about being the subject of one of his cartoons, let alone two."

Matt laughed. "Hilarious as they are, Bill drew them true to what happened. I got a medal for talking some Italian soldiers into surrendering and another one for capturing a band of German ponies. Those cartoons turned me into a laughingstock with the guys in the regiment and a war hero here at home. Go figure."

"That's it?" Mary asked, unconvinced.

"Pretty much."

"And your eye?"

Matt's sunny expression melted. "A horse blew up in front of me. It got spooked and stepped on a land mine."

"How awful that must have been for you and the horse."

Matt glanced at her in surprise. "You're the first person who ever expressed a hoot or holler about that poor critter. He was a big, handsome chestnut gelding with four white stocking feet, and as spirited, smart, and agile as they come. We took to each other right away. A day doesn't go by that I don't think about him, and the men I lost."

He saw the explosion in his mind's eye. Abruptly he averted his face, gave rein to Maverick, and started back toward the ranch. "We need to take these ponies down to the pasture and give them a good run. Are you game?"

The time for questions had passed. "I am," Mary said, turning Peanut to follow.

They galloped the ponies in the pasture until they began to lather up and then cooled them down at a walk before taking them to drink deeply at the trough. By the time Mary got to the barn with Peanut, the night air had chilled her, but once inside and out of the breeze she soon warmed up.

"You're a good rider," Matt said as he led Peanut to her stall and put oats in her bucket. He gave Mary a towel to wipe her pony down.

"I'm rusty and sore as hell," Mary corrected, trying to ignore the painful kink in her side as she rubbed Peanut dry.

"You'll survive," Matt predicted with a chuckle.

He guided Maverick to his stall, spilled oats in his bucket, gave him a quick wipe, and closed the gate. The pony promptly lifted his tail and dumped a smelly load of horse apples on the straw-covered floor.

Matt hoisted his saddle and headed for the tack room. Lugging her gear, Mary followed. In the tack room he turned on the wall switch that illuminated a bare electric lightbulb that dangled from the ceiling on a cord. A series of built-in saddle racks lined one wall directly opposite a crudely fashioned wooden bunk with a thick straw mattress covered in gunnysack. Against the far back wall stood a large old trunk and a tall Mexican cabinet on sturdy legs. Above the saddle racks a row of wall pegs held bridles and halters. Cracks in the lumber on the interior side of the outside wall were stuffed with old newspaper to insulate against the cold.

Matt put the tack away and turned back to Mary. "You've never said anything about your family."

"I don't have much of one to talk about," Mary replied.

"Were you an orphan?" Matt asked somberly.

"Not technically or legally," Mary replied breezily, trying to organize her thoughts. "The best way I can put it is I have an older brother who's a selfish bully and parents who barely tolerated me from the day I was born. Sometimes, they couldn't even do that. They weren't happy with each other, and I think I was a big mistake they wished would just go away, which is exactly what I did when I got up the courage. I haven't seen any of them since the day I left for the navy."

"That sounds miserable."

"It's not something I like to talk about."

With a soft rag, Matt cleaned the dust off the saddles and changed the subject. "How long did you serve in the navy?"

"Four years." She told him she mustered out in '47 as a chief petty officer, and that except for recruit training, she'd been posted at the Treasure Island Naval Station in the San Francisco Bay. Then she paused, waiting for the typical snide comment combat vets usually made about toy soldiers who pulled easy stateside duty during the war.

"A c*hief* petty officer," Matt said, visibly impressed. "You must have been some humdinger to make rank that fast."

Blushing, she almost hugged him. "That's very nice of you to say. I was good at my job. I thought about staying in and making it a career."

"I'm glad you didn't, otherwise we never would have met."

"Well, we did and here I am," Mary replied, reluctant to get caught up too quickly by his obvious interest in her. "Do you have a copy of the story written about your mother?"

Matt opened the Mexican cabinet and handed her a dog-eared magazine, already turned to a page titled "Emma Makes a Hand."

She sat on the edge of the bunk with Matt beside her and started reading. From the opening sentence to the very end, the story engrossed and entranced her. How lucky Matt had been to have such a woman for his mother. It made her a bit jealous.

"Patrick used to say she was one of a kind," Matt remarked. "She died too young."

"I would have loved to have known her."

"Yeah," Matt said, stifling any further thoughts of Emma. Abruptly, he took the magazine from Mary's hand and put it away in the cabinet. "That's my reading copy for interested parties," he explained. "Hidden away in my desk I've got a brand-spanking-new issue of the magazine I'm keeping for posterity, except to date there are no future generations of Kerneys on the horizon."

Mary raised an eyebrow. "Really? What about the woman with the young daughter who touched Patrick's heart?"

"Now, that's not fair. I already told you about Beth, and that wasn't easy to do. But to be clear, that little girl wasn't my daughter, although I would have gladly adopted her." He gave her an appraising look.

"What?" Mary asked.

"Most gals I know don't need to be prodded to talk about themselves."

"Most guys don't either," Mary countered. "What do you want to know?"

"Everything," Matt replied. "But I'll let you off the hook for now. What was the navy like?"

"At the time, it was exactly what I needed." She stopped and angrily shook her head. "That sounds so selfish. The world went to war, millions died, and I got what I needed."

"You contributed and served honorably," Matt said. "That matters."

"You're sweet to say that."

Matt swiveled to face her straight-on. "You're not ready, are you?"

"Ready for what?"

Matt stood. "To trust me. Never mind, I understand. I'll walk you to the house."

Mary grabbed his hand. "Sit down. I'm not very brave when it comes to talking about myself. I get tied up in a knot."

Refusing to let go of her hand, Matt sat close to her and waited.

She drew a deep breath, smiled, and said, "Okay, here goes."

They talked for hours. Mary told him about her love affair with Brian Sullivan, their plans to marry after the war, his family's

Montana sheep ranch, where she'd expected to live after their wedding, and how his death on Iwo Jima had shattered her.

Matt understood. He spoke about Anna Lynn, the woman who had stood by and cared for him during his slow recovery from his wound, and how in spite of his honorable intentions she steadfastly refused to be anything more than his lover and how slowly over time she distanced herself from him. He didn't mention the cause—her killing of Fred Tyler. Instead he described her daughter, Ginny, the sweetest little girl imaginable, and how he was weary of losing the people he loved, starting with his brother and his ma.

It made Mary yearn for a family to love. She shared painful memories of her father's rages, her mother's coldness, her brother's constant taunting and teasing that she was ugly and stupid, and her steadfast belief, until she met Brian, that she was unlovable. Just putting it into words exhausted her.

Matt described the nightmare memory of Patrick, drunk and yelling at Emma and CJ outside a hotel, denying he was Matt's father, scaring him half to death. He recounted Patrick's drunkenness and mean-spiritedness, and their fistfight on the college campus, in retrospect about nothing much at all, on the very day he met Beth.

They laughed that it was all too melodramatic and decided Matt was the lucky one to have at least one parent to love, twice lucky to have had an older brother to adore, although their bond was tragically cut short, and fortunate a third time to have made peace with Patrick, something Mary never expected to achieve with her parents.

Talked out, they walked to the veranda and said good night. Impulsively, Mary hugged him before hurrying inside. She slipped into her nightgown and, with moonlight cascading through the window, lay awake in bed thinking. In college, she'd had unsatisfying sex several times with a college boy who'd been unsure and awkward. Certain her own unattractiveness was at fault, she hesitated before trying sex again with another student several years older who had aroused her with his lively mind, only to be disappointed by his desire to satisfy himself with no thought to her. It wasn't until she met Brian that lovemaking became a wonderful, shared pleasure that now was mostly a receding memory.

In Las Cruces, she'd been discreet, choosing carefully whom to sleep with. But those few men fell far short of what she knew was possible between lovers. She wondered if Matthew Kerney would be any different.

She'd diligently tried to contain her sexuality, or at the very least to mask it, but it was undeniable and unrelenting.

She decided she was being stupid. She'd wanted Matt to touch her, hold her—no, dammit, she wanted him inside her. Come what may—be it good, bad, or indifferent—she decided to give it another try. At the worst, it would only be another disappointment.

She threw off the blankets, dressed, made her way to the barn, tiptoed into the dark tack room, found her way to the bunk, and whispered, "Are you asleep?"

"Not even close," Matt whispered back.

She undressed, slipped under the blanket, and reached for him as his arms enfolded her. They kissed softly, gently, their hands exploring, their legs entwined. She could sense his eagerness, feel her own quickening pulse. She guided her hand to his hard member, slowly caressing it as he turned on top of her. She spread her legs to receive him and gasped with pleasure as a wonderful erotic pulse vibrated inside her when he entered.

* * *

Over the weekend, they made love at every possible opportunity: in his truck, in the barn on bales of hay, late at night in the bedroom, during their horseback rides. On their return to Las Cruces, they even detoured to the village of Hot Springs on the Rio Grande and rented a motel room for several hours, leaving the bed a moist tangle of sheets.

Back in town, they saw each other every chance they could; usually at Mary's apartment, where Erma, if she was home, would stay discreetly in her bedroom unless Matt was invited for supper and to spend the night, or when they double-dated at the movies with Erma and one of her many beaus who constantly buzzed around her in hopes of winning her hand or gaining access to her bed—which was a rare but more likely possibility.

Matt spent most of the Christmas holidays in town with Mary, returning to the ranch alone for a few days while Mary frantically prepared lesson plans for her teaching job at the elementary school, which would start when classes resumed after the first of the year.

His hopes for the state livestock inspector position were dashed when the job went to the nephew of a powerful state senator who owned a big outfit in the Bootheel. Without the GI Bill to pay his living expenses, he was hard-pressed to stay in town without a job. Gus Merton had generously offered to advance Matt's name for a position at the college in the Ag Department's equine program, if he would only apply, but while he wanted nothing more than to be with Mary, he felt that he'd renege on his responsibilities at the 7-Bar-K if he did so.

They talked it over and decided Matt should go back to the ranch, take stock of what needed to be done to make the operation profitable, and come to town when he could. Once Mary had settled in at her job, they'd switch back and forth between town and the ranch on the weekends.

Soon after returning to the ranch, Matt drove to the Rocking J to visit with Al Jennings about their cattle partnership. With the understanding that Matt would immediately pick up his share of the work managing the mingled herd, Al agreed to an equal split of profits based on the livestock tallies at shipment. They'd continue to use the pasturelands on both spreads to keep down overgrazing, and jointly maintain the fences, help with the calving, ramrod the spring and fall works, and do all the major maintenance at the windmills, dirt tanks, and live water sources. It was as close as they could come to combining the two ranches without legally merging.

At home, Matt was in a quandary about Jim and Millie. Their pay stretched the budget, but it was clear that Jim did most of the manual work and the place would be a mess without Millie. Patrick mostly puttered, took naps, showed up for meals, and in the evenings listened to his radio in the living room. Matt didn't fault him; any man with three-quarters of a century under his belt, who'd spent a lifetime working sunup to sundown and got stove up badly more than once while doing it, deserved his retirement.

To keep things as they were, he asked Patrick to contribute his entire veteran's pension to cover Jim and Millie's salary so they could stay on. He readily agreed.

"Hell yes, I'll do it," he said as he picked up a livestock bulletin and headed for the bathroom. "Just keep me in victuals, feed me a good meal, let me sleep in my own bed, don't boss me around, and I'll be plumb happy."

"I can't promise the last one," Matt replied.

"Didn't think you would," Patrick grumbled.

Every week, Matt made his first priority to honor his agreement with Al Jennings. Alternating between the Rocking J and the 7-Bar-K, the two men met regularly to divide up the chores. One weekday morning over coffee at the Rocking J, he learned from Al's wife, Brenda, that she was pregnant with their first child. They'd been trying unsuccessfully for years to have a baby.

Matt whooped in delight at the news.

"I never thought we'd do it," Al said with a sly grin. "What with the doctor saying it wasn't likely gonna happen after all this time."

He slapped Al on the back. "I knew you had it in you, old horse. Congratulations." He pushed back from the kitchen table and gave Brenda a hug. "When are you due?"

"Six months," Brenda replied, radiating happiness. "But my doctor says I'll need to spend the last three months in town off my feet. We'll rent a small place close by in Hot Springs. I have an old friend from school days who lives there. She'll look in on me from time to time and keep me company when she can."

"That sounds perfect," Matt said, knowing they would need more help than someone occasionally looking in on Brenda while she stayed in town. That meant Al would have to be away from the ranch more than usual. With his pa long dead and his mother recently passed away due to old age, when Brenda's time came someone would have to jump in and help manage the Rocking J. It meant giving up some weekends in town with Mary.

He looked at his chum, who appeared both thunderstruck and excited about the prospect of fatherhood, and said, "You're gonna want to be with Brenda as much as you can, so I'll look after things here when you need to be gone."

With tear-filled eyes, Brenda kissed him on the cheek. "You're a one-in-a-million friend."

Al squeezed Matt's shoulder. "We're obliged."

"Enough of that," Matt replied, reaching for his hat. "We've got feed cake and salt licks to put out before we throw the cattle over to the fresh pasture."

The two friends set aside their impromptu celebration and got to work. It took them two full days to move the cattle due to some cantankerous mother cows protecting their premature calves, a difficult birth that resulted in the loss of a 7-Bar-K calf, and the discovery of a bloated Rocking J heifer dead from eating poison weed.

They parted company with the cattle scattered over the high pasture Patrick had bought years earlier from a sheepherder and later sold to Al's pa. With Maverick in the bed of the truck, Matt drove home unhappy over the loss of the calf. It not only hurt financially, it was also a damn shame. And although he accepted the fact that nature ultimately took its toll on all life, he fervently hoped Brenda's pregnancy wouldn't end in catastrophe. His friends deserved better.

* * *

At home after dinner, Matt put the kettle on the cookstove and took a hot soak in the bathtub before settling behind his desk to read the mail. All of the tension in his neck and shoulders that had soaked away in the tub came roaring back as he scanned a registered, typewritten letter from White Sands Proving Ground. It read:

> *Dear Mr. Kerney,*
>
> *Pursuant to the March 1, 1946 special use permit signed by the Secretary of War providing for the expansion of White Sands Proving Ground, you are hereby advised that a*

recently concluded aerial and ground survey of the 7-Bar-K Ranch conducted with your written permission by personnel of the U.S. Geological Survey has determined that certain lands presumed to be part of the original patent secured by one John Kerney are in fact within the White Sands Proving Ground boundaries and thus fall under the jurisdiction of the United States Army.

Enclosed you will find a map prepared by the Corps of Engineers showing the revised survey boundaries for your ranch. You have thirty days from receipt of this letter to remove any and all private property located outside the 7-Bar-K boundary lines. After that time said property will be seized and disposed of by the government.

Should you have questions please contact my office.

Maj. John Reynolds, US Army
Adjutant
White Sands Proving Ground

"Dammit," Matt snapped.

From across the room, Patrick turned down the volume on the *Amos 'n' Andy Show.* "What's stuck in your craw?"

Matt stepped over and showed him the letter. Patrick snarled, crumpled it, and threw it on the floor. "It's robbery and I say we fight it. Otherwise we're gonna lose a fourth of our land to those bastards."

"I bet they're just getting started." Matt picked up the letter and smoothed it out. "I'll see a lawyer pronto and have him talk to the army."

Most of the land the army wanted to take was marginal at best, but it included one good, small pasture. If the army prevailed, it meant Matt would have to reduce the size of his herd after spring works.

Patrick grunted. "The business end of my horse pistol would be more convincing than any lawyer's fancy words."

"You'd go to war with the army?" Matt asked incredulously.

"Hell yes and why not? This country was born in rebellion."

Matt sighed. "Let's try the peaceable way first."

"Suit yourself," Patrick replied, reaching for the volume knob on the radio.

* * *

On his way to see a lawyer, Matt detoured to the Rocking J to give Al the news about the army's land grab. Al had news of his own, showing Matt a letter he'd received from the army challenging the title to the two sections of pasture Patrick had sold to Al's father. According to the letter, the sheepherder who originally homesteaded the land had recorded his deed on the wrong county plats, thus invalidating Al's title to the land. He had thirty days to remove his cattle.

"They want control of every blasted acre from the San Andres east to the Sacramentos," Al said.

"And north of Carrizozo as well, I reckon," Matt added. "If they can't steal it, they'll lease it and never give it back. If we lose both pastures, we won't have enough grazing land to get us through to fall works."

"Can we stall them through to the fall?" Al asked.

"That's a question for a lawyer, and I'm on my way to see one."

"I'm going with you," Al said, rising from his chair. He gave Brenda a quick kiss, told her not to worry, and piled into Matt's truck for the drive to Hot Springs.

Along the way they talked about the trouble losing land to the army would cause. They'd have to move the herd off the Rocking J pasture, where the grass was good, and probably spend money on feed to fatten them up. Spring works were coming, and that meant gathering all the mother cows and their babies for doctoring and branding at either the Rocking J or 7-Bar-K headquarters. For convenience, they decided the Rocking J would do best. First, they'd throw the heifers, yearlings, and steers onto the 7-Bar-K north pasture, where the windmill produced a steady flow of water and the fencing was secure. Matt would send his ranch hand Jim Sawyer to stay at the line cabin to look after the cattle. Maybe Patrick would agree to go as well.

If in the end they lost the land permanently to the army, they'd have to cut back on cattle production in order not to further degrade the remaining rangeland. Matt thought it might be time for him to give up cattle altogether and return to raising ponies. A top hand with horses, Al suggested that if Matt made the switch they should still keep their informal partnership going. They sealed it with a handshake.

In Hot Springs, they met with Charlie Hopkinson in his downtown storefront office. The eldest son of a rancher with pioneer roots in the Lake Valley hill country, Charlie had chosen the law over livestock. In his thirty-year career, he'd been retained for one reason or another by just about every rancher in five counties. A rotund, bookish man who loved poetry over ponies and literary conversation over cattle, Charlie was known to be a fierce courtroom adversary. After reading the letters sent by the army, Charlie peered at Matt and Al over his spectacles.

"Save your money, boys; it's a fight you can't win," he counseled.

"Why is that?" Matt asked, agitated by Charlie's quick dismissal of their grievances.

"Because they've got proof that your title to the lands in question is invalid." Charlie leaned back in his chair. "Hear me out. To mount a case it would take a complete new survey of the 7-Bar-K to prove them wrong—if they are wrong—and a judge to set aside the army's claim that the Rocking J technically doesn't own those two sections. No judge I know is going to do that."

"Why not?" Al demanded.

"Because none of them wants to be branded as taking an unpatriotic stand against the army. No matter who I approached on the bench to hear your case, I guarantee he'd take it under advisement, wait until the army assumes possession, and then wash his hands of the whole matter by kicking it over to federal court."

"You know that for a fact?" Matt queried.

Charlie nodded. "I do. I play poker with every one of them the third Thursday of the month."

"What about the ranchers that are signing new lease agreements with the army?" Al asked.

"The government isn't questioning the title to those lands." Charlie tapped his pen on the desktop for emphasis. "And that's because either the state or federal government controls over ninety-five percent of it leased out for grazing. Even with a new lease, those folks forced off their ranches aren't going to be allowed back for the next twenty years—probably never, if you ask me. All they get is some money, and in most cases not a lot of it either."

"What can we do?" Frustration tinged Matt's question.

Charlie pondered the question for a moment. "As far as I know, you two own the only remaining privately held ranches in the San

Andres Mountains. My best guess is that eventually the army will come to one or both of you with a purchase option."

"You're telling us we won't have a choice," Matt declared.

"Pretty much." Charlie swung his chair around, searched through a bookcase, unfolded a large map of the Jornada and Tularosa Basin on his desk, and asked for the exact locations of the two ranches.

Matt and Al pointed out their boundaries. The 7-Bar-K was now completely encircled by the proving ground. With the loss of the two sections, the Rocking J sat right on the western edge of the military installation, most of it stretching into the Jornada tablelands.

"You can hang on for a while or sell out when the army comes a-calling with an offer," Charlie proposed with a sad smile.

"How long is a while?" Al asked.

Charlie raised the palms of his hands skyward. "Who knows? Next year? Five or ten years from now? But if you want to dig in your heels and stick it out, I'll gladly represent you. The best I can do is slow them down once they decide to come after you. What we don't want is for the government to condemn your property. Cash money at a fair price will be our goal. It's up to you to decide if my time is worth it."

He folded the map and put it aside.

Matt and Al exchanged looks. "We're sticking," Matt announced. "How much is your retainer?"

"At this point, with everything so uncertain, a retainer isn't necessary." Charlie got to his feet. "We'll take it step-by-step as the need arises. Just make sure I know about everything that transpires between you and the government from here on out. And I mean everything."

The three men shook hands.

"For now, as far as I know, you're some of the last holdouts the army can't bully off their land," Charlie said. "I'm proud to represent you."

"Ain't that being unpatriotic?" Al jokingly chided.

Charlie laughed. "Maybe, but it sure isn't un-American."

Matt and Al drove back to the Rocking J without much jawboning. When they turned off onto the Rocking J ranch road, Al asked Matt what he was going to say to Patrick.

"Nothing, except that we've hired Charlie Hopkinson to look out for our interests. That should keep him calm."

"That old boy isn't gonna budge off the land," Al predicted. "Neither would my pa if he were still with us."

"I'm not inclined to budge an inch myself," Matt said. "I already gave them my left eye. That should be good enough."

Al nodded sympathetically. "But it puts a pall over just about everything we do from here on out, doesn't it?"

Matt nodded. "As if drought and not enough pasture for the cattle we've got isn't bad enough."

"Are we gonna stick to our plan?"

"You bet we are," Matt said emphatically.

Al smiled. "I feel better already."

Matt smiled in return. "Me too, partner. Me too."

15

A week after meeting with Charlie Hopkinson, a carbon copy of a letter he'd written to the commanding general of White Sands Proving Ground on Matt's behalf arrived by mail. In it, Charlie complained about a lack of adequate warning to remove Matt's property from the "disputed lands" and the "unconstitutional" refusal of the army to allow Matt to challenge the findings of the new 7-Bar-K Ranch land survey. Attached to the letter was a note from Charlie explaining he'd sent it to start a paper trail of protest that might prove helpful in any future legal actions against the federal government. The next time Matt saw Al, he learned Charlie had done the same for him.

Moving the herd from Al's pasture to the 7-Bar-K north pasture meant trailing the stock a far distance over mountainous terrain unsuitable for vehicles. As a result the enterprise took on most of the trappings of an old-time cattle drive on horseback. Patrick proved to be a big help putting the chuck wagon back into shape, stocking it with necessary victuals and firewood, and volunteering to serve as the camp cook. Matt enlisted Jim Sawyer to resupply the high-country cabin, tune up the north pasture windmill to ensure adequate water for the arriving cattle, truck sufficient feed cake and salt licks to last at least a month, and then meet them along the trail on horseback to help with the drive. All in all, money and time that could have been well used elsewhere went into satisfying the army's demands. It got Matt's blood to boiling and put Al into a foul mood as well.

Charlie's letter of complaint to the general did generate some unexpected help in the sudden appearance of the two range riders employed by the army who arrived with orders to assist in the removal of cattle from the Rocking J pasture. The men, Jamie Kyle and Marcos Vasquez, known to both Matt and Al, were experienced cowboys once employed by the San Augustine Ranch, a 150,000-acre spread now 90 percent owned by the army. They were genuinely sympathetic about the unhappy situation that had caused their arrival and readily fell to the task of gathering cattle for the drive.

Once under way it went slowly. Mother cows with their new babies couldn't and wouldn't be prodded or pushed, and about once every day a pregnant cow would drop a newborn calf, causing everything to come to a complete stop. In three days they reached the cabin in good spirits in spite of everything, moods turned around by the sheer enjoyment of working at a job they loved on a piece of beautiful high country, with panoramic glimpses of distant mountains crowned by pure white clouds in crystal-clear, turquoise-blue skies.

Jim Sawyer joined up with them at the cabin and they rested the herd for a day before pushing on to the north pasture. As they plodded along, the number of newborn calves increased. Matt and Al decided to establish a camp at the north pasture to complete spring works there rather than moving the herd once again downslope to the Rocking J headquarters.

They reached the pasture at midmorning on the sixth day of the drive with every cow and calf accounted for. Before Jamie and Marcos departed, Matt asked them to mail a note he'd quickly scribbled to Mary explaining his long absence from town. He hadn't been in touch with her since his return from the meeting with Charlie Hopkinson in Hot Springs.

After setting up camp, he sent Patrick and Jim back to the 7-Bar-K to restock and bring what was needed for branding and doctoring. Al left for the Rocking J to do the same and check on Brenda's well-being, which left Matt alone to enjoy some solitude. He turned Maverick out to graze and used his saddle as an improvised writing table to pen a long letter to Mary, describing all that had happened since their last weekend together almost a month ago.

Finished, he sealed the letter and put it away in his saddlebags, wondering if letters from her awaited him at the Engle post office, where the 7-Bar-K now got mail because of the army's permanent closure of the state highway from Tularosa to Rhodes Canyon. When he could, Matt made twice-weekly mail runs, but he hadn't been able to get to Engle during the past ten days.

They'd been writing to each other on the average of three times a week, and Matt sorely missed her letters. He hoped she hadn't stopped because of his silence, or lost interest in him for that very reason. He didn't like thinking of that possibility at all.

It riled him to think how much the blasted army had inconvenienced him, both in the pursuit of his livelihood and in his personal life. If both got ruined, he just might have to take up Patrick's horse pistol and join him in armed rebellion against the government.

The cattle, lazy and thickheaded by nature, had clustered around the water tank. Shaking off his ill humor, Matt saddled

Maverick and went to scatter them, certain he'd find a mother cow or two about to drop a calf and possibly in need of assistance.

* * *

Mary arrived home to find a letter from Matt in the porch mailbox. She dropped her purse on the couch and tore it open. It read:

Dear Mary,

I'm sorry to be so lax in writing to you recently but I've been forced by the blasted army to move the cows Al and I pastured on land that has now been taken from him for the proving ground. Because of all the time and effort that's gone into gathering and moving the herd, we've decided to do our spring works right where we are rather than trailing them down to the Rocking J. It means I'll be camped here and out of touch for about another week.

I've been missing you and your company. I'll come to see you as soon as I can, promise.

Affectionately,
Matt

Mary sat on the couch and read the letter again. Even with the endearments it seemed so formal. Had he written it in a rush? Was he backing away from her? Nearly three weeks had passed with no communication from him other than this brief note. She had no way to know if he still cared until she saw him again. She wondered if she'd ever.

She examined the envelope. It had been mailed from Alamogordo. If he'd gone there, with the state road across the proving ground now closed, he would have most likely driven south to Las Cruces and then east to Alamogordo. Why would he pass through town twice going and coming and not stop to see her?

The idea of it made her want to cry. Her last two letters had urged him to visit as soon as he could. She'd even written him on a Monday two weeks ago asking him to call her from the Engle train station on Saturday morning next, promising to wait until noon for his call, underlining that it was very important to speak with him. He didn't call or even write back to say that he couldn't.

All she could believe was that it was over between them. A feeling of abject misery froze her in place.

Erma found her sitting bolt upright on the couch in the fading light of day. "What's wrong?" she asked.

Mary handed her the letter. She switched on the table lamp, read it, and glanced at Mary. "You're crying over this?" she asked disbelievingly.

"A little," Mary admitted.

"That's silly. He's working, that's all. He hasn't got a telephone, he's probably miles from anywhere, and he hasn't had a chance to pick up his mail."

"That's one way to look at it."

"That's the only way," Erma countered. "Let's go out there this weekend and track him down. You'll see that I'm right."

Mary shook her head.

Erma sat and took her friend's hand. "Why are you so intent on believing Matt will run like the dickens once you tell him you're pregnant with his baby?"

"I just am."

Erma looked at Mary sternly. "If you're that convinced, why

don't we drive to Juárez this weekend and find an abortionist? That way the school board won't fire you for being a pregnant, unmarried teacher and you can start looking for Matt's replacement. Next time, will another cowboy do, or should it be someone who conveniently lives in town?"

"I'd never get rid of the baby!" Mary snapped. "And stop being so mean."

Erma stroked Mary's hair. "Think this through. Do you want to move far away and start over again with a baby and no job?"

"I have money set aside," Mary replied defiantly.

Erma wrapped an arm around Mary's shoulder. "You're scared, honey. I know I would be."

Mary leaned against Erma and nodded.

"Why don't you give Matt a chance to prove he isn't a cad?"

"Do you think he is?"

Erma took a deep breath. "After Hank, I'm suspicious of all men, but Matt has always struck me as one of the good guys. Frankly, I've always been a bit jealous that he went for you and not me."

"You never told me that before."

"I never thought you'd let go of him before."

"Is that what I'm doing?"

"You're planning for the worst instead of hoping for the best. Give him a chance to show his true colors."

"Waiting isn't my strong suit."

"Do you love him?"

"Yes, very much."

Erma gave her a squeeze. "Then you can do it. You're the bravest person I know."

* * *

Al and Patrick had spread the word about early spring works at the Rocking J and 7-Bar-K and over the course of the next few days, folks came to help, including Earl and Addie Hightower, who'd been displaced from their ranch, Miguel Chávez from Tularosa, and James Kaytennae and Jasper Daklugie from Mescalero. Brenda took charge of feeding the crew with Millie's able assistance, and Jim helped Patrick gather firewood and care for the ponies. Even Marcus Vasquez and Jamie Kyle came on the sly and worked for a day before riding off in early dusk after chow.

It was a bittersweet gathering of friends and acquaintances that put a sparkle in Patrick's eye and a spring in his step, and made Matt pause to recall many happy memories of times past. It also brought out the army by way of a small reconnaissance airplane that flew overhead several times a day to make sure no schemes were underfoot to plot sabotage or mount an armed incursion onto the proving ground.

Matt wondered what the pilot thought while circling around an encampment of wagons, people, horses, and cattle clustered near a hastily thrown up corral on the high side pasture of a remote mountain. From where he stood, it looked right off the page of a Eugene Manlove Rhodes novel set some seventy years in the past.

He took it all in. He loved the smell, feel, sight, and sound of it almost as much as the pleasurable companionship it fostered.

On one such flyby, Jasper Daklugie looked up at the single-engine plane with stars on its wings and wondered aloud if the army would let him ride in one.

"You're not in the army," Matt reminded him as he freed a bawling calf Jasper had just branded.

Jasper smiled. "Soon, I go." He touched the red-hot branding iron to another calf dragged over by James Kaytennae and the scent of seared hair again filled Matt's nostrils.

"But there's no new war to fight," he replied, remembering James Kaytennae's prophesy of an armed conflict to come.

"Soon it comes," James Kaytennae announced confidently as he roped an unbranded calf Earl Hightower hazed over to him from the far end of the corral.

The calm look of certainty on both men's faces gave Matt good reason not to challenge their predictions. Right or wrong, there was always a place in the world for oracles. And besides, on such a perfect day, he didn't want to think too deeply about the insane prospect of another war. Instead, he imagined that these remote, beautiful mountains would never again host such an old-fashioned assemblage of cowmen, womenfolk, ponies, and cattle. When spring works were done and all had departed, an invisible curtain on the old west would close once and forever. With a sudden pang, he wished Mary had been with him to see it.

16

With the army's closure of the state highway across the Tularosa Basin and the demise of Engle to virtually a ghost town, Matt had switched all of his business dealings to Hot Springs, the Sierra County seat nestled in low, rock-strewn, sandy hills along the Rio Grande. The natural mineral springs drew some tourist business to the town, as did the nearby Elephant Butte Reservoir, which when finished in 1916 created a manmade lake forty miles long and tamed a long stretch of the often wandering, sometimes destructive river. But mostly the town thrived on local commerce, government services, and a hospital to treat children with polio that had been built during the Great Depression. A number of motels on the main drag catered to motorists traveling along US Highway 85, a major roadway now completely paved that more or less paralleled the river from Las Cruces to Santa Fe, and there was the usual mix of bars, diners, and assorted stores and businesses that supplied the various needs of the citizenry. Yet the town remained devoid of charm to the point that it rarely made a favorable impression on anyone, including the folks who lived there.

With the completion of spring works on the 7-Bar-K, Matt left Jim Sawyer at the cabin to keep an eye on the cow and calf herd in the north pasture, said goodbye to a rejuvenated Patrick at the ranch house, who'd promised to take good care of the ponies, and headed first to Engle to pick up the mail, then on to Hot Springs to do banking and pay some bills before driving to Las Cruces to see Mary.

In Engle at the little general store that also served as the post office, he collected his mail and sat outside in the truck reading Mary's letters. There were six, all dated before he'd sent her a short note apologizing for his delay in corresponding. He read them in order and as the tone changed from Mary's usual cheerful affection to her worry about his silence, Matt's alarm escalated. In one letter she asked him to call on a Saturday morning and promised to wait by the telephone until he did so. Why would she want to do that? Had something bad happened? Was she sick? He shuddered at the thought of losing her to some illness. Or did she ask him to call so she could politely throw him over by long distance to avoid any face-to-face unpleasantness?

Why not? Matt speculated. An absent boyfriend who lived to hell and gone on a ranch outside of nowhere wasn't the greatest catch for an educated, good-looking woman who could have her pick of any of the eligible town bachelors. The mere thought of losing her to another man depressed him. What had he done to screw up so badly, other than by necessity being out of touch for a very short time? Surely, it wasn't just that.

Early March winds had kicked up on the Jornada and dust whipped through the open truck windows, coating Matt and everything inside. The hell with going to Hot Springs. He put her letters in the glove box and cranked the engine. Ranch business could wait; Mary was too important. He thought about trying to call her from the pay phone outside the train station, but most likely she was still in her classroom at school. He wheeled south, anxious and troubled to learn what awaited him in Las Cruces.

* * *

It was long past school hours when Matt arrived in Las Cruces. At the apartment, Erma's car was gone from the street and there was no answer to his knock at the door. The landlady, Mrs. Lorenz, told him the girls had left earlier all dressed up to go out, although she had no idea where—but after all it was a Friday evening. For several hours, until hunger got the best of him, he waited in the truck for Mary to return while Mrs. Lorenz every now and then suspiciously peeked at him through a window. He decided to leave the truck parked in front of the apartment so that Mary would know he was around in case she arrived home before he returned, and walked the few blocks to a diner on Main Street, where a group of noisy soldiers from the proving ground had commandeered three booths at the back of the establishment and were chowing down on food that was at least a peg or two better than the usual army mess-hall fare.

He sat at the counter eavesdropping on the boisterous jabbering of the young men in uniform as he ate a meal of broiled pork chops, green beans, and mashed potatoes with gravy. Finished, he left two dollars on the counter to cover the check and the tip and returned to Mary's apartment. The lights were on inside, cars were arriving, and Erma was at the open front door gaily greeting several well-dressed couples. Record-player music and the hum of lively conversation drifted from inside.

Matt balked and retreated to the street corner. It was most definitively a party that he hadn't been invited to attend. More cars arrived, filling up parking spaces on both sides of the street. Gus and Consuelo Merton showed up, as did several other college professors Matt recognized.

For better or worse, he decided to get it over with. He used his handkerchief to wipe his boots clean, brushed the dust off his jeans, took a deep breath, marched to the front porch, and knocked on the door. Erma appeared, blocked the doorway, and looked him up and down.

"Oh, it's you," she said flatly.

"Sorry to intrude on the party, but I'd like to speak to Mary if she's free."

Erma stood aside. "Come in."

Matt stalled. "What's the occasion?"

A hint of delight that Erma couldn't suppress danced in her eyes. "We're celebrating the opening of the inaugural student art league juried show on campus. My watercolor of the Organ Mountains took a first-place blue ribbon."

"Congratulations," Matt said, sincerely pleased for her accomplishment. He knew how much her art meant to her. "That's wonderful."

"Thank you." Erma's standoffishness cracked a tiny bit and she managed a smile. "Mary's inside. Last I saw her she was in the kitchen."

"Should I duck when she sees me?"

Erma stepped back. "That will be entirely up to you."

The front room was filled with guests clutching wineglasses, smoking cigarettes, and chatting to one another with great gusto. He was halfway across the room when Gus Merton intercepted him.

"Where have you been?" he thundered, clasping a hand on his shoulder.

"Wrestling with overprotective mother cows and skirmishing with the US Army," Matt replied with a grin.

"Ah, the plights of the modern-day rancher in the wilds of New Mexico," Gus replied with a sympathetic smile. "I want to hear all about it. Are you here for the weekend?"

"I plan to be."

"Good. Come to dinner at the hacienda tomorrow. Bring Mary."

Matt shrugged. "I sure will, if she's free."

Gus raised his chin in the direction of the kitchen. "By all means, find out if she can join us. Consuelo will be sorely disappointed if she can't."

He gave Matt a gentle push toward the kitchen as he turned to speak to a matronly woman obviously eager to gain his full attention.

In the kitchen Mary was deep in conversation with a good-looking fella Matt didn't know. When she saw him, she broke away and hurried over.

"I saw your truck when we got home," she said tonelessly. "Let me get my jacket and we can talk outside."

Matt nodded. "Okay."

On the sidewalk, she silently led him away from the party.

"Are you upset with me?" he asked as they reached the corner.

Mary stopped, turned on her heel and faced him under the dim glow of the street lamp. "I have something to tell you. I'm pregnant."

Matt took a breath and sighed in relief. "That's it?"

"Excuse me?"

A smile lit up his face. Relieved and delighted by the news, he grabbed her by both arms. "I thought you were going to dump me. We're going to have a baby?"

Mary could hear the pleasure in his voice. She bit her lip to keep from crying and nodded. "Yes, we are."

Matt wrapped her in his arms. "Marry me."

He didn't question her, doubt her, or retreat from her. All her fears that he might do so evaporated. His instant and complete commitment to her was so overwhelming it felt almost surreal. "Are you sure that's what you want to do?"

His arms tightened around her. "Yes, I am. Will you?"

"Yes, yes, yes," Mary answered.

"Gus and Consuelo have invited us to dinner tomorrow night. Other than Erma, I'd like them to be the first to know."

"That's perfect," Mary said, squeezing his hand. "But tonight you're all mine."

Giddily, she led him back to Erma's party.

They entered the apartment and spotted Erma across the room, who took one look at their silly, lovestruck smiles and rushed over to hug them both.

* * *

The next morning, Erma was gone from the apartment when Matt and Mary got up. The party mess had been cleared away and there was a pot of fresh coffee on the stove along with a note from Erma saying she had gone off to meet with her Saturday-morning drawing group and would be back early in the afternoon.

Over breakfast they discussed how they wanted to get married. They decided on a simple ceremony with a few friends in attendance, including Gus and Consuelo Merton; Mary's landlady, Mrs. Lorenz; and Jimmy Kendell, the navy vet they both liked. Of course, Erma would be the maid of honor and Matt wanted Al Jennings as his best man.

Matt asked Mary about inviting her parents, but she had no desire to do so. However, she wanted Patrick to give her away.

"He can be mulish. What if he refuses?"

"If you tell him he's going to be a grandfather soon, he'll come," Mary predicted. "I'd also like Jim and Millie to be there."

"Anyone else?" Matt queried.

Mary shook her head. "Not right now, but we have to keep it small since we have to pay for everything ourselves."

When the breakfast dishes were done, they walked to a downtown jewelry store, where Mary decided, much to an eager salesperson's dismay, that she didn't want a diamond engagement and wedding ring set; just a plain gold band would do. She picked one that fit perfectly. Given the difference in price between diamond rings and a gold band, Matt gladly paid for it on the spot.

They got back to the apartment before noon. Once inside, half-starved for each other and in a trembling rush to make love, they started tugging at their clothes, laughing, falling half-naked on the couch. They'd barely put themselves back together when Erma burst through the front door.

"Am I interrupting?" she asked innocently, taking in Mary's disheveled hair and the lipstick smudges on Matt's face.

Mary bounced off the couch. "Nope, your timing was perfect." With a mischievous grin, she reached into her purse and showed Erma the gold band.

"Oh, my, you two didn't waste any time. It's beautiful." She faked a pout. "Hank never gave me one, the bastard." She shook off the memory with a brilliant smile. "But on to happier matters. So when are you getting hitched?"

"We haven't gotten that far yet," Matt replied with a grin.

"Except you're my bridesmaid," Mary added.

"Of course I am." Erma dropped her sketchpad on the side table and sank into the easy chair opposite the couch. "Let's dream up something for your wedding."

Over the next hour they made a list. They'd need a license, the names of people to invite, a date, time, and place for the wedding and the same for a small reception to follow. What should they serve at the reception? Did they want a preacher, a judge, or a justice of the peace to marry them? What about flowers? Certainly a new dress for Mary and a new suit for Matt were called for. And what about the wedding pictures? Did they want music at the reception?

Finally, Matt threw up his hands. "Whoa."

"What?" Erma asked, looking quickly up from the notebook she was using to keep the list.

"I don't mean to throw cold water on the plans, but we need to keep this shindig small and not too expensive."

"What do you suggest?" Erma asked sternly, unwilling to budge from her personal idea of exactly what her very best friend's wedding should be like.

Mary gently took the notebook from Erma's hand. "We don't have to rush. We'll figure something out."

Erma sighed, stood, and reached for her sketchbook. "My first and probably only attempt to actually plan a wedding and I get shot down." She sniffed her hand and made a face. "No matter, I have to bathe and change anyway. We were out all morning sketching cows at the college Ag barn. What lovely, smelly creatures they are, but Maynard Dixon I ain't."

She charged up the stairs before Mary could accuse her of being melodramatic. "We can pare it down," Mary reassured Matt. "I have some money set aside if we need to use it."

Matt shook his head. "You hold on to that money. Tonight at dinner, we'll ask Gus and Consuelo for their advice. I bet they can at least put us on to a judge willing to marry us, and give us some ideas on a place to rent for the reception."

Mary nodded absentmindedly, cocked her head, and listened. "Hush, Erma's running the tub." She slid close to Matt and started unbuttoning her blouse.

* * *

That night, over a glass of wine in the library before sitting down to dinner, they announced their engagement to Gus and Consuelo, who, delighted by the news, demanded that the wedding and reception be held at their casa. Gus would arrange with a friend who was a retired district judge to officiate, Consuelo would oversee preparations for an early afternoon wedding ceremony in the large, high-walled, enclosed courtyard, with a reception immediately to follow near the adjacent outdoor kitchen, where tables and chairs would be set up for the guests. Consuelo would choose the menu and do the cooking, Gus would select the spirits, and the food and drink would be served buffet-style. It would all be very easy and informal. In case of inclement weather, everything would simply be moved inside to the spacious living and dining rooms.

Matt's offer to pay for the cost of the reception was dismissed out of hand. All they needed from the couple, Consuelo announced, beaming with pleasure, was a date for the wedding and the number of invited guests. Mary decided on the last Saturday in March, three weeks hence. She required at least that much time to prepare. She needed to buy a dress, pick out shoes, select the proper stationery, address and mail invitations—plus do a dozen other little things.

At the dinner table, she announced she'd finish out the school year before resigning her teaching position. Surprised, Matt hadn't thought that far ahead, but her decision made sense. Remaining in town, close to medical care if needed, was a sound idea. He wondered if it might be best for her to stay in Las Cruces throughout her entire pregnancy.

All of a sudden he realized that he didn't have a clue as to when the baby was due. He didn't even know if Mary had a doctor, if her pregnancy was normal, what the hospital would cost, or what they'd need to buy for the baby. He was so over the moon in love and excited about becoming a father, he hadn't done any hard thinking about the situation.

The growing awareness that he faced a brand-new reality drained the color completely from his face. Across the table a worried Consuelo asked if he felt all right. He covered it up with a cough and a swallow, fibbing that something had momentarily gotten stuck in his throat.

They finished a wonderful evening at the front door saying good night with hugs from Gus and Consuelo and promises made by all to stay in constant contact so that everything would proceed smoothly. On the drive to Mary's apartment, Matt learned that the baby was due in late September or early October, and that according to her doctor everything was normal. In addition, she had already started setting aside money to buy baby clothes and other necessities. At an appropriate time in the early summer Erma would host a baby shower. Furthermore, on one of his future trips to town, they needed to shop for a crib. She'd recently spotted several in good shape at reasonable prices in a local secondhand furniture store. She asked him to stay over through Monday. That way they could go to the county courthouse after school to apply for their marriage license. Oh, and they needed to start thinking about boy and girl names for the baby. She would start a list. And what did he think once the baby was born about asking Jim and Millie to move from the casita to the ranch house? The casita might be a little cramped, but would afford them more privacy. And she'd already decided that since the ranch now had electrical power, she would get a new washing machine with her own money, which would make the chore of keeping the baby in clean diapers a lot easier.

After verbally tussling over who would pay for the washing machine and finally conceding to Mary's wishes, Matt realized he was no match for a woman fully engaged in nest building.

* * *

For Matt, the weeks preceding the wedding passed quickly and for the most part without a lot of demands on his time. Mary, Erma, and Consuelo took charge of all the preparations and necessary details like a trio of combat-hardened field marshals mounting a major campaign against Matt's bachelorhood. They kept him informed every step of the way, mostly after the fact because of his frequent time away at the ranch, where he spent a good deal of effort putting the casita in tip-top shape after relocating Jim and Millie to the ranch house. He didn't see the need to wait until the baby was born to move into the casita, and besides, like Mary, he wanted the privacy it afforded.

Jim and Millie were happy to oblige, and Patrick enjoyed having them closer at hand for kibitzing, company, and nightly sessions in front of the radio.

As they shopped for the crib, the washing machine, and other baby necessities, Matt happily discovered that Mary was very frugal with money—an extremely important virtue for any ranch wife. She even suggested they get married in their military uniforms to save the cost of buying wedding outfits. The idea of a military wedding also appealed to both Erma and Jimmy Kendell, who decided to join in and wear their navy blues. When told, Patrick wanted no part of it. Tickled at the thought of becoming a grandfather, he'd gladly give Mary away in a pair of clean, pressed jeans, a fresh white shirt, and polished boots, but he damn sure wasn't wearing his moth-eaten Rough Rider uniform.

In addition to her duties as maid of honor, Erma also volunteered to serve as the official wedding photographer, enlisting Ernie Downs, an aspiring artist and newly acquired boyfriend, as her assistant. Consuelo would prepare the bridal bouquet from the spring flowers blooming in the hacienda courtyard, and as a courtesy to Gus, retired Judge Horace Van Patten—the very justice who had sent Fred Tyler to prison years ago—agreed to marry the couple for one of Gus's good Cuban cigars and a glass of the twenty-five-year-old port he kept hidden away in his library.

Given the short interlude between the engagement and wedding, the three field marshals running the campaign agreed an announcement in the paper wasn't needed. Nevertheless, rumors about the reason for the sudden marriage started to spread, which Mary ignored with an easy grace. Matt kept an eye on her in case she was hurt by the rumors and faking it, but she appeared truly happy and immune to the gossip. Besides being a knockout, the gal had grit and gumption.

At Consuelo's urging, arguing that it was only proper to do so, Mary reluctantly wrote a note to her parents informing them of her engagement but made no mention of the wedding date. A week later, she got a terse letter back from her brother, Tom, wishing her good luck, and saying that her mother had died of cancer two years ago, her father was living in a church-run rest home because of severe, crippling arthritis, and Tom was about to sell the ranch and move his family to California.

Although it may have been unintended, her brother's message freed her from her last ties to her family and closed that painful chapter in her life. She felt a huge sense of relief. Now everything was brand-new, with a bright and exciting future with Matt ahead.

* * *

The wedding went off without a hitch. With his hair slicked down, neat and tidy in appearance, and a smile on his face, Patrick walked Mary from the hacienda to the old cottonwood tree in the center of the courtyard, where Judge Van Patten cleared his throat, asked them if they agreed to their pending union, and upon their unanimous assent, pronounced them to be married. Matt controlled his jitters, slipped the ring onto Mary's finger, and gave her a lingering kiss that the well-wishers greeted with whistles, catcalls, and applause, with Al Jennings among the loudest. After Erma's boyfriend Ernie finished taking the wedding-party pictures, Consuelo and Gus sprung surprise entertainment on the gathering by ushering in three musicians who rolled an upright piano to the patio and got the party under way with some really good dance tunes.

Matt had invited Rosella Gomez, his former landlady from the barrio. She had come alone, all dressed up and looking somewhat uneasy. Consuelo and Mary sat with her for a spell chatting in Spanish, which quickly put her at ease. Soon she was smiling and clapping her hands as the dancing couples whirled by. Matt made it a point to dance with her and she jokingly chided him for not marrying one of her nieces and moving back to the old neighborhood. She giggled with delight when Matt replied none of them had measured up to her. He returned her to her seat and took Mrs. Lorenz for a whirl next, who remarked in his ear that he'd married a true treasure of a girl and he darn well better treat her right. Matt promised to do so.

Jimmy Kendell, handsome in his navy aviator uniform, danced repeatedly with all the women, smoothly and expertly guiding them around and around with his one arm, much to the delight of Brenda Jennings, who loved to dance and was married to a man with lead feet. Al took it with good humor and even awkwardly shuffled through a slow tune with Brenda to prove his devotion and love. Matt tried hard not to laugh at the look of painful determination on his best friend's face.

Even Jim and Millie Sawyer, whom Matt figured would stay chair-bound at a table, kicked up their heels to a tune or two.

By six o'clock, most everyone was a little tipsy from making too many toasts, stuffed from eating too much good food, weary from all the dancing, and ready to call it quits. All except for Patrick, Judge Van Patten, and Gus, who'd long ago retreated to the library and had to be herded out to say goodbye to the newlyweds. With everybody assembled, they saw Matt and Mary off at the front door as they drove away to change out of their uniforms at the apartment and drive to El Paso, where they'd spend their wedding night in a deluxe room at the Hotel Paso del Norte.

They made love at the apartment and again immediately after checking in to the hotel. Mary had splurged on some frilly undergarments that Matt took no notice of whatsoever. She teased him about it over dinner at the best steak house in town. He promised to take a longer, closer, slower look when they returned to their room. Mary rather doubted it.

The manager, told of the special occasion by the hotel clerk who had booked the table, had their waiter serve dinner with flair. The food was delicious. Neither had had much to eat at the wedding and they cleaned their plates. The salads were fresh with a light, tangy dressing, the steaks grilled perfectly, the young asparagus crisp, the small, roasted potatoes tender, and it was all topped off by a glass of red wine each, compliments of the house. Other patrons at nearby tables, who'd been made aware of their newly married status, smiled and raised their glasses in congratulations. Mary blushed at the unexpected attention.

After dinner they ordered cordials and toasted each other privately for surviving their wedding day, which they admitted had been exhausting, fun, and no mean feat. Matt vowed to take her on a proper honeymoon someday when time and money allowed. Thinking of the baby to come, she smiled and told him the best honeymoon she could possibly ever have would be living with him on the 7-Bar-K Ranch. It was a dream come true and she was antsy for the school year to end so they could be together permanently. When he shook his head in mock dismay and said that she might quickly tire of him on a daily basis, she punched him hard on the arm and made up for it with a smooch.

They left the restaurant arm in arm and walked around the nearby old downtown plaza. Matt stopped in front of a saloon filled with Saturday-night revelers and told her that a speakeasy had once inhabited the building and charged customers a dollar for a one-day membership.

Mary peeked inside. "It just looks like an ordinary bar."

"Ah, but in its day it was filled with gangsters, rumrunners, and molls. Not a place for a respectable married woman," he teased.

At a corner lamplight, he kissed her and said she was beautiful. She truly believed it and it made her love him all the more. Although she'd thought she knew better, she'd started her wedding day hesitant about marrying, wondering if Matt really loved her or was merely acting honorably. But the feeling had passed, leaving her with the crystal-clear knowledge that she'd found her perfect mate and truest friend.

Strangely, now that it was done, she still didn't feel married at all. Perhaps that would come with time. In a way she hoped not; living with a lover seemed a much more enticing and interesting prospect than having a husband. She smiled at the thought of it.

"What?" Matt asked, wanting an explanation of her dreamy smile.

Mary raised his hand to her lips and kissed it. "Nothing. Just happy, that's all."

17

The promising spring of 1950 became the summer of war and the beginning of a punishing drought. By the time Mary moved to the ranch the grass was already scorched and the hottest temperatures on record had been reported in towns and villages surrounding the Tularosa Basin. On most afternoons the thermometer Patrick had tacked to a post on the veranda hovered near the hundred-degree mark and clouds in the sky were as rare as the sound of live water. Within weeks, North Korean soldiers began pouring across the border into South Korea, driving the South Korean army almost into the sea. There was speculation that the Chinese would join in the fight to ensure the entire peninsula became a communist state.

According to James Kaytennae, Pvt. Jasper Daklugie had completed his army basic training and was enrolled in an advanced infantry course with the hope of attending jump school to earn his paratrooper wings after graduation. James was sure Jasper would see combat and come home safe. Matt hoped so, and wondered aloud to Mary if the world had become a place constantly at war. She refused to believe it.

With the loss of pastureland to the army, the scarcity of grass, and the high price of hay, Matt and Al turned to harvesting cactus, burning off the spines, and mixing it with molasses to feed to their cattle. It was backbreaking work, but it kept the cattle from starving, although it was discouraging to see the weight drop off the animals so quickly on marginal feed. Supplements helped some, but not enough.

When the wells started to dry up and the live streams stopped running, they had to keep the thirsty cows from suffocating by digging the mud out of their nostrils when they rooted for water in the few remaining stagnant pools. Finally forced to move the critters to an overgrazed high pasture with the only reliable water source on both spreads, they were obliged to dig into their dwindling cash reserves to purchase hay. Al predicted if the rains didn't come by fall works, they'd be in debt and selling underweight cattle for next to nothing. Matt didn't doubt it.

On a day that promised rain and brought only lightning from a brief, passing thunderstorm that dropped a sprinkle of spit and sparked a fire in the high pasture, they lost the last of the native grass and all the hay bales they'd hauled for the cattle. Only the frightened critters were saved.

They were licked for the year, and they knew it. They cut their losses and sold most of the mixed herd, keeping only the best mother cows, calves, and the pick of the yearlings. The proceeds barely paid the bills. It meant if the drought didn't break come spring, they'd have to sell off all of the remaining cattle, which would put them flat out of the cow business.

Matt had already taken a hard look at switching over to ponies, and the prospect didn't look bright. Replies to letters he'd written to folks in the rodeo business that he'd sold horseflesh to before the war warned him off. The rodeo business had changed and now just a few trainers of top-flight cutting horses dominated the marketplace. Dismayed, Matt kept the news to himself.

Throughout it all, Mary's consistently high spirits offset Matt's occasional gloominess. The baby growing inside her and the joy of being with Matt on the ranch made her unshakably optimistic. She went about each day full of energy, helping Patrick with the few remaining ponies, fixing delicious meals from recipes she found in library cookbooks, sewing curtains for the living-room windows, and working diligently on a quilt for the baby, learning how to make it from an instructional pamphlet.

Matt worried that without her dear friend Erma's companionship and missing the attraction of town life, Mary would soon tire of the ranch. If she did, it was never mentioned and through back-and-forth visits with Brenda Jennings, Mary soon formed a strong friendship with her. Both were pregnant, exceedingly happy about the prospect of motherhood, and had endless things to talk about. Brenda favored a girl because she believed them to be easier to raise. Mary didn't care one way or the other as long as the baby was normal and healthy.

Mary's mood became a little less cheerful when Brenda left for Hot Springs, where she would remain until her baby's birth. Soon after Brenda's departure, Jim and Millie gave notice. Both had recently turned sixty-five and were qualified for old-age pensions under social security because of Jim's long-ago employment in a slaughterhouse and Millie's early work as a hotel housekeeper.

Although it was left unspoken, Matt figured if Mary hadn't arrived as the new lady of the house, the Sawyers would have gladly pocketed their monthly benefits and stayed on. From a monetary standpoint, Matt wasn't sorry to see them go. It meant Patrick's Rough Rider pension could now be used to help pay ranch bills rather than their salaries. It also meant more work for Matt, but since his labor didn't cost a cent all he'd lose was a little extra sleep. The only serious drawback was that Patrick would lose their company and friendship, which had come to mean a lot to him. But he held his tongue, wished them well when they left, and didn't grumble about it.

With the household down to three, Patrick decided to take over the casita as his domicile. With the house now hers to do with as she wished, Mary immediately started fixing it up. Matt's every free minute was spent helping on one project or another, the most important being turning his old bedroom into a nursery. When they finished all of her projects, the inside of the old place actually looked like a home and not an oversize, somewhat run-down bunkhouse.

To celebrate, Matt suggested they invite Erma for a visit. The notion thrilled Mary. Erma readily agreed and came up by train for a long weekend. The two gals gabbed constantly in the cab of Matt's truck on the drive to the ranch. If he hadn't known better, he'd have thought the two of them hadn't seen each other in years. Each night he went to bed while the two women stayed up late visiting in the living room. They were so compatible and shared so many traits, Matt figured the only thing that separated them from being biological sisters was the accident of birth. Before Erma returned to town, they agreed Mary would stay with her in Las Cruces during her last month of pregnancy and Matt would join them when her due date was near.

It didn't work out that way. Restless and uncomfortable on a late September night, Mary's contractions began. She waited for a time before gently waking Matt to tell him the baby was coming.

"Are you having contractions?" he asked.

Mary nodded. "Mild ones. They started two hours ago."

"How much time do we have?" he asked.

"I'm not sure," Mary replied. "Everything I've read said it can take hours."

"What can I do?"

"Heat a hot water bottle—my back is killing me."

"Shouldn't we leave for town right away?"

She kissed him on the cheek. "There's no rush. Besides, I have to pack."

"Lie down. I'll pack for you."

Mary gazed at him as if he were a rather dull, impatient child. "A hot water bottle would be very nice."

"Okay."

In the kitchen, Matt stoked the cookstove, put water on to heat, woke Patrick up, and sent him hell-bent over the mountain to fetch Al and Brenda, who'd recently returned to the Rocking J with their new baby boy. Matt knew mama cows could take hours to deliver; others could drop a newborn calf lickety-split. He would take no chances. He needed Brenda here to lend a hand.

He returned to find Mary in the living room walking in circles, pressing her fists against the small of her back. Her overnight bag was on the floor next to Patrick's easy chair. "It hurts," she said with a tight smile. "A warm bath would help, I think. Not too hot, though."

He put more water on the stove, laid out fresh towels and a clean nightie in the bathroom, and returned to find Mary squatting on the floor, her head resting on the couch cushion.

"Are you all right?" he asked.

Mary lifted her head. "It's nothing. The contractions are getting stronger and closer together, that's all. This helps relieve the pain."

"We should leave now, dammit," Matt demanded.

Mary shook her head. "It's not that bad, Matthew. The bathwater, please."

It took a while to get two large pots of water boiling. He ran cold water in the bathtub, mixed in the hot water from the stove, and checked to make sure the bathwater was warm before helping Mary ease into the tub. There was a blood-tinged stain on Mary's discarded nightie. He looked at her in alarm.

"Don't worry; it's just from the mucus plug." She sighed and reached for his hand. "Ah, this is nice. Thank you. Just let me soak for a while."

He stayed with her, watching her intently. When she was ready to get out, he helped her to her feet and toweled her dry. Dressed in a fresh nightie, she padded barefoot to the living room and started walking in circles again. She seemed better, no pain showed on her face. He watched from the kitchen door as she went round and round and round.

"The walking helps," she announced as she padded past his desk for the umpteenth time. "But I think I'd like that hot water bottle now. My back is killing me. And a big glass of water, please."

He filled the hot water bottle, got her situated on the couch with it tucked against her back, and gave her a kiss and a big glass of water.

"You're very good to me," she said, after draining the glass.

"I'm not sure I'm any good at all." His hand shaking, Matt put the empty glass on the side table. "Over the years I've helped a whole lot of mother cows deliver their babies, but this is different."

"My water just broke," Mary whispered, embarrassed. A murky stain appeared on the cushion. She gasped in pain.

"What is it?"

"Everything is speeding up." She howled, gasped, howled again, and didn't speak until the pain passed. "I can feel it moving."

He glanced at the desk clock. It had been four hours since she had shaken him awake. Where was Patrick? He should have brought Brenda by now.

He pulled her gently off the couch. "Squat, like you did before," he told her.

Instead she got down on all fours. An intense pain in her lower back whipsawed through her. She could feel pressure in her rectum and with each contraction she could feel the baby descending. She started pushing, taking in huge gulps of air, and pushing again. Each repetition wrung an explosive gasp of pain.

"It's coming." She pushed again. "Get the oilcloth off the kitchen table and take me into the bedroom now."

He got the oilcloth, guided her to the bedroom, spread the oilcloth on top of the blanket, and gently lifted her onto the bed. She gasped, pushed again, and the top of the baby's head appeared.

"I see it!"

"Get it out," Mary grunted loudly, her voice filled with pain.

"Keep pushing!" Matt yelled.

Mary pushed and the baby's shoulders appeared. Matt eased it out. The placenta discharged and Mary collapsed against a pillow, exhausted.

"It's a boy," Matt announced shakily. He cut the umbilical cord with his pocketknife and slapped the baby on the rump. And with Matt's pronouncement, bloody, red-faced Kevin Kerney, perhaps the last child to be born on the old Tularosa, entered the world, took his first breath, and began to cry.

18

Other than the town of Hot Springs renaming itself Truth or Consequences after entering a national promotion by a television quiz show and winning the right to do so, Matt didn't find much to laugh about in 1950. Soon after the historic event, locals shortened the name to T or C, which made it a little less onerous to some but still decidedly oddball at best.

In spite of it being a tough year, Matt was by no means unhappy: he had a beautiful wife who was an incredible partner and wonderful mother, a healthy and astonishing baby boy who brightened Matt's day with amazing smiles and giggles, and a once deplorable excuse of a father who'd transformed himself into a doting and kindhearted grandfather. In part, Matt figured he had little Ginny to thank for it.

Even with everything okay on the home front, little else prompted lightheartedness in Matt. Fighting in Korea cast a gloom over him every time he listened to the radio news or read a newspaper. And the iron curtain that had descended over eastern Europe half convinced him that another world war was imminent.

It depressed him that schoolchildren were being taught to hide under their classroom desks if and when the Soviet nuclear bombs fell. Finally, the drought he'd hoped would ease by year's end only deepened and intensified.

National radio news reporters called it a Texas drought and focused their stories there, but as always nature paid no heed to the state boundary lines drawn on maps. Throughout the year with no summer monsoons, no hoped-for late fall moisture, and only bone-cold, dry winter days, locals began griping that the Texans should have kept the damn drought to themselves.

The income from Matt's military disability and Patrick's Rough Rider pension barely covered the basic necessities, and when the water well at ranch headquarters dried up, Matt borrowed cash to drill a new one, which put him into debt to the bank with no reliable source of earnings on the horizon. Additionally, the cost of feed kept climbing. But he was forced to keep some livestock on the ranch or risk losing his agricultural property tax reduction, which would result in a much larger tax bill that they could ill afford.

1951 came hot, dry, and marked by pale-blue, cloudless skies. The ground was so desiccated it had sunk in spots from a lack of moisture, forming shallow, bowl-shaped indentations in the dusty pastures. Summer rolled in but the rain clouds never did, and the relentless sun fried what little grass was left and baked the ground into hardpan. Hot gusts whipped through the cottonwood windbreak, stripping leaves and sapping moisture from the thirsty trees.

Autumn and winter brought no relief, and Matt began to wonder if young Kevin, now on steady legs and constantly on the move, much to the consternation of his mother, would ever hear the sound of live water running in the stream bed by the corral. If he hadn't sunk a deeper well, the place would have been unlivable. Without water there was nothing of value to the land. The truth of it was driven home by an exodus of small ranchers on the fringes of the Tularosa moving permanently, lock, stock, and barrel, off their land into town.

Al and Brenda at the Rocking J were doing a bit better than that, but not by much. The wells on the west slope of the San Andres foothills still produced steady water, which he'd leased to a large producer who was running a small cow-calf herd across a twenty-five-thousand-acre pasture on the Jornada. Along with Al's occasional job driving a livestock truck, it brought enough in to pay their bills. They were staying put.

With no cattle to work, Matt went to the Roswell livestock auction and picked up three good-looking geldings at rock-bottom prices and trained them with the hopes of eventually selling them as cow ponies. He also took on occasional work as a wrangler on what once was the vast old Bar Cross Ranch that covered a forty-mile stretch of the Rio Grande and enclosed the rugged Fra Cristobal Mountains in the northern Jornada. The size of the outfit and the terrain required cowboys on horseback—not in pickup trucks—to bust cattle out of the thick bosque or haze them out of narrow slot canyons and off precarious rocky shelves. That necessitated running a remuda for the cowboys during both spring and fall works, a job Matt truly enjoyed.

Hoping for a break in 1953, the drought only worsened, and during the summer Matt took a job as an assistant horse trainer for a rich California doctor who dabbled in racing quarter horses at the Ruidoso Downs racetrack in the Sacramento Mountains. Matt liked the job but hated being away from Mary and Kevin, and he returned home vowing never to be gone that long again, although the money he'd earned paid off the bank loan for the water well.

A week after his homecoming, and a week before leaving for his wrangler job at the old Bar Cross, he sat with Mary on the veranda in the still summer night.

"I don't see how we can keep going like this," he said, looking out into the darkness, which suited his sour mood to a T.

Mary reached for his hand. "Except for when you're gone, Kevin and I are quite happy here."

"Sometimes I think I'd sell this place in a minute if the only potential buyer in the universe wasn't the US Army."

Mary laughed. "You'd have to shoot Patrick first."

"Probably," Matt allowed. "But you're here alone too much."

"It does get lonely at times," Mary admitted. "But Brenda and I visit back and forth as often as we can, and Kevin and Dale are as close as brothers. They're both very smart little boys."

"Wildcats when they're together," Matt countered.

"That too."

"I'm missing too much of him growing up when I'm away," Matt grumbled.

Mary squeezed his hand. "Are you complaining?" she chided jokingly.

"Not me. How about we pack some gear and trek to the line cabin in the next day or two? I haven't checked on our high pastures for months."

"I'd love it. So would Kevin."

"Good." The moon crested the Sacramentos, casting light on the dead cottonwood at the edge of the windbreak that his grandfather John Kerney had planted seventy-some years ago. With thick boughs bent low to the ground at a tilt, it had an almost eerie appearance in the moonlight. "I'm going to cut that dead tree down for firewood," he announced.

"Don't you dare," Mary warned. "Kevin loves that tree. He calls it the witch's tree. I often find him there, especially when Dale comes to play."

"Has he fallen out of it yet?"

"Once or twice," Mary admitted. "His only injuries have been a bruised knee and wounded pride. He now has strict orders not to climb above the first branch."

"Then it's unsafe," Matt said, remembering his boyhood friend Jimmy Potter, who'd died in his arms after falling out of a tree in the Las Cruces bosque after climbing it to inspect an eagle's nest. It had been a nightmare that haunted him for years. "I'm cutting it down."

"Can't you just trim it so he can't climb any higher?"

Matt mulled it over. The last thing he wanted was to argue with Mary about a dead cottonwood, or spoil the fun Kevin might have sitting in the branch of the tree with his best pal. "I'll take a look at it tomorrow."

"Thank you," Mary said, pondering if it was time to voice the plan she'd hatched during his absence. She decided to do it. "I don't think it's fair for you to be the only one working to keep everything together. I can contribute too, you know."

"You already do. This place would fall apart without you."

Mary waved off the compliment.

Matt was undeterred. "Did you discover the Spanish gold hidden at Victorio Peak while I was gone?"

For years, until the proving ground closed the range, treasure hunters had scoured the nearby mountain looking for gold and jewels allegedly buried by the Spanish.

"I'm being serious," Mary retorted. "I want to go back to teaching, and we can really use the money."

Matt opened his arms to embrace the vast, moonlit basin. "Teach where? There are no more schools on the Tularosa, because there are no more families with schoolchildren living here to teach."

"I know that," Mary replied tartly, unwilling to let Matt get off dismissing her idea so sarcastically. "I've been thinking that I could teach in T or C, live there during the week, and come home on weekends."

"You'd leave Kevin here with me and Patrick?" Matt asked disbelievingly.

"No, he'd come with me."

"Then I'd never see the two of you at all. Besides, who'd look after Kevin while you're teaching? You can't carry him off to school with you. And even if you could, I can't afford to rent a place for you to live."

"Didn't I hear you say earlier that we couldn't keep going on like this? If the ranch isn't making us a living, why stay? Wouldn't it be easier for all of us to live in town until the drought ends? Then we can come back and pick up where we left off."

"Patrick isn't gonna move to town," Matt predicted emphatically.

"So much the better if he stays here," Mary replied. "He already said he wants to."

Matt looked at Mary suspiciously. "So you two have already talked this over, have you?"

"Don't make it sound like I've been going behind your back," Mary retorted.

"Well, haven't you?"

"And don't get sore at me for trying to help, Matthew," Mary shot back. "Think about what I'm proposing: Patrick lives here, where he wants to be, looks after the place, and takes care of the ponies; Al and Brenda check on him from time to time and bring supplies if he asks, and we'll come out weekends and during school holidays."

"It makes sense," Matt admitted grudgingly. "But I already told you, we can't afford a place in town."

"Yes, we can," Mary countered. "I saved a good deal of money when I was in the navy and most of it has been earning interest in a bank since the day I arrived in Las Cruces. When I've offered in the past to contribute it to the ranch, you've always refused and urged me to save it for Kevin."

"What's wrong with that?"

"Nothing, but now it's time to use that money for all of us. After we come back from the line cabin we're going house hunting in T or C. I want us to buy a place in town, and don't you dare give me any grief about it. Your mother did exactly the same thing for you when you were much younger than Kevin."

Matt sighed. "Okay, I know when I'm outmaneuvered, outgunned, and utterly defeated."

Mary smiled sweetly. "You'll never be defeated. And I bet you'll find getting a job or at least landing some regular work a lot easier once we're settled in town."

"Speaking of work, what makes you so sure the schools will hire you?"

"What?" Mary asked, pretending she didn't understand the question.

"You heard me," Matt prodded.

"Because they already have," she reluctantly admitted.

“Oh, I see. What if I decide not to go along with this plan of yours?”

“I’ll turn down the job and cancel our house hunting, but you won’t have a very happy home life for the next year or two.”

Matt couldn’t help but laugh. In some ways she was a lot like Emma, his strong-willed mother he still dearly missed. “You’re tough as nails when it comes to getting your own way.”

“No, I’m very sweet, sexy, and obliging,” Mary corrected. She got up, settled down on Matt’s lap, and kissed him long and deep to make her point. “Now take me to bed.”

Matt tickled her all the way to the bedroom.

* * *

The next morning in the barn after breakfast, Matt told Patrick he was going along with Mary’s plan to move the family to T or C during the school year.

“It’s best for Mary and Kevin,” he added.

“You’re not selling the ranch to the army?” Patrick asked, relief showing on his face.

“Why would I do that?”

“I was scared you might, that’s all. Just to be done with it and get on with your life. This place is about to blow away.”

Matt shook his head. “That’s not gonna happen. This is more than just a place to live; it’s our history.”

Patrick looked out the barn doors at the family cemetery on the hillside above the ranch house. “Except for memories and the folks we have buried here, right now it’s not worth a bucket of spit to anyone but the government.”

“We’re not selling and you’ll be holding down the fort.” Matt hung his pitchfork on a peg. "Will you be all right here on your own?"

Patrick smiled. "Don't you worry about me. When are you moving?"

"Before Mary's job teaching school starts." Matt grabbed a cross-cut saw. "Help me prune back that dead cottonwood so Mary stays happy and Kevin can keep playing on it with his pard Dale."

Patrick pulled on his work gloves. "It's about time you figured out that your wife ramrods this outfit."

* * *

They rode ponies to the cabin, Kevin with Matt gripping the saddle horn on Maverick, Mary astride Peanut, and with enough grub and water for an overnight stay stuffed into the saddlebags. The die-off of the last of the tall pines that once had sheltered the cabin was a sad sight to see, the branches bare of all but a few needles, the cones, picked over by jays, lying broken apart and scattered in the duff.

Matt figured the drought would soon kill all the remaining old-growth evergreens and the mountains would be bare of everything except scrub. The pretty high-country dell where Cal Doran had built the cabin now teetered on the edge of forever losing all its charm under a harsh sun with no comforting shade. He'd return in the cool of autumn and harvest the wood before it lost all its pitch.

Matt's last visit to the cabin had been in early spring. Since the day it was built, the cabin had never been locked, and upon arrival he spotted evidence of recent use, including fairly fresh tire tracks, the cookstove ash box almost overflowing, and most of the stacked firewood used up and not replaced.

Even in earlier times before the ranch was surrounded by federal land, such findings would have been worrisome and unexpected. Folks who knew of the cabin, mostly neighboring ranchers, cowboys, or an occasional hunter, were free to make use of it; however, common courtesy dictated leaving it the way it had been found. But now with travel on the proving ground prohibited, Matt figured only army types who lacked good manners had ready access to the cabin.

That bothered him. If it was the army, why were they trespassing on the 7-Bar-K? What were they up to?

Resolved not to let his discoveries spoil the day, Matt had said nothing to Mary, and after cleaning out the stove and laying a new fire, he took Kevin to the corral and let him ride Peanut bareback as he led the pony at a walk.

Approaching his third birthday, Kevin sat relaxed on the pony, his little hands gripping Peanut's mane, a smile plastered on his face. Soon he'd be riding all on his own under watchful eyes. Matt needed to fetch the old child's saddle from the tack room and get to work restoring it.

"We need to get you a pony," Matt said.

Kevin nodded enthusiastically. "I know. Mom told me."

"She did?"

"Yes, and I want a gray one."

"It has to be gray?"

"Un-huh, and little enough for me because I'm still small."

"Is that what your mother said?"

Kevin nodded again, his blue eyes fixed on Matt's face. "Uh-huh."

"Well, I guess I've got my marching orders."

"What's a marching order?" Kevin asked seriously.

"A marching order is doing what your ma says, such as getting you a pony," Matt replied as he gently pulled Kevin off Peanut.

"When?" Kevin asked, his eyes bright with excitement.

"Maybe for Christmas," Matt replied, hoping to have some extra money by then.

Kevin's face lit up. "I have to tell Mom."

He dashed under the corral fence and raced to the cabin. When Matt arrived a jittery Kevin stood inside watching Mary chase an infuriated bull snake out the front door with a broom.

"Was that a bad snake?" Kevin worriedly asked Matt.

"Nope, a good snake," Matt answered. "It just wasn't invited for dinner. Later I'll draw you a picture of a bad snake so you can tell the difference."

"Okay." Kevin turned to his mom. "Can I go outside?"

Mary nodded. "Stay close."

Kevin scooted out the open door and Mary set aside her broom and gave Matt a kiss. "That's for promising Kevin a pony at Christmas."

"We should have enough money by then." Matt took out the holstered pistol he'd packed in his saddlebag and put it on the high shelf with the canned goods.

"What's that for?" Mary asked.

"You never know. Maybe some two-legged uninvited visitors will show up. Wave it at anyone suspicious who comes by while I'm gone. I'm going to take a quick look at the lower pasture. I'll be back in an hour."

Mary called Kevin into the house and Matt rode out, following the tire tracks that led down the cattle trail to the old Tularosa state road. Originally, he'd intended to go upcountry first and be gone for three or more hours, but the notion of unwanted visitors troubled him.

In ten minutes of easy riding he was at the pasture gate that had been deliberately knocked off its pins and moved aside. Littered around were a number of shot-up tin cans used for target practice, along with spent handgun and rifle shell casings. There were tire tracks from two different vehicles; one set stopped at the busted gate, the other set continued on to the cabin, maybe five or six times over a period of months from what Matt could see.

Who would want to be up here that often? If it was a stranger unfamiliar with the land, how would he know about the cabin in the first place?

He rode on a bit farther and found the bones of a deer scattered near the trail. A closer look proved it had been a young buck killed and field dressed for meat by someone who knew what he was doing, maybe a soldier but probably not.

He returned to the gate, flipped Maverick's reins over the top strand of barbwire fencing to keep him from straying, and got to work rehanging the gate using baling wire and nails to jerry-rig it.

He'd about finished when he heard the sound of a fast approaching vehicle. He turned to see an older, bearded man in a military surplus jeep brake to a stop and reach for a rifle resting on the passenger seat. The back of the jeep was filled with supplies.

"What are you doing there?" the man asked in a high-pitched voice, his rifle pointed directly at Matt's chest.

Maverick was twenty feet away with Matt's rifle in the saddle scabbard. "Fixing the gate."

"You're trespassing," the man said as he got out of the jeep, his gaze jumping from Matt to Maverick and back. "Don't try anything."

Matt looked the man over. He was maybe fifty or a bit older, thin but fit-looking with a sweaty face, narrow piercing eyes, and an odd head twitch that with all things combined made Matt uneasy.

"Raise your hands," the man said, waving his rifle. "Go on, get 'em up."

Matt did as ordered, thinking it best to say nothing.

"Who are you?" the man demanded, taking a step closer. "Tell me and don't you lie."

"My name is Matt. Who are you?"

"None of your business. How come you wear an eye patch? You a pirate or something?"

Matt shook his head.

"A thief?"

Matt shook his head again.

"You're a thief." The man paused and spat. "Where did you put it?"

"Put what?"

The man sneered. "The gold."

"I don't know what you're talking about."

The man pulled the rifle to his cheek and pointed it at Matt's head. If he twitched too hard Matt was dead. "I'll kill you for lying. Is it safe?"

"I don't have any gold," Matt said calmly, lowering his hands. "But I've got food on the stove at the cabin. Come on up, we can share a meal."

The man's eyes widened. "Nobody supposed to be here but me. Did Doc show you the cave before Charley Boswell killed him? Or maybe some of those army boys poking around from the proving ground found the passage and you killed them. Are you working with Babe? Have you got Doc's maps Babe says she lost?"

"I don't know any of those people," Matt answered. But it finally clicked that this was one of those treasure hunters who'd been snooping around Victorio Mountain and other places searching for Spanish gold.

The man glared at Matt as he brought the rifle away from his cheek. "Yes you do. You carried that gold out one bar at a time and then blocked the passage. Sixteen thousand of them. Where you got it hid? Tell me now or you die."

Convinced he was facing a loco treasure hunter, Matt remained silent, trying to figure a way to get the man to drop his rifle.

"What did you say?" the man asked with a sneer.

Matt shook his head. "Nothing. I didn't say anything."

The man shook his head in disbelief, his sneer turning into a crazy smirk. "Yes, you did, I heard you talking to yourself and all."

Matt decided he'd better play along. "Okay, you're right, please don't shoot me. I don't have the gold but I have the maps."

"I knew it," the man crowed gleefully, showing broken teeth, stomping his foot. "Where are they?"

"I'll take you to them."

The man waved the rifle at the jeep and took a step back. "Get in."

"The jeep can't go there," Matt replied, raising his chin in the direction of a nearby ridgeline with a switchback trail leading to the top. "I have the maps at my camp, just a short horseback ride away."

"Stay away from that horse and long gun," the man warned. "We'll walk. You go first."

Matt started out with the man three paces behind. Halfway up the trail it turned rock-strewn, eroded, and difficult, making it necessary to concentrate on climbing. Matt heard rocks tumbling down the trail behind him and turned to see the man looking at his footing, the rifle lowered. Quickly, Matt picked up a large rock, spun around, and hit him squarely in the temple. He dropped off the side of the trail and slammed headfirst into a boulder.

Matt stepped over and found him dead with a broken neck. The wallet in his pocket contained a driver's license in the name of Dalton Moore. He put it back and stood over the body for a moment, working out in his mind what to do before deciding to leave everything just as it was. He didn't want to tell Mary he'd just killed a man, or have his son see it, even though it had been done in self-defense.

And he sure wasn't going to admit anything to Patrick. Best to say he'd found the abandoned jeep at the gate and the body of the dead man on the switchback. It would be up to everybody to decide to take his word for it or not.

He was angry at Dalton Moore for putting him in the situation and not at all happy having to pad the truth, but it was the best and quickest way out of what otherwise could become a complicated predicament.

At the cabin, he called Mary outside away from Kevin, who was playing with some toy horses and a cast-iron wagon, and told her in low tones that he'd found a dead body, trying hard to believe it himself.

"That's terrible," Mary said after hearing him out. "We have to report it to the sheriff immediately."

"We can call him from Engle on our way to town tomorrow," Matt suggested.

"We can't just leave him out here."

"Of course you're right. I'll go back and cover the body with a tarp and rocks to protect it."

"We should go home right away," Mary said.

The aroma of dinner simmering on the cookstove did nothing for his appetite, which had been replaced by a tight knot in his stomach. "After I get back, we'll head home."

"Good. I'll have everything ready."

* * *

Five days later, the following article appeared in the Las Cruces newspaper:

TREASURE HUNTER FOUND DEAD

Dalton Moore, age 58, a local treasure hunter known to many in law enforcement for his repeated illegal attempts to find Spanish gold on White Sands Proving Ground, was discovered dead from an accidental fall on the remote 7-Bar-K Ranch by rancher Matthew Kerney.

Sierra County Sheriff Max Story said evidence showed Moore had been trespassing on the ranch and using a remote line cabin on the property for several months as a hideaway while searching for treasure around Victorio Mountain, a place rumored to contain a large hoard of precious metal and jewels.

At the time of his death, Moore, who had recently been hospitalized for mental problems, was wanted on an outstanding federal warrant for violating a court order prohibiting him from trespassing on White Sands Proving Ground. According to Sheriff Story, no foul play is suspected and the case has been closed. When contacted, Matthew Kerney referred all questions to Sheriff Story.

On the same day, the headline story on the front page reported accusations by high-ranking government officials that North Korea was still holding American POWs, violating the armistice agreement signed at Panmunjom a month earlier on July 27, 1953.

19

After the final bell on the last day of school, Mary Kerney and her young son, Kevin, now approaching seven, drove home to the T or C cottage she'd bought with her navy savings nearly four years earlier. Built before the start of the World War II, it sat on a double lot with a pleasant view of the nearby Rio Grande and the bleak yet striking Caballo Mountains that notched the sky to the east. Although close to downtown, the cottage was part of a quiet neighborhood away from the busy US highway that cut through the heart of town and the motels and bathhouses along the Rio Grande riverbank that catered to folks seeking medicinal relief at the numerous mineral hot springs that bubbled to the surface.

The cottage had a pitched roof, a covered front porch wide and deep enough for several chairs, two bedrooms, a bathroom, a living room, and a kitchen with enough space for a small dining table. It had all the modern conveniences: electricity, indoor plumbing, hot and cold running water, an electric range, a refrigerator, and—wonder of wonders—a telephone, which still remained only a remote, very unlikely possibility back at the ranch.

Because it was frame-built and not adobe, even with the insulation Matt had added to the attic it still got hot as the blazes in the summer. By the end of the school year Mary eagerly looked forward to a return to the 7-Bar-K and the relative coolness of the double adobe ranch house with its shady veranda.

Matt was away until Sunday working on a mesquite eradication project at the vast Armendaris Ranch north of T or C. With the drought persisting into a seventh year, invasive shrubs were taking over the desert grasslands at an alarming rate. Three years earlier, the Ag Department at the college in Las Cruces had recruited Matt to work with area ranchers to help improve deteriorating range conditions. Gus Merton had recommended him for the job and on the strength of his influential support, along with Matt's degree from the college, his service in the war, and his excellent reputation as a rancher, he got the position. It was a plum job that he took to with enthusiasm and quickly came to love. Not only did it give him flexibility to set his own schedule, it paid well enough to keep the 7-Bar-K going without needing to rely on Mary's salary or Patrick's pension.

Luckily, Mary also had a job she loved. She taught third grade at the T or C elementary school and enjoyed helping her sometimes enthusiastic, sometimes lackadaisical students explore the world through books and reading. Most every day they were a delight to be around—even the rowdiest and the neediest ones.

What she didn't save from her salary went into paying the monthly bills and improving the cottage with new windows, a new roof, painting it inside and out, planting more shade trees, and building a corral and horse barn to stable Kevin's pony, a gray gelding he'd named Two-Bits because of a quarter-size black spot on its left haunch.

A good deal of the renovations had been funded by an unexpected check from her brother, Tom, who upon their father's death had returned from his California home to settle the estate. Her share minus Tom's expenses was probably about a tenth of what she was due, but after getting into an initial snit about it she decided she really didn't care and was happy to put the inheritance to good use.

Soon after buying the cottage, she'd made a number of weekend road trips to Las Cruces, haunting the secondhand furniture stores and spending time with Erma while Matt looked after Kevin at home. What she couldn't buy used she bought new in T or C, including the kitchen appliances and a nice bedroom set for Kevin's room.

Little by little over time, she made the cottage comfortable and pleasing to the eye. She painted furniture, built a bookcase for the living room, made curtains for the windows, refinished the wood floors, and planted flowerbeds in front of the porch. It was a perfectly agreeable home in a small town, which, despite the laughable notoriety of being named for a TV quiz show, and civic-minded attempts to transform it into something grander, remained an ordinary, provincial, often wind-blown, dusty cowboy town. Mary figured the name would forever remain a joke to most New Mexicans as well as the many curious tourists who thought it amusing that a town would do such a silly thing.

She was frequently alone with Kevin during the week while Matt was away at his job. She kept busy after school with house projects, grading papers, preparing her teaching lessons, helping Kevin with his school work, and enjoying her son's company. He was a bright child, easy to be with, and surprisingly mature as well as tall for his age. He towered over his classmates and was at least a year ahead academically. Mary wasn't quite ready to have him skip a grade, although she feared he'd lose interest in school if he didn't do so in the next year or two.

Occasionally on the few weekends when the family didn't go to the ranch and Matt was home at the cottage, she entertained with small impromptu parties, inviting colleagues from her school, a neighboring couple she'd come to like, or the parents of Kevin's school friends. All in all, the people of T or C were mostly good, hardworking folks and Mary got along with them just fine.

Sometimes Patrick came for a visit and would bunk overnight on the living-room couch after keeping Kevin up late telling him stories and tall tales about the old days on the Tularosa. Erma came up from Las Cruces very rarely, and only after Mary was doggedly persistent with repeated invitations. They were still as close as sisters when they got together, but her career as an artist had begun to flourish and she'd taken on a part-time position at the college teaching two painting classes each semester.

Brenda Jennings occasionally stayed over during her trips to town and brought Dale along to play with Kevin, much to his delight. With Mary's help, Brenda was homeschooling Dale, but the two women had started seriously talking about the possibility of Dale living in town with Mary and Kevin starting in September so he could attend public school. The best of friends, the boys were hounding their mothers relentlessly in favor of the idea.

Mary was content with her life, but there were moments when she yearned for a new adventure, or at the very least a return visit to San Francisco. She longed to feel the moist, humid sea air against her face, see the grand, tall buildings and lovely Victorian houses, ride the cable cars, visit the museums, and enjoy the excitement of being in a cosmopolitan city once more. She fantasized about a day of shopping at the Emporium on Market Street, capped by dinner and drinks with Matt at a restaurant in Chinatown, or dancing with him late into the night at one of the smoky jazz nightclubs.

Arriving home, she parked the car in the driveway. Kevin leaped out in a hurry to tend to Two-Bits, who waited patiently in the corral at the back of the property, his head draped over the gate, his tail happily flapping. Inside the open horse-barn door, Matt's pony, Maverick, lounged in the shade, rubbing his shoulder against the doorjamb.

Matt had left Maverick behind, choosing to rest his pony and ride Armendaris Ranch horses during his stay there. Next to the corral he'd also parked the two-axle, two-horse trailer he'd bought in an auto salvage yard and rebuilt.

That week, every night after dinner in the cool of the evening, Mary and Kevin had gone riding along the riverbank, loping the ponies north out of town toward Elephant Butte Reservoir, where folks came from all over the state to swim, fish, and boat on the water. It had been grand fun, topped off with a cold soda pop bought at the service station along the road to the reservoir.

She watched Kevin climb the corral gate. Two-Bits greeted him with a shake of his head as Kevin scratched his ear and gave him the apple he'd saved from his lunch box. Like his father, he found caring for ponies a pure pleasure and not a chore at all. And like his father, he had a connection with ponies that seemed far from ordinary.

In the house, Mary kicked off her shoes, changed into blue jeans and a short-sleeved top, went to the kitchen, and made Kevin a snack. She was impatient for Matt to come home on Sunday, not just because they'd leave soon for the ranch but because she was feeling especially fertile and the timing was right.

For two years, they'd been trying to get pregnant again, without success. Supposedly nothing stood in their way; Kevin was clear proof of it. But all the examinations, consultations, and tests with specialists in Albuquerque had been fruitless. The doctors were mystified and stymied, but Mary was not quite ready to give up. A little girl had been floating through her dreams for some time.

She planned to start her summer at the ranch with a little seduction and had splurged on some sexy undergarments to set the mood.

* * *

The summer at the ranch started with Dale coming to spend the week with Kevin. When the boys weren't helping Matt with the ponies, a chore they both enjoyed, or out riding, they could be found at the camp they'd thrown up behind the barn, or dangling in the Witch's Tree with Matt's binoculars scanning the basin for signs of army activity. After supper, they sat with Patrick in the living room, listening to overseas shortwave radio broadcasts and making lists of the countries they could identify. At nightfall, Mary would order them off to bed and they'd scoot out the door to their camp with their flashlights to read under the stars in their bedrolls. Before turning in, she'd slip quietly to their camp to check on them and find them fast asleep.

Mary loved to watch the two young boys together. They were great friends, and seemed to have endless energy matched by prodigious appetites. She prepared three hearty meals a day and they packed the food away like starving stevedores. According to Dale, who was always first to clean his plate and hold it out for seconds, she was a really, really good cook.

On the third night of Dale's visit, a pelting rainstorm brought

Mary, Matt, and Patrick to the veranda in time to see Kevin and Dale running through a sheet of rain to the house as thunder boomed and lightning cracked across the sky. Dried off and in fresh clothes, Mary let them stay up until the last raindrop had fallen and the roar of floodwater in the pasture stream bed had eased to a trickle. They slept on the veranda on an old mattress covered in blankets.

In the morning, she found them mud-splattered, gleefully wading in the stream bed. She ordered them into the stock tank, clothes and all, and told them they'd get no breakfast until they presented themselves at the kitchen table washed and scrubbed for her inspection. She made them clean their fingernails twice before letting them take their seats.

It rained lightly on and off during the day. The boys moved their camp into the barn tack room, helped Matt and Patrick shovel mud out of the corral, and rode with Matt in the truck to inspect the ranch road. They returned an hour later, with muddy boots and dirty clothes, to report that it was washed out in spots but passable. She made them clean up and change again.

In between her cooking chores, she did the laundry with the veranda and kitchen doors wide-open to let a lovely, cool, moist breeze course through the house. Under a low cloud–covered sky, she hung out the wash just as the rain intensified. She hurried with her empty laundry basket to the veranda, where Matt, Patrick, and the boys were watching distant, horizontal lightning whip-crack above the silvery expanse of dunes at White Sands. Under the *rat-tat-tat* sound of rain on the veranda roof, everyone was smiling, but not a word was said about the drought lifting for fear of jinxing it.

The rain subsided until evening when a good, soaking shower settled over the ranch that lasted deep into the night. By morning the sky had cleared and a golden sunrise made the wet land glisten. It stayed dry and sunny all that day and the next, quashing Mary's hopes for continued showers. She knew better than to wish for days and days of constant moisture on the Tularosa. The basin almost always got its precipitation in spurts—sometimes drizzles, sometimes downpours. It could be weeks or months before the next storm arrived.

On Dale's last evening on the ranch, the sky turned dark and angry, a harsh wind whistled through the cottonwood trees, and thunder rolled behind massive clouds that towered above the Sacramento Mountains. The spectacle brought everyone out to the veranda, the boys perched on the top step, Patrick settled in his chair, Mary and Matt at the railing.

When the first spray of wind-driven rain splashed against Mary's face, she turned to Matt and said, "I think the drought has broken."

Matt grinned like a kid at Christmas as the storm unleashed a lashing downpour. "Now that the grass will start coming back, I'm going to buy us some cows."

20

On the afternoon of August 6, 1957, Matt, Mary, Kevin, and Patrick were at the T or C cottage preparing to leave for the ranch after spending the previous day shopping for new school clothes for Kevin, taking Patrick to see the doctor, and buying supplies for the ranch. The telephone rang just as they were at the back door. Matt answered to find an agitated Charlie Hopkinson on the line. He'd just returned from a court appearance in Albuquerque, where a district judge, at the request of the army, had ordered US Marshals to evict John Prather, Charlie's client, from his ranch on the Tularosa.

"Seems like nothing can or will stop them," Hopkinson added angrily. "Old John's ranch headquarters is but a mile and a half inside the government's boundary and they refused to budge an inch on the appeal to exempt it from condemnation. The judge had no choice but to rule for the government. But John isn't budging either; he vows to stay put. The marshals are going to be there in the morning with an eviction order. Word is that reporters from all over the country are coming to cover the standoff. I thought you'd want to know."

"Much obliged," Matt replied.

After apologizing for being abrupt as he had other folks to alert, Hopkinson hung up. Patrick nearly had a fit when Matt told him what had happened. Like Patrick, John was one of the last of the old-timers on the basin—a man who'd come to the Tularosa from Texas as a young child with his family in 1883, not long after Patrick's father had arrived.

"It's indecent," he sputtered, too upset to think of a better word. "It ain't right. I'm going over there to stand by him when the marshals show up."

"Is that wise?" Mary asked, concerned Patrick's agitation might kill him. He was eighty-two and had high blood pressure.

Patrick's face turned bright red. "Don't try to mollycoddle me. I'm going over to John Prather's and that's all there is to it. He'd do the same for us."

"Do what you think is best," Mary said, giving Matt a questioning look.

"Patrick's right," Matt said grimly. "Now that the army has won against Prather, I guarantee they'll come after us next. It's time to start digging in our heels."

The thought of losing the 7-Bar-K made Mary heartsick. "Kevin and I will stay here."

"No, Kevin goes with us," Matt countered. "I want him to learn firsthand that right and wrong isn't always about what the law or some judge says it is."

"That's the truth of it," Patrick snapped in agreement.

"He's a child." Mary looked at the two Kerney men and protectively wrapped her arm around Kevin's shoulder. "He could get hurt."

"This is a battle of wills, not a shooting war," Matt said. "You head on home to the ranch."

"I'll be fine, Mom," Kevin piped up, excitement flashing in his eyes. "I want to go."

Mary looked at the three Kerney men, all eager to join the fray. Although she'd never met John Prather, she'd read about him in the newspapers. Last year, after a judge in Albuquerque had ruled against him in condemnation proceedings, he'd become something of a local hero when he told reporters he wasn't about to move and anyone who tried to force him off his ranch risked life and limb.

The story made headlines across the country and several national papers ran profiles about him, detailing how for more than half a century he'd built his spread on remote rangeland south of the Sacramentos, scooping out tanks to catch rainwater, sinking a thousand-foot well, building fences, roads, and a house made of rock, and running cows on eight sections of deeded land and twenty thousand acres of leased government land.

All along, while other ranchers had caved in to the army's demands and sold or been forced out, only Prather on the south end of the Tularosa and Matt and Al on the north had stood pat. Since the day she'd married Matt and moved to the 7-Bar-K she'd known the ranch one day might get swallowed up by the army, but it hadn't preyed on her mind. The grueling six-year drought had been at the forefront of the family's concern.

"I'm going with you," she said firmly, unwilling to be so easily brushed aside.

Matt frowned and then smiled. "I wouldn't dare try to stop you. We'd better get going. It's a far piece and time's a-wasting."

"Throw some bedrolls in the back of the truck," Mary ordered. "I'll pack some clothes, make some snacks, and fill the canteens with water."

Within ten minutes, the four Kerneys were squeezed tightly in the cab of Matt's truck, with Kevin on Mary's lap, two rifles in the rear window gun rack, and bedrolls, clothes, and a small cooler filled with water and snacks in the truck bed, rolling south above the speed limit on their way to the Prather Ranch.

* * *

Close to the desert grasslands of Otero Mesa, nudged next to the southern tip of the Sacramentos, the Prather Ranch sat hard against the Fort Bliss McGregor Range bordering the White Sands Proving Ground. At dusk, after an afternoon of hard driving under the furnace of an August sun with only a quick stop for a meal at a small diner in the ramshackle village of Organ at the foot of the San Augustin Pass, the Kerneys arrived, hot, sweaty, and achy. Pickup trucks haphazardly parked in front of the solidly built rock ranch house announced that folks had already begun to gather. Several vehicles with Texas plates had press placards on the dashboards.

John Prather met them at the front door with a smile, a handshake, and a friendly howdy. A soft-spoken man, he was lean and deeply tanned. He wore thick eyeglasses and a sweat-stained cowboy hat pulled down low to the tip of his large ears, and appeared unperturbed by his predicament.

"You've come a far piece," he said as he gave a nod of greeting to Mary and Kevin.

"We've got to stand together," Patrick announced. "You and me are the last of the old-timers."

"We're almost extinct, I reckon," Prather chuckled.

"Not yet."

"Not yet by a long shot." Prather pointed at a tight-knit group of four sunburned men in white dress shirts and wrinkled pleated pants smoking cigarettes at the corner of the house. "Those newspaper boys over there will want to ask you questions and take your pictures. Shoo them off if it's a bother. They've already posed me holding my rifle. I think they'd be happy if I shot a US Marshal or two when they show up to evict me come morning."

"Will you?" Mary asked.

"I don't want to, that's for certain. Come on inside. There's coffee and grub if you're hungry. There's folks here you know that'll be glad to see you. More are coming around sunup. Things should stay quiet until then."

Before Prather could usher them inside, the press boys descended, several with cameras, all with notebooks in hand. Mary wanted no part of it. Dragging Kevin along she wound her way through a dozen people in the living room, saying hello to those she knew, and went to the kitchen to see if anything needed doing. Several ladies she didn't know were chatting at a table stacked with clean plates, glassware, and utensils. Two more were at the kitchen washbasin drying dishes. On the cookstove pots of beans and chili simmered. She chatted with the women for a short while, turned to look for Kevin, and found him gone. Outside, one of the newspapermen with a camera was snapping photographs of Kevin sitting against the side of the house clutching Matt's rifle. A camera flashbulb popped just before Mary yanked the rifle out of Kevin's hand and pulled him to his feet.

The reporter smiled at Mary's hostile look, told her it was a great human-interest photo, and gave her his card in case she wanted to write and have him send her a copy as a keepsake.

She tore the card up, put the rifle back in the truck, and looked Kevin square in the eyes. "Did you take your dad's rifle without asking his permission?"

"Yes, ma'am," Kevin admitted, staring down at his boots. "The man said it would be okay."

"Do you think it's smart to do what strangers ask?"

"No, ma'am, I guess not."

"What have you learned?"

"Don't act dumb," Kevin proposed, almost as a question.

"That's right." She tapped a finger against his temple. "Always use your noggin."

"Yes, ma'am, I will."

Mary gave him a reassuring smile and a quick hug. "Okay, you, get in the back of the truck, pull off your boots, climb into your bedroll, and go to sleep. Tomorrow's going to be a big day."

The men gathered at the corral, listening for news on a car radio and talking well into the night. Mary fell asleep on the truck bench seat. In the morning at first light, she woke up to the blaring sound of a car horn. She'd been covered with a blanket and her head rested on a pillow of clean clothes from the small suitcase she'd packed in T or C. Only someone as sweet as Matt would have thought to tuck her in like that.

Out the rear window she saw him asleep in the bed of the truck, snuggled next to Kevin. Patrick was nowhere to be seen. Down the dusty ranch road came a small caravan of vehicles, mostly pickup trucks. Reinforcements had arrived.

She rubbed the sleep from her eyes and went to help in the kitchen. Best to get folks fed before the marshals appeared and the showdown started.

21

There were more than twenty people at John Prather's ranch when three deputy US Marshals showed up later in the morning. They caught up with John just as he and a few of the visiting menfolk had returned from working his cattle in a nearby pasture.

"We're here to evict you, John Prather," Deputy US Marshal Dave Flack announced as Prather dismounted his pony. "I've got a court order from a judge." Uncomfortable with his assignment, Flack waved the paper in his hand above his head as though it were a shining beacon of jurisdictional might. He nervously eyed the folks clustered in front of the ranch house. Several of the men were toting rifles. Two others packed pistols on their hips. There were five women and a young kid no more than seven or eight standing next to an old-timer clutching a rifle in both hands. Four city slickers—most likely newsmen—hovered nearby.

Prather turned his pony loose, adjusted his thick eyeglasses, peered at Flack and his two sidekicks, pulled his sheath knife, and waved it at the deputies. "The hell with your piece of paper. Come and get me."

Flack put his hand on the butt of his holstered pistol. "No need for that." His two partners followed suit.

"Are you gonna shoot me for being on my own property?" John Prather asked.

"Let's just stay calm," Flack replied, decidedly unsettled. "The judge says you've got to go."

Leg weary, Prather hunkered down on his haunches. "I'm not moving an inch." He deliberately pointed his knife at each of the lawmen, one, two, three. "You get off my ranch. You're trespassing."

"You know we've got to do this, Mr. Prather," Flack countered, trying not to plead. Evicting the old man from the place he'd built up from scratch for over a half century was a miserable thing to do.

Prather spit in the dirt. "Show some smarts, young fella, and git off my land before I forget my manners."

"I can't do that."

"Then let me get my long gun from the house and we'll settle matters here and now," Prather proposed.

"I can't do that either." A good twenty-five feet separated Flack from John Prather. He took two steps closer and heard the sound of rifle rounds chambered in long guns.

"Don't come any nearer," Prather warned as he rose up from his crouch.

"I can wing him from here," a voice called out from the front of the house. Flashbulbs popped and camera shutters clicked.

Flack swung his attention to the old-timer standing next to the young boy. The man held a bead on him with a rifle. Reporters scribbled notes.

"What's your name, Marshal?" one of the reporters called out. "Who are those officers with you?"

"No gunplay!" Flack ordered his two companions, who were about to clear leather. The deputies froze.

"Lower the rifle, Pat," John Prather said. "We aren't killing anyone just yet."

"I've shot better men," Patrick Kerney growled. "And it would give me great pleasure."

From the look on the old man's face, Flack didn't doubt it.

"Lower the gun," Prather repeated evenly.

Grumbling, the old man did as he was told. One of the women, the prettiest of the bunch, rushed up to him, gave him a dirty look, and yanked the young boy into the house. Chagrined, the old man glanced away.

Flack smiled in relief and paused to regain his composure. "Let's start over, John."

Prather looked skyward. It was getting on to eleven o'clock and the sun was blazing hot. "Go right ahead and start," he said genially.

"I'd rather not arrest you." Flack pulled out a handkerchief and wiped his sweaty face. "Come to town with me, cash the check the government sent you, and live a comfortable life."

"What happens to my livestock? Who's gonna water my garden and orchard? What if thieves come and steal everything I own? Are you gonna protect my spread while I'm gone to town living comfortable like you put it?"

Flack shook his head. "You're acting muleheaded about this."

Prather smiled broadly. "Mules are some of my favorite critters, so I appreciate the compliment. But you're the one being disagreeable and foolhardy. Can't you tell when a man is standing his ground? I told the judge I wasn't moving, so either come after me with your leg irons and figure to get sliced doing it, or get gone."

He waved his knife again for emphasis.

"We have a job to do," Flack replied, realizing he was near the divide that separated seeking sympathy from outright begging.

"Find another line of work," Prather suggested, punctuating the comment with a snort and a spit.

"It's either us or the army."

"Go on and get those army boys," Prather challenged.

"Woo-hoo!" yelled one of the younger men in the crowd, a tough-looking cowboy. "You tell them, Uncle John. Bring on the army!"

Flack took a deep breath. "Let's just cool down," he said, facing the cowboy, his voice cracking from the dryness. He longed for a swig from the water jug on the backseat of his government vehicle.

The cowboy shot a nasty look in reply but stayed quiet.

Flack switched his attention back to Prather. "How about you ask your friends to look after the ranch until we can get things settled in town?"

"No need for any of that malarkey." Prather nodded at the dust cloud on the ranch road. "Company's coming. Otherwise I'd offer you a cup of coffee and send you on your way. If it's the army, maybe we'll be able to settle things right now."

Dave Flack looked at the crowd in front of Prather's rock house. They were as restless as a bunch of schoolkids waiting for playground bullies to start fighting. He prayed it was the army. Instead a small squad of reporters and cameramen arrived, piled out of three cars, and surrounded John Prather, filming and firing questions at him all at once. There was a television news reporter from Los Angeles and another one from Albuquerque. A newspaperman from Chicago and a radio newscaster from Washington, DC, had flown in to cover the story.

Deputy US Marshal Dave Flack turned to his two fellow officers and ordered a retreat, but before they could get to their vehicle, a reporter from the original group that had been watching since the moment they'd arrived waylaid them.

"What are you going to do now, Deputy?" Jack Flynn from the El Paso *Sun Times* asked Flack. Flynn had been dogging the Prather case since the beginning and had become a real pain in the ass.

"No comment," Flack replied.

"So my headline will read, 'Rancher Stands Off Three US Marshals.'"

"Write anything you want," Flack grumbled, trying unsuccessfully to step around the man. "Just don't forget to mention that nobody got hurt."

"John Prather stands to lose everything he's worked for these last fifty years. That's pretty harmful, wouldn't you say?"

"You know what I mean."

"So why didn't you arrest him?" Flynn demanded.

"And start a riot?" Flack shot back.

Flynn smiled and shook his head. "That would have been newsworthy."

"You're an asshole, Flynn."

Flynn's smile broadened. "Have you nothing else to add, Deputy?"

Flack pushed past Flynn, ordered his men into the vehicle, got behind the wheel, and drove away.

"What do we do now, Dave?" Deputy US Marshal Mike Saiz asked from the backseat. He was a rookie with less than a year on the job.

"Hand me the water jug," Flack replied.

Jug in hand, Flack took a long swig. "To answer your question, we're gonna kick this puppy up the chain of command and wait to get our butts chewed."

There was a long silence.

"That's okay by me," Deputy US Marshal Trinidad Romero said from the passenger seat. "I didn't sign on to this job ten years ago to kick an old man off his land, no matter what the courts decide."

"Amen," Dave Flack replied. "But try to keep that opinion to yourself."

In the village of Orogrande on the road to El Paso, Flack called his boss, Richard Bradford, the US Marshal for the state of New Mexico, and reported his failure to serve the writ and remove John Prather from his ranch.

"Just as well," Bradford replied wearily. "This has turned into a three-ring circus. Newspapers and TV stations from all over the country have been calling my office. Let the army take the heat. They're on their way from Fort Bliss as we speak. Go back to the Prather ranch and keep an eye on things, but take no action, understood?"

"You got it, boss," Flack said, relief flooding his voice. He hung up and turned to Mike and Trinidad. "We're in the clear with Bradford. I'm hungry, let's get something to eat."

* * *

Once a thriving mining community, Orogrande had fallen on hard times. Aside from a train depot, a roadside café, a few occupied houses in need of repair, and several dilapidated buildings, the village had almost ceased to exist. Flack figured the day would come when the only thing left would be a road sign at a lonely desert railroad crossing.

The three deputies were at a table next to the café's front window, sipping coffee and waiting for their meals to arrive when three military jeeps filled with soldiers roared by, heading toward the Prather Ranch. A stream of civilian cars followed closely behind.

Probably more reporters, Flack guessed. He got to his feet and threw greenbacks on the table to cover the cost of the food. "Let's go," he ordered.

"We haven't eaten yet," Mike Saiz complained.

"It won't kill you to skip a meal, and this is a show I don't want to miss," Flack replied.

On the straight, lightly traveled highway, with Flack driving at high speed in the government sedan, it took only a few minutes to catch up to the convoy. Off the pavement on the ranch road, the deputies ate dust all the way to the ranch house, where they discovered all the reporters clustered outside on the shady side of the house with everyone else forted up inside.

The army officers consisted of a light colonel, a major, two captains, and two lieutenants. Along with their three enlisted drivers, they formed a picket line behind their jeeps, while the newly arrived reporters spread out and got busy filming, snapping photographs, and taking notes.

Dave Flack approached the officer in charge, a light colonel with blood in his eye wearing starched fatigues and spit-shined boots, now covered with a film of dust.

During WWII as a dogface, Flack had fought from Italy to Normandy and had little love for spit-and-polish officers. He looked the colonel up and down, flashed his badge, and said, "Don't do anything stupid, Colonel. There are at least twenty people inside that house, armed and ready to fight."

The officer arched an eyebrow. "Now, how would you know that, Deputy? You just got here."

"No, I just got *back* here from Orogrande," Flack replied. "And I can tell you for a fact that John Prather, his kinfolk, and his friends aren't about to lay down their weapons and invite you inside."

"Wasn't it your job to evict him?" the colonel asked, eyeing the very sturdy-looking rock house. Against light weapons it was a formidable defensive structure.

"It was," Flack admitted. "But I didn't have enough manpower for a siege. Neither do you, from the looks of it, unless you plan to bring up some tanks and artillery pieces with reinforcements."

"I'll be the judge of what's necessary here," the colonel replied.

Flack shrugged. "Suit yourself, but if you start a war, I'll arrest you and your men."

The colonel sneered. "You don't have jurisdiction over the United States Army."

"Try me," Flack replied, silently cursing at himself for jumping feetfirst into a brouhaha he'd been told by his boss to avoid.

The colonel looked Flack over and decided he wasn't bluffing. "What do you suggest?"

"Ask John Prather to parley with you and then decide what to do." From what Flack had seen of the old man, he doubted a showdown with the army would faze him.

The colonel nodded a curt agreement and, using a handheld transistorized megaphone—a newly invented technological gizmo favored by the military and law enforcement—he called for John Prather to step outside the house.

Several minutes passed before the door opened and Prather appeared with a long gun in hand.

"John Prather, I'm Colonel Reinhart. I'm here to resolve this peaceably."

"Well, Colonel, you can go straight to Hades. I will kill the first man that steps through the door into my home. I'm staying here dead or alive."

"Surely you don't mean that," Reinhart replied.

"Get off my ranch," Prather snapped. He stepped back inside and slammed the door just as the barrels of several rifles appeared in open windows.

"Shit!" Colonel Reinhart said under his breath.

"He doesn't parley very nicely, does he?" Flack noted, biting back additional sarcasm.

Reinhart looked around at the reporters eagerly awaiting the action and at his men patiently awaiting their orders. He glared at Flack. "Arrest Prather," he ordered through clenched teeth.

"No can do," Dave Flack replied with a winning smile. "It's your ball game now, Colonel. But watch out. You could wind up with egg on your face if you force a showdown."

In a huff, Reinhart turned his back on Flack and had a hurried confab with his subordinates. After some back-and-forth hushed conversation, they climbed into their jeeps and left. As soon as they were out of sight, Flack told all the newsmen to leave pronto or be arrested.

"You can't do that," Jack Flynn blustered.

"This is technically federal land until a judge says different, and you're trespassing," Flack retorted.

"You'd arrest all of us?" Flynn scoffed.

"Yep, starting with you," Flack said. He raised his voice to be heard over the grumblings. "You fellas got your story, so now get going."

Slowly the reporters packed up and drove away.

From the front door, John Prather minus his rifle called out to Flack. "Are you still gonna try to evict me, Deputy?"

Dave Flack shook his head and smiled. "No, sir, my boss ordered me to take no further action against you."

"Are you fellas hungry?" John Prather asked.

"A mite," Flack allowed.

"Lose those *pistolas,* come inside, and you can have some brisket and beans," John Prather said.

"That's mighty kind of you," Dave Flack said as he shucked his sidearm. He was hot, hungry, and tired, but after all was said and done the day hadn't turned out half-bad.

* * *

Within a matter of weeks, on the recommendation of the US Army, a new writ was issued by a judge exempting John Prather's ranch house and fifteen surrounding acres from federal seizure with the understanding the rancher would cause no further trouble. It gave US Deputy Marshal Dave Flack great pleasure to serve it.

22

For some time after their return from John Prather's ranch, Matt and Patrick remained cautiously optimistic about their chances of holding on to the 7-Bar-K, if and when the army came calling with an eviction notice in hand. Although Prather's victory had been small in terms of all he had to give up, it proved that sometimes one man with gumption and grit could thwart the power of the government. It gave them reason to hope.

Toward the end of summer, Dale Jennings started living with Mary and Kevin in the T or C cottage so he could attend public school. Before he arrived with a satchel of brand-new school clothes, Matt had built sturdy bunk beds for the boys that fit perfectly in Kevin's bedroom. Brenda was excited to have Dale attending school with proper teachers, but simultaneously sad about the prospect of no longer having him at home with her on the ranch. She was determined to follow Mary's lead and buy a place in T or C so she could care for Dale and find work to help pay for the additional expenses.

Al was sympathetic to the idea but much more immediately

interested in using the continuing profits from the Jornada land he'd leased to a larger producer to get back into the cow-calf business, especially now that the drought had ended and the Rocking J high pastures were nicely greened-up. Additionally, they had started receiving cash compensation from the army under a program that reimbursed ranchers outside the proving-ground boundaries who vacated their property during missile firing. So far, they'd been paid for three test firings that had caused them to leave the ranch. The money went to catching up on unpaid bills. Also, he stood to take a larger cut of the profits as manager of the Rocking J and 7-Bar-K commingled herd. If beef prices held steady, in a year he might be able to swing a down payment on a house in town. All in all, Al was finally feeling upbeat about the future after a mostly dismal decade.

So far, he'd been able to go against the tide that had forced most small, family operated producers to rely on steady, outside employment to survive. Matt and Mary were lucky to both have reliable, full-time jobs that allowed them to keep their ranch without going into the red. But they were college graduates with education and skills he didn't have, and he had no desire to sell farm equipment, drive a livestock truck, repair windmills, or work in a feed store in order to keep the Rocking J out of bankruptcy. Ranching was all he knew, and he wanted no part of a six-day-a-week job working for somebody else.

To town folks it may have seemed muleheaded, but for Al it was a way of life he loved, and he planned to stick with it through good times and bad. He hoped to raise his son to do the same once the ranch passed on to him, only to do it smarter and better than his old man.

* * *

With the demands of his job pressing him for time, Matt was more than willing to relinquish the joint cattle operation to Al, who was by far the better stockman. He helped out with the cattle when time allowed and took on all the ordinary maintenance and upkeep chores at the ranch that Patrick no longer could do. During his time at the ranch, he soon came to realize the old man needed more looking-after than a weekend visit could provide. On top of growing deaf, Patrick suffered from chronic back pain, had frequent spells of forgetfulness, and was constantly plagued with pain in the leg he'd badly broken years ago in a crash while driving through Rhodes Canyon.

It took Matt several months to bully Patrick into the idea of accepting the notion of a full-time housekeeper. He finally relented after Matt gave him the ultimatum of a housekeeper or a permanent move to town. Victory in hand, Matt hired Marge Crowley, a divorced, older woman from Socorro who was butterball-round, built low to the ground, and full of nervous energy. Happily, the two hit it off right from the start.

Having Marge at the ranch quickly alleviated Matt's nagging worry of leaving the old man alone with no help in case of an emergency. It also forestalled the guilt he knew he would one day face when the time came to move Patrick into a nursing home. Matt dreaded the thought of what that would do to the old man.

* * *

Late at night, the day after Christmas, Al rushed Brenda from the Rocking J to the T or C hospital emergency room suffering from severe stomach cramps and heavy vaginal bleeding. After X-rays and overnight observation, the doctors performed a full hysterectomy.

While Matt kept Dale and Kevin occupied at the cottage, Al and Mary maintained a nervous vigil at the hospital. Al chain-smoked cigarettes as Mary thumbed distractedly through old magazines. The slightest sound of approaching footsteps brought them instantly to their feet. To everyone's great relief, Brenda came through surgery okay. Five days later, the doctors released her and she recuperated under Mary's care at the cottage until she was well enough to be up and around.

On her last night there, a tearful Brenda, devastated that she'd never have another child, broke down in Mary's comforting arms. It took all of Mary's willpower not to mingle her own tears with Brenda's. In spite of all her consultations with medical specialists and all the testing she'd gone through, she'd been unable to get pregnant again. It was mystifying and frustrating to have another child denied to her for no known reason. In the face of Brenda's grief over the same fate, she held her tongue.

In the morning Al came with Dale and carried Brenda home. With Matt and Kevin at the ranch so as not to be underfoot during Brenda's convalescence, Mary faced the remainder of the day and the next alone. In a frenzy to occupy her mind with only trivial matters, she cleaned the house, washed clothes, and rearranged the dishes in the kitchen cupboards before leaving for a walk downtown to buy a few staples at the market.

She truly didn't need anything from the market; it was simply a way to escape the memory of the dream that had haunted her since waking. In it, a little girl as pretty as could be, dressed in a summery party dress with a blue ribbon in her curly blond hair, stared at her with big, sad eyes, waved goodbye, and vanished into an enveloping ghostly mist.

The dream had repeated over and over during the night, each time slightly different but always with the same ending. Each time she woke up sobbing, knowing the little girl in the dream was the daughter she would never, ever have.

Dismayed by her premonition, hoping to clear her mind, Mary delayed her return home with a stop at the drugstore just prior to closing time, where she dawdled over the stationery section picking through boxes of discounted Christmas cards. On an impulse, she purchased a hand-tooled leather diary with a locking clasp and the image of a frisky colt on the rich grain cover.

She'd frequently thought to start a journal for Kevin so he'd have a record of her side of the family. He'd never shown much interest in the subject and she certainly hadn't encouraged any, but the day might come when he'd want to know more. Giving him a journal to read might be the best and safest way to share her past with him while avoiding all the lamentable parts.

She walked home in a chilling breeze under a low sky with darkness filling the slender river valley and masking the mountains. At the kitchen table, she stared at the lined empty page for a long time wondering where to start. Finally, she picked up her pen, wrote the date at the top of the page and began thusly:

> *Suffering from tuberculosis and dissatisfied with his studies to become a Presbyterian minister, your grandfather, Clyde Ralston, came from Chicago to Santa Fe in 1905 to work as an accounting clerk in a dry-goods store. Instead, he took a job as the bookkeeper at the largest ranch on the Galisteo Basin and eventually became a cattleman who loved to preach.*

She paused and read what she'd written. It was a good beginning. The touch of humor about her sanctimonious, hypocritical father pleased her. Even though it was a witticism that without further explanation would have no meaning to Kevin, she decided to leave it in.

She continued writing into the night, the words flowing more easily than she'd ever imagined possible. It felt good, even liberating in a way, but at the same time emotionally exhausting.

* * *

In late winter of 1958, Matt was loaned by the college to the US Fish and Wildlife Service to organize and conduct a wild mustang roundup on the San Andres National Wildlife Refuge in the mountains south of the 7-Bar-K Ranch. A band of fifty or more wild horses led by one dominant, crafty stallion had penetrated the refuge in search of water and browse during the long drought and had taken up permanent residence. Now they were competing with the bighorn sheep and other wildlife for the limited grass and water resources, and the government wanted them removed. If relocation failed they would be shot. Matt's roundup effort would be constrained by the Fish and Wildlife requirement that during the removal, only minimal damage to the land or the ponies would be tolerated.

Slightly more than 57,000 acres, the refuge was a haphazardly shaped rectangle twenty-one miles long, completely enclosed by White Sands Proving Ground and permanently off-limits to the public. Created just prior to World War II to protect native bighorn sheep, it was isolated, remote, and relatively untouched by human hands. Except for some disappointing hard-rock-mining ventures and a few failed ranching operations during the territorial days, the refuge contained a largely pristine mountainous slice of the far northern Chihuahuan Desert. Most people in the state, be they native-born or newcomer, didn't have a clue that it existed, and the few who did know about it had only a foggy notion of its location.

From the gentle western slopes of the San Andres to the juniper-studded mountainous high country, the refuge was a sanctuary not only for the bighorn sheep that had been decimated by the recent drought, but also for mule deer, mountain lions, and black-tailed jackrabbits. Rock caves sheltered colonies of bats. Long-legged lizards that Matt had never seen before scurried over scorched earth hot enough to fry eggs.

There was birdsong new to Matt's ears. Occasionally he got a glimpse of some bright tropical plumage flashing across the sky. Turkey vultures hunted overhead, and fleet-footed roadrunners darted through the bush searching for insects, seeds, or small rodents.

In deep crevices there were ancient rock-art drawings of bighorn sheep, sun symbols, arrows in flight, lightning bolts, and human handprint impressions in pale white pigment. They were poignant reminders of early hunters who'd come before, each as meaningful as the names of the conquistadors and explorers scratched into the stone face at Inscription Rock, a hundred miles away.

At the foot of a half dozen steep canyons in the refuge, water flowed from natural springs where ash and desert willow flourished along lush, gurgling stream banks teeming with birds that flittered from tree to tree. On the lower terrain, grasses, agave, yucca, and creosote peppered rolling pastures that climbed gentle foothills. On higher ground, piñon trees clung to rocky slopes, and Apache plume, bursting with delicate white flowers, flourished in crevices below steep, stratified rocky escarpments.

Matt delighted in the assignment. He'd picked three top-hand cowboys to assist him, all experienced horsemen, and with his assembled crew they made camp their first day on the refuge under the watchful eyes of four bored army MPs, ostensibly assigned to assist, but really there to contain any sudden rash of espionage that might break out among the cowboys. They saw no sign of the ponies that night, but in the morning they awoke to watch the silent passing of the band less than a hundred feet from the camp on the way to water in Ash Canyon.

Through binoculars, Matt counted fifty-two horses, including the reigning stallion, his mares, yearlings, colts, and three new week-old foals trailing close to their mothers. There was an old dappled gray in the band Matt was certain had been one of the wild ponies he had unsuccessfully tried to gentle back in the Depression years. It made him wonder what had happened to all those other mustangs he and Patrick had boneheadedly tried to tame.

At a distance, he followed the band on foot so as not to spook them and watched as they leisurely watered in Ash Canyon before moving on to graze in a downslope pasture that he'd already rejected as a gathering point due to an overabundance of mesquite, prickly pear, and tall ocotillo, which would hinder any attempt to haze the animals into a capture corral.

Wild critters used to ranging and browsing eighteen miles every day, the mustangs were sturdy, well-muscled, sure-footed animals, capable of scrambling quickly up rocky terrain and outrunning just about anything on four legs. They could easily disable, maim, or kill a man with their hooves, teeth, and strong bodies. Capture would be no easy matter. But with the prospect that the ponies would be slaughtered if not removed, Matt had no intention to fail at his task.

After the band moved on, Matt and his boys spent the day in search of a capture point, finally settling on a foothill pasture at the mouth of a slot canyon where horse tracks showed frequent passage to where live water beyond pooled in a rock basin and trickled down to a narrow, tiny, lush wetland.

That night they camped up above and in the morning were rewarded by the sight of the ponies passing by on their way to water. Forgoing breakfast, they saddled up and trailed the ponies for several hours to make sure they would be nowhere near the canyon while they built the capture corral. Matt didn't want the sound of their activity to cause the animals to vary their routine.

Back at the canyon, Matt laid out his plan for the corral. It was a simple design: gates at both ends with a pen large enough to contain the ponies without crowding and agitating them. The idea was to let them pass through the corral once or twice without capture so they could hopefully contain the entire band when they shut the gates. Once penned, Matt and his hands would lasso small numbers of the ponies at a time and trail them in groups of five to ten, depending on how aggressive the critters were, to waiting livestock trucks on the outskirts of the refuge.

With the help of Fish and Wildlife personnel and the army MPs, who grudgingly joined in, they set about sinking posts, setting railings, and hanging the gates. After the corral was up, they used tarps, shelter half tents, and surplus cot-size mattresses the army had supplied at Matt's request to conceal the fencing and pad the posts and the double swinging gates to reduce the chance of injury to the animals. Finally, they cut branches and boughs from a grove of junipers on higher terrain, carted it all to the corral, and tacked it to the posts and gates as camouflage.

By late afternoon the corral was complete, but Matt wasn't quite finished. He knew from experience that horses had an excellent sense of smell; any good cow pony would frequently cast for a scent when following cattle no longer in sight, especially if the tracks were hard to discern. The corral alone would be something new and disturbing on the route to water, and the lingering scent of man would unsettle them even more. He ordered the crew to move camp a quarter of a mile away and erase all traces of their presence.

There they waited.

Two days passed without a sign of the ponies. Each day Matt sent out riders to spot them and they returned with reports that the band was watering far to the north in a canyon at the edge of the refuge. Two days later, with the ponies drifting closer but still nowhere near the corral, Matt started to think the band had sensed the trap. Another no-show the next morning found him running out of options. With eight days left to remove the horses, there wasn't time to take down the corral and set it up at a new location. If the ponies didn't show soon, he'd be forced to attempt to drive the band into the corral, which had a decidedly dismal chance of succeeding.

Matt slept fitfully that night, imagining the footfalls of ponies, only to wake up in time to see a lone mare with her young foal enter the mouth of the capture corral. He had no idea if he'd missed the rest of the band, but a quick inspection of hoofprints told him a long line of ponies had slowly and cautiously traversed the length of the corral. Reassured that they were back, he decided to give the band one more safe passage before closing the trap.

From a distance, Matt and his boys trailed and kept a close watch on the mustangs during the day and throughout the night, shadowing in shifts of two. At daybreak from a nearby promontory they watched in great relief as the horses quietly appeared and meandered into the mouth of the open corral on their way to water.

The next morning, after another night of sentinel duty and a cold camp breakfast, saddled and ready, they nervously waited to spring the trap. When all but six stragglers were inside, Matt signaled the MPs to close the gates. He sent two of his men to chase down the stragglers, and they kicked up dust in pursuit of three mares, two colts, and a foal that tore out of the canyon. From inside the corral a deafening roar of spitting, snorting, stomping, angry, frightened ponies rose up.

Matt and his remaining cowboy, Les Leland, a top roper and savvy hand, took a quick look over the top railing at the distressed, agitated animals. The reigning stallion, a thick-chested black, was damn angry and snorting snot. With his nostrils flared and his ears pinned back, he pounded the ground with his powerful hooves and slammed his body against a younger stallion that had invaded a group of mares milling against the corral fence. Two of the mares snapped and bit at another youngster that also tried to intrude.

Matt hadn't counted on warfare between the males and told Les they needed to get the stallions out of the corral before they started killing one another. "Best we do it one at a time," he suggested.

Les eyed Matt speculatively. "Are you sure you want to go in there?"

Matt tipped his hat back, scratched his forehead, and checked the rounds in his six-shooter. "Let's go after that big, mean, black son of a bitch first."

Les grinned, checked his pistol, and nodded.

Matt felt Maverick quiver under him as he ordered the gate opened. He spurred his pony inside with Les hard on his heels, both with lassos twirling in long, flat loops.

The black wheeled to face them just as the loops settled simultaneously over his head. Maverick dug in as the black reared in protest and charged straight at Matt, almost pulling Les out of his saddle.

Maverick tried but couldn't get out of the way fast enough. The black slammed into the pony and he went down hard on his side with Matt's arm pinned under his shoulder. He felt something snap, saw the black rise up above him with murderous eyes, and heard the sound of gunfire just before he lost consciousness.

23

Matt's wreck in the corral resulted in a badly fractured left humerus. Maverick, on the other hand, wasn't hurt at all. After coming out of surgery, Les Leland told Matt that two of the army MPs had braved the rampaging ponies to carry him out of the corral to safety. They administered first aid and rushed him to the hospital, where an orthopedic surgeon pinned the bone in his upper arm back together. For the next two months it was encased in a plaster cast from his shoulder to his wrist, and made normal living almost impossible, especially when dressing. When he got his sense of humor back he joked to Mary that he seemed prone to ruining only the left side of his body. She didn't find it very funny.

As far as the pony capture went, Les had taken charge after Matt's wreck and successfully removed the band from the refuge. Only the black stallion and one colt had been lost; the colt crushed to death against a gate by a raging mare trying to escape. Awaiting further relocation, the mustangs now idly grazed amidst hundreds of large ammunition bunkers at the Fort Wingate army post outside of Gallup. Matt couldn't help but wonder what kind of hilarious cartoon Bill Mauldin would have dreamt up about such a sight.

A week after his cast came off, Matt and Mary received an invitation from Maj. Gen. Norbert Schroeder, commanding officer of White Sands Proving Ground, to attend an award ceremony and parade for the two army MPs who'd rescued him. PFC Fred Ely and Sgt. Tony Marshall were to receive the Soldier's Medal for heroism not involving conflict with an enemy.

They gladly accepted, not only to personally thank the two soldiers but to also get a firsthand look at the post headquarters that had blossomed from a few temporary, surplus buildings into a military complex spread out over several hundred acres of old ranch pastureland. The base now housed hundreds of enlisted soldiers in barracks and a large number of career military personnel and their families in residential housing. And it employed a growing number of scientists, technicians, civil servants, and office workers at various research facilities, laboratories, test sites, and office buildings in or near the headquarters complex.

For more than a decade, local motorists cresting the San Augustin Pass eastbound on the highway that ran from Las Cruces to Alamogordo could glimpse from a distance the rapid transformation of the proving ground into a small city. It was as close as most folks would ever get to actually stepping foot on the high-security base, which had turned nearby Las Cruces into a boomtown. The Cold War had brought continuing prosperity to southern New Mexico.

On the morning of the award ceremony and parade, Matt, Mary, and Kevin traveled the proving-ground access road from the highway, stopped at the security gate, and presented their letter of invitation to an MP at the guard station. He checked Matt's and Mary's driver's licenses, directed them to park in front of the nearby provost marshal's building, and asked them to wait there for their escort, who would arrive shortly. Within a few minutes an army staff car drove up and a smiling young first lieutenant dressed in starched khakis jumped out.

"I'm Lieutenant Terry, your escort," he said as he opened the passenger door to Matt's pickup truck and speculatively eyed the young boy who climbed out after Mary. "We didn't know you'd be bringing your son."

"I doubt Kevin will be any trouble," Mary replied. "He'd like to thank the soldiers who saved his father's life."

"Yes, of course he would," Lieutenant Terry replied, recovering quickly. "We should have included him on the invitation."

"I'm gonna be a soldier when I grow up," Kevin announced as he adjusted his cowboy hat. "But Mom thinks I'd like the navy better."

"I'm sure the army would love to have you," Lieutenant Terry said with a smile as he greeted the boy's father with a handshake. Father and son were dressed alike in pressed blue jeans, long-sleeved white cowboy shirts, go-to-town cowboy hats, and polished black cowboy boots. The boy was a smaller version of his father, with deep blue eyes, square shoulders, and a lean, lanky frame.

Lieutenant Terry motioned the Kerneys to the staff car, and once they were settled inside the olive-drab sedan he proposed a quick tour of the post headquarters, including some of the guided missiles that were on display. Kevin grinned with delighted anticipation.

* * *

Maj. Gen. Norbert Schroeder sat alone in his office at headquarters studying the large, detailed map of the proving grounds on the far wall. Schroeder had been on the job for slightly more than two years and very soon the base would officially become White Sands Missile Range—a more fitting designation for an installation that under his command had embarked on the development and testing of the Nike Zeus missile, a technological airborne marvel capable of seeking out and destroying enemy intercontinental ballistic missiles carrying nuclear warheads.

From the very first day behind his desk, General Schroeder had been bothered by the blotch of white on the map that signified the only remaining private inholding on the military reservation: the 7-Bar-K Ranch. A past commander had nibbled at the edges of the ranch, craftily finding a way to seize the public grazing lands the ranch had once leased, but all direct efforts since to entice the Kerneys to sell had failed dismally.

Schroeder saw the white blotch on his map as a potential major security risk. Because case law allowed the Kerneys access to their property, they had free egress to the ranch but were legally forbidden to trespass beyond the ranch boundaries without permission. However, given the hundreds of square miles of federal land surrounding the ranch, it was virtually impossible to enforce compliance, which meant they could easily roam throughout the mountains with very little chance of detection. That made the ranch a perfect jumping-off place for undetected espionage incursions onto the base.

He'd considered initiating condemnation proceedings against them, but had held off, not wanting a repeat of the public-relations disaster caused by the John Prather fiasco. The last thing he needed was a swarm of angry cowboys and their families staging another standoff.

Today, he'd meet Matthew Kerney and his wife, and use the

opportunity to take measure of the man. He already knew about his combat war service and that of the elder Kerney in the Spanish-American War. He'd also acquainted himself with Mary Kerney's exemplary stateside service in the navy. Also, he knew the couple was highly regarded both professionally and personally by influential community leaders throughout the state.

One more time, he paged through the dossiers on the family his staff had prepared before putting them aside and turning his attention to the award and parade ceremony. Most of the enlisted men who served under his command were college-educated draftees who disdained the discipline and orderliness of military service, so he'd cancelled all weekend passes and scheduled the parade on a Saturday morning to remind them that they were indeed still members of the United States Army.

Schroeder loved a good parade, and he'd had his detachment COs and NCOs drilling their troops for the last two weeks after evening mess call so that they'd at least look and act like soldiers when they formed up and marched.

They would fall in at thirteen hundred hours in fresh khaki uniforms for inspection and then march to the parade grounds across from headquarters, where they would pass in review after Private First Class Ely and Sergeant Marshall received their decorations, and Sgt. Maj. Jerome Zachary retired with the rank of full colonel after forty years of service with the Legion of Merit medal pinned to his chest.

The review stand would be filled with members of his senior staff, all the wives and children of the company and field grade officers, their senior NCOs, most of the high-ranking civil servants and their families who worked at the base, and members of the press from Albuquerque, El Paso, Las Cruces, and Alamogordo.

He would use the event to announce the official renaming of the base to White Sands Missile Range effective May 1, 1958, a mere three weeks hence.

But first, he'd lunch with Mr. and Mrs. Kerney in his headquarters conference room over a nice meal of brisket—favored, Schroeder understood, by ranchers and prepared by the chef at the officers' club.

* * *

An ROTC graduate from West Virginia, First Lieutenant Terry proved to be a well-informed tour guide. Recently promoted, Terry had eighteen months to serve on active duty before returning home to join his father's insurance business in Charleston. After a visit to the guided missiles that graced the entrance as statuary outside the headquarters building, Terry drove them by the service club, swimming pool, movie theater, library, post PX, the chapel, the health clinic, and around a compound of new brick barracks for unmarried enlisted men before taking them on a quick tour of the new housing development for senior NCOs and officers that consisted of neatly lined up, cookie-cutter homes on winding streets. As he drove, he talked about the many famous people and celebrities who'd visited the base, including a British field marshal, Hollywood starlets, and the comedian Jack Benny.

Back at headquarters, Terry guided them to an office, where they were greeted by a lieutenant colonel and quickly ushered into Maj. Gen. Norbert Schroeder's office, where he stood next to his desk smiling and ready for the introductions.

"I'm very pleased that you could come," Schroeder said, slightly miffed that he hadn't been advised that the Kerneys had brought their young son, who could be a distraction. He gestured at the several comfortable chairs and couch separated by a long coffee table in the middle of his office used for informal conversations and briefings, invited them to sit, and joined them.

"We have a few minutes to chat before lunch," he added.

"It was kind of you to invite us to the ceremony," Mary said.

Schroeder smiled broadly. "It means a lot to Sergeant Marshall and PFC Ely that you're here. We'd like to take some photographs of Mr. Kerney with the two soldiers for our base newspaper after the event, if that's okay with you."

"Yes, of course," Matt replied, deliberately terse, making Schroeder work at whatever agenda he had planned.

Schroeder smiled at Kevin, who sat between his parents on the couch. "Did you enjoy the tour?"

"Yes, sir," Kevin answered. "The missiles were really neat. The officer let me sit on the little one called the Corporal."

"We need to get a picture of you sitting on it as a souvenir."

Kevin grinned.

"Have you ever seen a military parade before?" Schroeder asked.

"No, sir, but I bet it's super."

"It is," Schroeder agreed, glancing at Mary Kerney. "I'm sorry your father-in-law turned down my invitation."

Mary laughed. "Patrick did you a favor, General. He would have shown up with blood in his eyes."

Schroeder nodded sympathetically. "Unfortunately in the past we haven't been very good at diplomacy with our neighbors."

"That's the truth of it," Matt said flatly.

The door to the adjacent conference room opened, signaling that lunch was ready to be served.

Schroeder stood. "The cook has fixed a nice brisket. Let's eat and talk of more pleasant things. I understand, Mr. Kerney, that you're quite an expert on restoring native grasslands in these parts. We need to do some of that here. Perhaps you could advise us."

* * *

After a pleasant lunch filled with good food and casual chatter, General Schroeder, accompanied by his deputy commander, his aide-de-camp, and Lieutenant Terry, escorted Matt, Mary, and Kevin across the road to the parade ground, where the troops and the spectators had assembled. Upon their arrival under a hot sun in a clear-blue April sky, the troops were called to attention, Sergeant Marshall and PFC Ely were brought forward, their citations were read, and Schroeder pinned medals on their chests. Then Jerome Zachary, the former sergeant major, now bird colonel, wearing his officer's uniform with five rows of ribbons, was called forward to receive the Legion of Merit. Before presenting the award, Schroeder summarized Zachary's combat service in both world wars, noting that he was one of a very few soldiers to have been awarded the Silver Star in each conflict. He then announced the upcoming name change to White Sands Missile Range, which was greeted with a murmur of approval from the audience.

After the troops passed in review and left the parade grounds, the reporters and photographers clustered around the Kerneys and the newly decorated soldiers, taking pictures and asking questions. Soon Lieutenant Terry called a halt to the interviews, and had an army photographer take pictures of Matt with Ely and Marshall, and another one of Kevin astride the Corporal missile, waving his cowboy hat in the air as though he was bronc riding. It made for a great snapshot.

Before Schroeder said goodbye on the front steps of the headquarters building, he took Matt and Mary to one side and said, "I want you to know the Pentagon has agreed to my recommendation that we pay you a fair price for your ranch as an alternative to seizing it through an eminent domain proceeding. You can use any appraiser you choose to do the valuation. I'd very much like to move forward on this."

Matt shook his head. "Sorry, we're not interested, General. I made a promise to my father that the ranch stays in the family until he says otherwise, and he's not agreeable to moving. I'm afraid you're going to have to live with things the way they are. Try to kick us off the land, and we will fight you."

"Perfectly understandable," Schroeder said, his jaw tightening. He touched the brim of his hat and nodded to Mary. "Good day to you, ma'am."

Mary smiled sweetly. "Thank you for your hospitality."

Back in his office, Maj. Gen. Norbert Schroeder sat at his desk and wrote out an order to his provost marshal instructing him to have MPs immediately begin stop-and-search procedures every time the Kerneys or any of their visitors entered or left the missile range on their way to and from the 7-Bar-K Ranch. It would require manpower to manage it, but it was time to send a first-strike message to Matthew and Mary Kerney that the kid gloves had come off.

24

The constant stop and search of Matt and his family was harassment, plain and simple. Most times the MPs took twenty minutes or more to inspect the 7-Bar-K vehicles entering the missile range reservation. The majority of the soldiers were deliberately slow and nitpicky as payback for pulling boondock duty they clearly disliked. Sergeant Marshall and PFC Ely were the exceptions; both hurried Matt and Mary through the checkpoint whenever they were stationed on the range road through Rhodes Canyon.

By summertime, the harassment escalated into an embargo when an official letter arrived from the judge advocate general at the base requiring all visitors and vendors wishing to visit or do business at the ranch to apply for a special permit and successfully complete a security background check. Estimated time for clearance was ninety days. Until clearance was granted, all would be turned away. Deliveries of gasoline, visits by the veterinarian, transportation of livestock and bulk supplies, and all social visits by friends were effectively shut down. The ranch became an isolated island.

Patrick's housekeeper, Marge Crowley, got her very own letter from the army that included a form for her to fill out and return so the FBI could investigate her background. It advised her that should she leave the ranch while the investigation was ongoing, she would not be allowed to return until her clearance came through, thus making her a virtual prisoner at the ranch. Fortunately, she was happy to stay put and take care of Patrick, whom she'd begun to treat as a surrogate spouse.

For his part, Patrick didn't seem to mind. In fact, Mary and Matt wondered if some spooning was going on between the two, but thought it impolite to inquire.

Even Al, Brenda, and Dale were banished from the ranch until they got cleared, but that didn't stop them from occasionally sneaking over the mountain on horseback to visit. Matt, Mary, and Kevin did the same, and all of them delighted in their illicit trespassing. Several times they got spotted by roving jeep patrols, but the ponies could go places jeeps couldn't, so they always made clean getaways.

To thwart such flagrant violations of national security and add to the nuisance value, the army started sending single-engine, fixed-wing aircraft on low-flying patrols over the ranch at odd times of the day and night. It had Patrick threatening to shoot the damn things out of the sky.

Fed up, Matt took the story to the newspapers in Las Cruces, T or C, and Alamogordo, hoping for some coverage about the army's heavy-handed tactics that might spark some outcry. The only result was a small article in the T or C paper saying tightened security measures at the missile range during test firings was causing minor inconvenience to some area ranchers on the northern end of the range. Frustrated, he wrote a letter to both New Mexico US senators asking them to intervene on his behalf and got responses from aides saying they'd look into his complaint and get back to him. A follow-up letter from one of the senators soon arrived stating that in light of national-security interests, nothing could be done. The senator wished Matt and his family all the best.

To keep travel to and from the ranch to a minimum, Mary and Kevin rarely went to town after school adjourned for the summer. It was heaven for Kevin. If he wasn't following Patrick around, doing his chores, or riding his pony, Mary found him perched on a low bough in the Witch's Tree, with a book in hand or scanning the vast Tularosa Basin with a pair of binoculars looking for spies. He was sure enemy agents were sneaking around the missile range communicating with one another by walkie-talkie, taking photographs of the strange, blocklike buildings that now dotted the landscape, or interrogating kidnapped scientists in secret camps hidden in the back reaches of the Malpais.

For Christmas, Matt had given Kevin two western novels by El Paso native Tom Lea, *The Brave Bulls* and *The Wonderful Country*. Set in Old Mexico and the Southwest, the books enthralled Kevin to the point that he constantly pestered Patrick to tell him stories of the olden days. Patrick readily obliged, spinning tales about the family back in the time when cattle roamed free and there was no missile range to keep people out.

One evening on the veranda after supper, Patrick told Kevin about Emma Kerney, the grandmother he'd never known, and read him the story Gene Rhodes had written and published about her. It opened up an emotional door in Patrick that had him talking nonstop to Kevin over the next several days about the Kerney family and the old Double K Ranch days. He took him to the family cemetery plot on the hill above the ranch house and told him about his ancestors, about John Kerney's partner, Cal Doran, and Kevin's uncle CJ, killed in combat and buried in France. He talked about the notorious characters and outlaws who'd ridden the range, some of the famous unsolved murders and heinous crimes that had been committed on the basin, the Indian Wars, the Mescalero Apaches he'd known, the Chávez family of Tularosa, and his days as a Rough Rider in Cuba with Teddy Roosevelt. After swearing Kevin to secrecy, he even showed him his pardon from the Yuma Territorial Prison.

"You were in prison under a different name?" Kevin asked, wide-eyed as he read the creased, yellowed document signed by the Arizona governor.

Patrick nodded affirmatively. "Back then, it was called a go-by name. I used it because I didn't want nobody to know what I'd done. I got sent up for stealing, when I was a young and foolish boy."

"Does my pa know?"

"He does, although I kept it from him for years, shamed as I was."

"What does getting a pardon mean?" Kevin asked.

Patrick sighed. "It means I was forgiven for my desperado ways."

Captivated by the notion that his very own grandfather had once been an outlaw, Kevin went to sleep each night dreaming about roundups, cattle drives, shoot-outs, bandits, and rustlers. He couldn't imagine a more exciting life and he was proud to be part of a family of such daring men, what with Patrick, CJ, and his pa all being war heroes. In fact, it made him swagger a bit and want to be just like them.

That evening, after an early supper, Patrick told Kevin to saddle up Two-Bits and join him on a horseback ride to the mailbox on the old state road.

"We get our mail in town now, remember?" Mary said as Kevin scooted out the door to call Two-Bits from the near pasture.

"I know that," Patrick replied, peeved at her insinuation that his memory was faulty. It hadn't gotten all that bad yet. "I'm feeling a need to have a horse under me, and besides I'd like to see how the cattle are doing on the far west pasture. Since they're prisoners Al can't move until the army says so, and Matt's away teaching a week-long class at the college, best that I take a look for myself."

"I'll come along," Mary suggested.

"And spoil my time with the boy?" Patrick replied. "I still have a few stories left to tell him."

"Like what stories?" Mary prodded.

"Haven't decided which ones yet," Patrick replied with a sly grin as he pushed back from the table.

"Don't be late getting back and make me come looking for you," Mary warned with a worried look.

Patrick smiled. "Just because I'm an old man doesn't mean you have to mollycoddle me."

"Fair enough," Mary said reluctantly with a wave of her hand. "I'll have the canteens filled and snacks for your saddlebags before you go."

"Thank you kindly, ma'am," Patrick replied. "We'll give our ponies a good workout and be home before dark."

"You'd better be."

* * *

They were halfway across the near pasture, loping the ponies along, when Patrick said, "Did I ever tell you of the time I went up single-handed against some cattle thieves right here on the ranch?"

"No, Grandpa," Kevin said, slowing Two-Bits to a trot. "Did it happen a long time ago?"

"Not too long. It was before your pa went off to fight in the army. We had this old boy named Shorty working for us who seemed okay until he slicked up a story about needing a few days off to see a lady friend in El Paso, all the time conspiring to trail a herd of our cattle down to the state road, where he planned to meet up with his two cronies in on the scheme."

"What happened?" Kevin asked eagerly.

"He would have gotten away with it, if I hadn't become suspicious."

Patrick explained how he'd met Shorty at the cabin just before his departure and noticed he'd let the woodpile get low, and had cleaned out all his gear and clothing for what was supposed to be a few days of relaxation. Figuring it was odd, he followed Shorty when he left the cabin supposedly to catch a train in Engle for El Paso.

"Where the trail meets the state road I found out he had our cows gathered and penned when they should have been upcountry."

"What did you do? Did you kill him?"

"Didn't kill him, but should have. After it was over, Shorty skipped out of the state and was never heard from again. Well, anyway, once I got closer I spotted two livestock trucks on the road waiting to haul those critters away. So I snuck up a hill, shot holes with my long gun into the truck engines to disable them, and winged one of the drivers. That caused that lying coward of a cowboy to turn tail and run. I sent the other two shank's mare down the road, where they got arrested in Alamogordo after stumbling in half-dead of thirst and sunburned to a crisp. Sheriff said it was the first time hereabouts rustlers had tried to steal cattle using trucks. The newspaper even did a story about it."

"Wow!" Kevin exclaimed. "Can I see where it happened?"

Patrick paused, looked skyward, and shook his head. "Nope, it would get us home too late."

"Please," Kevin begged.

Patrick grinned. Having a young button around who seemed genuinely interested in what he knew and what he'd done just tickled him pink. "Well, if you're man enough to take the scolding you'll get from your ma, I guess I can take my licks from her too."

Kevin broke Two-Bits into a lope. "Yippee!"

They entered the far pasture and cut upslope into the mountains, following an old cattle trail that led to an occasional stream, and got to the site of Patrick's gunfight as the light faded behind the San Andres. They dismounted and Patrick showed Kevin the old stock pen where he'd found the cattle, the ridge where he spotted the trucks idling on the road, and the narrow arroyo he'd taken to cut them off before they could load the critters. Because of the growing darkness, they walked their ponies down the arroyo to the old state road.

"This is where the shooting started." Patrick pointed to the spot on top of the canyon where he'd held sway over the bandits. The sound of an approaching engine and the glare of headlights coming around the bend cut his story short. "Looks like we've got some army boys about to check on us," he said.

The jeep ground to a stop. "Stay where you are and don't move," a voice ordered.

"No need to get bossy," Patrick retorted. "I'm Patrick Kerney from the 7-Bar-K, and this is my grandson, Kevin."

"Stop talking and stay put," 2nd Lt. John Spence snapped, his hand firmly on his holstered handgun.

It was his first rotation to the Rhodes Canyon outpost since arriving at the missile range two weeks ago fresh out of MP school. Leaving the enlisted men behind so that they wouldn't see how miserable he was about being in the army—in retrospect ROTC had been a big mistake—he'd taken a jeep out for a drive hoping to restore his spirits.

Lt. John Spence had a dilemma; he'd been told about the Kerneys and their ranch, but he'd also been ordered to strictly enforce any trespass on the reservation. "Do you have any ID?" Spence asked.

"Not on me, unless you take into account the brands on our ponies," Patrick replied, squinting into the bright beams of the headlights.

"That won't do," Spence said, making a quick decision to follow the letter of the law. "Walk toward me."

"What for?" Patrick demanded.

"I'm charging you with trespassing."

"Are you arresting the ponies too, or can I send them home?"

"They can go."

Patrick slapped the ponies on their haunches and they trotted off in the direction of the arroyo. He figured it would be a good three hours before they wandered into the near pasture at the ranch house. By then, Mary would be about ready to kill him. "Now what?" he asked.

Lieutenant Spence considered his next move. He'd left the outpost with only his .45 on his hip and carried no handcuffs. He figured the young boy wouldn't be a problem, but he'd heard that the Kerney men were feisty characters. If he could get them to the outpost peaceably, he'd send them to the Sierra County Jail under MP escort.

"Will you cooperate?" Spence asked.

"I reckon so," Patrick replied.

"Get in the back of the jeep."

Patrick nodded and took Kevin's hand. "Are you doing okay, boy?" he asked.

"Yes, sir," Kevin replied quietly.

He led his grandson to the jeep. "I guess we're both outlaws now, just like in the old days," he whispered.

Anticipating his first jeep ride and his newly minted status as an outlaw, a smile lit up Kevin's face.

* * *

The army was building something at the outpost, but Patrick couldn't figure out what it was other than a big hole in the ground that was smack-dab in the center of the old road running through Rhodes Canyon. They had even built a short, temporary bypass around the hole in the ground so vehicles could travel around it. Up close, it looked a good thirty feet deep, blasted out of rock. Sometimes when the wind was right, he'd heard the explosions at the ranch.

When they reached the outpost, consisting of a portable barrier across the road, a cook tent, a flimsy barracks to house the soldiers, and an outhouse tucked behind some shrubs, the officer who'd arrested them, a shavetail lieutenant by the looks of him, told an MP sergeant to take Patrick and Kevin to the Sierra County Jail and charge Patrick Kerney with trespass.

"I don't think you really want to do that, Lieutenant," the sergeant cautioned, staring at the most sorry-ass excuse of an officer he'd ever had the displeasure to meet in his eight years of active duty, including a year of combat in Korea.

"That's an order, Sergeant," Spence said. "Pick a soldier to accompany you."

The sergeant paused a beat, deciding whether to try one more time to save the lieutenant from a serious butt-chewing by the post provost marshal.

"What are you waiting for?" Lieutenant Spence snapped.

That sealed it. "We're on our way, Lieutenant." The sergeant turned on his heel without saluting, motioned to a corporal to accompany him, piled Patrick and Kevin into a jeep, and drove off.

From the front passenger seat, Patrick asked the sergeant why they were going to the hoosegow in town and not the post stockade.

"Because we can't lock up civilians in military prisons," the sergeant replied with a glance and a laugh.

"What's so funny?" Patrick asked.

"You're not going to the hoosegow anyway," the sergeant replied. "You see, what the lieutenant forgot or didn't know in the first place, is that I can't charge you with trespassing because I personally didn't witness it. Only the lieutenant can do that."

"You're gonna let us go?"

The sergeant laughed again and shook his head. "Nope, I'll let the sheriff decide, so it's official that we followed the lieutenant's orders."

Patrick looked over his shoulder at Kevin sitting in the backseat next to the corporal. "Seems we're not gonna get to be outlaws after all." He shook his head sadly. "Too bad; going to jail was about the only good excuse we'd had with your ma to stay out of trouble."

"Being arrested is almost as good as going to jail," the corporal suggested.

"Have I been arrested?" Kevin asked.

The corporal nodded. "Yep, you could say so because you're in our custody."

"Then I'm an outlaw," Kevin announced happily.

"That might calm your ma down some," Patrick offered, tongue-in-cheek.

In the middle of one of the best adventures of his young life, with the wind from the open jeep in his face, a corporal with a pistol sitting next to him like he was some sort of criminal, and the prospect of being questioned by the sheriff, Kevin smiled and said, "I don't mind if I get in trouble with Ma. It's worth it."

* * *

In T or C at the Sierra County Sherriff's Office, the MPs and Patrick drank coffee with the deputy on duty while waiting for the sheriff to arrive. At Kevin's request, the deputy let him hang out in the unlocked empty holding cell, where he studied all the names scratched into the walls and came to the conclusion that the county wasn't lacking in outlaws. He thought about adding his name to the list but changed his mind because of a sign above the built-in concrete bunk that read: ANYONE CAUGHT DEFACING COUNTY PROPERTY WILL BE PROSECUTED TO THE FULL EXTENT OF THE LAW.

The sheriff arrived and rolled his eyes in disbelief when the MP sergeant told him what happened. After the army boys left, he called the missile range to report the incident and had his deputy drive Patrick and Kevin to their cottage in town. For Kevin, a ride in a patrol car was the perfect ending to the day.

As soon as they were inside, Patrick called Al at the Rocking J and told him about getting arrested and detained by an MP. The news sent Al on horseback over the mountain to tell Mary. Next, Patrick called Matt in Las Cruces, who laughed at hearing the news and talked with Kevin for a spell to make sure he was okay. Before hanging up, he wished Patrick luck getting out of the doghouse with Mary.

By six in the morning, Mary was at the cottage. As soon as the riderless ponies had come home, she'd been out in the truck searching. It had taken Al most of the night to track her down. She was too relieved and too exhausted to give them what-for. Patrick made it all the more difficult for her by fixing her a good, hearty breakfast.

As they were eating, a neighbor came by with the morning newspaper that carried the front-page headline RANCHER AND GRANDSON ON HORSEBACK ILLEGALLY DETAINED BY ARMY.

Patrick read the article, which gave an accurate accounting of the events, and chuckled. "I figure the sheriff must have put a bug in the newspaper editor's ear."

Kevin cut the article out of the paper to keep as proof of his budding outlaw credentials.

Mary, her ire now fully focused on the army, was simply relieved nothing terrible had happened to Kevin and Patrick.

* * *

At White Sands Missile Range headquarters, Maj. Gen. Norbert Schroeder's morning took a bad turn when his public-affairs officer, Capt. Raymond Peck, laid down a copy of the T or C newspaper article that had been picked up by the wire services.

"Probably every paper in the state will carry it," Peck said.

Schroeder clenched his jaw. "Has the information been verified?"

"It has, sir. I personally and privately spoke by radio to the lieutenant and the sergeant, and they both confirmed the information. The sergeant also noted the lieutenant was not inclined to accept his advice about the matter."

Schroeder huffed in disgust. The article painted a sympathetic picture of the Kerneys and characterized the army as stumbling buffoons. It was a PR disaster.

"Who is this officer?"

Peck flipped open a notepad. "Second Lieutenant John Spence, age twenty-two, an ROTC graduate who arrived here a little over two weeks ago. His academic record is far from sterling and his MP training scores weren't much better."

Schroeder held up a hand to stop Peck. "I want him reassigned to the enlisted men's service club handing out Ping-Pong balls until his active-duty obligation expires. And tell him for me, he will remain a second lieutenant until that blessed day comes."

"Wouldn't offering him a general discharge serve just as well?"

Schroeder shook his head. "He doesn't get off that easy. There's an important lesson for Lieutenant Spence to learn, and the army is exactly the right place for him to learn it."

Captain Peck closed his notebook and stepped to the door. "I'll ask the provost marshal to send someone to relieve Lieutenant Spence and have personnel cut new orders for him ASAP."

"Very good. Tell Captain Jaworoski at Special Services, with my apologies, that I'm sending him a dud."

"I'll fill him in, sir."

Peck closed the door and Schroeder let out a big sigh as he stared at the white blemish on the wall map of WSMR denoting the continued existence of the 7-Bar-K Ranch. If the Kerneys were already gone, the incident with the dumbbell lieutenant never would have happened. Short of eviction through the courts, which would certainly be another PR mess, what was it going to take to force them out?

25

Nineteen Sixty, a year of growing prosperity, saw Eisenhower deep into his second term as president with the general election looming in November. More people were working at decent-paying jobs, going to college, starting families, and entering the burgeoning middle class than ever before. Folks were optimistic about the future, even with the constant overshadowing threat of the Cold War.

For Patrick it began as a year of growing confusion. The more forgetful he became, the more of his painful past he remembered. One late morning out of nowhere, after waking from a dreamless nap, the sudden realization hit him of what a god-awful, sullen, angry child he'd been, refusing to show any appreciation or affection to the father who'd searched for and rescued him, or for Cal Doran, the man who ultimately raised him. He pictured watching John Kerney die in that terrible wagon accident while he stood by mute and unfeeling. The image was immediately replaced by a stab of self-loathing for falsely damning Cal Doran at the time of his death for his acts of great kindness. The truth of his meanness clutched his heart like a vise.

Several times in early summer he'd mistakenly confused names, thinking Kevin was CJ, Marge was his second wife, Evangelina, and Mary was Anna Lynn. His slipups earned him worried looks and questions from the womenfolk as to the state of his health. He briskly brushed aside all such inquiries as silly, unnecessary pestering.

Embarrassed by his blunders, he took to writing their real names on a piece of paper every morning before breakfast and practicing them so as not to forget. Still, he lapsed occasionally, especially with Kevin, which made him more and more cautious about saying anything that might cause additional probing into the state of his well-being.

He took to mentally measuring his words twice before speaking, much as a carpenter would before sawing a board. It made him appear slow and dull, which drew more thinly veiled looks of sympathy and worried expressions of forbearance from Mary and Marge that only served to further depress him.

One day when he called Kevin CJ by mistake, he had to swallow tears as the memory of his drunken fight with CJ in the corral stampeded through his mind. He'd driven CJ forever from the ranch that day and ultimately to his death in the trenches of France. Pure meanness had killed that wonderful boy just as it had earlier ended his marriage to Emma, the only woman he'd ever truly loved. Fortunately, successfully lying to a nine-year-old about a grain of sand in his eye was easy enough to do.

Since her death, Emma had been fixed like a center post in his head. The woman had endured more pain and suffering than anyone he'd known and yet she'd died impeccably, if there was such a thing, slipping away with love in her eyes and a beautiful smile on her face.

Until recently, he hadn't given much thought to his own demise, but now he wondered if he could do it as well. In the back of his mind, the idea of nothingness had always annoyed him and he'd quickly shucked it off, but the growing aches and pains in his creaky old body told him that leaving the world might not be such a bad thing.

In preparation, he consoled himself with reminders that he was no longer a drunk, no longer violent in word or deed, that he'd made permanent peace with Matt, had a lady friend in Marge, who genuinely seemed to like him, a grandson who willingly and regularly sought his company, and a daughter-in-law who had shown him only kindness from the very first day they met.

Surely that counted for something in his otherwise self-inflicted ruin of a life. In the shadowland of his existence, he was a better person than he'd ever been before or ever thought he could be.

On one summer morning, a writer fellow came to visit unannounced, hat in hand, uttering apologies and asking for a bit of Patrick's time. He was a professor of some sort at Texas Western College in El Paso with a foreign-sounding last name Patrick couldn't pronounce, and he was interested in interviewing oldtimers on the Tularosa for a book he hoped to publish about the territorial years after first putting together a pamphlet for the army on the history of the missile range. Patrick almost sent him packing but changed his mind at the chance to tell a bit of the family story for Kevin and posterity, especially some of the tales maybe he'd forgotten to recount. He also warmed to the idea of setting the record straight about misconceptions folks might have about his life and times.

But it got hard once the questions started coming. To begin, he couldn't remember if he was born in 1872 or 1875, so he picked the earlier date, which made him eighty-seven years old. He got confused about the location of Double K, thinking it was some forgotten ranch John Kerney had started before the 7-Bar-K. When the writer asked, he couldn't recall that Eugene Manlove Rhodes had ever worked for the spread until he found the copy of the story Gene had written about Emma and let the fellow read it. He did get a story out correctly about meeting up with Oliver Lee when he was chasing down cattle rustlers and coming upon one of the dead men Lee had killed fair and square out on the far reaches of the Tularosa.

The writer really liked that one. It was a good one all right, as was the one about Gene Rhodes hiding some of his pals on the ranch who were wanted for murder. He tried to recall who Gene had sheltered from the law but the names escaped him. However, much to Patrick's relief, the writer knew who he was talking about.

He was asked about the Rough Riders, and Patrick allowed he'd known Teddy Roosevelt and had killed a few men on San Juan Hill, but refused to say more, as the image of Jake Jacobi dying at his feet—an image never far from his mind—choked him up. He still missed that old boy and the good times he had with him wrangling in Arizona.

When talk turned to more recent past events, such as the mysterious disappearance of Vernon Clagett, the killing of army deserter Fred Tyler, and the accidental death of treasure hunter Dalton Moore found trespassing on the ranch, Patrick clammed up tight, thinking the damned army would try any trick to get information of wrongdoing and use it to seize the 7-Bar-K.

No matter how hard the fellow tried, Patrick refused to budge, but when he switched to asking about old-time neighbors now long gone from the basin, Patrick obliged, rambling on about this and that person. He also talked a lot about the atom bomb that was exploded out on the Jornada, a subject of keen interest to the fella.

After the writer closed up his notepad, put away his pencil, expressed his appreciation, and left, Patrick sat on the veranda wondering why he and Matt had never talked about going to war or what it had done to them. To his way of thinking, it didn't seem unusual; war talk never made for polite or easy conversation.

All told, Matt seemed to have done a good job of getting over it, but you never knew about another man's private thoughts. Patrick still had an occasional Technicolor nightmare about the bloody fighting he'd witnessed in Cuba with shells exploding and body parts flying, and he still got phantom shivers about the terrible stateside hospitals where he recovered from his wounds watching hundreds of scared, delirious men die morning, noon, and night. All that was clear as a bell from more than sixty years ago.

He imagined the same would hold true for Matt. Memories etched in killing and obliteration are indelible, eternal.

As the summer edged on, Patrick took to sleeping more and more, sometimes in the sun on a mild day like an old hound dog spread out to cool his parts in a gentle breeze. He napped pretty much out of boredom. When he felt drowsy he tried to stay awake by tinkering at some easy odd job that needed doing. Sometimes it worked and sometimes it didn't. Reading didn't help at all; it just put him to sleep faster and he could never remember where he'd left off anyway.

About all he managed to do day in and day out was get himself dressed, clean himself up, eat his meals, putter around a bit, take naps, and stay out of everybody's hair. Even that wasn't enough to keep worried looks off Mary and Marge's faces or stop them from constantly trying to look after him.

With Matt and Kevin it was different. To the almost-ten-year-old Kevin he was just Gramps. Young'uns by their nature just don't have the time or inclination to worry about old folks getting older. Patrick appreciated that. And Matt's approach of simply checking in to see how he fared, done usually without comment, was a helluva lot more evenhanded than all the unnecessary fussing. He appreciated that as well.

Late in the summer, a week before Labor Day and the start of school for Kevin, Patrick woke with a start in the dark of the night in great need of the bathroom. When he discovered that his legs didn't want to move, he remained motionless and tried not to panic, his eyes fixed on the sliver of moonlight knifing through the open window. Slowly, he threw the bedsheet back, sat upright, and rubbed his hands over his legs, relieved to feel the sensation.

Figuring he wasn't paralyzed, just slow to get things working, he waited a spell before swinging his legs to the floor and standing. He chuckled with delight until he took his first step. His head spun and he almost crashed to the floor. Only his hand on the bedpost saved him.

He waited until the dizziness passed before starting out again, this time on steadier legs, taking small steps but still managing to bump his shoulder against the door frame as he made his way out of his bedroom. He got to the bathroom just in time, happy to have avoided embarrassing himself, and sat on the toilet far longer than he needed, wary his legs might fail him again when he got up.

Finally ready to risk it, he returned to his bedroom feeling ancient, creaky, and out of sorts. He sat on the edge of the bed and practiced standing up until he was satisfied everything was working as it should. But it didn't relieve his anxiety. He stayed awake until it was time to get up, wondering when his body would fail him next, which part would cause him to take a nosedive.

With Matt at the ranch for a week on vacation from his job with the college, everyone was gathered at the kitchen table for breakfast when Patrick arrived. Of course, other than a smile and a howdy to all, he didn't say a word about his nighttime troubles.

His hopes that the incident with his legs was nothing more than a one-time episode rose throughout the day. His head stayed clear, he walked without difficulty, neither shuffling nor stumbling, and by evening time he was encouraged that it had been merely a freak event.

He turned in for bed optimistic that all was well. Except for one trip to the bathroom, he slept throughout the night, getting out of bed with both legs working, pausing for only a second to remember his name and where he was. Another good day followed. He helped Matt clean and oil saddles in the tack room, rehang several loose railings on the corral, and prune some low-hanging, dead branches on the windbreak cottonwoods. By dinnertime he was tired and hungry, but he felt useful and like his old self. The day had been his best in months.

After supper with the dishes done and put away, Mary asked him to go on a stroll up to the family graveyard. Patrick figured it was mostly to see how he was doing, but he didn't mind at all. They left Matt and Kevin listening to the radio in the living room and Marge relaxing on the veranda, and walked up the hill. He'd been deliberately avoiding Mary lately, scooting around her at a distance so as not to get her worrying about him. But today he felt so damn good, she could badger him with questions about his health to her heart's content and it wouldn't bother him at all. He felt lucid and energized—hell, even sprightly. The day had eased his aches, pains, and worries.

It had been some time since his last visit to the family plot, and he was pleased to see that Kevin had been keeping up with his chore of maintaining everything in good order. All the markers were upright, the fence enclosing the graveyard had been touched up with paint as needed, all the weeds had been pulled, and the native grass was trimmed back a bit. For his work, Kevin received one dollar a month cash money paid straight out of Patrick's pocket. It pleased him to see how reliable the boy was and how well he met his responsibilities.

Outside the fence next to an old tree was a grassy mound where long ago Patrick's pa had buried one of his favorite ponies. A big rock near the mound served as a bench and they sat looking out on the Tularosa. When once it was a serene desert just beginning to come alive at dusk, the modern world now intruded and disturbed it. Electric lights winked at seemingly random locations across the basin. Concrete buildings, blocky and blind to the outside world, sat on bare unadorned ground surrounded by miles of scrub and sand; signposts of hush-hush research dedicated solely to blowing up cities, maybe even the world, if a few powerful men decided it necessary.

Born well before the marvel of airplanes that touched the sky, Patrick saw little value in the modern world other than for a few conveniences such as his pickup truck, electric lights, and the radio.

They sat together in silence as darkness gathered.

"You seem to be in fine fiddle today," Mary finally said.

"I am."

"That's nice to see."

"It's nice not having you fretting over me."

Mary laughed. "You'd be happier if I just didn't care?"

Patrick chuckled. "Now, I didn't say that."

"Earlier today, Kevin told me that years ago you'd been to prison. Did you make up that story for him?"

Speechless, Patrick froze. Nobody alive in the world but Matt knew about his time in the Yuma Territorial Prison. Nobody. "You say Kevin told you?"

"Yes."

"Well, that's a load of bull," Patrick snorted, trying to understand how the boy had found out.

"Kevin's not the kind to make things up," Mary replied calmly.

"He's lying," Patrick thundered, figuring Kevin must have snooped through his things and found the governor's pardon. He grunted in dismay. The boy he believed to be so decent and respectful was nothing more than a worthless, thieving, snot-nosed kid.

Mary got to her feet. "Why would he lie about it?"

"I don't know, but I'll have no further truck with him."

"Let's go talk to him together," Mary suggested, touching Patrick's arm.

He pulled back and rose up. "Leave me be, woman." Then he slapped her hard across the face.

Stunned, her cheek stinging from the rough blow, Mary retreated. She couldn't see his expression in the darkness, but his breathing was harsh and labored.

He lurched past her down the hill. "What did I just do?" he wailed mournfully to himself, his voice full of distress.

With tears in her eyes from his blow and startled by the unprovoked attack, Mary waited until she heard the screen door slam shut before starting down the path to the house. The time had come for the family to face the hard reality of Patrick's diminished capacity.

Matt met her halfway. "What happened?" he demanded, short of breath.

"Didn't he tell you?"

"He says he doesn't know what he did."

"He hit me, slapped my face."

"Why?"

"There wasn't a sane reason for it."

Matt opened his arms. "Are you hurt?"

Mary leaned against him, felt his warmth and protection as he embraced her. "Not really, but I'll probably have a shiner in the morning."

"We have to do something about him," Matt said with a sigh.

"Yes, we do." She lifted her face and searched his eyes. "And we have to do something for ourselves as well."

Moonlight through a rolling bank of clouds dappled the ranch. It never looked lovelier. "I know," he replied sadly.

26

Although the cause of Patrick's condition was unknown, perhaps the result of a brain tumor or simply the process of degenerative aging, the doctor's diagnosis was severe dementia. There was no cure, no medicine to treat it, little hope for remission, and no way of predicting how long Patrick would live in his present condition; it could be months or years.

Forced by the situation to take leave from their jobs, Matt and Mary spent two weeks investigating nursing homes around the state and finally got Patrick admitted to a church-run facility in Albuquerque that was going to cost a whole lot more than his monthly veteran's pension would cover.

Housed in a thick-walled adobe near the Old Town area of the city, the facility was clean, the staff polite and helpful, and the residential rooms, although rather small, were adequate for two. After reading the physician's medical report and diagnosis, the administrator explained that Patrick could live in the home as long as he didn't become violent or run away. If that happened, he'd have to go elsewhere, perhaps to one of the state institutions.

Not sure where they would get the money to cover the additional costs, Matt and Mary signed the contract anyway, packed Patrick up, and moved him in with a chipper ninety-year-old man who smiled and talked mostly gibberish. While Matt arranged Patrick's few belongings on the nightstand and hung his clothes in a small closet, Mary settled him into a padded armchair next to his bed and promised they'd come to visit at least monthly. Patrick, who'd completely stopped talking days before, looked at her with empty eyes, said nothing, and stared out the window at a dirt lane at the rear of the home bordered by a dry arroyo.

Kevin took Patrick's removal from the family the hardest. Unwilling to believe that his gramps would never be the same, he'd begged Matt and Mary not to send him away, and got angry when they did. He'd bunked with Dale at the Rocking J so as not to miss the start of school, and when they came to fetch him he was still fuming. Their explanations about Patrick's illness had no effect on him. It took a visit to the nursing home the following weekend for Kevin to realize that his grandpa wasn't the same person anymore. Seeing Patrick in such a reduced mental state sucked the visible anger out of him. He sat sullenly in the truck on the way home to T or C looking out the window, his usual good spirits deflated.

During the rush to get Patrick the care he needed, Marge Crowley, the housekeeper, agreed to stay on until everything got settled. With Patrick gone, Matt wasn't surprised when Marge expressed a desire to leave the ranch. Without kin to turn to or friends to lean on, she decided to move to Albuquerque, find work, and look in on Patrick as often as she could. Her obvious affection for the old man touched Matt's heart, and he gave her three months' salary and spent a Saturday driving her to Albuquerque, where she settled into a small, furnished apartment on

Central Avenue near the high school, close to a convenient bus route to Old Town.

While there, Matt made a quick stop to see Patrick and found him the same as before: withdrawn and mute, but freshly shaven and dressed in clean clothes. He sat anchored to his armchair staring out the window at the dirt lane. His roommate's bed was stripped down to the bare mattress and the personal items on the nightstand were gone. The nurse on duty told him the man had died and a new resident would be moving in on Monday. She also said that their best efforts to get Patrick to socialize often failed, except at mealtime, which he always looked forward to—for the food, not the companionship. So far, he'd shown no inclination to wander off, nor had he exhibited any aggressive tendencies.

Matt tried to make jovial small talk with Patrick, asking if he'd made any friends, if he enjoyed the cooking, or if he was getting enough exercise. Patrick stared out the window, stock-still, stiff-necked, and mute. He was permanently missing in action. Matt realized the chances were slim to none that he'd ever have a meaningful conversation with his father again. An overwhelming feeling of sorrow came out of nowhere. Matt knelt down, squeezed his father's shoulder, and said goodbye.

"Maybe you can't hear this, but I hope you can," he said in a whisper. "We've had our differences, but that's been behind us for a long time now. Mary and I truly appreciate how much attention and affection you've given to Kevin. You've been a real good grandpa to him. He misses you and sends his love. We all miss you."

To Matt's surprise, Patrick turned his head and eyed him seriously. With a hint of a smile at the corner of his mouth, he nodded slightly and softly patted Matt's hand.

Matt left the nursing home thinking he should have thanked

Patrick years ago for the man he'd become and forgotten about the man he'd once been. It made him feel small-minded for being so unforgiving over so many years.

* * *

A month passed before Matt, Mary, and Kevin had a chance to return to the ranch. Already there was a feeling of abandonment and neglect about it, as well as troubling evidence of trespassing. Al Jennings had moved the few remaining 7-Bar-K ponies to his ranch headquarters. With the cattle they'd held over for spring works currently grazing on Rocking J pastures, it meant for the first time in the history of the spread, no 7-Bar-K livestock grazed on the land. That reality stabbed Matt like a cactus spine.

Somebody had shot up the windmill blades and tromped through the house. Although nothing appeared to be missing, Mary thought the food pantry had been raided for some canned goods. There was no evidence that trespassers had slept in the house or used the kitchen, but still it was an invasion that put them all in a snappish mood.

While Mary swiftly set about changing the sheets on all the beds as a precaution, Matt hurried to the barn to see if any of the saddles or tack had been stolen. He found the gear all where it should be, but Patrick's old trunk had been busted open and ransacked. Missing were his old Rough Rider uniform, assorted military equipment, and his army medals. Back at the house he searched to see what else might have been taken, and discovered Patrick's old horse pistol that he'd kept in a drawer of his bedside table was gone.

He took a walk around the ranch house looking for tire tracks and footprints, but strong, gusty winds had covered any traces with fine sand blown up from the Tularosa. He figured the interlopers were from the missile range. Who else but soldiers would have easy access to the ranch? Who else but army boys, who didn't know the value of a well-made saddle, would pass up stealing something worth good money? Why take only some military memorabilia and an ancient handgun?

It irked Matt that part of his family history had been stolen. He wouldn't forget it. He'd file a report with the sheriff when they got back to town, but doubted anything would come of it. From now on when they were at the ranch, he'd sleep with an unloaded shotgun next to the bed, shells close at hand.

* * *

After sweeping out the place, dusting the furniture, doing the laundry, and remaking the beds, Mary fixed a dinner of sandwiches and salad with groceries they'd brought from town. Over dinner, she waited for Matt to raise the subject of the ranch, but he didn't say a word. With evening covering the land, no critters or ponies to care for, and no chores that needed doing other than washing a few dishes to air-dry, the ranch felt hollow and empty to her. She joined Matt on the veranda wondering if Patrick's absence had somehow withered the place, much as drought could dry and stunt the land. Or maybe the thieving vandals had sucked the life from it.

She sat in Patrick's old rocker. A fleeting vision of him with his feet perched on the railing made her smile. "Where's Kevin?"

"Down at the Witch's Tree trying to spot secret agents and guided missiles through my binoculars," Matt replied.

"I'm sure they're out there," Mary said. She paused for a moment. "Are we going to talk about what we have to do with the ranch?"

"I've been putting it off, haven't I?"

"Understandably."

"But for a little too long," Matt admitted.

"Yes."

Matt's gloomy sigh was swept away by a slight wind through the cottonwood trees. "It's just hard to let it go."

"With nobody here to care for and protect it, there won't be much left after a while."

Matt nodded. "It's already looking a little run-down. I wish we could sell it to anyone other than the army."

"They're going to take it from us if we don't sell to them." Mary leaned closer. "Either they'll steal it through the courts, or we try to get some money out of it—at least enough to pay for Patrick's care and maybe a little more."

"Yeah, this old homestead owes him that much at least." Matt stood, walked to the veranda stairs, and looked at the star-filled sky. "Once, I hated this ranch, wanted nothing to do with it. I even swore I'd never live here. Now, it breaks my heart to let it go."

Mary went to him, wrapped her arm around his waist, and leaned against him. "We'll make our own happiness wherever we are, whatever we do. Isn't that already how it is for us?"

Matt smiled at her. "You bet it is." His smile faded as he gazed at the empty pasture. "Back before the war, I had a real good run selling cutting horses and top cow ponies to ranchers and rodeo cowboys. After a long day working them, I used to love to come out here in the cool of the evening and see my ponies lazing in the pasture. God, they were as pretty as they come. Having them here made the harshness of the land somehow more civilized and peaceful." He turned to Mary. "More beautiful."

"We can make another place like this for ourselves," Mary suggested.

"I feel like I'm giving up, quitting, to let this go."

"If you want to stay and fight, we can."

"Like old John Prather." Matt studied Mary's face. "You'd do that?"

"I would, Mr. Kerney."

Matt kissed her softly. "Hard as it is, I think it best we move on and make sure Patrick is well cared for."

"Let's not move too far," Mary pleaded.

Matt laughed. "Not on your life. I'm too much of a desert rat. Let's collect Kevin from the Witch's Tree and start making plans."

* * *

Before approaching the army to discuss the sale of the 7-Bar-K to the government, Matt and Mary met with Craig Gridley, an Albuquerque attorney who specialized in real-estate law. Through his many contacts, Matt had learned of Gridley's successful handling of several high-profile civil cases against government agencies attempting to condemn private property at below-market value.

A tall, thin man in his thirties with a full head of unruly brown hair and thick, droopy eyebrows, Gridley sat behind his desk and studied the titles, deeds, and survey documents. When he finished, he looked up, smiled, and told Matt and Mary that based on the army's own land survey and the fact the ranch was owned outright with no liens or other encumbrances, the government wouldn't be able to get away with making a lowball offer for the ranch.

He added that using the value of comparable ranch properties on the north end of the basin where ranchers had lease agreements with the missile range would give further credence to a just-compensation argument before the court, if it came to that.

"But I don't think it will go to court," Gridley concluded. "Obviously, the army wants your ranch and is willing to buy it. Where the niggling comes in is with what Uncle Sam is willing to pay. If you wish, I can put everything together you need to get the price up as high as possible and negotiate the deal on your behalf."

"How soon can you do it?" Matt asked.

"Give me thirty days."

"How much will your services cost?" Mary asked.

"I require a five-hundred-dollar retainer and I'll bill you by the hour. You can pay any balance owed me once the proceeds from the sale are deposited in your bank account. Let's set a limit of no more than twenty-five hundred dollars of billable hours and my reasonable expenses. If I have to exceed that amount, I'll ask for your approval in advance."

"That seems fair," Mary said.

"We want to be at the table when you close the deal," Matt said as he wrote out the check for the retainer.

Gridley nodded and stood. "Understood. I'll make contact with the judge advocate office at White Sands Missile Range today and open discussions."

"So soon?" Mary asked.

Gridley shrugged. "In many ways, the peacetime army is just another cumbersome government bureaucracy. Advance warning will help them get under way. Besides, they need to know we're coming at them with some heavy artillery, namely me."

"You talk like a vet," Matt said.

Gridley grinned. "Marines, Korea. I applied for a commission before they could draft me. The GI Bill paid for law school."

Happy with their choice of legal counsel, Matt and Mary shook Gridley's hand and left his office convinced they'd found the right man to tussle with the army.

* * *

Two weeks passed before Craig Gridley called the T or C cottage on a Saturday evening. Gridley reported the army had made a chickenshit offer for the 7-Bar-K. He was about to launch a counteroffensive.

With the telephone receiver tilted away from his ear so Mary could listen, Matt asked, "What kind of counteroffensive?"

"I'm mailing a letter to the army advising them that you are entering into preliminary discussions to sell the ranch to either the New Mexico College of Agriculture or the US Fish and Wildlife Service."

"We are?" Matt asked in astonishment.

"Both organizations are interested in looking at the property for range research and wildlife preservation, much like the experimental range on the Jornada and the San Andres National Wildlife Refuge."

"How did you pull this off?" Matt asked.

Gridley chuckled. "Through my good offices as your legal counsel. But don't get your hopes up. This is a ploy. Neither the college nor the federal agency think they have a chance in hell to keep the land out of the military's grasp. They're simply willing to take a serious look at the property and consider making an offer."

Mary took the receiver from Matt's hand. He bent his head near to keep listening. "What was the army's initial offer?"

"Trust me, you don't want to know," Gridley replied. "I'll have something firm to present to you by the end of the week. The JAG lawyers at the missile range will be scrambling to come up with a better deal. Keep the last weekend of the month free. If all goes well and you like the terms we'll close on the agreement here in Albuquerque."

"Not at the base?" Matt asked. He'd been looking forward to giving the brass a piece of his mind about all the unnecessary harassment and endless inconvenience they'd caused.

"This is lawyer stuff, not brass-hat business," Gridley explained. "I'll start a title search and begin gathering courthouse documents on Monday."

"What do you think a fair offer would be?" Mary asked.

"Six figures. I'm hoping for something around a quarter of a million. A source of mine says the army plans to operate the ranch as a way station. Civilian and military personnel who need to be up-range for extended periods of time would use it for temporary housing. They want it badly. I'll call as soon as the army's next offer comes in."

"Thank you," Matt said.

Gridley laughed. "It's my pleasure."

After hanging up, Matt and Mary sat on the couch in the living room, shocked into temporary silence by the sudden realization that the 7-Bar-K would soon be gone from their lives forever.

Finally, Mary said, "What do we do next?"

"Ranching is hard," Matt ventured. "We're lucky to both have decent-paying, reliable jobs, and this cottage, bought and paid for, to call home."

Mary looked at him skeptically. "You want to give up ranching forever?"

"There are ten sections adjacent to the Rocking J that just came on the market. The land isn't in good shape, but with some work it could be brought back."

"Good or bad, we can't ranch on ten sections," Mary argued.

"I know it. I'm thinking we ask Al if we can buy into the Rocking J as full partners. With the 7-Bar-K pastures no longer available, we need more land to graze our commingled herds. I know

Al would love to buy those sections but doesn't have the wherewithal to do it. Even if he could, it's still gonna cost a pretty penny and some hard work to restore the grassland."

"Could we build a little casita on the Rocking J ranch headquarters for our own use?" Mary asked.

"Or maybe expand the small cabin near the ranch house," Matt replied.

"Do you think Al would consider it?"

"I do, but before I even ask, I want to know what you think of the idea."

Mary slid close to Matt and kissed him. "It's perfect, and Kevin will love it as well."

Matt pulled her close and grinned. "That's what I wanted to hear."

27

Craig Gridley's frontal assault against the army's bureaucracy failed miserably. Not only did the government lawyers obtain a federal court ruling based on national security barring any entity other than the military from purchasing the 7-Bar-K Ranch, they immediately withdrew their cash settlement offer on the ranch. In its stead, they proposed a year-to-year co-use lease agreement, much like the one Al had with the Rocking J, which would require Matt to vacate the ranch during missile test firings. Based on the total acreage of the ranch and the estimated number of days the army wanted control of the skies above it, an annual payment of three thousand dollars was proposed.

Dismayed and embarrassed at being out-finessed by the government, Gridley dug in his heels and got the annual lease amount doubled. He immediately filed a lawsuit in federal court on behalf of Matthew Kerney and Al Jennings asking the judge to lift restricted travel across the missile range to and from the 7-Bar-K for all members of both families, any current or future employees, and all authorized suppliers or others conducting legitimate business with the plaintiffs. Again, the court sided with the army, the judge noting that even with proper authorization to cross portions of the base, searches could continue if there was reasonable suspicion of a national-security risk.

The back-and-forth haggling and court appearances took months, and just after the lease paperwork was signed and the first payment received, Matt got a telephone call from the Albuquerque nursing home administrator reporting that Patrick had wandered off from the facility. The police had picked him up several hours later a mile away sitting on the curb in front of a home for unmarried mothers. Matt had twenty-four hours to come and fetch him or he'd be sent under an emergency court order to the state mental hospital in Las Vegas for a competency evaluation.

Fortunately, Patrick had picked a Saturday to wander off to visit the unwed mothers, and the call from the nursing home had come while Matt and Mary were at the cottage instead of the ranch. Within minutes Matt was in his truck and on his way to Albuquerque. Mary remained behind, calling every nursing home in southern New Mexico and West Texas searching for another place that would accept her father-in-law.

In Albuquerque, Matt rescued Patrick from a police holding cell, gathered his possessions that were packed and ready to be picked up at the nursing home, and drove back to T or C, hoping Mary had worked a miracle. He arrived to find her waiting on the cottage porch. She hurried to him as he pulled into the driveway.

"Take him to the hospital right now," she said, eyeing Patrick as she got into the truck. He stared blankly ahead, his hands folded neatly in his lap, unmoving. "Doc Blaine has agreed to admit him overnight for observation."

"Where's Kevin?"

"Inside with Brenda and Dale. They came down from the

Rocking J in case you needed my help." She reached out and touched Patrick's sleeve. "How is he?"

Matt wheeled the truck in the direction of the hospital. "I have no idea, he hasn't said a word and has barely moved a muscle since I picked him up. Did you get something lined up?"

Mary shook her head. "I've been calling everywhere, even places we can't afford. I've put him on every admission waiting list there is."

At the hospital, Patrick, hunched over and shaky, shuffled slowly inside holding on to Matt's arm. It broke Mary's heart to see him so frail and incapacitated. She wondered if he was drugged. Matt turned him over to the admitting nurse at the reception desk, who led him gently by the hand much as she would a frightened, lost child.

"He seems docile enough," Matt noted hopefully.

"Meaning?" Mary asked, wondering what prompted such a ridiculous observation.

"Meaning what the hell do we do with him if he isn't?" Matt sputtered. "What if he wanders off again? Or tries to hurt you or Kevin? What if no place will take him in?"

Mary stayed silent, her expression guarded.

"I suppose we could leave him alone at the ranch in the hopes he'd wander off and die," Matt added.

Mary looked at him with rank displeasure. "What a preposterous thing to say."

Matt shook his head in frustration, ran a hand through his hair as if to brush away all of the conceivable unpleasant possibilities he'd thought of, and smiled apologetically. "I shouldn't have said that. But I've been brooding about what the hell to do with him ever since I left Albuquerque with him sitting next to me like a stone statue."

Mary's expression softened. Of course Matt would make Patrick his personal dilemma to solve. "He's family and he needs us—all of us," she said. "One way or another *we* have to find a way to take care of him. You really wouldn't want it any other way, would you?"

In the face of Mary's reasoning, Matt's anger with Patrick evaporated, replaced by the realization that he'd been feeling sorry for himself.

He grinned and kissed her. "That's my girl. You keep me honest, and I love you for it. But you've got to admit the damn old coot is nothing but trouble and always has been."

Mary laughed. "That may be so, but he's our trouble," she said.

* * *

It took months before they could get Patrick admitted to the Fort Bayard Veterans Hospital outside Silver City. During that time, they cared for him with the help of a retired practical nurse Doc Blaine had recommended, who looked after him during the weekdays. After school, Mary took over and if Matt wasn't traveling for work, he'd spell her. Kevin, who was bunking on a cot in Matt and Mary's bedroom, chipped in by taking Patrick on walks, reading him stories, and keeping an eye on him while Mary fixed meals, went to the store, or did her household chores.

Patrick seemed to enjoy Kevin's company the best, although the television Matt bought proved to be his favorite diversion. He'd sit in front of it for hours watching anything and everything. The weekends they took him to the ranch was when he seemed his most settled and content, never straying. He could usually be found on the veranda in his favorite chair staring out at the basin. He rarely spoke or showed any sign that he knew where he was or who he was with. Gradually, they all got used to the peculiarity of living with a person who dwelled in an unfathomable, unreachable shadow world.

Even on Patrick's best days it had been like prison for all of them, and when Fort Bayard called with news of an opening it brought a feeling of great relief for Matt and Mary. In almost a holiday mood, she packed a picnic lunch for the trip to the hospital, made sure Patrick was wearing his best clothes, and insisted that Kevin go along, although he'd expressed no desire to do so. On a rough, winding road outside the once-thriving mining town of Hillsboro, they drove through the Black Range into the Gila Wilderness and stopped to eat along a stream in the cool pines of the high country before continuing on to Fort Bayard. It was the first time Kevin had actually been in the mysterious westerly mountains he'd seen so frequently from the 7-Bar-K high country. He marveled at the thick stands of tall pines that climbed steep canyon walls to towering summits.

There were no tears or sullenness on Kevin's part when he hugged his grandfather goodbye inside the stark, three-story hospital that dominated one end of the parade grounds of the old historical frontier army fort where the famous Buffalo Soldiers had once proudly served.

"Will we ever see him again?" he asked soberly as they drove away.

"Of course," Mary said. "We'll come as often as we can."

"Do you think it matters if we do or don't?" Kevin asked.

Mary studied her son's face. "Does it matter to you?"

"Yes, ma'am," Kevin replied.

"Are you saying that just to please me?"

"No, I'll miss him."

Mary took her son's hand. "I bet he knows that."

"I bet he does too," Kevin said with a smile.

* * *

Patrick's health continued to decline over the next year, to the point that the doctors at Fort Bayard believed only his willpower and a strong physical constitution forged by eight decades of hard work kept him alive. For Mary, it didn't matter that he showed not the slightest hint of comprehension during their regular visits; she refused to let Matt stop going, although they'd reached the point of not staying long. Kevin always willingly went with them, and Mary was convinced it was his presence alone Patrick somehow sensed as they sat at his bedside.

In the spring of 1963, the army made an offer on the ranch. This time Matt went to see Charlie Hopkinson for legal advice. He thumbed through the paperwork and told Matt to take the deal, which was exactly half of what the Albuquerque lawyer Craig Gridley had hoped to get.

"You weren't ever going to get what that place is worth," Charlie mused. "But those army lease payments you've been getting these past several years have probably helped to soften the blow."

Matt agreed and asked Charlie to handle the transaction. "Get us ninety days to vacate, if you can."

"Can do," Charlie replied, offering a hand to seal the deal.

Matt left with a sour feeling in his gut. When the original deal with the missile range fell through, he'd lost the opportunity to buy the ten sections adjacent to the Rocking J. Now for the first time since John Kerney staked his claim on a slice of mountain wilderness overlooking the Tularosa nearly ninety years before, the family was about to become landless. He had half a mind to get stinking drunk in the first bar he could find. Instead, he drove to the desert outside of town and sat in the truck until it was time to go home for supper.

Four months before Kevin's thirteenth birthday, Patrick suffered a massive heart attack and was transferred to the VA Hospital in Albuquerque. He died there quietly in his sleep on the day White Sands Missile Range took possession of the 7-Bar-K Ranch. The army denied Matt's request to bury Patrick in the family cemetery, so he had his remains cremated and hatched a plan to return him to the 7-Bar-K, the missile range be damned.

A week later under cover of darkness, accompanied by Mary, Kevin, Al, Brenda, and Dale, and with Patrick's ashes in his saddlebag, Matt led his small company of riders onto the missile range through a narrow, almost invisible, boulder-strewn slot canyon and up the faint trace of an old Apache path to the Kerney family cemetery. There he bared his head and buried Patrick's ashes next to Emma's grave.

No one said a word. When he rose they all stood for a moment gazing out at the majestic sky brimming with stars above the great, lonesome Tularosa, now bereft of the last of the true, old-time cowboys, the last ranch sitting abandoned and silent below.

THREE

Kevin Kerney

28

The year Kevin Kerney was about to turn thirteen, he and Dale skipped the eighth grade and started high school. That same year, Raymond Edward Cannon, owner of the Willow Creek Ranch located at the base of the Sierra Cuchillo Mountains in the northern part of Sierra County, inaugurated an annual working cowboy and kids' rodeo on his spread.

In a cottonwood draw on a wide rift valley at the foot of the elongated north-south range, the ranch was a rich-man's getaway built for Mr. Cannon after the war by the best craftsmen, using the finest materials.

The Sierra Cuchillo Mountains were named not for their knife-like shape but for the legendary Apache leader Black Knife of the Warm Springs Band. On their northern slopes, they had once contained a ponderosa forest that long ago had been harvested for mining operations. Pockets of piñon and juniper trees dominated the gentle, gravelly eastern gradient that rose up to a steep, barren, western escarpment.

The ranch house was the fanciest and biggest dwelling Kevin

had ever seen. More a sportsman's lodge than a home, it had been constructed with massive timbers that supported a soaring, vaulted ceiling. An eight-foot fireplace at one end was bracketed by large windows that gave a panoramic view of the mountains. Arranged throughout the room were conversation areas with handmade chairs, couches, tables, and ottomans upholstered or decorated in western and cowboy motifs. It boggled Kevin's mind that the house had a half dozen huge bedrooms, all with individual full bathrooms. The dining room adjoining an enormous kitchen contained a handcrafted table with matching chairs that could easily seat two dozen people.

The nearby guesthouse also had a huge cook's kitchen, along with two full bathrooms and four separate bedrooms. A few steps away, near a stone and adobe horse barn, stood the foreman's cottage, built of milled lumber covered by a sloping bright-red metal roof. It had a spacious porch that looked out on a set of corrals near a horse pasture and brand-new rodeo grounds complete with a judge's stand and a small covered grandstand in close proximity to the chutes. During the events, folks who weren't able to snare a seat in the grandstand backed their pickups against the fence and watched from lawn chairs in the truck beds.

From the very get-go, the two-day rodeo drew hundreds of folks from the surrounding area, including a contingent of city and county elected officials from T or C. At the conclusion of the first day's events, Mr. Cannon and his wife, Polly, threw a barbeque on the front lawn for the contestants and spectators that was more a rally for Cannon's preferred political party candidates than it was a neighborly get-together. Still, the food, spirits, and company were great and nobody minded the glad-hand politicking.

Kevin figured the foreman's cottage was almost as big as the old 7-Bar-K ranch house. Behind it, no more than a hundred feet away, stood the bunkhouse, a long, low-slung adobe building with living space for six cowboys who worked cattle during the calving and shipping seasons and after fall works guided hunters into the mountains who anted up a pretty penny for the chance to bag a buck deer, a black bear, a wild turkey, or a mountain lion.

Cannon had made his fortune as a lawyer specializing in corporate acquisitions and was known for always turning a profit no matter what enterprise he undertook. Accordingly, the ranch operated in the black. While touring the ranch headquarters, Kevin and his parents were flabbergasted at the opulence of the place. When his dad half-jokingly advised him to go to law school first if he wanted to be a rancher, Kevin said he'd give it some thought.

That first year Kevin and Dale competed only in the team roping event and they came away with a second-place ribbon but no belt buckles. Kevin's dad, however, took the cowboy all-around title with a first in bronc riding, a second in steer wrestling, and another first in team roping with Al Jennings as his partner. He won a cash prize, a silver buckle, and a new saddle. Amid catcalls and cheers, he raised the saddle over his head and with a grin on his face and an ache in his side from getting stepped on by the steer, he promptly announced his retirement from competition. Bursting with pride for his dad and determined to match his success, Kevin decided to win the top prize in the kids' rodeo next year. Maybe he'd even get a peck on the cheek from Mr. Cannon's granddaughter, Melissa, a dark-haired thirteen-year-old charmer with bright-blue eyes who handed out the prizes.

During the school year, a number of cute girls in his classes helped Kevin quickly forget about Melissa Cannon. He trained with his dad every chance he got to improve his skills in calf wrestling and calf roping, and when he was at the Rocking J, he and

Dale worked tirelessly on their team roping—the only event Dale had any real interest in.

Keeping his grades up, practicing his rodeo skills, and pulling his share of chores at home and at the Rocking J took up most of his free time, so girls weren't a high priority, although he was starting to think they should be. Maybe next year he'd meet one he really liked.

* * *

Although the Rocking J kept its original brand, the ranch was now officially the J&K Land and Cattle Company owned jointly by Al and Brenda Jennings and Matthew and Mary Kerney. Kevin's parents had taken the money from the sale of the 7-Bar-K and invested a chunk of it in the enterprise to improve the pastures, upgrade the breeding stock, drill two new deep wells, replace fencing, and expand the small cottage at the ranch headquarters. As before, Al managed the cattle operation and Kevin's dad continued to work for the college as a range and equine specialist, helping out during gatherings and on weekends. In addition, he bred and trained a small herd of cow ponies in his free time that he sold to area ranchers.

The summer after his freshman year, on a day when both sets of parents were in town on business, Kevin and Dale saddled up, left the Rocking J, and snuck onto the missile range to visit the old 7-Bar-K, traveling through the narrow slot canyon well hidden from any soldiers scanning the San Andres through binoculars. They reached the ranch undetected and found it unoccupied with the front door wide-open. Although the army had moved cots, gray metal dressers, chairs, tables, and a dented steel file cabinet into the ranch house, all the warmth of the place was gone. There was evidence of rodent droppings in all the rooms and a slithering impression of a snake on the dusty wood-plank floor in the living room that gradually disappeared on the steps to the veranda. Paint was peeling off the wood window frames, and there was a large water stain on the kitchen ceiling from a roof leak around the stovepipe.

A heavy padlock secured the entry to the adobe casita off the courtyard. The boys debated busting in to see what was inside, but gave up the notion so as not to advertise their trespassing.

The barn, corrals, and sheds looked no better than the house, and the once-welcoming cottonwood windbreak below the veranda was dying of thirst from a lack of moisture. At the end of the windbreak, the long-dead Witch's Tree tilted precariously, and the rock-lined, hand-dug channel Kevin's great-grandfather had trenched to water the trees was bone-dry. Soon all the beautiful old trees with thick branches filled with lime-green leaves quaking in the soft breeze would be dead and cut up for firewood.

At the family cemetery on the hill, part of the fence was down. At first glance, Kevin thought it had been deliberately damaged until he discovered a critter hole next to one of the posts had caused the collapse. He got a shovel with a broken handle that had been left behind in the barn and with Dale's help reset the post and repaired the railing. He doubted anyone staying at the place would notice, and if they did he didn't care.

Before leaving, the boys pulled all the weeds inside the fence so that it looked cared for. If his gramps was watching, Kevin knew he'd be pleased. On the ride back to the Rocking J, he stewed over the notion that what mattered most to some people didn't count for spit to others. His family history lived in the hand-dug water channel, the thick-walled adobe house, the stoutly built corral, the slat-board barn, the large stone water tank, the stately, silent windmill, and the land so carefully tended. It meant nothing to the army. What kind of men ran the army? Whoever they were, he didn't think much of them.

They started for home over the mountain, not caring a lick when the MPs on jeep patrol spotted them coming out of a grove of trees at the top of the steep eastern escarpment. They were too far away to get caught. They drew rein and waved their hats at the soldiers before dropping out of sight down an old game trail.

"We're gonna catch hell at home if our parents find out what we did," Dale predicted.

Kevin shrugged. "Maybe not."

"Why is that?"

"Because I bet my dad has been to the ranch at least once since we buried Gramps's ashes."

"How do you figure that?"

Kevin smiled. "If we can't stay away, I doubt that he can either."

Dale nodded soberly. "It's a hard place to forget. Let's go back again someday."

"Yeah, lots of times," Kevin added.

* * *

At the next Willow Creek Ranch Kids' Rodeo, a sixteen-year-old took the top prize. But Kevin and Dale came away with buckles for first place in team roping. They also got a photograph in the T or C newspaper showing Melissa Cannon presenting their awards. Dale's grin lit up the photograph and Melissa posed like a starlet, smiling prettily at the camera. Disappointed at his narrow second-place finish for the all-around title, Kevin glared glumly into the lens. He'd lost the championship with a disqualification in calf roping by breaking the barrier too soon. He started the first day of his second year of high school determined to never make that mistake again.

The first day at school also brought Eunice Williston into his class. A transfer student from Socorro, she was a mixture of tomboy and tease. She was natural and uninhibited, with short-cut blond hair, a slightly crooked nose, and a devilish laugh.

Her father had retired as a captain from the Socorro Police Department and recently taken a job as a Sierra County deputy sheriff. He'd been on the police force before the war and had returned to his old job after getting discharged, where he'd met his wife and started a family. Eunice lived with her parents on a leased ten-acre horse property south of town along the river. She had an older, married sister who lived in San Diego with her navy husband, and a handsome pony named Lucky. She was a year older than Kevin, but that didn't seem to matter. They hit it off right away. They were the tallest and brightest students in their class, shared a mutual love of horses, and liked the same kind of music.

At the first teen hop of the season at a local church, they danced only with each other, which got them teased about going steady. Kevin secretly liked the idea of Eunice as a girlfriend, but she wanted nothing to do with it. He had hopes that time would change her mind.

They quickly fell into a routine of searching out each other's company during lunch hour and soon started visiting back and forth to do homework, talk, and listen to records. Kevin got to know her parents, Ben and Donna, who were likable but a little reserved around him. He chalked it up to a parental suspicion of his motives, which wasn't completely unfounded.

Eunice's dad was a slender man with the same slightly crooked nose as his daughter's. Unlike many of the town and county cops

Kevin had met he didn't strut his authority, and Kevin appreciated that.

On one occasion, he showed Kevin his collection of frontier law-enforcement memorabilia that he kept and displayed in a small spare bedroom he used as a study. It included a number of valuable old six-shooters, antique police and sheriff badges, and a large assortment of official police uniform patches from agencies throughout the southwest. Many of the badges and patches were in shadow boxes mounted on the walls. Also framed and hung were two rare Wanted posters for Black Jack Ketchum and Billy the Kid.

As Kevin admired the collection, he told Mr. Williston how Gene Rhodes had come to write a story about his grandmother. Kevin's family connection to Rhodes got Mr. Williston talking enthusiastically about Rhodes and his frequent alleged run-ins with the law. It turned into a conversation Kevin thoroughly enjoyed and got him thinking he might like police work.

Some time later, Mr. Williston told Eunice she'd made a good choice in Kevin as a friend, and while he was pleased to hear of it, it still didn't get him to first base with her. He soon gave up trying and in the end it didn't matter. She was great company, had a wicked sense of humor, a quick mind, and was fun to be around. Although he looked forward to seeing her every day, he still yearned to have a girl in his life who was more than just a real good buddy. He sometimes wondered if it would ever happen. He really, really hoped so.

29

Late in September, a letter arrived in the mail from Erma Fergurson, inviting them to a Halloween party on Saturday, October 31, at her home in Las Cruces. In it, she ordered the Kerney clan to arrive on Friday afternoon and stay as her guests over the weekend. Regrets would not be acceptable and costumes at the party were required, including masks. And no, Matt and Kevin couldn't come as cowboys; that would be cheating.

The invitation delighted Mary. Erma was her oldest and dearest friend, and now that she was back from the Art Institute of Chicago with an MFA in studio art and teaching at the college, they stayed in touch much more frequently.

When Matt came home she showed him the invitation and said that they were going, no quibbling and no questions asked. His only grumble about it was trying to think of a costume he could stand to wear.

"How about going as a pirate?" Mary suggested.

Matt laughed. "Why didn't I think of that?"

Matt made arrangements to take off work early the Friday before the party, and on Thursday night Mary packed what they needed for the weekend so they could leave for Las Cruces as soon as school let out. Except for Kevin, who didn't appreciate being strong-armed into going and forced to miss the Halloween dance at the high school, they drove south in high spirits, the autumn sun glaring brightly on the western horizon. However, Kevin's mood improved as they drew closer to the city and the prospect of escaping T or C for the weekend became more appealing. He liked his friends and all, and school was okay, but sometimes the dusty desert town of five thousand was boring, with not much for kids to do. It catered to health seekers eager to be cured at the hot springs and mud baths, and to the customary trade of the townspeople and area ranchers, but it had no nightlife other than the movie theater and the bars. Strangers on the streets were either lodgers staying at one of the health spas, motorists stopping overnight at one of the car courts, or folks camping at Elephant Butte Lake. Illegal gambling had supposedly been cleaned up in the bars along Main Street, but along with drinking and watching TV, it was still the most popular adult entertainment in town.

Las Cruces, on the other hand, was eight times larger, more modern, and much livelier. The city teemed with college students and was home to hundreds of scientists and engineers who worked at White Sands Missile Range. Army boys on weekend passes chased after the local girls, and hotrods roared up and down dirt roads outside of town, occasionally pursued by the sheriff. There were nightspots with bands that played rock 'n' roll, not just country music, and at the bars along Main Street there was bound to be at least one Saturday-night fight between cowboys from the area ranches and soldiers from the missile range. The town even had a real public library and a fancy country club and golf course that bordered the highway to Alamogordo. Kevin was seriously considering attending college there after high school.

Erma's house was in an old neighborhood of Victorian and pueblo-style homes near downtown. In fact, it was the same one she'd shared with Mary during their college years, except Erma moved out of the attached apartment into the main house when she bought the place after the death of her landlady. Renting out both the main house and the apartment had helped pay her living expenses during the time she was in Chicago attending the Art Institute.

Kevin always enjoyed visiting Erma and considered her his aunt. She was perhaps the most unconventional person he'd ever met, with a wisecracking sense of humor and a mile-a-minute mind. She was always on a tangent about something or other and willing to argue about it. And she was pretty as well, with short hair that made her look a lot younger than his mom, although they were almost the same age.

Her home was equally unusual. On the outside it was a stately two-story house with a steep roof, brick cladding, and a welcoming front porch on a large lot. Tall trees in a carefully tended front lawn towered above the roofline. The inside was filled with objects Erma had bought at flea markets, junk yards, and estate sales and turned into collages, mobiles, or abstract sculptures that decorated the walls, hung from the ceiling, or stood on floor pedestals. The front room served as a constantly changing solo exhibition of her shimmering, impressionistic paintings of New Mexico landscapes.

Upstairs, she'd turned the largest bedroom with the best light into a studio, choosing to sleep in a sparsely furnished small room that had originally been the nursery. The remaining two bedrooms were kept ready for guests and an occasional drunk friend unwilling to crawl behind the wheel after attending one of Erma's parties.

The term "avant-garde" always came to mind when Kevin thought about Aunt Erma. Once he'd asked her why she wasn't married, and she'd said that after trying it once she found it didn't suit her, adding most men turned rather boring when they married, although she exempted his father from her generalization. She finished her lecture about matrimony with a pat on his cheek, a smooch, and the suggestion that he not be in a rush to get hitched.

"And watch out for the girls who are," she counseled.

They arrived at Erma's to find a note pinned to the unlocked front door inviting them in and saying she'd be home soon from the market. Inside, cut-out paper Halloween skeletons, pumpkins, and witches danced on garlands strung along the walls. In the kitchen, a pot of delicious-smelling spaghetti sauce simmered on the stove. On the counter sat an open bottle of red wine and three wineglasses, along with another note ordering them to unpack and have a drink.

Kevin smiled. Since turning thirteen last year he was allowed a glass of wine at Erma's by way of—as she put it—her hostess prerogative. At home, maybe he could have a sip from his mom's glass at Thanksgiving and Christmas. There he was still a kid; at Erma's he was almost a grown-up.

Erma arrived with a bag of salad fixings, and they celebrated with a glass of wine in the kitchen, after which Matt and Kevin headed downtown on foot to stretch their legs and leave the ladies to visit without interruption.

Most of the stores were closed, but Kevin spotted a thirty-dollar wristwatch in a jewelry-store window that he really liked. It was military-style with large numerals and a sweep second hand on a brown leather strap, but he only had ten dollars in his pocket. His father watched him eye it but didn't say a word. Kevin didn't either.

At a flower shop open late they bought a bouquet of chrysanthemums and daises for Erma, which, upon their return, she accepted with much delight and smooches. She placed them, snipped and arranged in a vase, as the dining-table centerpiece.

Before sitting down to eat, Howard Conway arrived to join them for dinner. During introductions, Erma mentioned Howard had been a soldier at the missile range, but pleaded not to hold that against him. She got a laugh and a ready agreement from Mary and Matt.

A tall guy with an easy smile, a square chin, and a wide forehead with thick eyebrows and light-brown hair, Howard was an engineering graduate student at the college. Originally from Tennessee, he was a good fifteen years younger than Erma, which wasn't surprising, as she liked her boyfriends young.

Howard had been drafted after college and because he had a degree in engineering, had been sent to the missile range immediately after basic training. Vague about what he'd done while on active duty, he admitted to having spent most of his time up-range at some of the test sites on the basin. He jokingly said he'd been a sad sack of a soldier with a bad attitude who almost didn't get promoted to PFC.

"At least you weren't an MP or a general," Kevin said.

Conway laughed. "Not me. But I did fall in love with the area, so I stayed."

Kevin asked him what costume he would be wearing to the Halloween party, but Erma called a time-out before he could answer.

"No fair," she said, wagging a finger at Kevin. "You're supposed to keep costumes a surprise. That makes it more fun."

She turned to Matt and Mary. "Gus and Consuelo are coming."

Matt grinned happily and Mary lit up.

Erma refilled their wineglasses, sneaking a dribble more into Kevin's glass. "I thought that would please you."

After dinner, Howard stayed and helped with the dishes, and Kevin retired to his bedroom, where Erma had thoughtfully left a small stack of new books for him. He picked up *The Spy Who Came in from the Cold* and got caught up in the story right away.

Although he didn't know the exact time, it was late when he stopped reading. It made him wish he'd had the extra twenty bucks he needed to buy the watch he'd seen downtown. He sure did like it and it would look great on his wrist.

He undressed and slipped into bed, lulled to sleep by the voices of his mom, dad, and aunt Erma wafting up the stairs.

* * *

On Saturday morning, Mary and Erma got started on the party preparations while Matt took Kevin on a tour of the college, which was now known as New Mexico State University. Even on the weekend there were students everywhere; studying in small groups on the lawns, walking to and from the library, talking in the student union over coffee, and wandering through the shelves at the college bookstore. On the steps outside the college radio station, a young reporter was interviewing an antiwar activist surrounded by a small group of supporters holding END THE WAR signs. He was fervently proclaiming that the Gulf of Tonkin Resolution passed by Congress earlier in the summer would only escalate American military involvement in South Vietnam.

Kevin had been on the campus before, but only during the summer, when classes weren't in session. Then it seemed like nothing more than a collection of interesting buildings on a pretty campus with a nice view of the Organ Mountains. Today, it felt vibrant and fascinating, making the idea of going away to college all the more intriguing.

"I think I'd like to go here," he said to his dad.

Matt nodded approvingly. "It's a good school, and it would make your mother happy if you weren't too far from home."

Kevin watched a foursome of students pile into a car and peel out of the parking lot. "If I had a car, I could come home once in a while on weekends."

Matt laughed. "Don't get ahead of yourself, son."

They spent the remainder of the morning away from the main campus at the Ag Complex, where Matt kept an office. Outside the big barn, Kevin watched grad students drawing blood from quarantined cattle suspected of having bovine tuberculosis. His dad explained that when the skin test results are inconclusive, a special blood test was necessary to make a final diagnosis. Fortunately, the infected cattle came from a small herd that had no contact with other livestock, so there was little possibility the disease had spread.

They wandered around the Ag Complex until Kevin got hungry, then had lunch at the student union before returning to Erma's, where they were recruited to do a final cleanup of the front room before the party, carve the pumpkins to be placed on the front porch, and string orange and black bunting on the porch railings. Late in the afternoon, they all walked downtown for an early meal at a popular Mexican restaurant on Main Street—Matt's treat.

After returning, Kevin dressed in his policeman costume. Eunice's father had given him a Socorro Police Department sleeve patch and lent him one of his old badges and police hats to wear. His mom had sewed the patch on a black shirt and added epaulets to make it look more authentic. His dad had cut down an old baseball bat, painted it black, and put a strap on the end to make a nightstick. A long look in the dresser mirror convinced him it was a pretty cool costume.

He went downstairs to find Erma dressed as a flapper in a short, black sleeveless dress with a matching headband, a long strand of pearls, and glittery high heels. Mary was wearing a Clarabell the Clown outfit she'd made that consisted of a one-piece floppy suit with a high ruffled collar. She had painted an upturned grin around her mouth and penciled exaggerated eyebrows on her forehead. Matt was a pirate, wearing one of his best eye patches, ballooned pants stuffed into cowboy boots, a shirt with billowing sleeves Mary had found at a thrift store, and a purple sash around his waist. Except for the cowboy boots he looked okay. As required, everybody wore masks.

The first guests to arrive were Gus and Consuelo Merton, who came as Albert Einstein and Queen Isabella. Mary, Matt, and Erma spent ten minutes talking with Gus and Consuelo about old times before the party heated up.

Kevin was the only teenager there, but he didn't mind. Erma's friends, none of whom he knew, treated him like an adult, which made the party a lot of fun. And he got to sneak some wine when his parents weren't looking while talking to one of Erma's art students, a very pretty coed who came dressed as Peter Pan.

By eleven o'clock the party was still going strong, but Kevin was more than a little tipsy and bushed. He said good night to Erma, who gave him a kiss and teasingly asked if she should send the pretty coed up to tuck him into bed. He said sure, told his mom he was turning in, and climbed the stairs.

As he unbuttoned his shirt, he heard his father's voice in the backyard through the slightly open bedroom window.

"Let me see your hat," Matt demanded.

Kevin opened the window wide and peered out. His dad stood in the glow of the back porch light with a man wearing a Rough Rider uniform.

"Let me see the damn hat!" he repeated.

"What's the big deal?" Howard Conway replied. "I told you inside it was my grandfather's uniform."

Matt snatched the campaign hat off Conway's head and turned it over. "Were your grandfather's initials PK?"

Conway didn't answer.

"You're a liar."

"Okay, so it wasn't my grandfather's," Conway admitted. "I just said that for the fun of it. I bought it in a secondhand store."

Matt yanked the pistol from Conway's holster, checked to make sure it was unloaded, and waved it in his face. "And you got this from a pawnshop, I suppose."

"What's bugging you?" Conway pleaded. "It's just part of the costume."

"Be glad this horse pistol isn't loaded, or I might just shoot you. You stole it and the uniform from my old ranch."

Conway shook his head. "No, no, not me, I swear." His voice quivered.

"Prove it."

"I got it from a guy who served with me in the army. He said he found it in an abandoned homestead on the base."

"Aren't you forgetting the secondhand-store story?"

"I swear I'm not lying."

Matt grabbed the pistol by the barrel. "Strip down to your skivvies."

"What?"

"Do it or I'll beat you bloody."

"Are you serious?"

"Try me," Matt replied.

"Okay, look, I took it and I'm sorry. It was just a lark. Can't we leave it at that? I'll give the uniform back to you tomorrow, promise."

"One more time: take off the uniform," Matt growled.

Defeated, Conway removed the uniform. With his keys and wallet in his hand, he asked if he could just leave.

Matt motioned with the horse pistol at the back door. "Yeah, but you have to go through the house."

"That's ridiculous," Conway said.

"Either you leave through the house in your skivvies or I file a police report with the sheriff on Monday. I'll tell everybody here you lost a friendly bet to me. That will help you save face."

"A bet about what?"

"I'll make something up," Matt answered.

"Promise?"

Matt opened the back door to the sounds of party merriment. "I promise. Now, go."

Conway nodded, put on his boots, and stepped inside.

Kevin burst out of his room and reached the bottom of the stairs in time to see Conway's skivvy-covered backside darting for the front door past stunned partygoers.

For the first time since Friday he didn't even remotely mind missing the school dance. Not at all.

30

For Kevin, the holiday season of joy and happiness lost some of its cheer. Just before Christmas, Eunice's dad resigned from the sheriff's department to become the Socorro police chief. He started his new job right away, and left Eunice and her mother behind in T or C to prepare for their move back home after the first of the year.

Eunice was overjoyed to be returning to Socorro, and while Kevin was devastated to be losing a friend, he tried hard not to show it. But it bothered him that in all the time he knew her she had never explained why her parents had moved to T or C. When he asked, she blithely told him when her father had been passed over for chief, he retired in disgust, and moved the family to T or C to take a deputy sheriff position. She never in a million years thought he'd be offered the chief's job.

While it all made sense, Kevin couldn't shake off a feeling that she hadn't been completely up-front with him from the start. He wondered what else she wasn't sharing. Maybe, in the end, it wasn't his business.

About the only good thing Christmas brought was the watch his parents gave him that he'd spotted in the Las Cruces jewelry-store window. What a surprise that had been. For the first week he had it, he couldn't stop admiring it on his wrist.

He saw Eunice once the weekend before she moved. She was still flushed with excitement about leaving T or C and returning home. She promised to write him, but he sensed a growing detachment that dimmed his hope they'd continue to remain in contact. Although he couldn't put his feelings into words, he felt a sense of loss about her leaving until he realized she had considerably brightened his life.

He heard from her once about a month after she left in a chatty letter about how happy she was to be back in Socorro with her old friends. No longer glum about her departure, he wrote back not expecting a reply and didn't get one. He was too busy to worry about it. He'd thrown himself into the pursuit of the all-around title at the next year's Willow Creek Ranch rodeo, and when he wasn't doing homework or weekend ranch chores, he worked on his calf roping and honed his steer-wrestling and bronc-riding skills. As a junior he'd be eligible to compete in the annual all-state high school rodeo, and he had his eye on winning that championship as well.

He continued working with Dale on team roping, who had no interest in entering any other event now that he'd made the football team as a starting tackle. They were the same age, but Kevin had passed him in height. Where Dale was thick in the chest with legs like huge lodge poles, Kevin was square in the shoulders, lean, and quick on his feet.

Several of the boys he practiced rodeoing with at the county fairgrounds also played football, and as winter turned to spring, they started encouraging him to try out for the team. The previous year they'd taken the district title but lost the state championship, and they wanted another crack at it in their senior year. Even Dale got into the act by encouraging him to speak to their coach, Mr. Bradley, the science teacher.

"You'd make a good running back, and we need more speed," he added.

Not interested, Kevin continued to decline their invitations. One day during lunch recess, the team captain, Joey Stewart, caught up with him in the cafeteria.

"You need to try out for the team," he ordered. A burly two-hundred-pounder wearing his letterman's jacket, the thinly veiled threat was clearly visible in his eyes.

"It's not something I have time to do," Kevin replied.

"Show some school pride," Joey replied gruffly. "I'm asking you nice."

"It's not that I don't care about our school," Kevin answered. "I'm just not interested in football."

Joey snorted. "That's stupid. Nobody gives a damn about rodeo. Hell, we don't even have a rodeo club, let alone an official team."

"That's true, but it's the sport I like."

Kevin walked away and heard no more about it until Coach Bradley posted a team-tryout announcement on the school bulletin boards. Joey Stewart showed up again during lunch recess.

"Either you agree to try out for the team or meet me after school behind the gym." The sneer on his face was pure ugly meanness.

Kevin laughed. "The threat of fighting you isn't going to make me change my mind. Don't wait for me."

"Coward," Joey spat as Kevin walked away.

* * *

After school, Dale intercepted Kevin on his way home. "One way or another, Joey will make you fight him," he predicted sourly.

"That's plain dumb," Kevin replied. "I'm not going out for the team."

"Look, he's a bully—that's all he knows how to do. He wants you on the team. So do a lot of the guys. Plus, we need depth if we're gonna win state."

"I bet he makes a great team captain."

Dale winced in agreement at Kevin's sarcasm.

"Did he send you to come and get me?"

"Yeah, sort of," Dale replied sheepishly.

Kevin stopped in his tracks and gave Dale a disapproving look for being Joey's messenger boy.

Dale grimaced. "I ain't afraid of him."

"I didn't say you were." Kevin pondered his options. True, Joey outweighed him by more than fifty pounds and had bigger muscles, but he wasn't the brightest kid in town. "Tell him if he wants to fight to meet me at the county fairgrounds arena in an hour."

Dale raised an eyebrow. "What are you going to do?"

"Just give him the message."

Dale nodded. "Okay, I'll see you there."

He hurried off trying to decipher what the mischievous look in Kevin's eyes meant. He didn't know for sure, but he wasn't going to miss what his pal had planned for Joey at the fairgrounds.

* * *

Kevin got to the arena early, tied Two-Bits out of sight at the rear of the stock corral, unlatched the gate to the calf-roping chute, hunkered down behind a fencepost, and waited. In a few minutes a line of cars appeared on the dirt road to the fairgrounds. He backtracked to Two-Bits, got his lasso, and did a quick head count of the students who spilled out of the vehicles and tromped behind Joey into the arena. It looked like the entire team, the water boy, the student manager, and half of the cheerleaders had come to watch the fight. They formed a loose, noisy semicircle behind Joey and waited for the show to begin.

Joey didn't keep them waiting. He walked to the center of the arena, put his clenched hands on his hips, took an aggressive stance, scanned for his intended victim, and boomed out Kevin's name.

Kevin took his cue, threw a leg over Two-Bits, broke the pony into a fast lope, bent low to push open the unlatched gate, and bore down on Joey, his lasso in the air. The crowd behind Joey began to scatter, but he stood his ground just long enough for Kevin's perfect loop to settle over his shoulders. He quick-wrapped the lasso on the saddle horn, and Two-Bits skidded to a perfect dime stop that jerked Joey off his feet.

It knocked the wind out of him and he lay still for a minute before struggling upright, a murderous look on his face, his arms bound tightly at his sides by Kevin's rope.

Kevin gave Two-Bits a little jig and the pony fast-stepped backward, pulling Joey facedown in the dirt. Joey's teammates and the others stood in stunned silence, although Dale and a few of his football pals were smiling.

"Do you want more?" Kevin asked as Two-Bits snorted impatiently.

Red-faced with anger, Joey struggled to his knees.

"I could drag you around the arena a few times," Kevin suggested as Joey continued to glare at him. "It would skin some of the hide off you and probably hurt a bit."

"Let me go," Joey demanded after considering his options, his husky voice no longer filled with bravado.

"If I do, it ends here," Kevin said, with a firm tug on the lasso that made Joey freeze. "That's the deal, otherwise you're gonna eat a lot of dirt."

Joey stiffened and the color drained from his face. "Okay."

"You all heard that," Kevin said to the watching crowd as he jigged Two-Bits forward. Everyone nodded in agreement.

"Are we square, Joey?"

Joey answered through clenched teeth. "Yeah, we're square."

Kevin reached down, freed Joey, and trotted Two-Bits toward the gate, holding in check a growing need to smile. It wouldn't do to openly gloat about his victory, but it sure felt good nonetheless.

He waited until he was loping along halfway home before letting out a victory hoot.

* * *

Outside the high school principal's office, Mary Kerney waited with her unrepentant son on the uncomfortable seat of a wooden bench, worn smooth over the years by the bottoms of mischief-makers due for a scolding or reprimand. Across the hallway on an identical, equally worn bench, sat a sullen Joey Stewart, Kevin's opponent in the fairgrounds fight that didn't happen. With him was his father, Owen Stewart, the owner of a local car dealership and a big booster of the high school football team. He paid for the game-day programs and the GO TIGERS banners strung at the top of the stands, made up the shortfall in the team equipment budget, and sponsored all the newspaper ads announcing the team's home and away games. Heavy in the jowls, he had the look of a man ready to pounce.

According to the school secretary, who'd called Mary at home to bring Kevin to the principal's office immediately, the incident between the two alleged miscreants was already being talked about as a rumble of mythic proportions in which the school's most notorious bully had been laid low. From what Kevin told Mary about the episode, it was a one-sided fracas with her son coming out on top over a rather dimwitted opponent. And while she'd never admit to it, she would have loved to have seen it.

A two-minute wait brought Principal Lloyd Becker to the door. With a serious look at the boys and a polite nod to Mary and to Joey's father, he ushered everyone into his office, sat them in front of his desk, and launched into the reason for the meeting—namely the violation of the school rule prohibiting students from fighting on or off campus.

"We simply can't tolerate such behavior," he said.

Livid, Owen Stewart pointed a finger at Kevin. "I want him expelled!"

"For refusing to fistfight?" Mary asked sweetly.

Stewart curled his upper lip. "Just because you're a teacher at the elementary school, Mrs. Kerney, doesn't mean you or your son have special privileges here. He tried to run my boy down on horseback."

Mary studied Joey. "Your boy looks none the worse for wear."

"He assaulted him," Owen Stewart thundered. "That's against the law."

"I'd hardly call it an assault; more a creative way to avoid a fight. And it worked, as I understand it. Joey and Kevin have agreed to peacefully and permanently settle their differences."

Mary smiled warmly at Joey, who sneered at her defiantly. She kept smiling.

Owen Stewart snorted in disgust and turned to Principal Becker. "Do something," he commanded.

Becker faced Owen Stewart directly. "Yes, of course." He paused and then turned to look seriously at Kevin. "There is no question you violated school policy. However, since this is your first disciplinary infraction of any kind, I'm giving you a warning. Next time, the consequences will be greater. Do you understand?"

"Yes, sir, I do," Kevin replied solemnly.

Becker switched to Joey. "There is no question you also violated school policy. In addition, this is the third time this year you have been sent to me for aggressive behavior. For that reason, I'm suspending you for three days."

Owen Stewart shot to his feet. "You don't want to do that."

Becker rose. "Yes, I do," he replied patiently. "And the next time I see Joey in my office for any school infraction, no matter how minor, he'll no longer be on the football team."

Owen Stewart's eyes narrowed to thin slits. "The school board will hear about this."

Principal Becker nodded. "I'm sure they will, and I'll continue to tell them how much we appreciate your strong civic support of our athletic programs." He smiled genially at his guests and gestured at his closed office door. "Thank you for coming, and good day to you all."

Mary waited to giggle until she got in the car with Kevin for the short drive home.

"You're not mad?" Kevin asked.

Mary shook her head. "I've been trying to think of a reason to give you a good dressing-down, but I can't." She reached over and patted his knee. "Just go easy on the hijinks from here on out."

Kevin smiled in relief.

* * *

At the end of the school year Kevin brought home a report card with lower letter grades than usual in both math and science.

"My grades are still better than most," he argued as Matt grimly inspected the report card over dinner.

"Is that what you want to be when you grow up, just a little better than most?" his father replied, staring Kevin down.

Kevin dropped his gaze to the table. "No, sir."

"We expect more from you," Mary added. "Right now high school may be easy, but college won't be. You've gotten lazy."

"I may not go to college," Kevin said impulsively, without thinking. The announcement vibrated like a noiseless explosion in the room. "At least not right away," he modified.

"What?" Matt demanded.

Kevin shrugged. "A lot of kids don't go. Dale says he's enlisting in the air force when he graduates. Maybe I'll do the same."

"That's not being very smart," Matt countered.

"Why not?" He glanced from his father to his mother. "You both enlisted and served, and you're proud of it. Anyway, I'll probably get drafted when I turn eighteen, so why not get it over with?"

"You'll just be turning seventeen when you graduate," Mary said. "And we won't sign the papers for you to go in early."

"Why not?"

"Because we want you to go to college first," Matt replied. "If the military still needs you after college, so be it. Better to serve as an officer."

"Exactly," Mary echoed.

"Maybe I'll rodeo for a year and volunteer when I turn eighteen," Kevin replied.

"Got it all figured out, have you?" Matt said sarcastically. "Who's going to stake you to be on the circuit? How will you pay for a truck, a trailer, at least two good ponies, the entry fees, your expense money, and all the rest? Have you got that kind of cash?" He tapped his finger on the table as he made each point.

Kevin shook his head. "You know I don't. I figured to get a start working as a hand for a rodeo stock contractor."

"At a buck and a quarter an hour, if you can find the work," Matt predicted reproachfully.

"I'll bunk at the ranch between jobs," Kevin proposed.

"If you're not in school, you'll pay us room and board," Mary said, her expression tight-lipped and unsmiling.

Kevin bit his lip and pushed back from the table. "That's fine with me. May I be excused?"

"No, you may not," Matt replied.

They continued arguing over Kevin's future for a time until it ended in a stalemate. Sticking to his plans to forego college, Kevin's only concession was a promise to improve his grades in math and science next school year, or not be allowed to enter rodeo competitions.

"Maybe it's just a phase," Mary said hopefully after Kevin left the table. Her boy, who had been just about the best child a parent could hope for, had suddenly morphed into a defiant adolescent.

"Some rebellion is part of growing up, I reckon," Matt replied as he stood to help clear the table. "Let's hope it doesn't last too long."

Mary gave him a doubtful look.

* * *

That summer, Jeannie Hollister came along and captured Kevin's full attention. Petite and small-boned, Jeannie was quiet and serious except when she was on the dance floor. She was a year younger than Kevin, and he might not have noticed her if he hadn't been dragged by Dale to a weekly sock hop put on by a local church in an attempt to keep teenagers out of summertime trouble. It didn't stop the underage drinking at the favorite hang-out spots along the river, or kids making out in the cars along the stretch of abandoned pavement outside of town where the hot-rods raced, but it did give them an opportunity to get turned on and sweaty once a week in public.

He pretty much monopolized Jeannie from that first night, dancing with her to the Stones, the Beatles, and the other popular groups. Starting out, he shuffled around the dance floor self-consciously, but just by watching her he began to relax and loosen up. She had a natural sexiness in the way she moved and there was a look of pure delight on her face as she swirled to the rhythm. It enticed him to follow along. When they slow danced to songs like "You've Lost That Lovin' Feelin'," she molded herself against him.

Stuck at the ranch most of the summer, Kevin made sure to be in town for the Saturday-night weekend hops, riding with Dale, who'd gotten his driver's license and was seeing a girl he was stuck on named Becky Taylor. After the long workdays at the Rocking J in between the Saturday dance nights, both were eager to see their gals.

Jeannie's parents owned the best gift store in town, which featured the work of local potters, high-quality Native American jewelry, handmade leather goods, greeting cards, stationery, writing implements, and a selection of national and regional bestselling books. When she wasn't helping her parents in the store she roamed around town and along the river taking pictures of people and places with a single-lens reflex camera she'd received for her birthday. Her ambition was to travel the world as a *Life Magazine* photographer. She was saving her money to buy darkroom equipment so she could develop film in a small part of the cellar below the store that her father had walled off for her use.

Originally, she'd hoped to join the New York City Metropolitan Ballet Company, but abandoned the dream when she realized there was no place within hundreds of miles where she could seriously study classical dance. She planned to graduate as the high school valedictorian, get a presidential scholarship, and attend the University of New Mexico in Albuquerque, which had the best fine arts program in the state. She'd live there with an aunt and uncle. She thought Kevin crazy for thinking about enlisting after he turned eighteen and they argued about it, but never to the point of serious disagreement.

"Why not go to college first?" she asked after they left a matinee that had showed a short newsreel of the first major ground operation by US combat troops in South Vietnam. "You don't want to fight in a war and get killed, do you?"

Kevin shrugged nonchalantly, but secretly he was both half-afraid and half-enthralled at the prospect of war. The Technicolor footage of paratroopers patrolling though a rice paddy with their rifles at the ready was dramatic and exciting. "My parents say if I have to serve, I should do it as an officer. I'd have more choices that way. Maybe they're right. They both were in World War II and should know."

"Then you should listen to them," Jeannie said, her brown eyes serious. "Besides, I don't want you to go."

"I could never be a draft dodger or join the antiwar movement."

Jeannie stopped outside her family's gift shop. She was scheduled to look after the store so her parents could attend a late-afternoon meeting for business sponsors of the annual county fair. "Why not?" she asked.

"Pride, I guess. My parents, my grandfather, and my great-grandfather all served. My dad says that shouldn't matter to me, but it does. Are you against the war?"

"I am," Jeannie said gravely. "I'd march against it in Washington if I could."

"You're a peacenik," Kevin teased.

"That's right." Jeannie smiled sweetly and made the peace sign. "Ban the Bomb."

Kevin grinned. "I'm all for that."

"There's hope for you yet." With a coquettish look she said, "Guess what? My parents are going to take me to the Willow Creek Ranch rodeo so I can watch you compete. I told them you were my steady boyfriend and I just had to go."

Kevin fought off a blush. "Thanks for letting me know."

"About going or you being my boyfriend?"

"Both."

"You're welcome." On tiptoes she gave him a kiss, opened the store door, and disappeared inside. Through the glass window he waved at Jeannie's parents, who had been watching all the time.

* * *

With the Willow Creek Ranch rodeo scheduled less than a week after fall works, Matt felt bad about keeping Kevin away from the preparations and practice he needed for the competition. But the ranch came first and Kevin understood that, as did Dale, so no complaints were made.

This year, Matt had expanded the old foreman's cottage into a larger, more comfortable and modern residence that matched Al and Brenda's ranch house in size and conveniences. He'd kept the 7-Bar-K brand to use for the small herd of cow ponies he'd been training, and for the first time since leaving the Tularosa he was ready to market a half dozen of his best stock.

The day after the beef shipped to market and the remaining

cow-calves had been thrown over to fresh pasture, everybody went into high gear preparing for the sale of the first crop of 7-Bar-K cow ponies in years. Word had spread fast that Matt Kerney was back in the cow-pony business. On the day of the sale a sizable crowd gathered at the Rocking J, including Jeannie Hollister and her parents, Scott and Amy, all of whom Kevin had invited to the barbeque Mary and Brenda were putting on for the event.

Jeannie was a tiny girl with liquid brown eyes, dirty-blond hair cut short, and a serious demeanor that evaporated every time she smiled, which was often. Matt was quite charmed by her looks and personality and when the opportunity arose he complimented his son on his good taste in women. That made Kevin grin. A few minutes later, his mom gave Kevin a wink and a thumbs-up when he walked past with Jeannie. Even from a distance Matt saw both of them blush.

It took less than a half an hour to sell all six ponies at auction at prices beyond what Matt had hoped for. During the sale, Jeannie shot at least three rolls of film with her camera. Matt approached her as she was reloading her camera and asked if he could buy some of her photographs to advertise his next horse sale. A smile danced across Jeannie's face, and she wanted to hug him. He would be her first paying customer.

"Now that my darkroom is finished, I can get prints for you to look at right away," she said in a rush.

"No hurry," Matt replied. "Kevin says you're going to the Willow Creek Ranch rodeo. Pick out what you think are the best and bring them with you. We can strike a deal then."

Jeannie beamed. "I will. The editor at the *Herald* said he can't go this year and if I take some good photos, he'll use them in the paper and give me a freelance credit."

"Well, that will make you a bona fide professional photographer, won't it?"

"No, you will." Jeannie answered gleefully. "I'm doing the newspaper photos for free."

Matt smiled. "I'm happy to be your very first customer. I'm sure there will be a whole lot more." He looked over her shoulder and saw Jeannie's folks at the buffet table talking to Mary and Kevin. From all the smiling faces it appeared that everybody seemed happy with everyone else. "Selling all those ponies made me hungry," he said. "Let's join Kevin and your folks and get some grub."

Jeannie's smiled widened. "Great."

* * *

The first thing Kevin heard when he arrived at the Willow Creek Ranch was that Raymond Edward Cannon's granddaughter, Melissa, would not be handing out prizes and kisses to the rodeo winners. She'd opted to spend her summer in Europe instead.

Kevin didn't care. On the far side of the rodeo grounds he spotted Jeannie Hollister at the stock corral sitting on the top railing, peering through the viewfinder of her camera shooting pictures of the milling critters. Dressed in jeans, boots, and a floral embroidered cowgirl shirt, she looked scrumptious.

First up in the juvenile category was calf wrestling. Kevin had been practicing on full-grown steers and was determined to win it. But even a second place would serve in his pursuit of the all-around title if he scored high in team roping with Dale, won either the individual calf-roping or bronc-riding events, and made no disqualifying mistakes.

He unloaded Two-Bits from the horse trailer and watered and brushed him down before turning his attention to his tack and equipment. When he finished, he looked around for Jeannie but she was nowhere in sight. He spotted her parents about to enter the front door of the ranch house and figured she was already inside, touring the multimillion-dollar western-style palace.

He went looking for his dad and found him down at a horse pasture near the barn talking with Mr. Cannon about ponies. They were striking a deal to have Matt's stallion, Double Seven Johnny, stand at stud with some of Cannon's mares. Kevin knew that once the word got out, the asking price for the next crop of 7-Bar-K cow ponies would go higher. He could see the pleased look in his dad's eyes.

Together they chased down Jeannie, who stopped taking pictures long enough to show Matt the prints she'd selected for him to choose from. There were a dozen to look at, and he bought the five he liked best at ten dollars apiece. He could use them in his ads as long as he gave Jeannie credit as the photographer. They shook hands on the deal, and Matt wrote out a check on the spot. The smile that danced across her face was luminous.

The ranch bell rang for chow call. Cannon had slated the youth rodeo to start after the lunch, with five events scheduled. Calf wrestling kicked things off and bronc riding was next, followed by girls' barrel racing, individual calf roping, and team roping as the finale. His stomach churning from nerves, Kevin passed on lunch and occupied himself roping a stumping post in a corral away from the rodeo grounds. Dale joined him after a while and they sat under a shady willow until the first event was called up over the loudspeaker. Kevin had drawn the largest calf and was last to go. When his turn came, he waited on Two-Bits behind the barrier. He broke cleanly after the calf was released, caught up with it quickly, launched himself out of the saddle, and missed the critter completely, scoring no points.

He jumped to his feet, found his cowboy hat in the dust, and walked away amidst polite applause for his failed effort. He'd have to win every other event outright in order to claim the overall title. A second-place finish in bronc riding and a third in calf roping torpedoed his chances. His only win came with Dale in team roping.

He was totally deflated, and all the outpouring of sympathy from his mom, dad, Jeannie, and her parents couldn't lift his sour mood. He put on a cheerful face and forced a smile as Jeannie took his picture with Dale holding their team-roping championship belt buckles. He sought out and congratulated Tray Munson, the all-around title winner, and stood for another photograph of all the contestants taken for the next quarterly newsletter of the New Mexico Cattle Growers' Association.

He hadn't boasted he would win, hadn't crowed about how good he was at rodeoing, and hadn't made himself out to be something he wasn't. Still, he'd fallen short of his personal goal and badly embarrassed himself. That wouldn't happen again. He rode in the bed of the pickup truck on the way home, his head resting on his saddle, eyes fixed on a cloud-filled sky that promised rain. It was time to look ahead. He'd dig in, work hard, and redeem himself the following year at the all-state high school rodeo.

31

After his disappointing performance at Willow Creek, Kevin worked hard to improve. Realizing he needed to get stronger, he got permission from Coach Bradley to work out in the gym weight room after school, and when his chores and homework were finished, he diligently practiced his roping and riding skills. By October, at a regional rodeo held in Portales on the eastern plains near the Texas line, he'd packed on some additional muscle. It made a difference; he took a second in saddle bronc, a third in calf roping, another third in steer wrestling, and a first with Dale in team roping.

Encouraged but not content, he increased his weight work, adding another pound by Christmas. He'd also grown an inch to an even six feet and filled out in his upper body. To build stamina, he started running early in the morning three days a week.

He delivered on his promise to his parents to improve in math and science and at the end of the fall term he brought home a report card that put him back on the honor roll. The only thing he wanted for Christmas was help with the entry fees to at least two more regional rodeos so he could qualify for all-state. His parents willingly obliged, if he promised not to let his grades suffer.

Jeannie's life was just as hectic. She'd started an antiwar group with some friends, which wasn't making her popular among the student body or with the vast majority of citizens who staunchly supported the government's strategy in Vietnam. Some recently transplanted, self-styled hippies living in a dilapidated old homestead outside of town joined the group, and soon there were letters to the editor in the paper decrying the dropouts and drug users who were infiltrating the community, spreading antigovernment propaganda, and corrupting the town's youth. The police put the hippies under surveillance, openly tailing them around town, and started photographing all of the poorly attended antiwar rallies in the downtown park. There were rumors that the FBI had placed an undercover agent in town, but nobody could think of any newcomer or stranger who fit the bill.

The only public support for the peaceniks came from the local Methodist pastor. He was a World War II combat veteran and the father of one of Jeannie's girlfriends who'd helped start the group. Attendance at his Sunday services dropped considerably until the church council convinced him to be less vocal in his criticism of the war. After his daughter abruptly dropped out of the movement, word had it the pastor had been threatened with the loss of his job if he or his daughter continued their antiwar activities.

Out of loyalty to Jeannie, Kevin attended the rallies and some of the meetings when he could, but his heart wasn't in it, and he knew she could tell. One day she caught up to him in the hall between classes and asked if he'd help put up posters around town announcing that a well-known UNM professor and peace activist from Albuquerque would be staging a sit-in at the army recruitment office in Las Cruces on Saturday.

Across the top of the poster were the words STOP THE KILLING! It listed the time and place for the event and noted that New Mexico State University Professor of Art Erma Fergurson would also be participating.

"I won't do it," Kevin said.

"Why not?"

"Because soldiers aren't killers."

"Haven't you seen the news footage on television? The combat pictures in the magazines?"

Kevin nodded. "Maybe some ugly things happen; that doesn't make them killers."

Jeannie eyed him disparagingly. "But that's what soldiers do; they kill."

"I thought we had a deal not to argue about the war. You know I'm not for it; I'm just not willing to hate every guy who gets drafted and has to put on a uniform and go fight."

"How can you be so wishy-washy about the military after what the army did to your family?"

Not wanting to argue, Kevin nodded at the posters in Jeannie's hands. "Can I have one of those?"

She peeled one off the stack and handed it to him. "Why do you want it?"

"Erma Fergurson is a friend of the family. She served with my mother in the navy during the war. I think my mom would like to know about it."

"Maybe your mother will want to come to the sit-in."

"I don't think so. Are you going?"

Jeannie smiled. "You bet I am. Should I tell Professor Fergurson that I'm your girlfriend?"

"Are you still?"

Jeannie brushed up against him just as the tardy bell rang. "I'd better be."

* * *

When his mother got home from work—she was now the assistant principal at the elementary school—Kevin showed her the poster. It got a laugh out of her.

"I guess Erma's been radicalized against the war," she said. "Good for her."

"You mean that?"

"I do," Mary answered.

"Jeannie asked me if you were going."

"Maybe I should. I haven't seen Erma in a while."

"Are you serious?"

"I'll think about it. Are you planning to go?"

"Nope," Kevin replied. "I'll be at the ranch. Dad wants me to lend a hand with the ponies and I promised Dale we'd practice our roping."

"Well, then Brenda can look after all you menfolk if I decide to go."

Kevin grinned. "Are you turning into a peacenik like Jeannie?"

"Any soldier, sailor, or marine worth their salt is a peacenik at heart." Mary put on her apron. "I'm amazed that girl still likes you, as little as you see her."

"I'm irresistible," Kevin replied.

Mary shook her head in mock disbelief. "If you want dinner, stop bragging and help me peel the potatoes, Mr. Irresistible."

* * *

After mulling over whether to go to the sit-in at the Las Cruces army recruitment center, Mary decided to do it. Matt and Kevin got back from the ranch late Sunday afternoon expecting to see her sedan in the driveway, but it wasn't there. Nor was there a note left on the kitchen table that she was off doing some quick errand at the grocery store before it closed. They waited a good hour for her arrival before the worrying set in. Matt called Erma at her home but got no answer. They were about to take off for Las Cruces in search of her when the phone rang.

"We're just now back," Mary said when Matt answered.

"From where? I thought the sit-in was yesterday."

"It was," Mary replied cheerily. "We had an impromptu party at Gus and Consuelo's hacienda this afternoon after they bailed us out of jail."

"You were in jail?"

"With fifteen other protesters. Are you angry?"

"Not as long as you're all right."

"I'm fine, just tired. We stayed up all night singing Woody Guthrie songs."

"Well, you had us worried," Matt said. "Don't try to drive back tonight. I'll call in sick for you at work in the morning."

"That's perfect."

"You sound like you had a good time."

"I've discovered civil disobedience can be great fun," Mary replied. "I love you both. See you tomorrow."

Matt hung up, gave Kevin the news, and offered to buy him a steak dinner at De Santo's Grill, the only decent restaurant in town open on Sunday night.

"You can drive," he said, throwing Kevin the keys.

"So now mom's a peacenik and a jailbird," Kevin said as he climbed behind the wheel.

"That should get you to second base with your girlfriend," Matt predicted. "I hope she has the good sense to make you stop there."

"Oh boy, does she," Kevin replied.

* * *

On Sunday night, the Albuquerque television stations broadcasted the story of the Saturday arrest of antiwar protesters in Las Cruces, along with footage of the police handcuffing the peaceful demonstrators. Mary Kerney's image flickered across the screen. On Monday morning, the *Albuquerque Journal*'s statewide edition ran a feature story about the demonstration, along with a list of the people arrested by the police, minus the name of one juvenile. When Mary got home she confirmed to Kevin that the minor arrested had been Jeannie. He called and spoke to Jeannie's mother, learned she'd been released to her parents without charges, but would have to meet with a juvenile probation officer to prove she wasn't a delinquent. She wouldn't return to school until after her parents met with Principal Becker.

By Tuesday morning, Mary Kerney was the talk of the town. On Wednesday, she was called into the school superintendent's office and fired. As an assistant principal she served at the pleasure of the school board and had lost all rights to tenure and collective bargaining. There was nothing for her to do but empty her desk and go home. Many of the teachers at her school tearfully hugged her as she left.

Matt and Kevin were waiting for her when she arrived home. She dumped the box of personal stuff from her desk at work on the floor and sunk into a living-room chair. "I never should have gone to that sit-in."

"It was my fault for giving you the poster," Kevin said glumly.

"Stop it, both of you," Matt ordered. "Don't worry, we'll do just fine. I've got a pot of spaghetti on the stove. How about a glass of wine before we eat?"

Mary smiled weakly. "I'd like that."

"Maybe it's time for you to take a break from working anyway," Matt said.

"I've got homework," Kevin announced, heading for his room. He pretended to close his bedroom door, left it open a crack, and sat on the floor to listen. There was silence while Matt poured the wine, then he heard the glasses clink in a toast.

"How are we going to pay for his college?" Mary asked.

"He's not in college yet. But if we have to, we can take a mortgage out on this place, or even sell it and move to the ranch when he graduates high school. Neither of us are that attached to living in town, are we?"

"How I miss the ranch." Mary sighed.

"I do too," Matt replied.

"I can cash in my retirement from work if we need it."

"Let's not be drastic," Matt said. "We stick to the plan of sending Kevin to college. If he keeps his grades up, he can get a scholarship. Plus, if he goes to State, he qualifies for reduced tuition because I'm on staff."

"Maybe Erma could take him in if need be. At least when he's starting out."

Matt laughed. "She needs to do something for causing you to become a criminal," he joked. "We'll make it. We always have, haven't we?"

"Yes, we have. I feel better already," Mary said, relief flooding her voice. "Come here and smooch me."

Quietly, Kevin closed the bedroom door. He felt like a selfish ingrate. Right on the spot he decided to give up rodeoing, make the honor roll every term, and start looking for a part-time job. If times were still tough at home when he graduated, maybe they'd relent and sign the papers to let him enlist. A junior army ROTC program was starting at the high school in the fall and he would have one elective to fill in his senior year. He'd sign up for it. If nothing else, it would help him be ready when it came his time to serve.

He'd talk to his dad about his plans next weekend at the ranch, where the chances were always better that he'd get a fair hearing. It hadn't truly sunk in how much his parents had given up on his behalf. Both of them were happiest ranching. It was what they loved, and he'd kept them from it.

It was time to be a man, not a kid anymore.

* * *

Two months after the arrest of the "Las Cruces Fifteen," as they were called by the media, a district court judge dismissed all charges against the defendants and censured the police department for unlawfully disrupting a peaceful, legal gathering. With a clean slate, Mary petitioned the school board to be reinstated in her job as assistant principal at the elementary school. She submitted a letter signed by all her former colleagues at the elementary school supporting her request.

In a closed personnel hearing, the newly elected school board president, Owen Stewart—local car dealer, foremost Tiger varsity football booster, and Joey's father—looked Mary in the eye and with the slightest hint of a smirk on his lips said, "It doesn't matter what the judge ruled in your case, your behavior was unprofessional and reflected badly on this board, our school district, our dedicated staff, and our children. I think I speak for the entire board when I say that we only want true American patriots working in our schools and teaching our children."

In unison his fellow board members nodded their agreement as he called for the vote. Unanimously, and with the full support of the school superintendent, a twerp universally disliked by the teachers, Mary's request to get her job back was denied.

32

Matt nixed Kevin's proposal to drop rodeo and look for work after school. He thanked him for the offer, explained there might be some belt tightening with Mary no longer working, but not enough to worry about. They were a ranching family and naturally cautious about money and debt. With a pleased smile he predicted Mary would love being at home for a spell, and it would be a good thing for all of them.

His notion that Mary would enjoy staying home proved true. No longer saddled with the burdensome paperwork she'd carried home daily from work, finding substitutes for teachers who called in sick at the last minute, or dealing with the assorted emergency maintenance problems of a school building long overdue to be replaced, she happily adapted to being a full-time mother and housewife.

Within her first week of not working, she rearranged the living-room furniture, cleaned the house top to bottom, pruned neglected shrubbery at the property line behind the horse barn, and reorganized the pantry. Always a good cook, she put even better meals on the table. Sometimes she used recipes clipped from magazines to make special salads and sauces. Often she whipped up her own version of delicious stews, soups, and casseroles.

When she wasn't busy with housework or cooking, she got lost in a book, drew up lists of home-improvement ideas, or took on a special project such as—with Kevin's help—laying a flagstone walk from the driveway at the side of the cottage to the back porch.

It didn't seem to bother her when the school board refused to hire her back, although as a decorated navy veteran she was put out at being called unpatriotic by Joey Stewart's father. As time passed, her normal sunny disposition got sunnier. Even when she bossed or nagged him about his homework or her latest new undertaking she needed his help with, she did it with such good humor that Kevin never felt put out.

Some things she'd do on her own when he was at school. He came home to find she'd repainted the bathroom, or rearranged the contents of the kitchen cupboards or was in the midst of cleaning out the junk stored in the small attic. One day, he walked into the kitchen, where she was on a stepladder installing a newly purchased globe-shaped ceiling-light fixture. After she deftly attached it to the fixture base, he jokingly asked her what she planned to do next to the place.

She climbed down from the ladder and ran off a list of things: plant more shade trees, paint the exterior trim, re-roof the horse barn, and make new curtains for the bedrooms. Except for curtain making, she expected his help on the major projects.

"Are you fixing to sell the place?" Kevin asked.

Mary hesitated before answering. "Eventually, someday. I'd love to see your father do what he loves best. If he left his job with the university and returned to raising and training ponies, I know he'd be successful."

His parents' wistful conversation he'd overheard about their dream to someday return to ranching popped into his mind. "Then you and Dad should do it."

His mother smiled pensively. "We'll see."

After years in town with only part of the summers and some weekends at the Rocking J, she still missed the vast Tularosa sky, the quiet, peaceful nights, the cradling solitude far from all the hustle-bustle of town, and the feeling of belonging to a place. All of it was lacking in dusty T or C—a cramped, dreary outpost of civilization hunkered down along a tame river that meandered through desolate hills and a busy highway filled with travelers going everyplace else but there.

"You and Dad are just not cut out to be town folks," he ventured, knowing it was true.

Mary laughed. "I suppose you're right. Is that true for you as well?"

"Mostly," Kevin replied with a grin as he put down his schoolbooks. Outside the kitchen window a truckload of rock sat in a pile at the side of the house next to the driveway. Mary had checked out a library book about farm crafts that gave step-by-step instructions of how to build a freestanding dry stone wall. With Kevin's assistance, she was about to try her hand at it by building a flowerbed under the kitchen window.

"We're trenching the footing after you change out of your school clothes," Mary said, giving him a quick kiss. "So don't dawdle."

Kevin eyed the rock pile. "Do we have enough rock?"

"For now," she said jovially as she stowed her toolbox under the kitchen sink.

* * *

In the last high school association rodeo before the annual all-state competition, Kevin cracked three ribs in a fall during the saddle-bronc event that ended his chance to make a run at the state title. He didn't like it but had no choice; without medical clearance he was barred from competing. Besides the pain of missing out, his side hurt like the blazes every time he tried to throw a loop or urged Two-Bits into a gallop. His only small consolation was winning a first both in steer wrestling and team roping with Dale before the bronc sent him flying. Until his wreck, he'd been moving up in the standings and that was something, but certainly not enough worth cheering about yet.

He reluctantly urged Dale to find another partner for the team-roping event. "There are some good ropers around," he added, "and you could win it."

Still basking in the glow of being the first-string starting right tackle on the state championship football team, Dale opted to pass on finding another partner. "I can wait until next year, as long as you don't go and get stove up again," he replied with his customary lopsided grin. "Anyways, I don't plan to win the team roping title at state with anyone else but you."

Kevin punched him affectionately on the arm to signal his delight at having such a good friend.

In reply, Dale punched him back.

* * *

Depending on her classmates' political leanings, Jeannie was either heckled or applauded for being part of the Las Cruces Fifteen. Unfortunately, in conservative T or C, the hecklers dominated. Her few friends and supporters at school were ridiculed as well, but they stuck by her. At first she took the name-calling and jeering with forced good humor, but when some of the popular boys on the football team, egged on by Joey Stewart, started spreading rumors that she was having sex with the peacenik weirdos who were part of the local antiwar protest group, the heckling soon turned into taunts.

They called her a slut, a whore, a pussy, and a cunt. Girls who had been somewhat friendly started shying away, and boys who'd never before given her a second look started pathetically buzzing around, hoping to get laid.

Kevin got word of it early from Dale and pushed back at Jeannie's tormentors hard enough to stop most of the name-calling, but Joey and a few others persisted.

"Don't let them goad you into doing anything," Jeannie pleaded as they left school after the dismissal bell. "I don't care what they think."

"Joey and his pals won't let up," Kevin replied. Just then Jeannie's major tormentor drove by with a carload of his buddies. Joey slowed down so his passengers could yell, whistle, and make lewd gestures.

Kevin replied in kind as Jeannie stuck her tongue out.

"Don't start any trouble," she pleaded.

"Joey's already started it."

"My dad said he'll start picking me up after school if the harassment continues."

"No need. I'll walk you home every day."

"You'd do that?"

Kevin put his arm around Jeannie's waist. "I would."

Snuggled close, Jeannie smiled up at him. "Maybe you are my white knight."

Kevin laughed. "Hardly."

As they strolled down the hill to Main Street, Jeannie told him that business at her parents' gift shop had fallen off since she'd started protesting the growing war. Hoping to reverse the trend, they'd put a big sign in the store window supporting the troops fighting in Vietnam.

"That stinks," Kevin said. "You'd think people wouldn't be so small-minded."

"It's all my fault. I can't wait to leave this town," she said fiercely.

"Are your parents mad at you?"

Jeannie shook her head. "No, just worried about their business. It's hard owning a small retail store."

They walked the rest of the way to the gift shop talking about a classmate who'd dropped out of school and run away, supposedly to California. Jeannie was jealous of the boy's courage and wanted to do the same thing. Kevin threatened to go after her and bring her back home if she tried it.

"I'd miss you too much," he added.

He got a smooch for that.

After leaving Jeannie at the gift shop he hoofed it home and found his mom in the horse barn looking after Billy, one of Dad's ponies he'd brought down from the Rocking J in preparation for his planned visit to the remote Indigo Ranch in the Black Range, where he was to supervise reseeding a high country pasture. It would take him half a day in the saddle to get there from the ranch headquarters and Billy was his best trail pony.

Kevin put on his boots, and as he mucked out the stalls, he told his mother about his conversation with Jeannie. She scowled at the news, put the empty oat buckets aside, took off her gloves, grabbed her cowboy hat, and started for the house.

"Where are you going?" he called after her.

"I have an errand to run. Won't be long. Finish up here."

She was in and out of the cottage in a jiffy and wheeling her car onto the street before Kevin was half-done with the stalls. Within thirty minutes, she was back unloading two large paper bags filled with stuff from the gift shop. She unpacked at the kitchen table, setting out a crystal salt-and-pepper set, a new butter boat that matched her blue-and-white dinner dishes, a package of three deep-blue dish towels, a large pottery flower pot, an electric slow cooker, a bunch of artificial flowers, the newest edition of a Betty Crocker cookbook, and a novel by James Michener.

"There," she said, gazing with pleasure at her purchases. "Jeannie's parents say hello."

Kevin shook his head in amazement. "You're something else, Mom."

Gleefully, Mary waved a finger at him. "Don't you dare forget it, kiddo."

* * *

Over time most of the annoying and hostile comments made to Jeannie by other students died down, but Joey Stewart and two of his cronies didn't let up. More than once it left Jeannie on the verge of tears during their walk home after school. Angry at seeing her browbeaten by three Neanderthal bullies, Kevin confronted Joey in the hallway one morning between classes.

"You and your pals stop badmouthing my girlfriend," he snapped.

Joey smiled maliciously. "Stuff it, Kerney. Maybe I can't pick a fight with you, but that doesn't mean I have to lay off your slut girlfriend."

"We'll see about that." Fuming, Kevin walked away.

That weekend at the ranch while he was helping his dad tune up a windmill, he explained his dilemma about Joey and his desire to protect Jeannie from his bullying name-calling.

"I probably would get my butt kicked if I fought Joey, and I made a promise to Principal Becker not to get in any more trouble, but I can't just let it go," he said as he inspected the windmill tail vane from his vantage point on the small platform below the blades.

"Are you seriously considering taking him on?" Matt asked as he tightened the connection to the pull rod that drew water from the well.

"Probably. I've got a few inches on him, but he's way stronger than me. I've seen what he can bench-press in the gym. He's a bull."

"How are your ribs?"

"Okay, still a little sore."

"Then you'll have to be careful." Matt thought back to his boyhood days when he'd decided to fight a kid pestering a girl he liked and how his friend Boone Mitchell had showed him some moves. "Kick him in the nuts," he said.

Surprised, Kevin stopped in the middle of tightening a loose bolt. "Should I?"

Matt nodded. "You've got to protect yourself and put him down fast. From what I've heard, Joey Stewart isn't too bright and if he's like most bullies he's used to intimidating his victims. Act uncertain and scared at first, draw him in to striking distance, and kick him in the balls hard as you can. Do it again if need be. And if you have to hit him, lay into him with your elbows, not your fists. Use a knee to the gut for good measure if he's not down for the count."

Kevin nodded. "I think I can do all that. But, if I'm caught, Principal Becker will suspend me for three days."

"Just don't get expelled."

Kevin smiled. "I won't."

"And don't tell your mother we had this conversation."

"I won't."

Back on solid ground, Matt released the brake and the blades started turning. Soon water began gushing gently into the nearby tank. The sound of it brought a squawking blue jay eager for a drink to a low rung on the windmill ladder.

"Wrap your ribs tight around your midsection before you fight him, so you don't get re-injured," Matt advised. "Maybe I should be there."

Kevin shook his head. "That won't work. I'll ask Dale to back me up."

"Okay." Matt studied his boy, now almost a man. "I should tell you not to do this. Would that stop you?"

"No."

Matt threw an arm across Kevin's shoulders. "I didn't think so. Be careful, son."

"Don't worry, I will."

Matt flipped Kevin's cowboy hat down over his eyes. "But I do worry; that's what fathers do. Let me show you some moves."

Kevin pushed his hat up and grinned at his dad, thinking he was the best. "That would be great."

* * *

For two weeks, Kevin tried to speak to Joey Stewart alone to set up a showdown, but he was always with his buddies. Frustrated and impatient, he impulsively decided to visit Joey at his father's car dealership on Main Street, where he worked detailing new cars for display in the small showroom. During those two weeks, the fighting in Vietnam had escalated and more kids at school had gotten behind the antiwar protest movement. Only Joey and his sidekicks continued to spread lies about Jeannie and harass her. Additionally, they were now mocking Kevin behind his back for dating a girl who gave it away to anyone, first come, first served.

He'd promised Jeannie not to fight Joey, so he figured to arrange for it on the sly and face her disapproval after the fight was over. Before leaving for the car lot, he looked for Dale to go with him, but he was off somewhere with his girlfriend. He got there to find Joey hosing down a freshly washed, new coupe behind the two-bay service garage at the rear of the dealership. Neither of his sidekicks were with him.

"I thought you'd lost your nerve," Joey sneered as Kevin approached. The garden hose dangled in his hands, squirting a steady stream of water from the spray nozzle onto the concrete pad. A bucket of soapy water was at the rear of the coupe.

"I'm here now," Kevin replied. "Name your time and place." He could hear the sound of a revving engine through the open service garage doors and hesitated. Suddenly he realized he hadn't wrapped his ribs the way his father had said. But he'd come only to arrange a fight, not to start one. The look on Joey's face told him he'd made a mistake.

He gauged the distance to Joey; he was twelve, maybe fifteen feet away, standing behind the left fender of the coupe. He decided to retreat and began backing away. "That's all I came to say. Name your time and place."

Joey smirked. "Why not right here and now?" In one quick movement he raised the hose and sprayed Kevin in the face with a hard blast of cold water. Instinctively, Kevin blinked and Joey was on him. Joey's fist slammed into his cheek, once, twice, each blow delivering a jarring pain that had him reeling. He took another sharp jolt to the chin as he pulled back and tried to knee Joey in the groin, catching him on the thigh instead, the blow hard enough to make him wince and momentarily stop punching. Kevin kicked again, this time on target, and Joey dropped to his knees.

The garden hose on the concrete pad continued to spew water and both of them were soaked. Wobbly, his face smarting and his head reeling, Kevin staggered to the bucket of soapy water, threw it in Joey's face, and kicked him in the gut. Joey grabbed his stomach as air rushed out of him like a deflating balloon. Shaking from a last burst of adrenaline, wet from head to toe, Kevin turned to find two shop mechanics staring at him.

"Better skedaddle, boy, before Mr. Stewart gets here," one of the mechanics said.

Kevin took off at a slow trot up the hill behind Main Street. His jaw hurt, his right eye had started to swell shut, and his breath was jagged. He probably looked a mess but didn't care about that. What an idiot he'd been. He hadn't remembered half of what his dad had shown him to do. He worried about the trouble that awaited him at home, what would happen in the morning when Principal Becker called him to the office, and how angry Jeannie was going to be with him. The immediate future didn't look very bright.

* * *

He told his mom the whole sad story while she patched him up and inspected his ribs to make sure there was no further damage. He talked her out of a trip to see the doctor with a promise to tell her if anything besides his swollen-shut eye or his bruised jaw started to hurt.

She didn't yell at him, only pausing once during her ministrations to remark that he'd been dimwitted to go alone looking for Joey at his father's car dealership.

"I didn't plan on fighting him there," Kevin explained through puffy lips. "I just went to set it up on the QT so I wouldn't get in trouble when we did fight."

Mary chuckled. "Asking Joey Stewart to make an appointment to fight you isn't the smartest thing you've ever done."

"I know it," Kevin groaned.

A phone call from Principal Becker's secretary ordering Kevin to appear in his office at seven thirty in the morning with at least one parent in attendance proved her point.

"You're grounded for a week," Mary said calmly as she watched him swallow two aspirins. "And I imagine your father might have something to say about your behavior when he gets home."

Kevin nodded, hoping his dad might be more pissed at him for not using his advice, rather than for getting roughed up by Joey.

After arriving and getting the scoop from Mary about Kevin's bad behavior, Matt ordered him to the horse barn.

With a look of pure panic on her face, Mary blocked the back door. "Don't you dare whip him!"

"We're just going to have a heart-to-heart," Matt promised as he guided Kevin around her.

Outside and out of earshot, his hand gripping Kevin's arm, Matt marched him to the horse barn. "Thanks for not squealing on me back there, otherwise we'd both be in trouble," he said.

"That's okay."

"We'll stay out here with the ponies for ten minutes and when we go back I'll tell your mother that I gave you a good talking-to, understood?"

Kevin sulked. "Mom grounded me for a week. I'll miss the big school dance and the town fiesta." The annual town fiesta ran the whole weekend with live music, bull riding and team roping, parades, contests, and a funky boat race on the river. Everybody turned out for the party. It was just about the best fun you could have in T or C year-round.

"We'll let it stand for now," Matt said. "I'll plead your case in a day or two, but no promises. If your mother holds fast to her decision, so be it."

The glimmer of hope raised Kevin's spirits. "Deal."

* * *

Principal Becker kept his early-morning meeting with Kevin and his parents short and sweet. Because Kevin had gone to Owen Stewart's place of business, thus causing the fracas, he was officially suspended for three days. And because Joey had not been the instigator, he would receive no censure or discipline.

Neither of Kevin's parents raised a fuss about his decision, although their boy looked pretty knocked around. With great relief Becker ushered them to the hallway, secretly thankful to Kevin for screwing up so that he could find a way to avoid expelling Joey for the rest of the school year. The last thing he needed was a raging, tyrannical school board president breathing down his neck.

33

Although Matt shared an office on the university campus in Las Cruces, he was rarely there. Since his original appointment as an equine and rangeland specialist in the Ag College he spent ninety percent of his time in the field working directly with ranchers, county extension agents, and farmers on a variety of projects to improve degraded agricultural lands, manage wild horse populations in conjunction with federal and state officials, restore pastures invaded by woodland junipers and piñon trees, and supervise containment protocols to combat infectious disease outbreaks among livestock.

While there were other tasks that got his attention, including assisting aspiring doctoral candidates and graduate students at remote research locations managed by the university, by and large he worked with the men and women who either made their living on the land or devoted their careers to improving and protecting it—and he loved doing it.

The job was a perfect fit for ranchers, the children of ranchers, or anyone with a strong connection with animals. Those with a love of the land, an appreciation of wildlife, and an enjoyment of the outdoors were drawn to the work. Starting out, those were exactly the kind of people who'd joined Matt in the field. But times were changing and the new hires were up-and-comers with master's degrees specializing in subjects such as the moisture content of rangeland soils, the analysis of botanical matter found in steers grazing on desert grasslands, and the foraging preferences of sheep on irrigated pastures. Most of them moved quickly into PhD programs with the hopes of landing tenure-track faculty appointments at Ag colleges. And while Matt didn't doubt the value and importance of such research, it didn't attract his full interest as much as the hands-on, get-the-job-done work that he did.

In the time he'd worked for the university, he'd been promoted twice, and for the past several years he'd been area supervisor of the southwest quadrant of the state. Because of his position, he was often asked to judge 4-H competitions and FFA contests, serve as an official at county rodeos, award plaques to ranchers for their conservation efforts, and speak to civic and farm groups about the latest federal and state wildlife regulations, rangeland restoration practices, and emerging trends in modern livestock-production techniques. He never turned down an invitation unless it interfered with work, and when he couldn't go, he made sure to send a substitute.

For many years, his old boss at the university encouraged his participation at local events. He considered it an essential part of the job for his staff to spread goodwill for the Ag College by promoting community understanding of the important work it did to sustain agriculture in the state. But since the arrival the year before of Dr. Julius Nicolls as the new head of the Animal Husbandry Department—a transplanted Midwesterner from a larger, much more prestigious university—that attitude had changed. Now rather than informally accepting an invitation from a community group and simply showing up, Matt had to first submit a form detailing the specifics of the event and secure permission in advance. If the event was considered too important for an area supervisor to handle, someone higher up in the department with the right credentials or degree got the assignment.

Never a fan of unnecessary bureaucracy, sometimes Matt accepted last-minute requests from a group to meet with them without securing permission, figuring the goodwill he created far outweighed his failure to fill out a silly form. Sidestepping the new rules worked fine until he agreed to be a substitute speaker at a meeting of the Catron County Cowbells, a ladies' auxiliary of the New Mexico Cattle Growers' Association. In that neck of the woods, getting the cooperation of the old-timers who were set in their ways about ranching and not eager converts to modern practices was a challenge, so he never wanted to miss an opportunity to make more inroads, especially if he could influence the wives to influence their husbands.

Unfortunately, his appearance was reported in the Las Cruces paper and brought to the attention of Dr. Nicolls. For the infraction, Matt received a verbal reprimand by phone from a department underling. Never in his life had he been slapped on the hand by a supervisor for any reason. Over such a trivial matter, the censure smarted.

Matt had met Nicolls in person only twice: once at a gathering of personnel to welcome him to the Ag College, and soon afterward during his fact-finding tour of all projects, research stations, and off-site field operations under his direct organizational control. Unlike his predecessor, Dr. Ervin McAlister, who'd been affectionately called "Mac" by everybody who worked for him, Julius

Nicolls preferred being addressed as "Dr. Nicolls" and allowed no such informality among his staff.

He was a tall, skinny, stuffy man with a narrow face etched in a permanent frown. Matt doubted the man had ever willingly smiled. Word from the campus soon confirmed that he was autocratic, unbending, and punitive. He quickly surrounded himself with people of like minds.

Unlike the slower pace on campus during the summer, Matt's workload in the field always picked up in advance of fall works when the ranchers had not yet gathered, shipped their livestock, and tallied their once-a-year payday—if they were lucky enough to have one after the bills got paid. When ordered in the middle of July on a day's notice to travel to Las Cruces and meet with Nicolls, Matt was both surprised and slightly wary.

With Nicolls it was SOP not to inform those summoned as to what the purpose might be, so Matt called the other area supervisors to see if they'd also been ordered to appear. Learning he was the only supervisor invited, it left him wondering what was up. His annual job performance evaluation was a good four months off, and he knew of nothing of a political nature happening in his bailiwick that might create concern for the higher-ups.

He shrugged off worrying about it, got on the telephone, cancelled several appointments and a meeting, and called Mary, who was at the ranch with Kevin. When he told her he'd be heading to headquarters to meet with Nicolls early in the morning, purpose yet unknown, she thought it odd.

"It's probably nothing," Matt reassured her. "I can't think of anything that should worry me."

Not fully reassured himself that there was nothing to worry about, and thinking it best to be as prepared as possible, Matt hit the highway early enough to arrive on campus before the end of the workday and check in with a couple of guys in the department he knew and trusted. They had no idea why Matt had been called down so unexpectedly, and could think of no pressing reason Nicolls needed to see him. They reminded him that Nicolls was notorious for nitpicking about trifling issues. That was enough to let his worries slide.

Erma was in Europe for the summer studying French Impressionist painters and had rented her house out, so a free place to crash for the night was out of the question. He took a room at a mom-and-pop motel on Main Street and chowed down on some good New Mexican food at a nearby diner before taking in an early evening movie at the Rio Grande Theater, a John Wayne Western he'd missed in T or C.

In the morning, he presented himself to the department secretary ten minutes early and was kept waiting an additional twenty minutes before Nicolls made an appearance at his office door.

Given a quick nod of greeting and motioned into a chair, Matt sat. "What can I do for you, Dr. Nicolls?" he asked pleasantly.

Busy scrolling through a sheaf of papers, Nicolls didn't answer immediately. He put the papers aside, folded his hands together and peered at Matt. "Mr. Kerney, as you know the department has been upgrading the area field supervisor positions over the past year," he said without preamble.

"So I've noticed," Matt replied.

"Yours is the last position to be reclassified and now calls for the incumbent to hold a master's degree. I've decided not to grandfather you into the position."

"What exactly does that mean?" Matt asked sharply, knowing full well he was about to be bumped.

Nicolls frowned at Matt's retort and held up a hand. "No need for you to worry. Based on your satisfactory employment record with the department, your exemplary war record, and the fact that you are a university alumnus, I have found what I believe to be a very suitable assignment for you."

"Which is?" Matt inquired tersely, not giving an inch.

Matt's insubordinate tone earned him a suspicious gaze. "You are to be appointed the resident supervisor at our Fort Stanton Experimental Ranch in the foothills of the Sacramento Mountains."

"I am?"

Nicolls pursed his lips before answering. "As you may know, it consists of almost twenty-six thousand acres used for wildlife, livestock, and range research studies and experiments. It's quite a lovely area. With your background in ranching, we find you particularly well suited for the job."

"Do you?"

Nicolls stiffened, squared his shoulders, and gave Matt a stern look. "Are you dissatisfied with my offer?"

"Surprised is more like it."

Nicolls relaxed slightly. "You'll keep your current salary."

Nicolls wasn't doing Matt any favors. He would lose his present pay grade and be at the top of the salary scale for experimental station ranch managers, which meant no more annual increases based on seniority and job performance. It was a dead end for any future advancement.

Matt paused. He could delay accepting the offer and talk to Mary first, but there really wasn't anything to discuss. Nicolls wanted him out, didn't have a legitimate reason to fire him, so he'd carefully orchestrated a move to make him quit. It had worked on several other ex-employees, but it wasn't going to work on him. Not yet, anyway.

He looked across the desk at Nicolls and smiled. "I'll take the job."

Nicolls didn't flinch at Matt's unexpected acceptance. He cleared his throat and eyed Matt expressionlessly. "Very well. There will be a stipend to help defray your moving costs, and a housing allowance will be provided until you're re-settled. You start on September first. My deputy director, Dr. Virden, will provide particulars. We're finished here. Thank you."

Dumbfounded and amused by the man's arrogance, Matt stood. "Is that it?"

"Yes, you're excused." Nicolls returned his attention to the papers on his desk. After a few seconds, he looked up as if startled to see Matt still standing there. "Is there something else?"

"September first is six weeks away. If you want me on the job at Fort Stanton by then, I'll need some administrative time off with pay to make all the necessary arrangements to move my family from T or C."

Nicolls tapped his fingers together. Moderately irritated by the man's tone and his unwillingness to graciously resign, he did not feel generous. "You have adequate accrued vacation time to cover those activities, I believe."

Matt shook his head. "No, sir, I'm not using my vacation for this, nor do I have to. I want administrative time off with pay starting on August first and I want it in writing."

Nicolls snorted in irritation. Employees who had a smattering of knowledge regarding their personnel rights were invariably troublemakers. He'd have to find another way to get rid of him after his transfer went through. "University rules allow for two weeks of administrative leave with pay in such cases. I can authorize no more."

"Okay, put that in writing like I asked," Matt said.

Nicolls stifled a grimace. "I'll have Dr. Virden give you a memo."

The men locked eyes. Matt wasn't about to thank Nicolls for screwing him. As he turned and left to find Dr. Virden, Nicolls reached for the phone.

* * *

Matt met with Virden, got his memo, picked up some mail in his office in-basket, and called Mary at the ranch. Without railing about Dr. Nicolls, he briefly told her what had happened. After she recovered from the news, they agreed to meet at the cottage as soon as possible to hash things out. He got home to find Kevin in the driveway changing the oil in Mary's car.

"About done?" he asked.

"I just finished up," Kevin replied, closing the hood to the car.

"Good, come inside. We've family business to discuss." He looked over to see Mary at the back door impatiently waiting.

"Mom says they want you to work at Fort Stanton."

"Yep, but we've got a lot more to talk about than just that," Matt said. "Come on, jingle those spurs."

"Are you in trouble?"

"Not by a long shot," Matt answered, smiling at Mary as he walked up the back steps with Kevin at his heels. The delicious smell of a fresh-baked apple pie greeted him as he gave Mary a kiss.

"Did you make a pie for me?" he asked.

"No, it's an experiment," Mary replied, straight-faced. "I'm thinking I'll bake twenty pies each week and have Kevin sell them door to door all over town so we won't be homeless when you tell Nicolls to stuff the job he offered you."

"Is that what I'm going to do?" Matt asked with a grin.

"I don't know, is it?" Mary asked arching her eyebrow.

"Let's talk about it over a slice of that pie," Matt countered as he guided Mary to the kitchen table, his arm around her waist.

She pulled away. "You damn well better tell Nicolls to stuff it. For a man of your caliber and reputation, a forced transfer and demotion is unthinkable."

Matt settled into a chair and examined the huge apple pie, the perfectly browned crust rising almost three inches above the pie tin. "I agree, but we need to plan what comes next. With no more paydays, getting back to ranching isn't going to be without risk. And we can't ask Al and Brenda to carry us while I build up our horse business."

She sliced into the pie and put a wedge in front of Kevin, who had his fork at the ready. "We cash in everything, sell this place, and just do it!" she announced, her tone suggesting argument would be fruitless.

As Kevin attacked the pie, Matt grinned at Mary.

"What?" she demanded.

"Is there a piece of that for me?"

"Only if you promise me that we'll do it."

"I promise."

Mary smiled sweetly. "That's better." She slid a second slice onto a plate and handed it over. "Okay, now let's make a plan," she said, her eyes dancing with excitement.

Over pie—two wedges for Kevin—they discussed what to do. The cottage would get spruced up and go on the market within a week. Anything they didn't want or need at the ranch would be sold through classified ads in the newspaper. They'd both cash in their retirement pensions and Matt would take his accrued vacation time in a lump-sum payment. They'd sell Mary's car, used mostly for trips around town, and put the money on a new ranch truck with Matt's old truck as trade. Mary still had money in savings that they'd continue to keep as reserve. Finally, Matt would pay off all the odds-and-ends bills he could while he was still drawing a paycheck, allowing them to make a fresh start with almost a clean slate.

Throughout the discussion, Kevin stayed quiet, watching and listening. What had started as depressing news about his dad's job predicament had become a full-blown, optimistic scheme to return to ranching. If it meant he probably wouldn't have to go to a new school and live in a new town during his senior year, Kevin thought it was a perfect plan. Matt busily wrote stuff down: how much the cottage might sell for, what he expected to earn before he quit his job, how much they had in savings, what a new truck would cost, and how much it would cost to buy more ponies to increase the herd.

They talked about the Rocking J land. As a full partner with Al and Brenda, Matt had used what he'd learned working in the field to improve both the west slope high-country pastures and the predominantly low-lying Jornada desert grasslands. Fully recovered from the drought of the fifties, the land was now in good shape with live water in several canyons and draws, capable of sustaining additional ponies.

Listening, Kevin could hear their growing enthusiasm. Their excitement made him realize that with the loss of the 7-Bar-K there had been a void in their lives.

He decided to pipe up and pitch in. "I can drop out of school if you need me to."

Harsh looks seared into him from across the kitchen table.

"You'll do no such thing," Mary said emphatically.

"And forget about asking us to let you join the service," Matt added ardently. "Your job is to finish high school and go to college."

"But if you're not working for the Ag Department anymore, I'll have to pay tuition. And then there's books, room, and board," Kevin countered.

"Keep your grades up and you can qualify for a scholarship," Mary replied.

"I've been thinking about joining junior ROTC as an elective my senior year," Kevin said. "They offer scholarships for college students, and according to my guidance counselor I'd stand a good chance to get one if I took the class. But if we're not living in town anymore . . ." He let the potential impediment hang in the air.

Matt sighed. "We'll work it out."

"The school bus still stops at Engle for the ranch kids from the Jornada," Mary said. "You and Dale can use Patrick's old truck at the ranch to drive back and forth to the bus stop. On days when you have extracurricular activities, you can either drive to school or we can come fetch you."

"Can I keep rodeoing?"

Matt pushed the pen and paper aside. "I don't see why not. We're making changes, not eliminating what's important in our lives. Besides, having you compete will be great advertising for our ponies. Especially if you do well at state."

Kevin grinned. "I'll do my best, promise."

"Will you miss town?" Mary asked.

Kevin shrugged. "A little bit. Jeannie mostly."

Dad smiled sympathetically. "That's understandable."

Mary put a thoughtful finger to her lips. "Gus Merton might be able to help us with information about financial-aid programs at the college."

"We don't have to jump on that right away," Matt replied.

Kevin grinned in agreement. "Yeah, Mom, let me at least start my senior year first."

Studying the calendar on the refrigerator door, Mary wasn't listening. "Erma gets back from France in three weeks. I wonder if she'd consider boarding Kevin during his freshman year."

Kevin felt a rush of excitement. Erma threw the best parties with the best-looking coeds and dozens of other interesting people. Plus, she was one of the coolest and most popular professors at the university. And living off campus sounded a heck of a lot better than sharing a dorm room with guys he didn't know. Suddenly, maybe it *wasn't* too soon to start making plans for college.

She turned and looked at Kevin. "Unless of course you'd rather stay in a dorm with boys your own age."

Kevin shrugged nonchalantly and tried to sound impartial. "I don't know. Maybe we should see what Erma says when she gets home."

Dad pushed back from the kitchen table. "Let's take a break from all this figuring." He dug for his car keys and tossed them to Kevin. "Since we've already had apple pie for dessert, I suggest we all go to Larry's Drive-In for cheeseburgers and fries. You're driving."

* * *

Larry's Drive-In sat on a bend in Main Street just before the entrance to the Carrie Tingley Hospital. Drivers parked under a long metal canopy, where carhops took their orders from large printed menus mounted on posts in each parking space. Off to one side was additional, uncovered parking next to several picnic tables with umbrellas, where folks who didn't want to sit in their hot cars could dine. Inside was a small, air-conditioned dining room with a long counter where carhops picked up orders for delivery. Still early enough to not be packed with customers eager to avoid the heat, Matt snagged an empty table near the front window. He ordered double cheeseburgers, fries, and soda pop for everyone.

While they waited for their food, he told them he'd been granted two weeks of administrative leave to move the family before starting the job at Fort Stanton, but instead of taking the leave he would simply resign, and give Nicolls two weeks' notice instead.

"Why did you ask for the administrative leave in the first place if you knew you weren't going to use it?" Mary inquired.

"I wasn't about to simply cave in to Nicolls and quit on the spot," Matt explained, glancing from Mary to Kevin. "Plus, I wanted to make sure that we were all in this together."

"Are we keeping this a big secret until the day you quit?" Kevin asked.

"I'd like to," Matt replied.

"What else are you up to?" Mary prodded, convinced Matt was plotting something a little more cagey than figuratively thumbing his nose at Nicolls.

Matt smiled. "Nicolls loves to trumpet his latest efforts to professionalize the department. He'll probably issue a press release announcing my transfer weeks before I'm due to report to Fort Stanton. Quitting unexpectedly will leave him with some explaining to do."

"Don't you have to give a reason?"

"Nope. But if I'm asked officially I'll say it's for personal reasons."

Mary clapped her hands. "I love it."

"It might not cause Nicolls any grief, but I can privately rub his nose in it."

Mary laughed. "Oh, for heaven's sake, please do it."

"Can I tell Jeannie?" Kevin asked.

"On the day I resign," Matt answered. "Keep it under wraps until then."

Jeannie was visiting with her aunt, uncle, and cousins in Albuquerque for two weeks, so until she returned staying mum wouldn't be a problem. "What about telling Al, Brenda, and Dale?" he asked.

"We'll let them in on it," Matt said.

"Cool," he said, accepting his mom's barely touched bag of French fries.

* * *

By the time Jeannie returned home in early August, rumors had already spread across the region that Matt was being transferred to Fort Stanton. The fact that their house was on the market and they were planning to hold a garage sale was proof enough that the rumors were true. Matt's staff began asking about his job change, and in early August he confirmed it. The news broke in the local paper causing Nicolls to officially announce Matt's transfer and the appointment of his successor. His comment that Mr. Kerney would do a great job at the Fort Stanton Experimental Ranch made Matt chuckle.

During Jeannie's visit with relatives in Albuquerque, she'd attended several teach-ins at the university and participated in campus peace vigils organized by students. She returned excited about the growing antiwar sentiment in the country. Because she was one of the youngest activists to have been arrested, she'd been treated as some kind of celebrity. Her head swirling with newfound popularity, she was seriously thinking about dropping out of school, leaving T or C, and joining the antiwar movement full-time.

"You can't be serious," Kevin replied as they sat in their favorite drugstore booth waiting for the waitress to come and take their order.

"Why not?" Jeannie replied, her voice filled with resolve. "You're moving to Fort Stanton with your parents, so there's little to hold me here."

Kevin leaned across the table. "It's a secret, but my dad's not taking the job. He's going to resign and we're moving to the ranch instead. So I'll still be around."

The waitress approached. Jeannie ordered a Coke and onion rings to share. Kevin asked for a ginger ale.

"Why all the secrecy?" Jeannie didn't sound very excited that he wasn't moving away.

"I better not say any more."

Jeannie scowled at him. "I'm your girlfriend and you can't tell me?"

"I promised my dad."

Jeannie eyed him warily. "You don't trust me?"

"I didn't say that."

"That's what it sounds like to me."

Kevin sighed. "Okay, he's being pushed out of his job and told to go to Fort Stanton. He doesn't like the way it's being done so he's keeping his resignation secret from his boss until the last minute."

Jeannie shrugged indifferently. "That wasn't so hard. But I don't see what the big deal is."

"There isn't one, I guess," Kevin said. He paused while the waitress delivered the sodas and onion rings. "It's sure not as important as stopping the war in Vietnam."

Jeannie reached for an onion ring. "No, it's not. Let's not get started on that subject, okay?"

"What do you want to talk about?"

"I don't care."

Kevin sipped his soda. He'd thought he knew her well, but now wasn't so sure.

* * *

The day Matt drove to Las Cruces to personally tender his resignation and put in his paperwork to cash in his retirement account, an offer at almost full asking price was made on the cottage. The buyers wanted to close by mid-September.

His resignation caused a short-lived stir among the ranchers, farmers, and community organizations he'd worked with over the years. According to old friends in the department, Dr. Nicolls appeared unaffected by his abrupt departure and the slight embarrassment it may have caused him. Matt didn't care; he'd made his point.

Two days after registering for his senior-year fall classes, which included signing up for Junior ROTC, Kevin got a note in the mail from Jeannie breaking up with him. She blamed it, as she put it, on his decision to "support a militaristic government." A week later he learned from one of her friends the real reason was a college student at UNM she'd met and fallen for during one of the teach-ins. He thought to ask her directly to tell him the truth, but her chilly attitude dissuaded him.

By the middle of September, the family was settled on the

Rocking J and into a good daily routine. It surprised Kevin how quickly he seemed to be getting over Jeannie and how much he enjoyed being back in the country. Maybe, when it came to girls, he was getting the hang of not letting his feelings get the best of him.

34

Since he'd been cut loose by Jeannie, several other girls were showing interest, but with the start of the new school year, Kevin didn't have time to mope about losing a girlfriend or find a new one. His days, including the weekends, were filled. Each school day morning he drove with Dale in Patrick's old pickup either to the bus stop in Engle or on to town because of their after-school activities. Sometimes it was Spanish Club or Junior ROTC drills for Kevin, and for weeks Dale had football practice that kept them in town late. Kevin used the time at the town library to study and do his homework. When they did take the school bus, the frequent stops between Engle and school took over an hour each way.

At the ranch, he had daily chores helping his dad with the ponies and his mom around the house. In what free time he had, he practiced team roping with Dale and worked hard at getting better at steer wrestling and calf roping. It got so that Al jokingly made him rotate the critters he practiced on so as not to wear them out. When he could, Matt gave him tips on saddle-bronc riding. Sometimes late at night he'd fall asleep on the small desk in his bedroom and wake up with his head on an open textbook. Some days, staying awake in his last afternoon class was barely possible.

Dale and his parents lived in the original Rocking J ranch house that had been expanded over the years into a long, L-shaped, low-slung, pitched-roof home snugly nestled behind a grove of tall pine trees and surrounded by a split-rail fence. It sat facing a meadow about seventy-five yards away from Kevin's front door. Having started out as a small cabin used by Al and Brenda when they first married, from the front the Kerney house looked much as it did the day it had been built. But over the last few years Matt had expanded it out the back and more than tripled the size. It now had a large eat-in kitchen, a sizable bathroom, two roomy bedrooms, and a small mudroom off a deep screened-in porch, which gave a nice view of the San Andres to the east rising above. The renovated front room served as the living room. Windows bracketing the front door gave an unimpeded view of the ranch road winding up from the Jornada to the entry gate, where both the Rocking J and 7-Bar-K brands were prominently displayed under a sign that read: J & K LAND AND CATTLE COMPANY.

Some evenings, sitting on the back porch, Kevin could clearly visualize the 7-Bar-K ranch on the other side of the mountains and the sweet ranch house that sat perfectly situated on the shelf overlooking the Tularosa. He missed the old place and held close the memories of the good times he had there with his gramps. He and Dale still snuck onto the missile range whenever they could, ostensibly to scout for strays—that was their agreed-upon story in case they got caught—but mostly to poke around the 7-Bar-K homestead and watch what the army was doing at the rocket launch pads and tracking stations that peppered the basin. Occasionally Matt and Al went with them. It was great fun to outfox the roaming MP patrols, hide from the choppers, and search for the various electronic gadgets installed on the fringes of the missile range that the army used to detect interlopers. The loss of the ranch to the army still remained an unspoken hurt to all of them, Al, Brenda, and Dale included.

Although the days were long and work was often hard, there was a sense of contentment to ranch life that wasn't easy to find within the confines of town. His parents never left the ranch unless they had to, and the only time Kevin truly missed living in T or C was when he got to longing for a girlfriend.

The ranch kids on the surrounding Jornada spreads, some of which were twenty or more miles distant from the Rocking J, were all a lot younger than he was, and while there were some really cute girls around his age involved in FFA and 4-H, he simply didn't have the time to participate. He looked ahead to the future thinking surely he'd someday get lucky, but that didn't cure what ailed him.

At school, he enjoyed JROTC, especially studying military history and learning proper military etiquette. He was particularly keen about orienteering and marksmanship training. The instructor, James Bingham, a retired army major who'd fought in Africa and Italy during World War II, soon had the class of eighteen students marching like regular soldiers and passing his spit-and-polish uniform inspections. By the middle of the term, they'd twice been to the Sheriff's Posse shooting range, practicing for the rifle qualification test. So far, Kevin had posted the highest scores in the class, which would have qualified him as an expert marksman in the regular army.

Along with his other classmates, he was required to wear his uniform once a week, sometimes more, and no one at school dared make fun of them about it. Principal Becker made it clear at the first assembly of the year that any ridicule directed toward JROTC students would be dealt with harshly. Barred from open demonstrations of scorn, Jeannie and her tight circle of antiwar protesters would turn away in silence whenever anyone wearing the JROTC uniform passed by. Kevin always made it a point to give her a cheerful hello when it was his turn to be shunned by her and her pals in the school corridors.

Since the start of school he'd gained another pound of muscle, added a half inch in height, and healed up nicely from his cracked ribs. The upcoming fall rodeo was to be held on the university campus in Las Cruces, and he was raring to go. Excused from classes early by Principal Becker on the Friday before the weekend rodeo, Kevin and Dale caravanned with their parents to Las Cruces towing horse trailers filled with ponies and equipment. Both boys got to drive the whole way, which added to their excitement and enthusiasm for the weekend ahead. No longer were they being treated like kids.

After arriving, they registered with rodeo officials, paid their entry fees, unloaded and took care of the ponies, unhitched and parked the horse trailers, and found a motel on the west end of Main Street that offered reduced room rates to rodeo contestants and their families.

Erma had asked everyone over for drinks and an early dinner after their arrival in town, so they unpacked in a hurry and made the short drive to her house, where she greeted them at the front door with hugs and kisses all around.

Because they'd be competing in the morning, Kevin and Dale were served soft drinks, while Matt and Al opted for beer. They gathered in the living room, the women on a large couch with glasses of red wine and the guys on easy chairs clustered near a long coffee table that fronted the couch.

"I can't wait to watch you two compete," Erma said, raising her glass in salute to Kevin and Dale.

"We'll do good," Dale said, tipping his pop bottle in reply. "Promise."

"Well, you'd better. I told all my friends to come out and root for you."

"That will sure help," Kevin said, remaining cautious. Rodeo was a sport with too many unknown variables, especially when it came to the horse, the rider, the livestock, and the luck of the draw.

"Of course it will." Erma beamed agreeably, turning her attention to Mary. "I'm building a new house."

"You're what?"

"In the hills east of the university. It will have wonderful views of the valley and the Organ Mountains."

"Are you selling this place?" Mary asked, somewhat amazed by the news.

Erma looked shocked at the mere suggestion. "Heavens no. It's too valuable as a rental property."

Matt grinned and slapped his leg. "That's the way to do it. I swear, you remind me of my mother. In her day I believe she owned more property than any other woman in Las Cruces."

"That's my kind of gal." Erma stood. "Would you like to see the plans?"

An affirmative chorus greeted her. She went upstairs, returned quickly, and spread architectural drawings on the coffee table. Everyone gathered close as Erma guided them through the drawings. The house would have a deep living room with a wall of windows facing southwest and a spacious detached studio on the north side tied into the house by an enclosed courtyard with entry gained from a large kitchen and dining area. To the rear of the living room through a long hallway there would be two bedrooms, each with a full bath. Bedroom windows would look out on the Organ Mountains to the east. A curved driveway would lead to the attached garage on the south side of the house, above which would be a small one-bedroom apartment that Erma planned to rent out. The builder would break ground in a week.

Finished with her explanation, she turned to Kevin. "I expect you to be my first tenant when you start at the university."

Kevin's eyes widened. "Me?" he idiotically replied.

Erma laughed and poked him in the side. "Yes, you. It's already been arranged with your parents. They just didn't know you'd be living in a different house."

"Lucky stiff," Dale grumbled.

Erma glanced at Al and Brenda. "Should I make it into a two-bedroom apartment?"

"That's very kind but there's no need," Brenda replied. "Dale has decided to enlist in the air force when he graduates in June."

"Oh," Erma said politely, holding back on her impulse to criticize Dale's decision. "Well, it will be here for him when he gets out and decides to continue his education."

Dale smiled at the idea. "Cool."

Erma rolled up the drawings and put them aside. "I've roasted a couple of chickens for dinner and made a chocolate cake for dessert. Who's hungry?"

* * *

In the morning after the opening ceremonies, which included all the contestants cantering around the arena and the playing of the national anthem, the first event of the day was steer wrestling. By the luck of the draw, Kevin was slated to go last. The stands were packed with spectators. Just about every ranching family in the southern part of the state was in attendance, along with a large number of Aggie college students, faculty, and staff. In addition, townspeople, mostly families with children, had come out to watch the show. Over the next two days, two go-rounds for each event would decide the winners, including the all-around title.

Kevin watched his competition anxiously from behind the chutes as they took their turns, assisted by hazers who kept the steer running straight so the contestant could drop from his horse, grab the steer by the horns, and wrestle it to the ground. The clock stopped when the animal went down. Most of the contestants had good times and only one got disqualified. It took coordination, technique, and strength to post a fast time in the event. The cowboy with the best combined times would win. Dale was his hazer and did a great job, but Kevin fell short with a time of 6.1 seconds, which put him in second place. Still, it was a good start for his all-around score.

Barrel racing was next, which gave Kevin a breather before the team-roping event with Dale. After the cowgirls finished their go-round, they were up first. Kevin made a perfect break out of the box, dropped his loop neatly over the steer's horns, and swiftly turned the steer so Dale could rope both hind legs. It was picture perfect and both boys were grinning with pleasure as they doffed their hats and left the arena. They were in first place with a two-second lead that would be hard to beat if they stayed consistent on Sunday.

He took a third in saddle-bronc riding, barely reaching the eight-second mark before tumbling off the pony. He was pleased with the ride, although he thought the judges had scored him a little bit low. He was still in contention, however, and figured he needed at least two wins and maybe two second-place finishes for a shot at the all-around title.

His last event of the day, calf roping, came after bull riding. It was a timed event that required chasing a calf on horseback, roping it, flanking it onto its side, and tying down three legs. Kevin's calf proved uncooperative and he finished the go-round in last place, which dimmed his prospects of winning the all-around buckle. But in rodeo, spills, penalties, disqualifications, and ornery livestock could quickly reverse the standings. Tomorrow would be another day. He stayed encouraged.

On Sunday, Kevin climbed in the all-around standings with a first with Dale in team roping, a first in saddle-bronc riding, and a second in steer wrestling. His only hope to take home the buckle rested with the calf-roping event. He needed a great time to offset the previous day's last-place finish. Kevin did his best and turned in a respectable performance, but he couldn't overcome the deficit from the day before. The title went to Todd Marks, a cowboy from Glenwood. He got the buckle and Kevin got a plaque, presented to them during the closing ceremony by Dr. Julius Nicolls, chair of the Animal Husbandry Department at NMSU. Matt thought that was a hoot.

* * *

At the awards assembly at the end of fall term, Kevin made the scholastic honor roll again and received four JROTC uniform ribbons for physical fitness, academic excellence, orienteering, and serving on the rifle team. After the cheerleaders got their letters and Coach Bradley passed out varsity letters to all the jocks, Principal Becker took the stage, called Kevin and Dale up, and in a surprise announcement awarded them varsity letters in rodeo.

"Although we don't have a rodeo team or even a club, both Kevin and Dale have represented our school with honor, winning a number of events," he said, handing them the letters and accompanying certificates of achievement. "They will compete as Hot Springs Tigers at the all-state high school rodeo championships in Deming next spring, and I want you all to wish them well."

The cheers, whistles, clapping, and foot stomping made both boys blush. The football team, including Joey Stewart, the basketball team, the track team, and the baseball team all gave them a standing ovation. Soon, the entire assembly was on its feet. From the corner of his eye Kevin could see even Jeannie Hollister was standing and applauding.

The editor of the weekly paper took their photograph. It made the front page of the next edition with the caption: HOT SPRINGS TIGERS RODEO COWBOYS HONORED. Mary and Brenda got copies of the photograph from the editor and had them framed.

* * *

By the start of the Christmas holidays, the small horse barn and paddock Kevin had helped build was finished. Soon after the Las Cruces rodeo, Matt had driven to Mexico and purchased two stud stallions from Delfino Díaz, the owner of El Pajarito Ranch in the foothills outside the small Mormon community of Colonia Dublán. The Kerneys had done business with the Díaz family all the way back to the frontier days, when Patrick and Cal Doran had pushed a herd of cows across the border to sell to Delfino's father, Emiliano.

El Pajarito Ranch raised some of the finest quarter horses in North America and their prize stallions were coveted by breeders on both sides of the border. After close inspection, Matt bought two horses and had been waiting impatiently for the government livestock import papers from the Department of Agriculture to arrive in the mail so he could go fetch them. The documents came two days before Christmas.

He'd brought back photographs of the horses. One was a five-year-old chestnut named Petreo and the other a six-year-old gray named Centavos. "Stony" and "Cents" had been named by Díaz's young granddaughters. Both stallions were fine-looking animals proven at stud. He was eager to have them service his mares and had already contracted with two ranchers to stand them at stud for their brood mares.

On the Monday after Christmas, Matt and Kevin left for El Pajarito towing a new two-stall horse trailer. Arriving in Las Cruces, they headed west to the town of Deming and south to the border town of Columbus. They stopped so Kevin could tour some of the few remaining buildings of old Camp Furlong, the US Customs House, and the remnants of the first combat airfield in the United States. During the Mexican Revolution, Pancho Villa and his raiders attacked the town, which later became the headquarters for General Pershing's punitive expedition into Mexico. Kevin knew about the battle from his JROTC class and planned to write about it to fulfill the military-history requirement in the spring term. For an hour, he took snapshots, made notes, poked around some adobe ruins on the outskirts of the tiny village, and made rough sketches. At a small general store he bought six postcards with neat photographs of the old camp and airfield. Back at the truck, Matt, who was eager to collect his ponies, fired up the engine as soon as Kevin came into sight.

At the border crossing, they waited their turn to be questioned by a Mexican official who stood outside a small guard station with a sign on it warning that it was illegal to bring any kind of firearms into the country. When Matt reached the checkpoint, he presented his driver's license, proof of auto insurance, and the government papers needed to transport livestock into the United States. After inspecting the horse trailer carefully, the officer waved them through and they entered the dusty, dirt-poor town of Palomas, populated mostly by *braceros*—farm workers and their families who legally crossed into the United States at harvest time. With no one to stop them, the rest of the townspeople usually just sauntered across illegally at will. A few wealthy families in the town owned most of the businesses designed to snag US dollars from passing motorists, and they kept it all to themselves.

On the short main road through downtown they passed by a colorful array of brightly painted buildings that catered to tourists with large signs in English advertising discount prices on liquor, cigarettes, dental services, prescription drugs, handmade boots and saddles, and just about anything else you might need. Old men sat on the shady side of the street watching the traffic pass by. On dirt side streets, kids kicked soccer balls around or popped wheelies on bicycles. In front of the town grocery store, a hunchback beggar solicited change from customers. Matt told Kevin the several women loitering in front of a bar were probably in the flesh trade.

"The old-time cowboys on both sides of the border called them soiled doves," he added.

"That sounds almost flattering," Kevin mused.

"In a way, it was. For many of those old boys, the soiled doves were just about the only women they knew, and they were often treated with respect."

The houses on the outskirts of Palomas were mostly small, unfinished adobe structures or simple shacks with old tires on the roof to keep the tin sheeting from blowing away. Outside of town the land looked no different from southern New Mexico, except it was more expansive to the eye, with hints of distant mountains like vague violet specks tumbling westerly at the edge of a sea of desert grassland, dirty and pale yellow under a blue sky.

It was a good two-lane road with little traffic. About halfway to the rancho, Matt pulled off to the side of the road and they broke out the picnic lunch Mary had packed. They ate in the shade of the horse trailer under a cloudless, breezeless blue sky. The day had turned mildly hot, about ten degrees warmer than back home, and it was a welcome break from the confines of the truck. Only three vehicles passed them during the time they were stopped, all traveling south.

An hour and a half later they entered a pretty valley of farmland and orchards bisected by the Casas Grandes River and dotted with tidy houses and barns no different from the Victorian homes in the Las Cruces neighborhood where Erma lived. Settled by Mormons, the village of Colonia Dublán looked like it had been picked up intact by a Midwestern tornado and dropped gently into the valley.

Before the Mexican Revolution, Rancho Pajarito had virtually surrounded Colonia Dublán and nearby Colonia Juárez, another Mormon settlement. At its height, it embraced almost three quarters of a million acres. Now confined to mountain foothills and high pasturelands west of the villages, the Díaz family still controlled more than two hundred thousand acres. Beyond Sierra el

Pajarito, the place name taken for the ranch, the high Sierra Madres lurked to the west.

The rough and rocky road to Colonia Juárez cut through some low barren hills that gave way to an idyllic view of prosperous farms gathered along a small river that flowed downstream into the Rio Casas Grandes. They crossed it on a wooden bridge, followed a farm road through fallow fields, and climbed above the valley to a hacienda at the end of a long boulevard of bordering trees. The hacienda was long with an ornate parapet; tall, narrow windows; and massive, wooden double doors. It sat apart from a cluster of barns, paddocks, staff quarters, bunkhouses, and outbuildings—all pristine and gleaming white. Handsome ponies lounged in a nearby large fenced pasture and beyond the fence a small herd of cattle clustered near a stock tank. On the other side of the hacienda was an airstrip with an empty hangar.

Matt stopped at the ranch manager's house and was met by Claudious Whetten, also known as Claude, a Mormon whose family had worked at the rancho since before the Mexican Revolution.

Blond and blue-eyed, he spoke English and Spanish flawlessly. "Señor Díaz sends his regrets that he cannot be here," Claude said, shaking Matt's hand. "The family traveled to Mexico City for the holidays."

"That's perfectly understandable," Matt said, turning to Kevin. "This is my son, Kevin."

"*Mucho gusto*," Kevin said.

"You speak Spanish?" Claude asked in Spanish.

"I'm hoping to get pretty good at it," Kevin replied.

"*Que bueno*." He switched back to English, eyeing the afternoon winter sky. "You are welcome to spend the night."

"I appreciate the hospitality, but it's best we get back home pronto."

Claude nodded. "I understand. You'll be on the highway before nightfall and the traffic is always light, so there should be no problem reaching the border in a few hours."

He stepped off in the direction of the barns. "Let's go get your ponies. I just put them in their stalls and gave them oats after letting them roam in the paddock so they would not be restless on the journey to their new home."

"That's mighty thoughtful of you," Matt said.

Claude shrugged. "They deserve only the best treatment, which I know you will provide."

"You can count on it," Matt said.

At the stallion barn, Matt and Kevin looked over Petreo and Centavos before carefully loading them in the trailer. They said goodbye to Claude, who invited them back anytime, and drove down the tree-lined boulevard. A bright-orange sunset was behind them as they passed through the two Mormon settlements, reached the paved, empty highway, and turned north. An hour into the drive under a night sky and no moon, the left rear tire on the truck suddenly went flat, rubber thumping on the pavement, the rear end rattling.

The horse trailer started to fishtail but Matt slowed in time to keep from losing control and eased the truck off the road. He could hear Petreo and Centavos snorting in displeasure as he gently braked to a stop.

"Get those ponies out and hobble them while I unhitch the trailer," he ordered Kevin. "And stay with them."

Kevin nodded and jumped out. Matt waited until Kevin had the last pony unloaded before unhitching the trailer and pushing it back from the truck. He got the spare, fired up the Coleman lantern, and jacked up the rear end. He was loosening the lug nuts on the flat when the sound of an approaching vehicle and headlights appeared on the roadway. He stopped and stood.

"Stay where you are," he called to Kevin. "And only speak English if you have to speak at all."

The vehicle pulled off the pavement, the headlights on high beam. From the outline of the vehicle, Matt could see it was a pickup truck.

"You got a flat, hombre?" a voice asked in Spanish as a truck door slammed shut.

"What's that you say?" Matt replied.

"Norte Americano?"

"Yes," Matt replied, trying to see in the glare. Another truck door closed. Two men at least.

"You speak Spanish?"

"No."

"Okay, I talk in English." The man reached through the open truck window, switched the headlights to low beam, and in Spanish quickly told his partner to look into the trailer. "You got horses with you?" he asked.

A shadowy figure passed on the far side of Matt's truck. "Yes, two. They're nearby."

"Okay, that's good. My amigo will look after them while you change the tire."

"My son is with them."

"*Bueno.*" In Spanish he told his partner to bring the boy to him and then switched back to English. "Nice truck."

"Thanks." As the man drew near, Matt knelt and tried to remain composed as he removed the lug nuts.

The man stood over him. "I think once you've changed the

tire, we're going to take your nice truck, the trailer, and your horses too."

In the light of the Coleman lantern, the man smiled down at him with a pistol in his hand.

"Take whatever you want," Matt replied. Footsteps made him turn to see Kevin come into view behind the horse trailer accompanied by the second man, who was apparently unarmed. He had Kevin's arm twisted behind his back. "Are you all right?" Matt asked.

Tight-lipped, Kevin nodded.

"Tell me about the *caballos*," the *pistolero* said to his partner.

"Primo, two fine stallions from El Pajarito Rancho."

Matt removed the last nut, pulled the tire off, and let it clatter to the ground at the *pistolero*'s feet.

The man's smile widened as he poked Matt's shoulder with the barrel of his six-shooter. "Drop the tire iron."

Matt let it go.

"Give me your wallet."

Matt stood and handed it over.

The *pistolero* put the wallet in his shirt pocket.

"How much money?" he asked.

"About forty dollars."

"That's good. You got papers for your horses, *jefe*?"

Matt nodded, stood, and brushed dirt off his hands. "I'll get them."

"Send the boy."

"He doesn't know where they are. He can put the spare on while I get the papers."

The *pistolero* considered it, shrugged, and said in Spanish to his pal, "I'm going to kill them both anyway, so let the boy be helpful."

Kevin's captor pushed him toward Matt. White-faced, Kevin stumbled forward.

Matt smiled reassuringly. "Put the spare on, son. It's going to be all right."

The *pistolero* nodded. "Sure, everything is going to be okay, boy." He waved his gun at Matt. "Okay, I follow you."

Matt stepped to the open driver's door, reached under the bench seat, quickly unsnapped the holster to the horse pistol, turned, and shot the *pistolero* twice in the chest. Before he hit the ground, Matt fired a round in front of his amigo's feet.

"Don't move," he said in Spanish.

The hombre raised his hands and froze. Kevin stood motionless, staring at the dead man.

"Get some rope and hog-tie him," Matt ordered, waving the horse pistol at the startled Mexican.

Dazed, Kevin blinked. "What?"

"Hog-tie him, dammit!" Matt snapped. "Get on the ground facedown," he ordered the man.

The man dropped to the pavement and Kevin trussed him up as tight as he could.

Matt retrieved his wallet, searched both men for identification, and found police badges on both of them.

"They're Mexican cops," he told Kevin.

"What are we going to do?"

"Clean this mess up and go home," Matt replied.

They worked quickly. While Kevin changed the tire, hitched the trailer, and got the ponies loaded, Matt threw the body of the dead cop and his hog-tied partner into the back of the Mexican's truck, drove a half mile into the desert, and parked behind a thicket of agave plants that partially obscured the vehicle from the highway. He dropped the police badges and the cop's pistol on the floorboard, grabbed the Coleman lantern, rolled up the windows, got out, locked the cab, and threw the keys away.

"You're gonna leave me here?" the cop asked in Spanish.

"Yes, I am. You'd better hope someone finds you before the vultures or the coyotes discover your dead partner come sunup."

"*¡Chinga tu madre!*"

Matt laughed harshly as he started back toward the lights of his truck on the highway. "Good luck, amigo."

* * *

Kevin was ready to go. They scrambled into the truck, Matt behind the wheel, and drove away, hearts pounding, constantly shifting their gaze to the side mirrors expecting to see the flashing emergency lights of a police car coming up fast behind them. The border station was closed when they reached Palomas, and they crossed into New Mexico without incident. They passed through Columbus and on to Deming before stopping on the outskirts of town to give the ponies a breather from the trailer and feed them some oats.

"You're never going to mention one word of this to anybody *ever*," Matt said grimly as they walked the horses across an empty cotton field under a rising half-moon. "Especially your mother."

"No, sir, I won't," Kevin promised somberly. "Did you mean to take Gramps's horse pistol into Mexico knowing it was against the law?"

"Mexico is a different world," Matt said. "Anyone who goes there unarmed would be a complete fool."

Kevin stopped walking Centavos and looked at his father. "Did you kill that other policeman? I didn't hear any shots."

"I did not," Matt replied. "That would have been murder, not self-defense. I left him tied up in the back of the pickup. Hopefully, he'll be found."

"And if not, he'll die."

"That's possible," Matt replied. "Are you upset that I had to shoot the *pistolero*?"

Kevin shook his head. "No, I'm glad you did. Otherwise we'd be dead."

Matt clasped his hand on Kevin's shoulder. "That's right. Remember, not a word."

Kevin nodded solemnly. "I promise."

35

For weeks Kevin worried that the police would come to arrest him and his dad for murder. He kept waiting for a news story out of Mexico about one or two dead policemen, but there was nothing. His apprehension faded when he figured that if the other cop had survived, he wouldn't want to admit to any wrongdoing. Maybe he'd concocted a story about being ambushed by bandits. But reassuring himself didn't keep Kevin from having occasional nightmares about that night on the highway. The faces of the Mexicans were always ghostlike; only his father stood out clearly. Time and again, the horse pistol in his dad's hand spewed orange flames as the man fell dead on the side of the road in slow motion, his dad calm and expressionless as he pulled the trigger. Kevin wondered if he could ever shoot another human being without flinching or shaking. He doubted it.

After spring works, when the cattle had been gathered, the calves branded, and the herds thrown onto fresh pastures, ranchers traditionally took a breathing spell. To stimulate interest in his ponies, Matt took out ads in regional livestock and agriculture trade magazines using the photographs he'd bought from Jeannie, inviting interested parties to visit and look over the 7-Bar-K cow ponies that would be sold at auction in March. The ad also contained photos of Petreo and Centavos, with captions detailing their bloodlines and offering stud services at reasonable rates.

At the auction, all the ponies sold and the two stallions brought in a sizable amount in negotiated stud fees, enough so that Matt recouped half of what he'd spent to buy them from Delfino Díaz.

That night with Al, Brenda, and Dale joining in at the supper table to celebrate the successful auction and partake of one of Mary's special beef casseroles, Matt raised his beer bottle high.

"We're on our way," he predicted with a satisfied smile. "Along with the ranchers who bought, we sold to two pro rodeo cowboys who promised to come back again next year and bring their friends. That's a market that's only gonna get bigger for us."

"Stop gloating and eat," Mary said sweetly as she slid a plate heaped with beef casserole and green beans under his chin.

Matt's fork froze in midair as he grinned. "Is that what I'm doing?"

"He can't help himself," Al replied between bites. Everybody laughed.

As a conspirator pledged to silence, Kevin marveled at how guilt-free about killing the Mexican his father seemed to be. Was it really so easy to shake off taking a life? Did war teach a person how to do that?

Matt met his questioning gaze with a smile. Kevin smiled back, wondering if they'd ever again talk about what happened in Mexico. He didn't think so.

* * *

As always, the annual all-state high school rodeo coincided with spring break and Kevin felt ready. Both families packed up and left for the host town of Deming in the cool of the morning. They drove the back way to Hillsboro, then south through lovely grassy hills past the ghost town of Lake Valley, once the site of the richest silver deposit in the country, and finally west along a little used highway that ended just north of Deming.

The chamber of commerce had put welcoming banners announcing the rodeo on the streets and a local country-and-western radio station was broadcasting live from a popular diner. The DJ was interviewing favored contestants who'd won at regional events. As team roping contenders, Kevin and Dale were scheduled to be interviewed later in the afternoon.

They pulled into the arena parking lot, listening to Todd Marks, the current all-around state champion, modestly discussing his chances of repeating. He mentioned a few cowboys who worried him some, but Kevin wasn't among them. Kevin didn't know if he should take offense at the omission or be happy to be overlooked. He decided the latter. If he was *that* underrated, maybe Todd wouldn't see him coming.

After unloading the ponies, Kevin's and Dale's parents took off for the motel while they stayed behind to walk, water, and feed their restless animals. At the registration table they lined up behind two pretty cowgirls to sign in and pay their entry fees. The taller of the two had long dark hair under her cowboy hat. Her high cheekbones and intelligent, smoky eyes reminded Kevin a little bit of the folksinger Joan Baez.

He leaned closer. "Are you barrel racing?"

The girl turned and looked him up and down. "No, I'm here to sign up for prom queen."

Kevin blushed at the well-deserved sarcasm. "That was pretty stupid of me."

Next to him, Dale chucked. So did the girl standing with his tormentor.

"Not stupid," the girl replied. "Just inept."

"He hasn't had a girlfriend in a while," Dale explained.

Kevin dug an elbow in Dale's side, took a step back, and tipped his hat. "Sorry to have bothered you."

"No bother. Will you be at the dance tonight?"

"What dance?"

"At the American Legion Hall. It's a fund-raiser for the state high school rodeo association, but free to all participants."

"I reckon so, if you'll be there."

"I might be."

"Then I'll be there if you'll dance with me."

"I might."

"Would it be inept of me to ask your name?"

The girl shrugged. "Kim Ward."

"And I'm Loretta," Kim's companion said.

"I'm Kevin Kerney, and this here is Dale Jennings."

Loretta gave Dale a sweet smile.

"I know who you are," Kim Ward replied as she stepped up to the table. "If I don't see you tonight, good luck this weekend."

"We'd better go dancing tonight, old boy," Dale whispered in Kevin's ear as he dug an elbow in his side.

Kevin swatted his arm away.

* * *

Informed of the rodeo association fund-raising dance at the American Legion, both sets of parents decided to go as well. On their way from the parking lot, Kevin hung back and asked his father why he'd never joined a veterans' organization.

"I never saw much sense to drinking and telling war stories, most of which are BS," Matt replied.

"You never talk about any of your old army buddies."

"My war was a short one," Matt replied curtly. "I didn't have much time to make a lot of friends."

Inside, Kevin looked around for Kim Ward but didn't see her. Dale had cornered Loretta, the girl who had been in line with Kim. Kevin asked where she was.

"She'll be here," Loretta replied as Dale led her out on the dance floor.

The hall was festooned with bunting and banners put up by the rodeo association, and the band was playing two-step music that had the crowd filling the floor. The bar along a side wall was packed with men around Matt's age sipping longneck beers and watching the action.

Twenty minutes passed before Kim showed up, looking spectacular in a rose-red cowgirl shirt and tight jeans that showed off her firm, athletic figure.

"There you are," Kevin said, intercepting her as she crossed the edge of the dance floor.

"Do you know how to dance?" Kim asked.

"I do," Kevin replied, silently thanking Jeannie Hollister for teaching him how to move his feet.

"Let's see." She took him by the hand and pulled him onto the floor. "You better not be lying to me, cowboy."

As they danced, he learned she was from Deming, a senior about to graduate, and lived with her mom on twenty acres outside of town. When the band stopped for a break, they stepped outside to cool down.

"You're not too bad," Kim said as they stood in the cool of the night.

"That's because you made me look good," Kevin replied.

She stepped close and kissed him on the lips. "Want to go to a party?"

"Where?"

"Close by. Come on, I'm driving."

"I'll get Dale and Loretta."

"Just leave them be."

"Okay. Let me tell my parents first."

"I'll ask them," Kim proposed. "Point them out to me."

The band had started back up. Inside they found Kevin's parents dancing to an Elvis Presley ballad. With permission granted as long as Kevin didn't stay out too late, they piled into Kim's old Chevy. Five minutes later they stopped in front of a small farmhouse. One lonely lamplight shone behind the curtain of the front window.

"Where are we?"

"My house." She reached over and caressed the erection that pressed hard against the fabric of his jeans. "We're the party. My mom's at work." She nibbled his ear. "Come on."

He saw no reason not to and had no desire to resist. Still he asked, as he tumbled out the passenger door with Kim sliding across the seat behind him, "Are you sure?"

"I'm on the pill."

Later, when she deposited him at the motel-room door, he was no longer a virgin twice over. His parents were asleep in one of the double beds. Certain that he smelled of sex, he undressed quickly and got under the covers in the unoccupied bed, hoping it would go undiscovered. He fell asleep within minutes.

* * *

On Saturday, Kevin didn't see Kim until he'd completed the first rounds of team roping with Dale and saddle-bronc riding. Both events had been stellar, and if he kept it up he had a shot at leading the pack at the end of the day.

Barrel racing was about to begin when he approached Kim as she waited next to her pony.

"I've been looking for you. Good luck."

She eyed him cautiously and then turned away to adjust a stirrup. "Thanks. You're doing well, I see."

"So far, so good."

"Do you think I'm a slut?" she asked tentatively, her back rigid.

"No. I don't know you well enough, but I'm thinking you're one of a kind."

She turned and flashed a brilliant smile at him. "Perfect."

"What?"

"Your answer was perfect. Will I see you later?"

"I'd like that."

"No sex, though."

"That's okay."

"You're sure?"

Kevin hid his disappointment. "I'm sure."

She threw a leg up over her pony and settled into the saddle. "Okay."

She walked her pony away. When her turn came she took the lead in the first go-round and kept it.

At the end of his last event of the afternoon, Kevin stood tied with Todd Marks. He met Kim at the concession stand for a soda pop just as her mother was leaving for her job as the swing-shift supervisor at the telephone company. As she hurried away, Kevin commented that they looked more like sisters than mother and daughter.

"We hear that all the time. She was only seventeen when she had me. What are we going to do tonight?"

"My parents want to take us to dinner."

Kim's eyes lit up. "You mean it?"

"That's the plan."

She snuggled close. "You just might be the real McCoy."

* * *

On Sunday morning barrel racing was the opening event and Kevin cheered Kim on as she took the championship, running the cloverleaf flawlessly, her pony grazing only one barrel that teetered but didn't fall. When the final standings were announced, she whooped and threw her arms around Kevin before taking a victory lap on her pony. Her mother and a crowd of friends surrounded her after she returned and Kevin didn't see her again until he'd finished with a miserable run in the steer-wrestling event. With Todd Marks now clearly ahead, he tried not to sulk and look despondent.

He picked up some points in the all-around standing with another first with Dale in team roping, but didn't gain any ground in the saddle-bronc event. With calf roping, his last event, about to start, he was anxiously pacing behind the chutes when Kim found him.

"Are you going to write to me?" she asked.

Kevin stopped pacing. "Do you want me to?"

"Of course I do. After all, we'll both be at NMSU in the fall."

"You didn't tell me that."

Kim shrugged coyly. "Well, now I am."

"I don't know if I can wait that long to see you again," Kevin said with a grin.

Kim laughed. "Don't go and get all horny on me."

"I can't help it."

She leaned in and gave him a big kiss. From the corner of his eye he saw his dad at the arena railing trying to hide a grin. *He knows,* Kevin thought.

"Go get 'em, cowboy."

Kevin climbed onto Two-Bits. After this go-round he'd have to watch Todd Marks take his turn. No matter how well he did, all Todd needed was a run-of-the-mill performance to claim the all-around title again.

Two-Bits made a clean break, the calf was cooperative, and Kevin's tie-down went smoothly. There was some consolation in a strong finish, he thought, as he joined his father at the railing to watch Todd take the title.

Up in the stands, Kim was sitting with Mary, Al, Brenda, and Dale. Kevin wondered if his mom also knew. He figured so. Sexiness just oozed out of her.

Todd made a good run, flanked his calf onto its side, tied three legs, signaled time, and went to remount just as the calf kicked loose and stood. It was a clear disqualification. Kevin had taken the all-around title. Stunned, he couldn't believe it.

Grinning ear to ear, Matt thumped him on the back. "You did it!"

It was all he could do to keep from jumping up and down like a six-year-old kid on Christmas morning.

Grim-faced, Todd rode over to the railing, slipped off his pony, and shook Kevin's hand. "Congratulations."

"Thanks. I didn't think I had a chance."

Todd forced a smile. "Neither did I."

It took only a minute for the announcement to be made. The crowd in the stands roared when Kevin entered the arena to acknowledge their applause. He waved, doffed his hat, and smiled like a Cheshire cat. It was by far the best weekend of his life.

36

Through the end of the school year, Kevin and Kim stayed in touch mostly by letter and occasionally by telephone. Kevin expected that time and distance would wear down their interest in each other, but the reverse proved true. He wasn't sure why. Their letters were neither mushy nor sexy. Instead, they wrote about everyday things: Kim's part-time job to save money for college, Kevin rebuilding his grandfather's old pickup truck with Dale's help so he could take it with him to Las Cruces.

When he admitted to taking Betsy Reed, a girl in his Spanish class, to the senior prom, Kim wrote back jokingly accusing him of unfaithfulness before revealing she'd done the same with Corky Brazell, because "you only get to go to your senior prom once." Kevin felt the same.

Both of them had won scholarships. Kevin had two, a merit scholarship that covered tuition, books, and fees, and an ROTC scholarship that gave him a room-and-board stipend. In addition, Erma Fergurson was going to rent him the one-bedroom apartment in her new house for next to nothing in exchange for his handyman services. It meant he wouldn't be putting a big financial strain on his parents to go to college. He felt good about that.

Kim had also received financial aid, with a $500 New Mexico High School Rodeo Association Award she could use for incidental school expenses, and a presidential scholarship that paid her tuition, books, fees, and on-campus housing. Other than being required to carry a full class load and maintain a high grade point average in order to keep the scholarship, the only real downside was that she'd be forced to abide by dorm curfews and visiting restrictions. But with Kevin having his own place, she coyly told him it might be bearable.

After graduation, Kevin spent most of his time at the ranch helping Matt with the ponies and working cattle with Dale and both their dads. On a morning in July he accompanied Dale to Las Cruces so he could enlist in the air force. Dale requested flight-mechanic school after basic training, figuring the skills he'd learn would benefit him around the ranch or help him land a job after his discharge if need be.

Dale signed the papers, and the recruiting sergeant told him to report for induction in one week. Back in T or C, they stopped off so Dale could give his girlfriend the news. It didn't go over too well. From the cab of the truck, Kevin watched as they argued on her front porch. Finally, she threw up her hands in disgust, went inside, and slammed the front door in his face.

"What happened?" Kevin asked when Dale returned.

"She dumped me," he replied sheepishly. "I told her I didn't want to get married until after I got out of the service."

"She'll get over it," Kevin suggested, trying to bolster Dale's spirits.

Dale shook his head. "Nope, she wants to get married bad. If it isn't me, she'll find someone else."

"Is there some reason she's in such a hurry?" Kevin asked diplomatically.

Dale shook his head. "I didn't knock her up. It's always been 'wait until we're married.' That's just the way she's been raised."

"Nothing wrong with that."

Dale sighed. "I guess not."

Kevin fired up the truck. "Gals like guys in uniform. At least, that's what I've heard."

Dale chuckled disdainfully. "Yeah, you should know. Look how Jeannie Hollister stuck by you after you joined JROTC."

The following week, Kevin drove Dale to El Paso the day before he was to be sworn in at the induction center. They got a room at a cheap downtown motel, and upon the recommendation of the manager, parked the pickup, left most of their money hidden in their room, and walked across the border to Juárez, arriving in the city at dusk just as the nightlife was heating up.

Dale wanted a drink or two to celebrate his last hours of freedom as a civilian, so they wandered into a few noisy bars along the crowded main street that teemed with GIs in civvies from the nearby military bases. At one saloon Dale got to talking with two airmen from Holloman Air Force Base, who ragged on him about being stupid enough to enlist.

Dale told them he'd signed on for training as an aircraft mechanic, which he quickly learned would probably get him a tour in Vietnam. Neither of the airmen had gone there yet, but were due to deploy in a few months. Before departing, they recommended a visit to Casa Blanca, the best whorehouse in Juárez. Dale decided he had to see it for himself.

Following their directions, Kevin and Dale wandered a few blocks down the main boulevard to a side street that opened onto a large plaza. Directly across from a towering church with tall spires, a high, whitewashed adobe wall hid a large hacienda. A courtyard gate with a small sign above it discreetly announced the establishment.

Inside was a charming outdoor patio under thick, leafy shade trees. The lights of a brightly lit grand saloon beckoned through an open doorway. They settled at a long, polished bar and started drinking scotch whiskey, which Dale had a sudden need to try now that he was about to become a fighting member of the armed forces.

Although early, the bar was busy with a number of good-looking young women working potential customers. It wasn't long before two gals approached them and whispered suggestions of how they might be able to please them at a certain price.

Dale decided his transition from civilian life wasn't quite complete, so he quickly finished his drink, gave Kevin a silly grin, and left with his attractive escort down a hallway that led to a row of private rooms.

Kevin said no to the girl who'd almost crawled into his lap. Not because she was unappealing or suggested disinteresting acts, but because he didn't like the idea of buying sex. With her hand on his crotch and her tongue in his ear, it was hard to maintain his willpower. But he stuck to his guns and she eventually wandered away, which immediately made him begin to regret his decision. Fortunately it didn't take Dale long to conclude his tryst with the other girl. He returned looking smug and very pleased with himself.

They had another scotch to say goodbye to Casa Blanca, and ate dinner at a main-drag steakhouse, where Kevin had a change of heart about the "soiled dove" who'd propositioned him. By then it was too late. Most of his money had gone to buy Dale drinks and pay for dinner. He doubted Casa Blanca extended credit to gringo teenagers. Besides, Dale was a little too drunk to find his way back to the motel alone. With the last of what was left in his wallet, he piled Dale into a cab that took them to the international bridge. To keep Dale from weaving, Kevin guided him slowly across the bridge above the sluggish, brown trickle of the Rio Grande, and down the busy sidewalk to the motel. In their room, Dale reminisced about his time with the Casa Blanca whore before falling asleep fully dressed on the top of his bed. Kevin set the alarm clock for four in the morning and turned out the lights.

Shortly before six, after stopping for burritos for breakfast, Kevin dropped Dale off, hungover and pale-looking, in front of the induction center. He slapped him on the back and wished him well, a little envious of his friend and a little sad to see him leave. He watched Dale meld into the crowd of young men moving through the front door, reconciled to the idea that for him it was college before the military. Maybe he'd miss the fighting, but he'd made a promise to his parents that school would come first.

He drove away thinking it really wasn't all that far from El Paso to Deming—about a ninety-minute drive on a fast, good highway. The night at Casa Blanca had given him an itch to see Kim. He discarded the idea as harebrained. Instead, he headed north, home to the ranch.

* * *

Erma had offered to furnish Kevin's apartment above the garage of her new house, but Mary wouldn't hear of it. A full two weeks before classes started, she came down to Las Cruces with Kevin. They stayed as Erma's houseguests while haunting used-furniture stores and secondhand shops, buying what was needed at bargain prices. By the time they were ready to return to the ranch and prepare for his more permanent move, the apartment was fully furnished and ready. Kevin was itching to move in.

Mary and Matt followed him from the ranch the day he moved and Erma cooked a welcoming dinner for her "new tenant" and his parents that consisted of beef Stroganoff, French green beans, salad, and a peach cobbler. Before digging in, everyone toasted Kevin with a glass of wine to launch him on his collegiate journey.

Erma's new home was probably the most modern in town. It had the look of an adobe-style house, but the lines were sharp and clean with little inside or outside ornamentation. The floors were all tile and the walls all painted a soft off-white with a hint of yellow. She'd furnished it in Danish modern pieces that were sleek, low, and drew the eye. On the walls were some of her larger paintings highlighted by strategically mounted ceiling lights. A row of south-facing windows lit up the living room during the day, and opposite was a long, deep fireplace with a polished slab-stone hearth that made the room feel cozy at night. Her studio was where she let go and got messy, with paintings haphazardly hung here and there, stacked against a wall, or on easels in varying stages of completion in front of a bank of large north windows that drew in the beauty of the foothills and the soft, cool light of the day.

Kevin figured he was about the luckiest freshman at NMSU. He couldn't wait for Kim to see his apartment.

After his folks returned to the ranch, he had one day to settle in before Erma got serious about working him as her handyman in lieu of paying full rent. His first job, she informed him as they stood inside the double garage, still crammed with unopened packing boxes from her recent move, was to build floor-to-ceiling shelves along the back wall for storage. She handed him a drawing with the exact dimensions she wanted, gave him some money for the lumber and materials he'd need, and pointed to a toolbox on the floor near the garage door.

"You should find what you'll need for the job in there," she said. "But if not, buy it."

"What grade of lumber do you want me to use?"

Erma tapped her lips thoughtfully. "Nothing warped but nothing too expensive. Does that help?"

Kevin studied the drawing. What she wanted built was straightforward and easily done. "Yes. When do you want it finished?"

"Soon, so I can start unpacking these boxes, store things properly, and get this mess cleaned up. You can help me with that too." She patted him affectionately on the arm. "Oh, and I'll give you gas money when you run errands for me, okay?"

"Okay. I'll start today. But before I go for the lumber, I need to clear a path to the back wall and make room to work."

Erma smiled. "I'll leave you to it, but come inside before you take off. I have something your mother left for you."

"What is it?"

"A Betty Crocker illustrated cookbook. You can't live on twenty-five-cent hamburgers and ten-cent fries endlessly."

The mere thought of cooking every day made Kevin wince.

"It won't be so bad," Erma consoled. "And occasionally you have to help me in the kitchen when I have gatherings, so you'll learn."

"That's not my idea of being a handyman."

Erma laughed. "But it's mine."

* * *

Once the shelves were up, Erma helped Kevin put everything away. He removed the trash, cleaned up the garage, and asked what next. It turned out to be helping with a party she was throwing in the evening for some of her colleagues, friends, and graduate students. Not only did he learn how to dice, chop, and help prepare appetizers and canapés, he also had a good time when the guests arrived, especially when Sue Ann Bussey swooped in through the front door, her escort a forgotten tailwind.

Five-six with strawberry-blond hair and a flawless complexion, her arrival literally froze all conversation. She had a thousand-watt smile and a way of looking at you that said you were the most important person in the room. Kevin was more thunderstruck than smitten when Erma introduced him to her. He immediately wished he were at least five years older.

"Oh my," Sue Ann said, looking him over with a gleam in her eye. "Aren't you the handsome one."

"Enough of that," Erma cautioned.

Sue Ann turned her attention fully on Erma and gave her a kiss on the cheek. "Of course, you're right." She waved and winked at Kevin as her escort led her away to a nearby group of guests clustered in front of the living-room picture window. Outside, the valley was etched in vivid detail under a crystal-clear, late-afternoon sky.

"Stay away from that one," Erma said. "In fact, better yet, you are excused from your duties."

"I can go?"

"Scram," Erma replied. "Come for breakfast in the morning. I'll fix you waffles."

Kevin grinned and left. Erma's house rules were simple. With the exception of her studio he had free rein of the place unless she had an overnight male guest or told him otherwise. She in turn would honor his privacy when it came to any overnight guests, but he was forbidden from throwing large noisy parties without prior permission and he could not have a roommate move in unannounced.

He hurried in his truck to Kim's dorm. The last he'd heard she was scheduled to move into her room that day. He checked at the desk, discovered she had arrived, and asked the student resident assistant to ring her room. There was no answer. The girl didn't know if she was in the building but doubted it. There were just too many parties going on all over town.

He hotfooted it to the student union building and found it almost deserted, except for several students busy at a table making posters protesting the draft. He wandered around for a while checking all the outside areas where he'd seen students congregate hoping to find her. After one last try at the dorm thinking she might have just gone out for coffee or a snack with her roommate, he gave up and drove dejectedly back to his apartment.

Erma's party was still in full swing and he sat in his truck with the motor running, laughter and conversation pouring through the open living-room windows. It would be too depressing to stay up in his apartment listening to people having fun, and he was in no mood to join in.

He put the truck into gear and drove back to the dorm. He'd just stake the place out until Kim returned, *if* she returned—another glum thought. As he parked and walked across the lane a figure stepped out of the shadow of a nearby tree.

"Well, you sure took your time finding me," Kim said as she threw her arms around him. "Where have you been?"

"Looking for you." She smelled and felt delicious. He kissed her and kissed her again.

"Take me away from here. Show me your apartment. I'm dying to see it."

"When do you have to be back?"

"Midnight, but I've got a ground-floor room on the side of the building and a roommate who'll let me in through the window if I'm late."

"Let's go." Kevin pulled her by the hand to his truck.

She snuggled close on the ride to Erma's, where the party still continued in full force.

"Wow," Kim said as he led her up the stairs to the apartment. "This place is amazing. What a wonderful house. When am I going to see all of it?"

"Someday soon," he promised. "But first I'd like to show you my bedroom."

"What kind of girl do you think I am?"

"The best kind," Kevin said as he opened the door. "Smart, sexy, and sassy."

Kim stopped and scanned his face. "I think I really like you."

"I like you better," Kevin teased, pulling her along to the bedroom.

* * *

Kevin started college unsure of what exactly he wanted to do with his life. He loved ranching and could probably make a place for himself someday as Dale's partner at the Rocking J as well as take over the 7-Bar-K horse business from his dad when the time came, but it just didn't feel right. Even though the Rocking J was close to his roots, it just wasn't the same as the place of his ancestors. It had been founded by a Jennings, not a Kerney, and in that regard, he'd always feel junior to Dale and his family no matter how equal the partnership might be.

If he did decide to major in animal husbandry or range science, would he be able to someday have a ranch of his own? Or would he forever be the one who lived in the old foreman's cottage, no matter how nice it was? If he ranched, he wanted his very own place to start a family like his mom and dad had once had.

He remembered visiting Raymond Cannon's Willow Creek Ranch for the first time, where his dad jokingly advised him to become a rich lawyer first if he ever wanted to ranch. With land prices rising year after year there seemed a hard truth to that advice.

* * *

To put off deciding on a major, he stuck to the basics: freshman composition, math, European history, and Spanish, along with ROTC. It was a full load but manageable, and he got through midterms with a very creditable grade point average that was high enough to make the dean's list if it held. He'd adapted easily to college and prized the freedom it gave him. And although he wouldn't admit to feeling smug about it, his love life was also about as good as it could be.

On campus, there was a growing student protest movement against the war, with caravans of antiwar demonstrators traveling to Washington to join mass rallies demanding an end to the conflict. Not wanting to get involved because of his ROTC commitment, Kevin sidestepped the evening peace vigils and teach-ins. On those days when he wore his uniform, he was sometimes ridiculed and challenged as a war lover by some of the more strident peace advocates who wanted to argue with him. But he held his temper and moved on. Kim had made it clear she was against the war, but unlike Jeannie she didn't get on his case about being in ROTC, and he adored her for that.

Early in the semester he'd introduced Kim to Erma, and they'd hit it off immediately. Being with both of them during their first meeting made him realize Kim shared a lot of Erma's traits, especially her quick wit, smarts, and sexiness. On occasional weekends, Kim would sign out of the dorm on a Friday, ostensibly to go home for the weekend, and instead stay with Kevin. It didn't seem to bother Erma one bit, and he was absolutely certain she hadn't said a word about it to his folks.

Erma had a lover, Lewis Owens, whom Kevin had met briefly several times in passing. Sometimes his car was in the driveway overnight, but often he'd come and go in a matter of a few hours. Kevin figured him to either be married or traveling for work a lot. Kim thought it was likely Erma's lover was married, which made her the absolute coolest, most liberated woman she knew.

School, Kim, and Erma's handyman projects often filled his days and nights. A week might go by without Erma needing something done and then she'd have a flurry of projects for him, from installing new shades for the living-room windows to hauling and stacking a cord of firewood she'd bought for the fireplace.

He didn't get home until Thanksgiving, and then just for the few days he could spare with class assignments coming due and term papers to write. He'd only gotten one brief letter from Dale soon after his enlistment and he asked his folks how he was doing. Al said Dale would be home for Christmas before shipping out to his permanent duty station in Okinawa. He'd been promoted once and would have to wait a year to earn another stripe.

Looking forward to seeing him, Kevin wrote him a quick congratulatory note before he returned to Las Cruces. In some ways he was a little jealous, in some ways not. The fighting in Vietnam had escalated, with more American soldiers being sent there and a lot more coming home wounded or in body bags. Television news aired scenes of firefights, bombing runs, and civilian battlefield causalities. War correspondents were reporting increasing rumors of atrocities by South Vietnamese and US troops. On campus about the least cool thing you could do was wear an ROTC uniform.

In Las Cruces, another party was raging at Erma's, and an invitation to drop in was tacked to Kevin's apartment door. It was mostly the same mixture of faculty, staff, and grad students from the university, along with a smattering of Erma's artist friends. He was nibbling on the leftover appetizers in the kitchen when Sue Ann Bussey approached.

He'd met her twice more at Erma's and learned that she was twenty-one, had a degree in theater, and was in her first year of graduate school.

"There you are," she said liltingly.

Kevin blushed. It was automatic whenever he saw her. Along with the strawberry-blond hair, the creamy complexion, and magnetic personality, there was a supple roundness to her almost-perfect figure that invited fantasies.

Sue Ann stepped closer. "Erma tells me you have a very cute girlfriend," she whispered conspiratorially. "Is she here? I'd love to meet her."

Kevin took in her scent. "No, she's probably just getting back to town from Deming."

"I'm sure I'll meet her another time." She touched his arm. "You're a lucky boy to have your very own apartment. Do you know that?"

"Yeah, I do."

"Can I tell you a secret?"

"Sure."

"You're too good-looking to be so shy. I'd love to see your apartment sometime. Or maybe you'd like to see mine." She made her exit from the kitchen with a flip of her hair and a coy look over her shoulder.

Although he wanted to, Kevin didn't take her seriously, partly because he had a gal he really, really liked. But that didn't mean he wasn't aroused.

* * *

Kim's dorm roommate, Liz Hearn, was dating a basketball player, and when the season heated up in the second semester, they often went together to the home games. Kevin tagged along once and felt decidedly out of place sitting with all the players' girlfriends who staked out a row of cheap seats high above the home-team bench behind the courtside reserved seating for season ticket holders.

That semester Kim also joined the rodeo team. She'd been recruited earlier to join but had declined. She'd sold her pony because her mom couldn't afford to keep it and help pay for Kim's college expenses on a telephone company supervisor's salary. When the team manager found out, he arranged for a booster to cover the cost of a good pony and its upkeep for Kim to use. She was in heaven and encouraged Kevin to join the team as well, but he was short on time and didn't want to put any additional financial burden on his folks.

With team practices and meetings, hanging out with her roommate, and all the ongoing class work she normally had, Kevin saw much less of Kim as the semester wore on. His own busy schedule was much the same, so it was just the way things had to be. Yet when they were together it was still great, whether they were just walking and talking, taking in a rare movie downtown, having coffee at the SUB between classes, or fooling around at the apartment.

By the tail end of the second semester, Kim was ready to compete in a rodeo to be held on campus. Besides barrel racing, she entered the breakaway calf-roping event and had been practicing daily during every spare moment she had. It was a two-day rodeo held on the weekend just before finals week, and Kevin wasn't about to miss it.

Understandably, he hadn't seen her for two weeks. He'd left frequent messages for her at the dorm but heard from her only once when she called and made a quick apology for being so busy. The practices were grueling and she wasn't getting much sleep. Of course he commiserated. He knew what it took mentally and physically to prepare for the events.

His first final was in European history on Monday morning and he'd planned to attend only Kim's events, but the temptation to watch all the competitions was too great. After sneaking behind the chutes to wish Kim good luck, he joined the crowd in the stands and got caught up in the action. Kim took the lead in the first barrel-racing go-round but had only a fair time in the breakaway event, which wasn't bad for her first competitive crack at the event.

Kevin had competed against a number of contestants in the rodeo, many of whom were students at the university. He watched them with great interest, impressed with how much they'd improved. He began to miss being down there with them and being part of a sport where a rider and his pony had to act as one in order to win. When it neared perfection it was a sight to see.

He mulled over what might have been. Maybe he should have delayed college for a year and gone rodeoing on his own instead. It wasn't too late; he could finish out the year, drop out for a time, and see what he could do on the circuit. Maybe he could convince Kim to leave school and join him. The only problem with both ideas was money.

He put away his foolish notions. He'd made commitments to his parents, to the army to finish the ROTC program, and he sure didn't want to step too far away from Kim. He quit daydreaming just in time to watch his old nemesis, Todd Marks, in the saddle-bronc event. It was such an outstanding performance, it had Kevin on his feet and applauding before the announcer even gave the score.

The end of the rodeo on Sunday saw Kim with a first in barrel racing and a fifth in breakaway, which was darn good, and a first place for the team. As the crowd thinned out after the closing ceremonies, Kevin jumped the fence and went looking for her. She was with her teammates behind the roping chute celebrating their victory. He hung back, waited until she saw him, and then stepped over to congratulate her.

"Hooray for you," he said, giving her a hug. She barely hugged him back. "You did great."

"Thanks."

"Let's go get a bite. I'll wait until you're ready to leave."

Kim made a face and looked over at her teammates. "We're all going out together."

Kevin nodded. "Sure, have fun, you all deserve it. Call me when you're ready to leave and I'll come and fetch you."

Kim shook her head. "No, I can't. I'm seeing Todd now, Kevin." She kissed him on the cheek. "Sorry. Don't be mad."

"Oh" was all Kevin could muster as she walked away.

* * *

Kevin finished finals week miserable, hurt, and angry. Although he'd prepared well for his exams up to the minute Kim dumped him, he didn't give a hoot about how he did. To cope, he simply shut down. He'd go home and forget about her over the summer, guaranteed.

He got his grades two days before the end of the semester. The next day he'd be leaving for the summer, along with thousands of other students. He'd made the dean's list again, proving a broken heart hadn't made him stupid. He was packing to return to the ranch in the morning when Erma knocked at the door.

"Can I come in?" she asked.

"Sure."

It had been a while since Erma had visited and she took a quick look around. The front room was separated from the small kitchen by a partial wall with a built-in bookcase. It contained a desk, a chair, a small sofa, and a gently worn leather easy chair that faced a small black-and-white television sitting on a side table. On the wall over the sofa was a Johnny Cash concert poster. The room was clean and tidy. Knowing Kevin, Erma expected as much.

She settled on the sofa. "I haven't seen much of you lately."

"You haven't needed me to do anything."

"That's true." Earlier, she'd impulsively called Kim at the dorm to invite her to lunch before they both left for home and had learned about the breakup. She patted the empty cushion. "Come and sit."

Kevin eased down beside her. "What's up?"

"I spoke to Kim."

He jumped to his feet. "I don't want to talk about it."

"I do. I've come to give you some advice. It's not something I do often, so you'd better listen."

Kevin sank stiffly into the easy chair and stared at her. "What advice?"

"Don't be angry at Kim."

"Why not?"

"Because she was good for you and she was just what you needed. Everything I saw between the two of you was honest, loving, and caring. I'm betting you were faithful to each other right up to the end. It doesn't get much better than that."

"Faithful?" Kevin snapped. "What about you and your married lover?"

Erma broke into a laugh. "Is that what you think? Lewis is single and has a very sensitive government job that requires him to travel a lot. Sometimes I wish he was married, then I could see him more frequently."

"That's weird."

Erma rose. "Thank you for the compliment. You have two choices, Kevin. You can turn Kim into a cold-hearted bitch, or you can treasure her memory as your first true love. What you decide may well determine what kind of man you'll become. Don't screw it up."

She stepped over, kissed him on the cheek, and said, "Give my love to your parents."

"I will."

Erma left and for a long time Kevin sat silently considering her advice. He finally decided if he was going to be continually drawn to women with minds of their own, he'd best be prepared for the consequences.

37

Kevin prepared for his return to school pleased to no longer be a freshman and impatient to get back to living on his own. The summer had passed quickly; work with the ponies had kept him plenty busy. In some ways it had been a pleasure to step away from book learning and use his head and hands in the everyday ranch chores, helping his father with the challenges of turning frisky young horses into savvy cow ponies. He always learned something new working with his dad that was often far more satisfying than the large, somewhat boring classroom lectures he had to endure at college.

In the cool of the evenings he frequently joined his folks on the screened-in porch, where they talked mostly about their plans to expand the horse-breeding and training operation. His dad wanted to build a foaling barn to house mares with difficult pregnancies. Each baby they lost meant lost income, and if a brood mare died while foaling, the expense was considerable.

With profits being plowed back into the business, the gamble had yet to put them squarely in the black. However, they were no longer dipping into their dwindling cash reserves to pay the bills. From the look of his dad's patched jeans and his mom's faded blouses, Kevin could see they weren't indulging in any extras or spending money on themselves. And while both seemed fit and healthy, they looked a bit more worn down come the end of the day. Still, that didn't diminish their optimism about the future, or the joy of what they were doing.

For Kevin it had been a good summer. Being home with his parents, visiting with Al and Brenda, and catching up with some of his old high school acquaintances was the tonic he needed to get over Kim Ward. He even took Betsy Reed to a couple of Saturday-night movies, bought Jeannie Hollister a Coke when he ran into her at the drugstore, and went to Dale's old girlfriend's wedding in T or C. Part of him felt detached from it all as if he were a stranger visiting his old hometown.

Before he left for Las Cruces, his dad walked him to his truck and pressed fifty dollars into his hand. He refused to take it back.

"Unexpected things come up," he explained. "Besides, I know your ROTC stipend only covers the bare bones."

"Erma feeds me a lot," Kevin protested.

"You take it," Matt demanded. "And as a favor to me, call your mother once in a while. Reverse the charges. She misses you."

He turned to see his mom standing on the porch brushing a tear from her cheek and merrily waving at the same time. "I promise."

On his apartment door was a note from Erma saying she'd gone out of town with Lewis on an overnight road trip to Santa Fe and he'd find a landscape plan on his kitchen table that she wanted to discuss with him upon her return. It was a master plan drawn in her hand for the grounds immediately surrounding the house and the driveway. Most of the surrounding acreage on the property would remain untouched. It showed the exact location for every shrub, tree, bush, and planting bed, along with a list of the species or variety to be planted, mostly native. She wanted a great deal of rock work to be done, including sizable boulders, rock walls, and gravel pathways.

If she expected him to do it alone, it would likely mean working steadily during his free time over the course of the entire academic year. He didn't mind; it would give him a lot of satisfaction to see it come to fruition.

When she returned home they went over the plan together. It was to be his only handyman project for the year, and she would work with him when time allowed. Starting right away, all the rock, boulders, gravel, and plants would be delivered on an as-needed basis. When the time came, additional workers would be hired to help position the larger boulders.

"Do we have a deal?" Erma asked.

"You bet. It's the best project you've given me yet."

Erma laughed. "You're just glad to be released from making appetizers and hors d'oeuvres for my parties. Speaking of which, there will be one on Saturday night and you must come."

"I wouldn't miss it."

The party was one of Erma's standard affairs, only this time it had the addition of a Mexican guitarist, Gabriel Morales, who played and sang Spanish ballads on the courtyard. Kevin met him before the party while he helped Erma with the appetizers and hors d'oeuvres anyway, and discovered he was a muralist from Mexico City who had been accepted into the university fine-arts graduate program. They chatted in Spanish, which pleased Gabriel greatly. He talked about his wife and baby girl, who waited for him at their apartment in the old Hispanic neighborhood close to downtown. He was surprised and delighted to be in a place that reminded him of old Mexico, and to meet so many people who fluently spoke his native tongue.

He looked a little bit like the actor Fernando Lamas, with dark, intense eyes; a long, angular face; and a thin aristocratic nose above narrow lips. He had a ready smile, a strong baritone voice, and long fingers that flew over the guitar strings.

The minute Sue Ann Bussey arrived at the party, solo this time, she zoomed in on Gabriel like a heat-seeking missile, flashing her most brilliant smile, swishing by him as he roamed the courtyard taking requests for songs from the guests. Kevin's presence rated no more than a passing glance from her. He watched with amused interest as she tried to monopolize Gabriel's attention.

He charmingly deflected her. At the end of the party, when he packed up his guitar and left to go home to his wife and infant daughter, Sue Ann turned her spotlight on Kevin.

"Are you ever going to show me your apartment?" She pouted like a spoiled little Shirley Temple.

"It's such a mess, I'd be embarrassed for you to see it."

Sue Ann shook her strawberry locks. "I wouldn't mind."

Kevin studied her face. It was lovely, the smile magnetic, the look perfect for the camera, but it was empty of anything genuine. She could easily arouse him, but he found he really didn't like her. "No, I don't think so."

Her smile vanished. "You're kidding."

"No, I'm not."

"Jesus, what an arrogant kid you are." She snatched her clutch purse from the entry side table, said good night to Erma, and stormed out.

"I thought you'd sleep with her at least once," Erma commented dryly.

"So did I," Kevin said. "But there's nothing there. Why do you keep inviting her to your parties?"

"Entertainment value," Erma replied. "But now that I've discovered Gabriel and his guitar, you may have seen the last of her."

"That's okay by me."

Erma stepped close and gave him a motherly kiss.

"What's that for?"

Her smile was filled with pride. "Being the man my dear friend Mary has always known you would be."

"You aren't going to tell her about this, are you?"

"Goodness, no. Now go home before I ask you to help me clean up."

Kevin reached for the half-empty drink glasses on the entry table. "You don't have to ask. I'll help anyway."

* * *

After classes started, he saw Kim several times from a distance on campus but didn't try to intercept her. According to her roommate, who was in his English literature class, she was still with Todd, on the rodeo team, and as free-spirited as ever.

He had little time for dating or socializing. He managed to meet up for coffee at the SUB with several girls who appealed to him, but nothing came of it. He wasn't sure if they simply weren't interested or he wasn't, but the absence of any spark made it clear trying to turn it into something more wouldn't work. He took a town girl to a football game and slept with her once and that was the end of that. It was a monstrous disappointment compared to lovemaking with Kim.

In his second-year Spanish class there was a girl who intrigued him. He didn't know why, because she seemed the exact opposite of the type he liked. She sat alone, spoke little in class, and had a very shy air about her. She was tiny, dark-skinned with a small waist, had jet-black hair, obsidian eyes, and an oval face with high cheekbones.

He thought she was very good-looking but did everything possible to hide it. Her hair was always in a single braid that ran down her back, her clothing was drab and plain, she wore little or no makeup, and she hid her pretty face behind oversize reading glasses. She lived in the same dorm as Kim, because he'd seen her coming and going. During class introductions, she said she was from the Apache village of Mescalero. That was all he knew.

One day on a whim, he caught up with her outside after class. "You speak Spanish perfectly," he said with a smile as he walked with her. "Why are you taking the class?"

She stopped and looked at him with serious eyes. "Because it's an easy A and I need it for my grade-point average."

"That makes sense."

She nodded in agreement and began to walk away.

He caught up with her again. "I'm Kevin Kerney."

She paused again with the same serious look. "My name is Isabel Istee."

"From Mescalero, right?"

"Yes, I am Chiricahua." She eyed him critically. "You don't look like one of those hippie boys who wants to sleep with an Indian."

Her comment threw him off. "I'm not."

"Do you?"

"Do I what?"

"Want to sleep with me? I'm the only Indian girl living on campus, so it seems there's quite a competition going on about it." She said it without rancor.

Flummoxed, Kevin put his hands up in surrender. "I don't

know anything about that. I'm sorry if I've given you the wrong impression."

"Then why did you speak to me?"

"Is it forbidden?"

"No, it's just unusual. Most people leave me alone."

"I won't trouble you again."

"I don't mind, if you are honorable."

"I like to think I am."

"You study to be a soldier. I've seen you in your uniform."

"Is that bad?"

Isabel shook her head. "No. I must go now. I have another class."

He watched her walk away. He decided there was nothing shy about her at all. She moved with the grace of a woman, not with a bouncy, flouncy, college-girl walk. He figured Isabel Istee was not one to be taken lightly.

* * *

Isabel Istee thought about Kevin Kerney as she walked into her biology class, not quite sure of what to make of him. He seemed genuinely surprised to know there was a "Who would be the first to score with the Indian chick?" contest on campus. Was that on the up-and-up or just a ploy on his part?

She was the first in her family and one of the first women in her tribe to ever go to college. She wasn't about to dishonor her family or tribe in her quest to become a registered nurse with a bachelor's degree. Ever since she was a little girl she'd dreamed of helping her people, especially the teenagers. Among her generation a high percentage suffered from alcoholism and drug abuse, and the rate of pregnancy of underage girls was astronomical.

She'd noticed Kevin Kerney in Spanish class and appreciated that he was one of the few Anglo students who didn't speak over another person, rudely interrupt them, or fail to listen. She found these traits admirable and unusual in a White Eyes.

His family was known to her through Jasper Daklugie, who'd worked for a time on the Kerney ranch before he went to war in Korea. He had only positive things to say about the family. And Kerney's ancestors were known to her through the stories passed down from Jasper's uncle, who in the long-ago days knew and respected the Kerneys as decent people. The rarity of such a positive attitude among her people toward any White Eyes made Isabel disposed to withhold judgment. But experience had taught her that prejudice ran deep and was often unrecognized by virtually all White Eyes, including most of the students she'd met and many of the faculty.

Isabel was both Christian and pagan. She spoke three languages fluently, including her native Apache tongue, had a public name and a birth name known to few others, and was a member of an ancient matriarchal culture where women were more than just equals. It would take a special White Eyes to earn her regard. She decided if he persisted in his interest, she might be agreeable to it, but somewhat wary.

She settled down in her favorite chair at the back of the classroom where she'd be undisturbed and opened her notebook just as the professor cleared his throat to begin.

* * *

Without being pushy, Kevin persuaded Isabel to help him study for the midterm Spanish test, which would be to translate half a dozen English passages into Spanish. Conversationally he was okay, but when it came to the complexities of grammar, especially with words with multiple meanings, he often stumbled.

They met at the library and she tutored him for two hours, patiently correcting and encouraging him. On the walk back to her dorm, he invited her to Erma's annual Halloween party as his guest.

"Professor Erma Fergurson?"

"Yes, she's my landlady."

Isabel smiled in disbelief. She'd heard much about Professor Fergurson and had wanted to meet her. "She is your landlady?"

She rarely smiled, so Kevin took it as a good omen. "And my mother's best friend," he added, hoping it might win him a few points.

"I will go," she said as they stopped in front of the dorm. "Good night."

Hoping for more of an explanation as to why she showed such an interest in Erma, Kevin hesitated, but she'd already turned away.

"It's a costume party," he noted.

"I'll come as an Apache princess," Isabel replied over her shoulder.

And she did. When Kevin picked her up the night of the party, she emerged into the dorm reception area wearing a blue-and-red-beaded soft white buckskin dress with long tassels and knee-high matching beaded moccasins. Her hair, pulled into a braided ponytail, ran down her back to her waist. Draped around her neck were strands of colorful beads. Her eyeglasses were gone, showing off her lovely eyes. Her entrance stopped all activity. Guys waiting to pick up their dates unabashedly stared. She approached Kevin, looked him up and down, and smiled.

"Why did I know you'd dress as a cowboy?" she said.

"It seemed only right," he replied grinning. His chaps, hat, belt, boots, and spurs were the real McCoy, seasoned by his work at the ranch. Even his blue jeans had seen better days. Only the sparkling white, starched cowboy shirt was brand-new.

"What a pair we are," Isabel said with a soft smile as they made their way outside.

"You look spectacular."

"Thank you."

At the party, Kevin introduced Isabel to Erma, who'd dressed as a go-go girl in a miniskirt and boots. His date earned him a big wink of approval. Gabriel Morales and his wife were there as Diego Rivera and Frida Kahlo, along with a packed house of costumed revelers. Tables were laden with food and drink, and Beatles music poured from the hi-fi. Sue Ann Bussey was nowhere to be seen.

Isabel was the hit of the party, thus Kevin had little time with her. He entertained himself by jumping into conversations about art, the war, the peace movement, Aggie football, and complaints about some of the local politicians. When the party wound down, he rescued Isabel from a graduate student costumed as a turbaned sheik who had her cornered in the kitchen. As they walked to his truck, she took a long look around before getting in.

"You live here?" she questioned.

Kevin's hand froze on the ignition key. "In an apartment above the garage. Want to see it?" he asked hopefully.

"No, I just want to know where to find you."

He waited, hoping for clarification, but she was silent. He was still trying to figure what she meant when he got home.

* * *

Kevin's suspicion that Isabel was more interested in meeting Erma at her Halloween party than dating him was confirmed when she turned him down twice to go to the movies. He let the idea of anything more than a passing friendship slide, although he continued to remain intrigued by her. After their one date they always sat together in Spanish class and chatted briefly after, but never about anything personal. He didn't probe, nor did she seem interested to learn more about him. Occasionally he'd catch her looking at him as if she was trying to figure something out, and a moment of embarrassment would pass between them. She seemed to live inside herself more than anyone he knew.

During finals week they studied together for several hours the night before the Spanish exam. On their walk from the library to her dorm, she asked him when he'd be going home.

"Probably by the end of the week," he replied. "I earn most of my rent helping Erma with house projects, and I've fallen a little behind. And you?"

"Soon," she answered obliquely. "But I'll see you before I go."

Again mystified, Kevin said good night and watched her disappear through the dorm doors. When he saw her at the exam the next morning, he figured she only meant that she'd see him during the final. But it hadn't sounded that way the night before.

She finished the exam long before he did and waved at him as she left the classroom. He waved back, wondering if she'd be in his Spanish class in the second semester. If not, he'd miss seeing her.

Between studying and the exams, the days passed quickly. With his last final out of the way, he turned his attention to finishing the rock wall enclosing the circular planting bed in front of the house. The day started out mild and sunny, and he was making good progress until a fast-moving snowstorm blew in at noontime.

He'd promised Erma, who'd gone to Mexico on vacation, to finish the wall before he left for the ranch in the morning, so he put on his old barn coat, jammed a hat on his head, pulled on his gloves, and kept at it in the cold and wet until it got done. In the last flicker of twilight under a slate-gray sky, he admired his work briefly before putting away the tools and climbing the stairs to his apartment, eagerly anticipating a hot shower and something to eat.

When he emerged from the bathroom the wind was rattling the front-room window. He looked out to see heavy, wind-driven flakes pelting down and wondered if it was snowing at home. He wolfed down a can of warmed-up baked beans and a hot dog for dinner, too hungry to care about his culinary choices. He dumped the dirty dishes in the kitchen sink just as a knock came at the front door. He opened the door to a wintery blast. Isabel Istee, dressed in a heavy winter coat covered in snow, stepped quickly inside.

"I came to see you," she announced, shedding her coat. Under it she wore blue jeans and a bulky sweater over a blue cotton shirt.

"I'm surprised," Kevin said.

"I said I would." She looked him over. "Remember?"

"I wasn't sure what you meant. Did you walk here?"

"Yes."

"I could have come to get you."

"No, I needed the time to decide."

"Whether or not to come?"

"Yes." Her smile was almost playful.

"Well, here you are," Kevin said, still taken aback, wondering if he should do something, say something. "Now what?"

Isabel laughed and her face lit up. "I confuse you."

"Yes, you do."

"Take me to your bed," she said.

He opened his mouth to speak and she put her forefinger to his lips. "No talking."

In the bedroom, she undressed, let her hair down, stretched out on the bed, and waited for him. Nervous and a little shaky, he turned out the light and joined her. Within minutes, the quiet girl, the seemingly shy girl who lived so comfortably within herself, overwhelmed him with raw sexuality.

They did it twice again before she asked for a ride back to the dorm. It had stopped snowing and the desert town glistened under a blanket of white in a clear night sky.

"You can spend the night," he offered.

"No."

They dressed and left for the dorm. When he stopped at the front door, she looked at him and smiled. "You won," she said.

"Won what? Oh, you mean the contest."

Isabel nodded.

"But I didn't care about the contest."

"That's why I picked you."

"Now what?"

Isabel shrugged. "I'm not sure. I'll think about it while I'm at home."

"So will I," Kevin said.

"Good. That's the right answer." She got out, closed the truck door, and walked into the dorm looking prim, proper, and totally unaffected by their bout of incredible lovemaking.

* * *

At the start of the spring semester, Kevin returned to campus eager to see Isabel. He looked for her at registration, asked for her at her dorm, and left messages for her to no avail. Her roommate, a girl from Espanola, told him she would be returning to school late because of a death in the family. That was all she knew. Kevin asked her to have Isabel call him when she arrived. She said she would.

He worried perhaps some terrible tragedy had happened. She'd told him very little about her family. All he knew was that her parents were Ralph and Blossom, and she had a younger sister, Ramona. Her father was a high-ranking officer in the fire department and her mother was a member of the tribal council. She lived with her family in a house on a hill behind the tribal hospital near the village center.

He impatiently kept waiting for her to show up or call. After a frustrating week without hearing from her, he made another trip to the dorm hoping to find out more information. A resident assistant told him Isabel was back and attending her classes. The death in the family had been a cousin.

He wrote out a hurried note asking Isabel to call him at Erma's. The assistant put it in her mailbox behind the desk. Two more days passed with no response. He tried one more time to reach her by letter.

Dear Isabel,

I guess there really was a contest as to who would sleep with the "Indian" girl, only it was your contest, wasn't it? I was sorry to hear of your loss and I am sad if you feel we can no longer be friends.

Sincerely yours,
Kevin

He mailed it without a return address, hoping she'd be inclined to open an anonymous letter out of curiosity. Several days later between classes he saw her in the Student Union Building drinking coffee with her roommate. He approached their table.

"Did you get my letter?" he asked.

The roommate quickly gathered her books and slipped away.

Isabel nodded. "Yes."

Kevin sat across from her. "And?"

She studied him with her dark eyes. "We can be friends."

"Just casual friends, I take it."

"Yes, if you'd like that."

As he rose, Kevin stifled a sigh. "I'll see you around campus."

"Kevin."

He paused, waiting.

"I'll see you."

Holding back tears, Isabel watched him go. Over the holidays, she'd told her parents about Kevin Kerney, and how he was like no other White Eyes she'd ever known. She'd hoped, because of his family's long history of kindness and friendship shown to the tribe, they would be amenable to meeting him. It was, after all, the middle of the twentieth century and times were changing. She discreetly failed to mention that she'd seduced him and found him to be an intensely passionate lover.

Their reaction was immediate and harsh. They would not hear of it. The White Eyes were not brothers or sisters to the people. She could not make any pretensions of friendship to him; it would only damage her reputation at home. Should she persist, they would make her transfer to another college, perhaps the University of New Mexico in Albuquerque.

The forcefulness of their rejection stunned her. She argued with them for days, until she realized they were unyielding. Her mother was forever bitter about the White Eyes' internment of her Chiricahua grandparents at Fort Sill, Oklahoma, and her father, a good man at heart, instinctively and often with cause, distrusted all outsiders.

She considered abandoning her dreams, leaving the tribe, forging a life somewhere else with Kevin, if he would have her. Becoming part of the larger world. But her ties were too strong to break and she had made promises.

She had stood before the tribal council and asked to be sent to college so that she could return and serve her people as a nurse. With the support of the tribal president, they had agreed to pay for her education with the understanding that she would keep her promise. To break her vow would bring disgrace to herself and her family.

It would be hard, but she had to bend her will to the path she'd chosen. Seeing Kevin had unleashed an immediate desire to be with him. To stay strong she had to avoid him.

* * *

Forgetting Isabel wasn't easy. About the only way to do it was to buckle down, and Kevin did exactly that. He concentrated on classwork and finishing Erma's landscape plan, which was gradually taking shape. When he had a free weekend he went home to the ranch, where he was always happy no matter what.

He saw Isabel around campus and got a lump in his throat whenever they stopped to chat. The girl made his palms sweaty, but he pulled off nonchalance like a champ. At least he hoped he did. He often wondered if she felt a bit of regret for breaking it off, but her cool exterior gave nothing away. Either that, or he was just lousy at reading women.

One weekend at home, Dale was back stateside on leave and they went out drinking. Bartenders in T or C took a very liberal stance on underage drinkers, and in a smoky haven for drunks, they sipped longnecks, Dale doing most of the talking about his tour in Vietnam. He told tales of taking fire from enemy mortar rounds and fighting off VC incursions along the airfield perimeter. He related one story about an enemy mortar round that blew up a huge jet-fuel bladder tank, sending flames sky-high, killing three of his buddies, turning them into miscellaneous body parts. He would return to the Okinawa airbase when his leave was up and hoped never to see the Nam again. He was now an Airman First Class and had been awarded the Air Force Commendation Medal.

He joked that the air force gave out medals like candy canes at Christmastime, and said no more about it.

He was still Dale but different. The easy smile was still there, his sense of humor was intact, but the kid in him was gone, buried beneath a hard crust just below the surface. As soon as he landed stateside, he'd changed into civvies to avoid the taunts and insults hurled at servicemen by those who opposed the war. Dressed in jeans, an old work shirt, and his cowboy boots, only his regulation GI haircut and his military bearing gave him away.

"Are you gonna become one of those gung-ho officers hot to kill the commies and get medals?" he asked Kevin, half-seriously.

"I'm thinking of hotfooting it to Canada instead."

Dale rolled his eyes at the idea. "That ain't you."

"It's a stupid war," Kevin countered.

Dale nodded. "Just about every enlisted grunt who has served in Nam would agree with you. If we could mount a coup against the Washington politicians who got us into this fucking mess, we would."

"I don't know if I can handle it."

Dale snorted a laugh. "And you won't know until you're there. I was scared the whole time. Everybody is, even the hard-core lifers and the crazies."

"I guess I'll just have to find out," Kevin said.

"Don't go there," Dale advised. "Take your ROTC commission and get a desk job if you can." He finished his longneck and called for another.

"That would be the coward's way out."

"Or not," Dale said. "There's no rule that says you have to be a red-blooded, All-American hero just because a war is going on."

"You've gotten cynical."

"Maybe so. I'm thinking of heading down to Juárez next weekend to visit the ladies at Casa Blanca. Want to come along?"

Although it was tempting, Kevin shook his head. "Can't do it. Too much classwork."

Dale downed six more longnecks before he was ready to leave. Kevin had to lift his drunk, half-conscious friend into the cab of the truck and drive him home.

* * *

With the completion of Erma's master landscape plan, she had fewer and fewer handyman chores, telling him she didn't want to make up things for him to do and that he should concentrate on his classes. Of course, she hoped he'd still come to her parties when school resumed in the fall. He promised to be at every one. They were too much fun to miss.

With more time available in the upcoming fall semester, he decided to add another course to his schedule. Before heading off for his ROTC summer training, he preregistered for a Native American Survey class. Maybe he could learn something that might help him better understand Isabel.

He still smarted over her rejection. It was as if he was doomed to fall for women who ultimately dumped him. In Isabel's case, the reason remained unclear. He knew for certain she wasn't dating anybody at school. He could only wonder if there was a boyfriend back home.

He finished ROTC summer training in time to get to the ranch and help with fall works. He wasn't able to stay for the pony auction and was sorry to miss it, but eager to start his classes. He didn't see Isabel around campus until midterms. He spotted her staring at him from a distance, frozen in place for a long minute before hurrying away. He couldn't fathom her reaction.

The Native American class hadn't been very helpful in trying to personally figure out Isabel Istee. If he took into account the general duplicity, the outright thievery, and the mindless slaughter of Native Americans perpetrated by white men against Indians since the day they set foot on the continent, his guilt by ancestry might be enough to turn her off. But he'd never seen the slightest sign of small-mindedness on her part. He remained totally confused by the girl.

The semester ended without another sighting. By then he was

dating a town girl he'd met at a party Gabriel Morales and his wife threw at their house in the old Mexican neighborhood near downtown. Her name was Sofia Contreras and she soon lost interest when she realized marriage and children were not what Kevin had in mind.

By the start of his senior year, he'd convinced himself that he was over Isabel. One evening at the university library, he walked past her studying at a table with a guy who was one of the leaders of the students against the war movement. When she looked up and smiled at him, his heart skipped a beat. That minute, all he wanted was to be studying with her at that desk. He quickly walked away, wondering why she'd smiled at him, and what she was doing in the company of a campus radical.

The guy was a hardcore antiwar protester who liked to get in Kevin's face whenever he wore his ROTC uniform on campus. He was always spoiling for a shouting match to attract attention to himself and his cause. There were times Kevin wanted to call him out, times he was tempted to argue, but he held his tongue for fear he might slip up and agree that the guy was right—it was a totally screwed-up, unnecessary war.

He found what he wanted in the stacks, and gave Isabel and her companion a wide berth on his way out of the library.

* * *

Isabel had been unable to repress a smile when Kevin passed by. Every time she saw him, he awoke such strong desires in her. She'd tried several other boys over the last two years, had even slept with one to her great dissatisfaction. The few times she saw Kevin on campus, she froze to keep from running to him. She was tired of being wound up so tight about him. Her parents and the tribe could go suck eggs. In her dorm room she sat at her desk and wrote:

Dear Kevin,

I know you must think I've been terrible to you, but if you're willing to forgive me I'd like to see you again. You deserve an explanation and I am so sorry if I have hurt you. Leave a message if you're willing, if not, I understand.

Affectionately,
Isabel

She sat for a long time before sealing it in an envelope and addressing it. Holding on to her nerve, she mailed it in the slot at the front reception desk and returned to her room, fearful that he wouldn't reply.

Two days later, early in the evening, Isabel nervously waited for Kevin in the Student Union Building. When he appeared in the doorway, anxiety almost made her bolt for the ladies' room. When he sat down she thanked him for coming.

"I had to," he replied. "For the past two years I've been wondering what I did wrong."

"Nothing," Isabel replied. "You did nothing wrong."

She told him everything, and he listened without interrupting. When she finished, she reached across the table and touched his hand. "I've missed being with you."

"What's changed? Why can you see me now?"

"I've changed. It's too hard to not be with you."

She watched as he studied her face.

"Does that mean we can be more than 'just friends'?" he asked.

"Yes, if you're willing and you dare to believe me."

"I've learned that the Apache believe in something called life's circle."

Isabel nodded.

"I guess that could apply to you and me."

"Meaning?"

Kevin shrugged. "A circle has no end."

Isabel smiled and reached for his hand. "Just a beginning."

38

Over the course of their senior year, Kevin and Isabel were in each other's company almost to the exclusion of all others, Erma's frequent parties being the major exception. With their heavy course schedules, time together was limited, but they made the best of it with weekends at Kevin's apartment, and occasional Sunday-morning drives into the countryside, sometimes just to rubberneck and stop for a meal at a roadside diner, and sometimes to hike trails in the nearby Organ Mountains. As the weather warmed they picnicked along the river bosque, window-shopped the touristy stores in old Mesilla, and explored some of the abandoned historical sites, like the adobe ruins of Fort Selden near the village of Radium Springs. On those rare occasions when Erma felt a strong motherly need to check in on them, they'd share a thrown-together weeknight dinner with her, capped with a bottle of wine and good conversation. It was evident that Erma, who was not one to hide her opinions, thought Kevin was lucky to have captured the affections of such an intriguing, intelligent, and strikingly beautiful girl.

During school breaks and holidays, Kevin went home to the ranch and Isabel back to Mescalero. Kevin's parents, kept abreast of his involvement with Isabel through Erma's occasional phone conversations, never pried. They met her once during an unannounced, impromptu weekend trip to Las Cruces, when they arrived at Kevin's apartment and found her there still in her PJs. The chance meeting started out awkwardly but ended up very pleasantly with Kevin, his parents, and Isabel having lunch together at Matt's favorite Las Cruces hamburger joint. During Kevin's next telephone call home, his mom told him Isabel was classy and his dad pronounced her a stunner.

Fearing another explosive reaction by her parents, Isabel said nothing about Kevin to them. They were bursting with pride about her upcoming graduation and the proclamation the tribal council planned to issue on the day she was to receive her degree. Her mother had a big gathering in the works, with plans to invite almost half of the tribal membership. Along with Isabel's many aunts, she'd been working on it for months.

With Kevin scheduled to be commissioned in the army, and Isabel required to take the state nursing board exams before she could practice, neither of them spoke about future plans together. Kevin didn't want to discuss it until he either survived Vietnam or managed to avoid it, which he had no desire to do in spite of Dale's warning. But with the conflict dragging on and getting uglier by the day, like many others on campus he'd grown unhappy about the war and the government's policies. In spite of his mixed feelings, he had no choice but to honor his commitment to serve.

He figured Isabel had also sidestepped any talk of a shared future together because of her commitment to her tribe, which naturally had to come first. But the idea was never far from his mind that no matter what the difficulties ahead might be, eventually they'd be able to work something out as a couple.

In April they went to the Aggie team rodeo and watched Kim Ward and Todd Marks compete. Both had made it to the national collegiate finals the last two years and were returning again. They were the stars of a talented team, and highly touted to lead the Aggies to a national title.

Kevin usually ran into them once or twice a year on campus. They were still a couple and planning to join the pro circuit after graduating. Kevin had a slight pang of remorse about not sticking with rodeoing, but not enough of one to question the decisions he'd made. Once upon a time he'd competed on their level, but not anymore. They were extraordinary to watch, and he was proud to have once competed in the same arena with them.

After the final event, Kevin dropped Isabel at the dorm. She gave him a quick kiss before jumping out of his truck and waving goodbye. It had been a week since they'd been together, and he'd been hoping she would spend the night with him, but no such luck.

She'd been very quiet on the drive, with her eyes straight ahead and her expression thoughtful. It had been going on for a couple of days. He didn't think anything was wrong, but he couldn't be sure. There were times when she simply turned inward and everything else seemed to become miscellaneous static. He didn't know how she did it, but until she resurfaced she was almost unreachable.

Maybe it was just that and nothing more. At home, he settled down with his textbook, a compendium of some of the greatest war battles in history, and picked up where he'd left off with the fall of Constantinople in the middle of the fifteenth century.

* * *

Isabel's roommate had gone out to spend a half hour in the backseat of her boyfriend's car, and she had the place to herself. She undressed, stood naked in front of the mirror and turned sideways. Soon she'd start showing. If she didn't take action now, Kevin would soon be able to tell that she was pregnant.

If she told him, he would want to marry her—of that she was certain. And when he proposed, her resolve would most certainly weaken and she'd say yes. That would be disastrous for both of them.

She would not send him off to Vietnam married with a wife and a baby on the way, and remain behind waiting to be notified of his death. Nor could she heartlessly crush him with a cruel "Dear John" letter after he left. She knew in her heart it had to end now, and only she could do it.

She would have his baby—it was a boy, she was sure—and he need never know. Her child would be welcomed into the tribe, and she would not have to raise him alone. The Apache way made child-rearing a multigenerational family affair. The boy's grandmothers and aunts would civilize him and teach him etiquette and proper behavior. The boy's many male relatives would be called upon to teach him the ways of a man and his responsibilities to others. She would suffer no stigma except in the eyes of those few conservative Christian converts who'd abandoned their ancient traditions and beliefs.

Out of the blue, she wondered if she would ever marry. It broke her heart to think of being a wife to any man other than Kevin. How was she to tell him? It had to be a complete break, otherwise her determination would crumble.

She dressed in her PJs and sat cross-legged on her bed. She had to be strong, she told herself. She had to summon up all of her willpower. To make it work, she needed to be a warrior, she needed to be brutal.

She wrote:

Kevin:

I don't want to see you, don't want you to touch me ever again.

Stay away from me.

Isabel

When the note arrived, Kevin, in shock, showed it to Erma.

"You had no warning that this was coming?" she asked.

"Nope." His voice almost cracked. "What should I do?"

Erma studied the note. "Her tone says she means it."

"I know."

"Don't pursue her," Erma counseled. "Write her back, ask her to meet with you, and say you feel you deserve an explanation."

"And if she doesn't reply?"

Erma looked at him with sad eyes. "It will be hard, but let her go."

"Why do women do these things?"

"For the same reasons that men can be such idiots and jerks, present company excluded."

"In other words, you don't know."

"Exactly."

He wrote as Erma suggested and impatiently waited three days for a reply. When Isabel didn't respond, he couldn't let it drop despite Erma's counsel. He was desperate for an answer.

He called and left several messages, sent another letter, all with no results. He wavered between anger and depression. He couldn't make her disappear from his mind, couldn't shake off the callousness of her action, and couldn't discern any possible reason for the break. He was left thinking he must have done something wrong. But what?

Occasionally, he became hopeful. She'd done this to him once before. Perhaps her family had found out about them and pressured her to break it off. Maybe threats had been made, of what kind he couldn't imagine. She had stood up to them once; maybe she'd do it again. When it was clear that wasn't going to happen, he went through a period of feeling badly mistreated before he started to believe he'd get over her.

* * *

On graduation day, a hot and breezy late-spring morning, he filed into the Pan American Center, home of the Aggies' basketball team, and took his assigned seat on the arena floor. Excited families and friends of the graduates filled the stands. Seated alphabetically by last name, Isabel was two rows ahead of him.

After the speeches were finished, the university president began passing out diplomas. When Isabel's name was called, she walked to the stage with her head held high and a smile on her lips. In her cap and gown she looked heavier, like she had gained weight. As she passed in front of him to return to her seat, her face appeared puffy. He found it hard to believe she'd let herself go. That simply wasn't like her.

He blocked further thoughts of her by listening to the names being called and watching the students ahead of him rise and cross to receive their degrees. When it was his turn, he made sure not to look at Isabel. She was part of the past and today was the beginning of his future.

With his honors degree in hand, 2nd Lt. Kevin Kerney, who'd received his US Army commission the day before, left the stage with orders to attend Infantry Officer Training at Fort Benning, Georgia, starting in one week.

39

Kevin Kerney presented his orders to a three-striper sitting alone at a desk in the quiet, almost empty reception room of the Infantry Officers School Headquarters. The sergeant's name tag read GOLDSTEIN, and he wore the Combat Infantry Badge and airborne jump wings patches over the left breast pocket of his fatigue shirt.

Sgt. Abraham Goldstein, who was three years older than the lieutenant, studied the orders and eyed the officer. "Someone screwed up, Lieutenant," he announced in a heavy Brooklyn accent. "You're three days early. I suggest you get a billet at the BOQ until we start in-processing."

"Isn't there some temporary duty I can pull until then?"

Goldstein raised his eyebrows in mock surprise. Gung-ho new lieutenants wanting to charge ahead and impress the cadre were a dime a dozen. At their best laughable, at their worst embarrassing. "Look, Lieutenant, right now this post is bursting at the seams with junior and field-grade officers waiting for their permanent change-of-duty-station orders. We probably could take over and command a couple of banana republic armies with the idle infantry officers we got sitting on their thumbs around here."

Kevin didn't correct him.

He handed Kevin back his orders. "The army in its infinite wisdom has given you three days off, gratis. Don't look a gift horse in the eye, sir."

Again, Kevin didn't correct him.

"Grab a BOQ billet and enjoy yourself. A week from now you'll be glad you did."

Kevin smiled. "Thanks for the advice, Sergeant."

"One more thing, Lieutenant," Goldstein said. "Change into civvies, otherwise you won't enjoy yourself as much."

"Why is that?"

"Better to be a tourist on base than a freshly minted second Louie in uniform."

"You are a wise man, Sergeant Goldstein."

"I know," Goldstein replied with a grin. "All sergeants are."

With directions to the BOQ in hand, Kevin found his way, got a room, dumped his gear on the twin bed, and changed into his civvies. He'd arrived with no car, so over the next three days he poked around the base and surrounding area on foot. The huge military reservation spread out like an octopus along the Chattahoochee River. He hoofed through the neighboring city of Columbus, Georgia, that almost butted up against the main gate to the post, and strolled downtown Phenix City, the once-infamous gambling and fleshpot center just across the state line in Alabama.

Fort Benning was a city unto itself, with all you needed right at hand on the post, including stores, schools, recreation facilities, churches, a hospital, and a library. There were residential neighborhoods reserved for field-grade officers and above, with lovely tree-lined streets and tidy two-story homes. More modern, smaller, single-story homes in newer neighborhoods served married enlisted personnel and company-grade officers with families.

The land was different from New Mexico. There were large grassy fields, neat lawns in front of the houses, thick stands of trees on rolling, hilly terrain, and a river that gushed with water unlike the prone-to-drought Rio Grande. And unlike dry New Mexico, the weather was uncomfortably hot in a sticky, sweaty way, and it never seemed to cool down at night.

Columbus seemed to exist solely because of Fort Benning, and not in a good way. Everything that a soldier could possibly need—wedding rings, televisions, bedroom suites, pawnshops, payday loans, and divorce lawyers—was readily available. Retail stores stayed open late. Billboards saluted "Our Boys in Uniform" and offered great deals on just about everything. Tattoo parlors flourished. There were sleazy bars, cheap motels, acres of used-car lots, and American flags in profusion. It appeared that the army and Columbus capitalism had come together to form a more perfect union.

Allegedly reformed, Phenix City still offered all the illicit sex, drugs, and gambling a soldier would ever need, just in a more subtle way. The streetwalkers were gone, but a phone call would get you a woman to share your motel room for an hour or a night. In Columbus you could easily find the lonely wife of a soldier who'd deployed overseas to play house with for the duration. They were waiting to be picked up in every GI bar or hangout.

By the time Kevin processed into his Infantry Officer School class, he was eager to get started. He'd arrived thinking he was pretty well prepared for what the infantry would throw at him. He'd placed in the top ten percent during his month at ROTC Advanced Camp summer training. He didn't start out smug, but he soon learned he was wrong. The competition was stiff. Within twenty-four hours, his three days loitering around Fort Benning and Columbus were only a dim memory.

Of the 186 members of his class, there were OCS graduates with combat experience who'd come up through the ranks—some were ten-year veterans with two tours or more in-country. There were graduates of West Point, the Virginia Military Institute, the Citadel, and Texas A&M. There were guys who'd played first-string collegiate football, competed in track and field, and excelled at wrestling or some other sport like gymnastics. They were all hard chargers.

At the bottom rung of the ladder, where Kevin started out, were ROTC and National Guard commissioned officers. While none of the cadre verbally expressed it, Kevin and his ilk were obviously not very highly regarded as potential superior infantry officer material.

During in-processing, Kevin stood out because he was the only one who'd put down rodeoing as his sport. When it also became known that he was the youngest member of the class, everybody including the cadre started calling him Kid Kerney. He put up with it because there were worse labels draped on some of his classmates, including "Tweety Bird" for a skinny, undersize National Guard lieutenant, who washed out quickly along with twenty-eight others during the training cycle.

During the three-month course, Kevin moved up in the class rankings. He did well in land navigation, marksmanship, tactical planning, and written assignments. He improved in physical fitness and endurance exercises, and outscored some of the military-school graduates in the platoon-leader performance evaluation. Because of his academic marks and overall ratings, by the last week of training he was informed that he'd graduate in the top third of his class. Not high enough to be allowed to select his permanent-duty assignment, but good enough to have his preferences for a posting given some weight.

When he approached the officer assigned the task of recommending duty-station assignments and requested Vietnam, he was curtly told those postings would most likely go to West Point ring knockers and other career officers who needed a combat tour under their belts in order to move up through the ranks. Lieutenant Kerney, on the other hand, would probably get orders for an overseas tour in South Korea, an excellent infantry assignment.

Outside of headquarters a few days before graduation, he approached Sergeant Goldstein. Recently promoted to staff sergeant, Goldstein was a reliable source of straight-up information about all things infantry. As a last attempt to secure orders to a unit in Nam, Kevin decided to see if the age-old saying that sergeants ran the army held any water.

Goldstein threw him a snappy hand salute. "Lieutenant."

"A moment of your time, if you please, Staff Sergeant Goldstein."

Abe Goldstein smiled. "I do like the sound of that, sir."

"And it suits you well," Kerney replied. "I wonder if you know of an outfit looking for replacement lieutenants to send in-country."

Goldstein thought it over. He liked the lieutenant, who didn't seem to be in the army for the glory, had exhibited a real concern for those around him, and had a good grasp of what it took to lead. "It's now mostly an advisory role for the infantry," he mused. "I've got a buddy in personnel. I'll see what he says."

"Thanks, Staff Sergeant."

Abe Goldstein smiled and threw another salute. "No problem, LT."

He watched Kerney walk away. He'd read the lieutenant's background information forwarded from his ROTC college institution. His great-grandfather, his grandfather, his uncle, and his father had all seen combat from the Civil War through WWII. Whether the lieutenant knew it or not, he suffered from that strange and burdensome need to continue the family tradition.

Goldstein knew the compulsion well. His forefathers had fought on Flanders Fields in France, on the Italian beaches at Anzio, and on Pork Chop Hill in Korea. Silently he wished Lieutenant Kerney luck. The Nam had maimed and destroyed many good men. Goldstein was glad to be back in the world in one piece.

* * *

Kevin received orders to Schofield Barracks, Hawaii, with a posting to the 25th Infantry Division, and he had ten days to get there. Before he left, Sergeant Goldstein told him it might be his best shot to get in-country, and he'd let a buddy of his know the lieutenant was coming. Kevin thanked the sergeant for his help, hopped a plane to El Paso, rented a car, and drove to the ranch unannounced. His sudden appearance, along with the happy news that he wasn't going to Vietnam, was cause for celebration. Al and Brenda Jennings added their good news that Dale would soon be transferring from Okinawa to Holloman Air Force Base outside Alamogordo, where he'd serve out the remainder of his active-duty enlistment. For the first time in his life, Kevin got roaring drunk in the company of his parents and Al and Brenda, who were all equally wobbly by the time he hit the sack.

After a five-day homecoming, Kevin left for Hawaii, his parents watching him depart from the airport observation deck. The plane banked west, revealing the Tularosa and distant outline of Sierra Blanca towering over the Mescalero Reservation, and he felt a twinge of regret about Isabel. He still deserved an explanation.

At Schofield Barracks, Kevin cooled his heels in a replacement detachment for a week before a sergeant first class named Aldo Abruzzo found him lounging in a dayroom and handed him orders.

"You're going TYD to Nam, ASAP, Lieutenant," Sergeant Abruzzo said gruffly. Stocky and about thirty years old, Abruzzo had a permanent five-o'clock shadow. Along with jump wings and a combat infantry badge, he wore a ranger tab on the upper-left sleeve of his fatigue shirt. "And Abe Goldstein sends his regards."

Kevin glanced at his orders and cracked a grin. He was to be detached to a military assistance group tasked with advising ARVN units. "I'll be" was all he could manage.

Wondering why Goldstein had bothered to pull strings for the young lieutenant, Abruzzo looked him over and decided it didn't matter. He was just some more fresh meat to throw into the grinder of an unwinnable war, thanks to the stupidity of the Washington politicians.

* * *

2nd Lt. Kevin Kerney stepped onto the tarmac at Tan Son Nhut Air Base outside Saigon into a hot, wind-lashed monsoon downpour, wondering if he'd made a big mistake. The humid weather at Fort Benning had been barely tolerable, but this was ten times worse. Lugging his gear, he hurried into reception, where he presented his paperwork and was told to wait. He found an empty chair and watched a stream of happy-looking GIs scurrying through the sheet of rain to a civilian passenger jet about to take them home.

An hour later, when the monsoon had turned into an everyday storm, a first lieutenant tapped him on the shoulder. He wore a Signal Corps insignia on his collar. "Kerney?"

Kevin stood. "That's me."

"I'm Alan Enright. Grab your gear and let's go."

At six-six, Enright towered over Kerney. He had gray eyes and the look of a very tired man.

"Where are we going?" Kevin asked.

Outside, Enright directed him to a staff car. "To your new home. You're to be a glorified office boy. We're helping our South Vietnamese allies organize a new division. Knowing the capabilities of our friends, it will probably take a year to get it up and running. Fortunately, I'll be back home by then."

Disappointed, Kevin clamped his mouth shut.

Enright glanced at him from behind the steering wheel. "Don't despair—you're lucky to be among the many thousands of American soldiers in this shithole not required to fight, especially since we're going to be vacating the premises fairly soon."

"You make it sound like it's no fun to be here," Kevin complained, straight-faced.

Enright cracked up. "I can tell we're gonna get along, Kerney."

As Enright dodged through traffic around the airbase, he breezily told Kevin that the enemies of the Republic of Vietnam were everywhere. The Viet Cong were constantly skirmishing with the South Vietnamese ARVN troops at the outskirts of the city, assassinating political targets in broad daylight on the streets of Saigon, and blowing up airplanes at Tan Son Nhut. About one in four ARVN soldiers was either a spy, traitor, or a VC pretending to be loyal to the regime. Most of the ARVN generals were sitting on fortunes made by selling US equipment and supplies on the black market.

"It's like being a bit player in a parlor game that has dire consequences," he said as he pulled to a stop in front of a heavily fortified modern office building on the airbase. "We're home," he said. "This is the US Military Assistance Command. Come in and meet your fellow advisers."

Enright took him through a side door into a large bullpen area, where soldiers were busy at desks typing, filing, and talking on telephones. On a large wall were memos, diagrams, manpower requirements, tables of organization, and various equipment manifests. A sign on a secure communications door at the rear of the room noted that special authorization was required to enter. After quick introductions to the personnel on duty, Enright sat with Kevin at a small conference table away from the neat rows of army-issue gray steel desks.

"As you can see, I'm in charge of a platoon of clerk typists," he said. "You will be my assistant platoon leader. May I ask how you managed to get this temporary-duty assignment?"

"I know this sergeant who helped arrange the TDY," Kevin replied.

Enright's loud guffaw brought work in the bullpen to a momentary halt. "Of course. I should have guessed. And here I was worried that you were some general's illegitimate son."

"Not hardly," Kevin said.

"Good." Enright clapped his hands. "Let's get down to business."

He explained that the generals in their infinite wisdom wanted to create the best, most combat-ready, most highly trained, best-equipped, and best-led ARVN division ever in the entire Republic of Vietnam Army. It was to be fully supported by air, artillery, and armored units so it could operate with the same strike-and-response capacity of a US division.

His voice dripping with sarcasm, he went on to say that once the new division was fully operational it would become the template used to transform every other ARVN division, causing them to become equally effective and thus win the war.

"You sound slightly dubious."

Enright shrugged. "Even if it were possible, which it isn't, we'll run out of time long before it can happen."

Kevin said nothing.

Enright waited for a long minute before continuing. "Perfect, you're a realist. Let's get you settled in and down to work."

"And what is my job?"

"I've already told you, glorified office boy, and I wasn't kidding."

* * *

That first night in his billet, Kevin wrote home to tell his folks he was in-country but safe and secure in one of the most heavily guarded and fortified buildings in South Vietnam. He was doing administrative work—nothing dangerous—and they were not to worry. On impulse, he also wrote to Isabel telling her pretty much the same thing, and asked her to write back.

Enright put him in charge of shift and work assignment duty until his security clearance came through. From that point on, he was Enright's runner, taking sealed packets of confidential and secret documents from the secure communications center behind the locked security door to ranking officers throughout the command who were overseeing the development of the new division. Frequently he was out of the building with a briefcase cuffed to his wrist in a staff car, on his way to deliver sensitive documents to diplomats and generals, both American and South Vietnamese.

When he wasn't scurrying around the enormous military command compound, or in a staff car on the way to an embassy or government building, Enright had him writing up commendations for the clerk typists who were rotating home. He wanted every soldier to leave with a least one shiny medal in addition to the Good Conduct and National Defense decorations. With the brass hats upstairs passing out medals to one another left and right, Kevin understood Enright's reasoning, and he took to the task with enthusiasm. Twenty percent of the time, he was able to have the Army Commendation Medal awarded. Mostly he had to settle on getting the South Vietnamese to authorize one of their medals. He had good luck with the Republic of Vietnam Campaign Medal, the Technical Service Medal, and the Armed Forces Honor Medal, which was awarded for actively contributing to the formation and organization of the Vietnamese military. All requests for decorations had to go through normal channels, but when it came to run-of-the-mill Vietnamese awards, nobody upstairs gave a damn.

The morning Enright officially became a short-timer with less than sixty days left in-country, Kevin called the troops together and presented him with the Republic of Vietnam Armed Forces Honor Medal. It cracked him up. That night he got drunk with Kevin to celebrate his prestigious and most personally gratifying decoration.

When Enright had thirty days and a wake-up left before returning to the world, Kevin asked him to find a way to send him into the field.

"Worried my replacement will be some tight-ass butt kisser?" Enright inquired.

"Damn straight," Kevin replied.

"I don't blame you. Are you sure that's what you want?"

"I'm sure."

"Now that you've proudly served in a war zone, I could have personnel cancel your TDY status and return you to Schofield Barracks. Wouldn't that be better?"

Kevin shook his head.

Enright tapped a finger to his lip. "Okay, let me give it some thought."

A week before Enright was due to leave with his very own Army Commendation Medal pinned to his chest and a promotion to captain, he had one of his last official conversations with 2nd Lt. Kevin Kerney.

He spread a map out on the small conference table and said, "The new division we're creating for our Vietnamese brothers-in-arms will be headquartered at Miêu Giang, currently under our command. We inherited it from the marines, who didn't want to play there anymore. It's near a river valley seven clicks from the DMZ."

He traced the location on the map with his finger. "According to Intelligence, there's no heavy lifting going on in terms of serious enemy engagement along this part of the demilitarized zone. Orders are being cut for you to go to the Miêu Giang Combat Base and prepare an initial report on its readiness to be transferred to ARVN control sometime in the still-unknown future. As we speak, various forms are being created for you to use in this endeavor. The brass wants it spit-shined and standing tall when the time comes to troop the colors."

"I thought only the Brits did stuff like that."

"Don't be so damn picky." He folded the map and handed it to Kevin. "You'll have thirty days to conduct your review, fill out myriad forms, and file your report. Which I'm certain will be only the first of many to be conducted by a legion of officers with sequentially higher and higher rank. I'm sure your report will soon be forgotten. And gathering dust. I doubt it will qualify you for a combat infantry badge, but you never know."

Kevin grinned. "Thanks."

Enright waved it off. "The downside is you leave in two days and will therefore miss the drunken brawl of my bon-voyage party."

"How about I get you drunk tonight?" Kevin suggested.

Enright grinned. "Now you're starting to behave and think like an officer with some serious career potential. I'll have your efficiency report done before you leave."

The day before Kevin was to leave for Miêu Giang Combat Base, Enright got even with him by pinning the Vietnamese Armed Forces Honor Medal on his chest. Finished, he gave the shiny decoration a pat and said he was astonished by the willingness of the Republic of Vietnam to so quickly bestow such a very great honor on such a lowly yet richly deserving second lieutenant.

It took every ounce of Enright's self-control to keep a straight face, but when Kevin started laughing, he lost it, as did the assembled men in the bullpen, who hooted and hollered their approval.

In the morning, Kevin flew out on a chopper with fond memories of Alan Enright, certain he'd not meet his kind again during the rest of his time in the service. He was already missing his companionship. Before leaving he'd thought to write his parents to say he was going into the field, but decided against it. He was only preparing a report, not going into combat, so there was no need to worry them.

With the thudding eggbeater sound of the rotors vibrating through the thin skin of the helicopter, he suddenly thought about

Isabel. She'd never responded. So be it. For the first time he felt she was truly and completely in the past.

* * *

Master Sergeant Diego "El Mano" Ruiz scowled as he watched the lieutenant hurry across the LZ lugging a duffel bag and briefcase. He was expecting four way-overdue rifle platoon leader replacements, fully armed and equipped, not some junior pencil pusher from Saigon.

At five-six, Diego "The Hand" Ruiz was the toughest man in the brigade. Born and raised in Albuquerque, New Mexico, drafted early in the Korean War, he'd found a home in the army and had won the all-army boxing championship in his weight class three times in a row before retiring from the ring undefeated. Combat wounded twice in Korea and once in Nam, Ruiz owned virtually every award for valor except the Medal of Honor.

The young lieutenant slowed to a stop in front of Diego, who didn't bother to salute. He noted with interest the crossed rifles on the kid's fatigue shirt before glancing at his name patch over his right pocket.

"How can I help you, Lieutenant Kerney?" he asked.

Kevin pulled his TDY orders from his shirt pocket. "I'm here for a look around."

Ruiz plucked the papers out of Kerney's hand. At least the kid didn't spout a bunch of official-sounding garbage at him. He gave the orders a quick look. The base was to be evaluated for eventual handover to an ARVN division. Interesting. Ruiz returned the paperwork and pointed at a fortified bunker. "Wait in there, Lieutenant."

The young man nodded and double-timed to the bunker.

Ruiz went to the communications room and made a call to a friend at Military Assistance Command before seeking out brigade commander Col. Timothy Ingwersen, who, along with his deputy commander, was inspecting a newly reinforced section of the perimeter wire that the VC had blown up the night before.

"A moment, Colonel," Ruiz asked.

Ingwersen nodded. "What have you got for me, Top?"

Ruiz reported the arrival of Lt. Kevin Kerney, an infantry officer who had been sent up to inspect the camp for eventual transfer to an ARVN division. "I made a call and did a little snooping about him, Colonel. Distinguished ROTC graduate, in the top third of his Infantry Officer Class, recently received an excellent performance rating from his departing OIC, and awarded the ARVN Armed Forces Honor Medal, whatever that is. He's been in-country for four months at Military Assistance Command."

Ingwersen smiled. He was hurting badly for well-trained junior officers, and he was tired of waiting for the rifle platoon leaders promised to him weeks ago. It was as if the gods had dropped him an unexpected gift—a partial one, but a gift nonetheless. "What's the lieutenant's name?"

"Kevin Kerney. He's from my home state, but he doesn't know that yet."

"Get his TDY orders cancelled ASAP, have new orders cut permanently assigning him to my command, and put him in charge of 2nd Platoon, Bravo Company. Have it done by the end of the day."

"Roger that, Colonel," Ruiz said as he turned on his heel, wondering what 2nd Lt. Kevin Kerney would say when told his world was about to turn upside down.

That evening, before Kevin and his platoon turned out to stand watch, he scribbled a note to his folks.

Dear Mom & Dad:

I've been reassigned to a combat outfit as a rifle platoon leader and am just about to pull my first watch with a squad from my platoon. Don't worry about me. I'm at a very large and secure base with men who are seasoned veterans and officers above me who are all experienced field leaders. The top sergeant Diego Ruiz is from Albuquerque, so it already feels right for me to be here. He says our CO is in line for his first star so there will likely be a ceremony in his honor when his promotion comes through.

Anyway, that's it for now. Don't worry about me. I'll be fine.

Love,
Kevin

Two hours later, Kevin and a squad from his platoon repelled a VC attack at the northern wire perimeter. Lots of green tracers lit up the night. No one got hurt. Kevin's hands didn't stop shaking until he was off duty and alone in his bunk.

40

After sixty days as a Bravo Company platoon leader, Kevin still remained anxious and scared, whether he was inside the wire or out, on patrol or in his bunk, whether it was night or day, or whether the enemy was shooting at him or not. At first, he thought he was a complete pussy until he realized everybody was in the same boat—they just had different ways of dealing with it.

The rules about fear were straightforward and simple. You could joke about it, laugh about it, act indifferent about it, tease about it, but never, ever honestly admit to it. Kevin avoided the subject entirely. As a result, he found himself talking less, listening more, and saving his words for more important matters like giving and receiving orders.

The good news was he hadn't gotten killed or wounded, and neither had any of the men under his command so far. He had handled himself in combat without losing it, didn't take unnecessary risks, and was no longer considered just another boneheaded second lieutenant. His platoon sergeant had stopped constantly giving him advice, although Kevin continued to welcome it when it was offered. It was only after the men in his platoon decided he was okay that he learned he'd replaced an officer so terrified at the prospect of being killed he had to be relieved of duty and sent home early, a broken and depressed man.

The bad news was that he'd lost both his company commander and XO because of the Pentagon's stupid rule limiting officers to six months' service in a combat unit during their one-year rotation in-country. Their replacements were eager-beaver greenhorns looking for honors and promotions.

Things got worse when Colonel Ingwersen got his star and moved on, replaced by an officer out of the Pentagon who was more interested in getting his CIB ticket punched than he was in looking after his men. Word had it that he was one of those up-and-coming, field-grade types favored by the Joint Chiefs now flooding into Nam before the final pullout of combat troops so they could score some important war-zone time and maybe get a commendation or two to prove they were stud warriors. A Purple Heart for a minor wound was the best possible scenario.

Every member of the US armed forces and their allies knew the war was lost. Victor Charlie knew, the North Vietnam Army knew, as did all the politicians on both sides, plus the American public. Members of the Army of the Republic of Vietnam showed their shrewd understanding of the situation by deserting and abandoning their posts in droves. That didn't stop the VC or the North Vietnamese regulars from trying to kill all of the South Vietnamese troops that stumbled in front of their guns, many of them not-so-distant cousins. Kevin was convinced that in the recorded annals of armed conflict, blood feuds and tribal warfare had to be the worst of the lot.

Fortunately for the brigade, the new commander, Col. Bradley Douglas Rutherford, let Master Sergeant Diego "El Mano" Ruiz run the day-to-day operations while he and his senior staff entertained visiting congressmen, touring generals, news reporters, South Vietnamese dignitaries, and high-ranking ARVN officers—all interested in seeing where the new Republic of Vietnam division would be housed once it came online.

Kevin didn't give a shit. His immediate concern centered on bringing up to combat readiness the jittery, raw soldiers he received almost weekly as replacements for the seasoned troops in the platoon who rotated out back to the world because of the brainless Pentagon one-year-in-country policy.

The new soldiers, known as FNGs—fucking new guys—by the men, had to be slotted into a platoon of combat veterans who wanted nothing to do with them, didn't want to be near them, talk to them, know their names, or watch them get blown up or shot dead. Kevin sympathized and understood.

He despised land mines, booby traps, rocket attacks, and mortar rounds because they killed so indiscriminately and frequently without warning. If he had to face death, he favored it accomplished by a man he could see killing him with a gun. He smiled at his macabre thinking. Maybe he had a bit too much of the cowboy in him, courtesy of his hardscrabble Kerney ancestors.

Death was the other taboo subject. It was only tolerated in bull sessions if it came layered with sarcasm, bravado, or unusually inventive sidesplitting, sick humor. Again, Kevin held his tongue, but he'd come to believe that the experience of war was personal and different for each man. As much as they tried to find some common ground about dying, it was really a private matter impossible to be openly discussed. In the end, everyone died alone no matter who was around.

The base was nicknamed "The Rock Pile" after a nearby mountain that looked exactly like a pile of rocks tumbling skyward out of a valley floor. On high ground, it was a strange combination of fortified bunkers, tents, sandbagged defensive positions, prefabricated buildings, a large LZ, and observation posts completely surrounded by wire and a buffer zone devoid of vegetation. For Kevin the bleak, monochromatic, hunkered-down base was always a welcome sight when he was returning from patrol with his men.

He hated the jungle with a passion. It overwhelmed his senses with alien sounds, foreign vegetation, strange animals, putrid smells, and a forest canopy that turned daytime into darkness. It was most dangerous when there was silence. At times a shaft of light would dance across the undergrowth, freezing him into place, or a swarm of insects descended around his head, taking every ounce of his self-control not to swat them. He sweated buckets when it didn't rain, shivered soaking wet when it did, and dreamt of bloodred eyes staring at him through the black jungle.

He was dirty and didn't care; smelly and didn't care; had grown immune to picking off the leeches except for the fat, juicy one that tried to crawl into his ear and freaked him out. He froze up at the snakes that swam in the flooded rice paddies, the rodents that sniffed his nose in the darkness of the jungle, and the large insects that sounded like crinkling paper as they crawled across the backs of his legs.

He felt no kinship to his soldiers, no camaraderie with his fellow officers. He faked it to get along, but he survived by living within himself—his only safe place. Perhaps he now understood Isabel better, understood that the only way to withstand all things discordant, destructive, and repugnant to your nature was to detach and embrace the loneliness that ensued.

The one sound he looked forward to hearing was the engine of the fixed-wing army observation planes that flew along the highway every now and then searching for any signs of enemy movement. It reminded him of the days back on the Tularosa when they used to fly over the ranch. He sure missed that place.

At the end of his third month with the brigade, Kevin came down with a case of dengue fever that put him flat on his back for five days with a high temperature, headaches, muscle pain, and nausea. In between the bouts of fever and nausea he wrote a long letter home, mostly about his plans after the army. He was thinking of using the GI Bill to go back to school, although he wasn't sure what he would study. Maybe he'd apply to UNM and live in Albuquerque just for a change. He knew he'd come home to stay in New Mexico no matter what he did. He yearned for big skies, huge sun-kissed vistas, sprawling rock-strewn hills, majestic pine-clad mountains, and the clean dry heat of the high desert. He didn't say a word about Nam, just that he was doing fine and halfway through his combat tour.

Because of his viral infection, Kevin's platoon sergeant, a new NCO on his first rotation in-country, took the men out on an early-evening patrol of several nearby farms along the river, where some possible VC had been spotted during an overflight earlier in the day. On their return they were ambushed, with three KIA including the sergeant, and two others wounded.

It should have been Kevin out in front. He figured his life had been saved by a mosquito bite. He had to clamp down hard not to let the guilt overwhelm him. He should have been out there with them *listening*. Maybe he could have saved some of them.

By the end of his fourth month with the brigade, Kevin had revised his opinion about the Pentagon's six-month limit on combat assignments for officers. Since his transfer, so many had arrived and left that he was now one of the most experienced platoon leaders in the brigade, but with sixty days and a wake-up to go before he rotated out, he was fast becoming a short-timer. He pitied the enlisted men who had to pull double the time on the line, but he was happy it didn't apply to him. He was ready to go home.

* * *

On a day when the observation plane flew west over the highway and didn't come back, Kevin was called to the command post and tasked with leading a rescue mission to retrieve the downed pilot. His engine had quit and he'd crashed on the side of a mountain after radioing his location. An air force flyover confirmed the coordinates and the pilot was observed to be alive but wounded. Radio contact had subsequently been lost.

There was a clearing seven clicks from the crash site large enough to serve as an LZ. After insertion, Kevin would lead a squad with two additional light machine gunners, a radioman, and a medic along a nearby stream bed that ran to the foot of the mountain. Once there, traveling fast and light, they were to retrieve the pilot and return to the LZ for extraction. Gunships would hover nearby and fighter jets would be ready to strike at a moment's notice. If Victor Charlie was there, they'd know Kevin and his men were coming. The brigade stood ready to rock and roll if help was needed.

Rutherford shook his hand, wished him luck, and watched as Kevin and his men lifted off from the base. During the short flight, Kevin scanned the ground looking for any sign of VC movement. There was none along the highway, and as they approached the LZ the jungle canopy was too dense to see through.

Praying it wasn't a hot LZ, and half expecting to be riddled by automatic rounds, Kevin was the first man out the door. All was calm as he sprinted to the tree line with the squad spread out behind him, running for cover.

Away from the open LZ everyone dropped prone, weapons at the ready. With the thumping sounds of the choppers receding, Kevin listened hard. The jungle sounds he heard reassured him, but he was so jacked up for that one telltale sound of enemy movement he waited a bit longer than he should have before finally ordering his squad leader to send a man on point to the stream bed and have everyone move out.

With his squad leader at the rear to cover, Kevin followed behind point, slightly to one side, the men behind him in a strung-out, staggered line to avoid bunching up. They moved slowly into the brush, the riflemen loaded down with M16s and as many cloth bandoliers filled with extra ammo as they could carry, the machine gunners toting heavy M60s, the radioman with weapon in hand burdened by the weight of the radio strapped to his back, the medic with his canvas satchel crammed full of medical supplies and drugs lugging a litter, all of them with canteens clinking on their belts, broadcasting their position to anyone with ears close by.

Gripping an M16 he'd brought along for extra firepower, Kevin silently laughed at the notion that they were traveling light. And given the terrain, he sincerely doubted they could travel fast. He waited for the world to explode, but only jungle sounds prevailed.

Under radio silence they moved along the stream bed, Kevin yearning to stretch his gaze across a big slice of country with distant mountains lurking instead of straining to see through the dense, claustrophobic shroud of dark green that pressed down from above. They made it to the crash site on a small ledge a third of the way up the steep mountainside to find the pilot propped up against the fuselage, nodding out from pain, his .45 limp in his hand.

Kevin put the squad in defensive positions and radioed a report to brigade as the medic got busy examining the pilot. After a quick look, the medic gave him a heavy hit of morphine, rapidly treated a deep gash on his forehead, put a splint on his fractured left leg, and gave the okay to move him.

Kevin didn't waste any time ordering the pilot strapped onto the litter and everyone back down to the stream bed, where he took point and set a quick pace. As they moved through the jungle canopy, he wondered if it might be possible to finish the mission with his men unscathed. Less than a half a click from the LZ, a large, beautiful orange butterfly with an ivory stripe across its wings drifted out of the light from the clearing up ahead. It fluttered toward him and just as it neared, he caught sight of a slight movement in the bushes on the far side of the opening.

He stopped, motioned his radioman forward, told him to call for the extraction choppers and the gunships, and ordered everybody to drop. The kid looked ahead at the empty LZ and hesitated. Kevin hissed the command again as he yanked the radioman down and hit the dirt. Automatic fire tore through the trees above his head with a loud roar, shredding bark, leaves, and branches.

The radioman fell next to Kevin with a bloody hole in his upper thigh. On his belly, Kevin yanked the kid to cover, ordered the medic forward, grabbed the radio handset, and called in the gunships. To the rear he heard an M60 unleashing a torrent of fire against the slower cadence of several AK-47s. He swung around just as three grenades went off, silencing the AKs. He got a thumbs-up from his squad leader signaling it was secure, at least for the moment.

Fire still poured at the squad from across the LZ. Kevin gave the target location to the gunships and brought his machine gunners forward to rake and pin down the enemy position. The gunships came in low and fast, strafing Charlie pass after pass, cutting down the bush like deadly, thunderous great scythes until Charlie's weapons fell silent.

Kevin figured they were either dead, in retreat, or regrouping, but he wasn't about to take any chances. Holding the gunships nearby, he checked on his men before calling for a medical evacuation. Besides his radioman and the pilot, two more were wounded, one with a serious gut shot, the other with a shattered shoulder blade.

Kevin sent the wounded out first with half his squad at the edge of the LZ perimeter covering the lift-off. When the loaded chopper went airborne, Kevin carefully scanned for movement across the LZ. All was still.

He called in another chopper and when it landed, he zigzagged across the LZ behind his men, expecting all hell to break loose. It wasn't until everyone was safe and in the air on the way back to the base that he remembered the butterfly. Once upon a time, he'd been saved by a mosquito bite. This time it had been by a beautiful orange butterfly that had floated to him through the light. Who in the hell would believe that story?

Everybody survived, including the kid with the hole in his gut.

Ten days and a wake-up before he was due to rotate out, a general from Saigon flew up and pinned the Silver Star on Kevin's chest. His squad leader on the extraction team got the Bronze Star with a V for valor, and the rest of the men received commendation medals also with V devices. The wounded had already received their coveted Purple Hearts. Colonel Rutherford also got a medal for directing and commanding the successful operation from the safety of his command bunker. It was all a little ridiculous in Kevin's mind, especially Rutherford's decoration.

Later in the day, when he told his platoon the colonel's medal was richly deserved it earned him a big laugh. His platoon sergeant remarked that he didn't know until that very moment the lieutenant had a sense of humor. Smiling, Kevin promised it wouldn't happen again.

He expected to spend the last few months of his tour pushing papers somewhere in Saigon, but a big surprise came with orders promoting him to first lieutenant and sending him home early. Kevin figured a general's eager young son sporting new second Louie bars badly needed to qualify for a Combat Infantry Badge before the war wound down.

He couldn't care less.

He decided to wait to call his folks until he was safely out of the country. That night before turning in, he packed his gear and tore up his short-timer's calendar. In the morning he'd leave for Tan Son Nhut Air Base, the first stop on his way home.

He thought about the clear blue skies of the Tularosa and the vast landscape of desert and mountains that always filled his senses. He thought about the peace and solitude that awaited him, and the soft, lazy days ahead with family and friends. He was alive.

He fell asleep dreaming of butterflies.

DEDICATION

Playing soldier and building forts in the woods with my friend Max after the war. Helping Sonny and Shirley, who lived on the next farm over, bale hay. Taking care of Maggie's chickens long after they stopped laying eggs. Watching Leroy threaten to fall out of the tree and then couldn't do it. Frustrating Mrs. Morris, who tried to teach me how to square dance in a three-room schoolhouse and couldn't. Riding my one-eyed blue roan pony to school. Seeing the smoldering ashes of the big country house where we'd once lived.

Living in town and palling around with Joe Maggio; Skip Kinsey; Tommy Tom; Darlene Fox; Christine Lipinski; Linda Quick, the sheriff's daughter; and sweet Lorraine. Later in the city with Michael M., Chris, Kerry, Fred, Nancy, Jane, Josh Jr., Beverly, Isabel, Brandon, Leslie, Natalie, Mavourneen, and all the other rising young stars chasing fame long before it got made into a movie.

On the line in army green with Tony and Fred: two buddies who always had my back. Also Sug the lady-killer, Sergeant Toms, and the major who wanted me to reup and become a lifer. (Not the one with the cute daughter I tried to fall in love with.)

At UNM getting schooled by Hanrahan, Thygerson, Zudi, Bob Morgan, Sidney Rosenblum, and Jim Ruddle while partying with

Jim and Sally and Johnny, my roommate, who drove the coeds crazy. Tom McKenna, my navy vet buddy; Squirrel, who did a mean iron cross on the rings; Dee from the Hub City; Helen; Almut; and all the other party girls. For Gerry, who went CIA straight out of grad school; Mark, who died too young; Charney, who was way too wild; and Tony Hillerman long before he got famous writing mysteries. To Maxie Anderson at Ranchers Exploration and Development, who funded a start-up educational publishing company that rescued me from unloading freight cars for Railway Express at the Albuquerque rail yards and got me started writing.

In San Francisco during the first glimmer of the hippie movement thinking maybe I should become a cop. In Los Angeles for Hollywood nights with Penny and Hugh; Frank and Judy; Vernon, the best-dressed social worker in East L.A.; the beautiful Joann with the flaming red hair. Brian the neighborhood dealer; and Bruce, his sidekick. Steve the primo shrink at the L.A. Free Clinic and his lovely wife, Carol. And Jimi Hendrix's knockout social worker girlfriend, and sweet, motherly Henrietta who remembered the good old days in Southern California. Also Leslie, who wanted to be a movie star and did a TV furniture-polish commercial before vanishing forever. Living among the hippies in Sierra Madre Canyon watching Watts burn and El Monte riot. And our neighbor, Lanny G., another vet buddy now entrenched in Mexico making art. Marching against the war with other vets down Hollywood Boulevard, and that one hot summer night when the detectives from the Hollywood Precinct, who looked and dressed like movie stars, grilled me for a murder on my doorstep that I honestly didn't commit. And to our guardian angels: Dot, a true Southern belle and her husband, Vic, a streetwise taxi driver who pulled the night shift just for the fun of it.

Back in New Mexico, to my old friend Dave Hernandez, who

thought I'd make a good cop, and Bev, Ron, Roger, and Judy, four really good cops who did their jobs with pride. To Eddie Ortiz, one of the Santa Fe good guys. His funeral packed the cathedral.

Before that in grad school at Iowa City with fellow student Hildegard and my adviser Katie Kruse. Dr. Robert S., the kindhearted shrink who took a hard fall; Jim Styles; and Carol and Chuck in Cedar Rapids. And Flakey, wherever he may be; lovely Linda who sashayed off to Puerto Rico and back to Santa Fe on her way to who-knows-where; and F. Robertson, lost somewhere in Albuquerque shrinking heads.

A hand salute to Mark, a combat vet with a Bronze Star and an ace buddy who bounces back from fuckups at the speed of light. To MIA friends Bill and Peggy, Cliff and Inez, Perk and Alice, Tony and Connie, Brian and Judith, and Marty and Marti.

For good friends Elias and Susan, Bill and Debora, John and Jann, Joe and Valerie, Danny and Fala, Lucy and Roberto, Luis and Carmella, Wes and Maura, the irrepressible Betsy Reed, Terri and Polly, and the infamous St. Charmay of the Good Works. Also artist Peter Rogers, aka De La Fuente, and his lady, Beth; our great neighbors Lisa and Jim; and the unstoppable Dorothy Massey from Collected Works, who helps make literature and books blossom in Santa Fe.

For Robert, Marie, James, Richard, and Waldo, who all tried real hard not to be crazy but never quite made it, and to Cowboy Bob—in his day the best shrink in Santa Fe. To the brilliant Jeff Sloan, gone but not forgotten, and the equally brilliant Richard Bradford of *Red Sky at Morning* fame, also departed much too soon. You guys always made me think and laugh. To Carol, who moved away to Arizona to get happy. For George, the courtly lieutenant colonel with the Silver Star, and sweet, sassy Miriam at the Department of Health, who joked she taught me how to write. For

Carla Muth, who gave me a job when I needed one, and Larry Martinez, who thought my attempt to be a writer was cool.

But long before that, for Sammy, Betty, Judy, Bill, Johnny, Vicky, Mabel, Lucille, and Evangeline, who haunted the Santa Fe barrios with me back in the day when we tried to salvage glue-sniffing kids who didn't think anybody cared. And those few schoolteachers who really did care, especially Mary Ann, Dolores, Sue, Kathy, and Mary.

For Hilary Hinzmann, a classy guy and brilliant editor who thought maybe I could learn to write. For Di Bingham, my Aussie mate who runs our website from ten thousand miles away. And last, to Emily Beth, my sweetie and best friend these many years. Truly, every book has been because of you.

ABOUT THE AUTHOR

MICHAEL McGARRITY is the *New York Times* bestselling author of *Backlands, Hard Country,* the Anthony Award–nominated *Tularosa,* and eleven other bestselling Kevin Kerney crime novels. A former deputy sheriff for Santa Fe County, he also served as an instructor at the New Mexico Law Enforcement Academy and as an investigator for the New Mexico public defender's office. He lives in Santa Fe with his wife, Emily Beth.

Kerney Family Tree
1842–1972

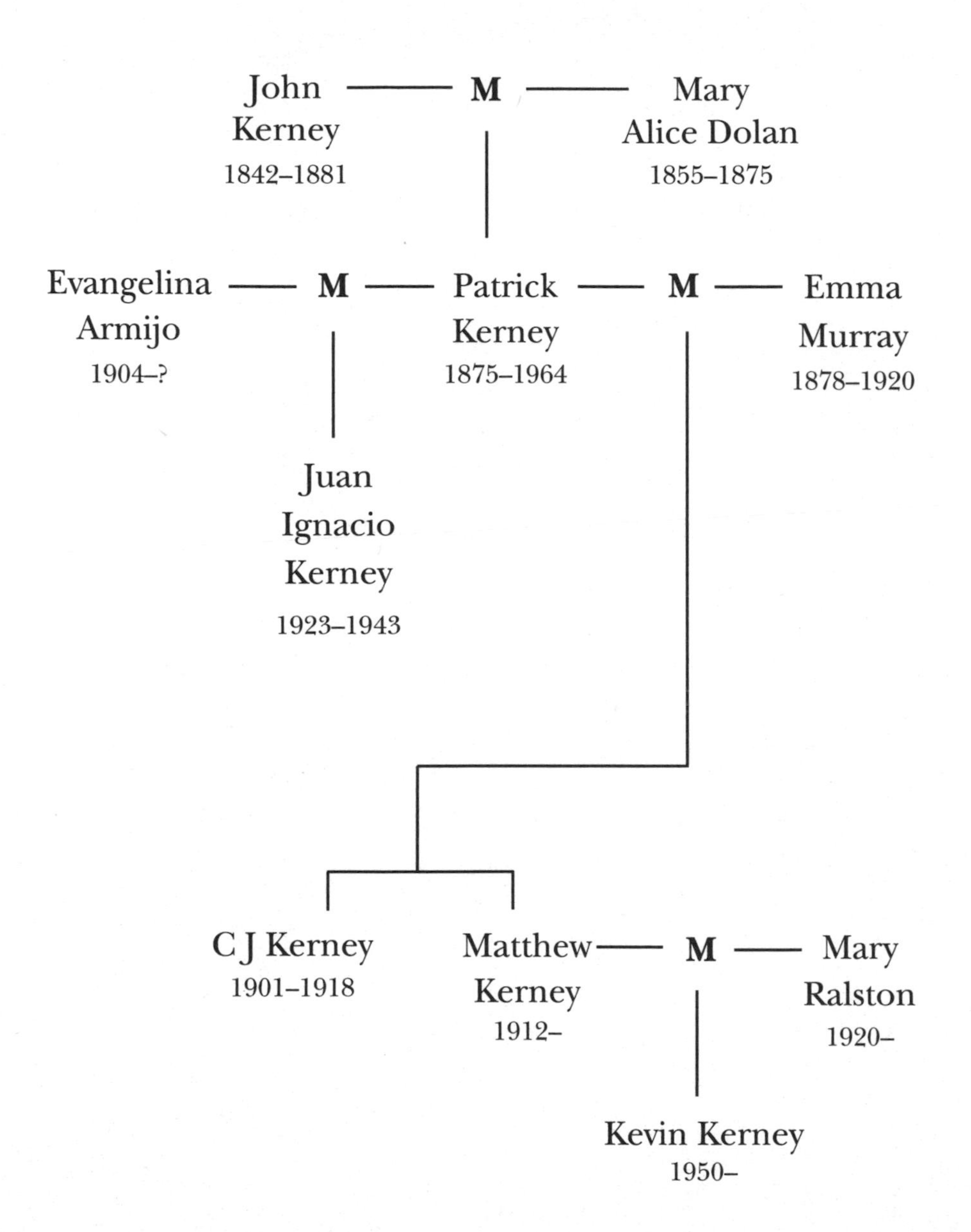